BLOOD IS THICKER

About the author

J.S. McGrath was born in Melbourne in 1971 and attended Good Shepherd Primary, Gladstone Park and St Bernards College in Essendon. He graduated with a Bachelor of Business at Swinburne University and is a CPA.

He has travelled extensively overseas with wife Lyn, and they currently live in Lilydale with daughter, Hannah and dog, Holly.

He writes as a hobby in his spare time.

Other works by J.S. McGrath

Inspector McAbbey series
Blood is Thicker
An Eye for a Tooth (2005)

Holly (picture book)
Holly and the Pussycat

Matt and Em (Teen fiction)
The Gruel Dare
The Nick (Coming soon)

Action adventure
The Last Testament (2005)

The author is available for public speaking.
For more information please see the website:
http://jsm.lightningweb.com.au

'If you think you can't, you'll prove yourself right'

Personal Motto

BLOOD IS
THICKER

Sharon,

Enjoy the book and
hope you enjoyed
Australia !

Cheers Jun

J.S. McGRATH

PenFolk Publishing, Blackburn Victoria
September, 2003

Published for J.S. McGrath in September 2003 by

PenFolk Publishing
21 Ronley Street
Blackburn Victoria   3130

Reprinted October 2004

ISBN 1 875894 35 7

McGrath, J.S., 1971–
Blood Is Thicker

Design and production by

Bill Ellemor, PenFolk Publishing

Cover design by

Jim Sultana, JS Designs (www.jsdesigns.com.au)

Acknowledgements

I would like to thank the following people for their support during this long process.

My readers and critics: Cara Sultana, Richard Orford, Hugh and Jacqui Neuharth, Peter Chladek, Danny Sarra, Rosslyn Abbey, Sarah Moore, Sharron Taylor, Bernie McGrath, Melanie Eyres, Anne Pedgeon, Glenda McGrath, Cathy Morrison, Vince Lescai, Andrew Bond, Ian Salek, Frances McGrath, Lorraine McDonnell, Gavin Mitchell, Anne Smith, Pat Comerford, Kevin McGrath, Justin and Kylie Oliver, Greg Symmonds, Charlie Hullin, Tim Turner, Emma McGrath, Danielle McGrath, Harry Van Der Zon, Ann-Maree Eastman, Phil Brierley, Carly Allen, Andrew Rule, Scribblers, Tom Pearce, Helen Casey, Susan Borg and the 'literary bitches'.

My mentors and editors: Lyn Abbey, Donna Cutler, Anne Wright, David Hart, Lorraine Emrich, Rebecca Constance, Bill Ellemor and Diana Reed.

Thanks to David Ranson and Shelley Robertson for their expertise and to the detectives in Homicide and the Major Collision Investigation Unit who love to help, but require anonymity.

Thanks to the following businesses: Jim Sultana's JS Designs (book cover), Bill Ellemor (layout and production), Mistral International and Lightningweb.

To everyone else unmentioned who has played a part, including my family, thanks.

Finally, with love to my wife, my staunchest supporter and harshest critic, this is for you.

For Lyn

signature *noun.* **1.** a person's name written in a distinctive way, used in signing something. **2.** the action of signing a document. **3.** a distinctive product or quality by which someone or something can be recognised.

Oxford English Dictionary, Oxford University Press 2002

'I don't believe in God,
so I can't be saved,
All alone as I've learned to be
in this mess I have made.'

Mess, Ben Folds

Prologue

The man pressed the intercom until a voice finally answered.

'Come on through,' it said. It was a young voice, faint above loud music, which blared through the tinny speaker like war-time propaganda.

The man lifted his finger from the intercom and reached for the handle. A buzzer sounded and it clicked open. He strode along a corridor to the apartment door. After a casual glance around, he jabbed at the door bell.

The music inside thumped loudly and the cactus garden on the windowsill shook. He held his finger to the bell and waited.

After a few seconds the music stopped and the door opened. A slim teenager, wearing a two-piece bathing suit with a sarong drawn around her waist stared up at him with the scowl of someone interrupted from a pleasant dream.

Her skin beaded with sweat from dancing and she sparkled with the studs and rings she had pierced through her lip, nose, ears and navel.

The girl wiped her shining brow and studied him. He was tall with silvery hair. His weathered skin reminded her of an old leather boot.

'Can I come in?' he asked with a smile.

She looked into his eyes and frowned, pulling subconsciously at her sarong to cover any bare flesh that might be showing.

'Sure,' she said with a sheepish grin. 'Mum will be home soon.'

He walked past her. In the clenched fist behind his back, he thumbed the base of an old vial. Its lid left an imprint of a crucifix in the heel of his palm.

1

Even though it was well after three am, Detective Inspector Ryan McAbbey was staring at the ceiling when the phone rang.

That was the way he slept these days. He didn't.

His wife stiffened in the bed beside him and he sighed. A late night call meant only one thing. He leaned over and picked up the handpiece.

'McAbbey.'

He listened for a moment then hung up, falling back onto the pillow.

It was better than in the old days, he mused, when he was called on in the early hours to a drug raid. Then the threat was real, his life was on the line and the tension from his wife was palpable. He remembered how he used to holster his pistol and check ammo. But in Homicide, the killer was gone long before he arrived.

McAbbey dressed, splashed water on his face and combed his hair.

On his way downstairs he checked on his daughter, Chelsey. McAbbey gritted his teeth as he approached her bedroom at the end of the hallway. Her light was on and she had school in the morning.

He tapped on her door and when there was no response, he opened it. Chelsey was rugged up in bed, just as she used to be after his bedtime reading duties. She had put a stop to that years ago—something to do with growing up.

She was fast asleep with a book in her hands. He took the novel, kissed her cheek and turned off the light.

Downstairs, he put bread in the toaster and boiled the kettle. He dropped an Earl Grey tea bag into a mug of hot water—black, no sugar and a touch of cold water to spare his tongue. He spread a thin layer of vegemite on the dry toast, downed his tea and left.

The police lights from the patrol car flashed across the street. They reflected on a row of elms in front of a new apartment block. There were no curious bystanders, but eyes peered from behind curtains and chained doors as a new white BMW screeched to a halt.

Detective Senior Constable Pete Vincent stepped from the car and walked towards the units. He followed a short cobblestone path to the foyer entrance.

A bored Senior Constable was surprised at the bold appearance of a young man dressed in a penguin suit with a brushed-back all-gel haircut. He stepped forward and blocked the way.

'Sorry, sonny. I'm afraid you can't …'

Pete Vincent calmly reached into his pocket and pulled out a new leather wallet and flicked it open. The seasoned officer stepped back and waved him through.

He walked across a carpeted foyer to an open-air courtyard, where the droning of air-conditioning units competed with crickets in the balmy stillness. Spotlights reflected on a large swimming pool surrounded by double storey apartments with views.

Pete followed the path around the pool until he came to apartment thirteen. He ducked under the police cordon and stepped inside.

The modern lounge room was painted a sea-blue with sandstone coloured drapes. A sofa, bloated like a puffer fish, faced a bay window with a view of the lit park opposite. Past the lounge and through an arch, he entered a modern kitchen with matching appliances in stainless steel.

A policewoman comforted a woman who was slouched on a stool weeping.

Pete stared at the distressed woman's long legs and short skirt, but looked elsewhere when the policewoman noticed. She nodded to the stairs and he went past them.

Pete took three steps at a time and glanced around at the top. He walked to the bedroom, being careful not to touch the walls or disturb furniture.

The girl was propped up against the bed head with the covers tucked tightly around her waist. He noted her pasty complexion and the stillness of her chest. Her eyes were dulled like frosted glass and her head had lolled to the left, cocked forward as though she was listening.

He moved closer. She was of slight frame and fair skin, with long blonde hair and small arms, which rested in her lap. The fall of her hair exposed an ugly red mark, which cut deep into the skin around her throat.

Pete checked the room. There was a matching pink wardrobe and vanity. A portable television sat on a wooden frame bolted to the wall with a stack of CDs and a small player below it. Next to the vanity was a window with drawn drapes covered with Disney cartoon characters. Above the bed dressed in scant clothing, the pop singer Kylie smiled from a framed picture.

Pete moved to open the wardrobe but stopped, realising that without protective wear he should not touch anything in the room.

He heard a car stop outside and went to the window to peer through the curtains. A standard issue white Commodore had parked down the street and the driver walked towards the patrol car.

'Morning, Inspector.'

McAbbey nodded a brief greeting to the seasoned officer. He was one of those Senior Constables who had worked the beat for thirty years without ever managing a promotion to take him off the streets he complained about so often.

'Where's my crew?' McAbbey asked.

'They called through to say they'd be a little held up. A car accident, apparently.'

'Fatality?' McAbbey frowned. 'Funny—I didn't hear anything on the way over.'

'Nope. Jack hit some old lady who pulled out of Coles without looking.'

McAbbey turned to the BMW blocking the driveway.

'Who the hell left their car in the way?' he snapped.

'Some ankle biter who works for your department,' the Senior Constable replied.

'No one in my squad owns a bloody Beemer. Who is it?'

'The Chief Commissioner's son. I heard a rumour he'd been promoted to Homicide.'

'Vincent Junior,' McAbbey groaned. 'His promotion, as you generously describe it, was nothing to do with me.'

McAbbey asked a couple of questions and then stormed towards the apartment.

2

When McAbbey entered the bedroom Pete Vincent was facing the vanity mirror with his hands in his pockets. McAbbey studied the newly-promoted Chief Commissioner's son and scowled. 'Just what the hell do you think you're doing?' he demanded.

Pete turned suddenly.

'I've just been posted to Homicide—I was on call this morning.'

'Nice. Perhaps you can explain to me why your Kraut-can is covering the driveway?'

'The girl was already dead,' Pete said, 'It's not going to make much ...'

'Never park within cooee—not in my squad,' McAbbey said. 'This ain't some bloody valet privilege; we're here to do a job.'

McAbbey turned from Pete and studied the window. He pulled a glove from his pocket and put it on before drawing back the curtains. Taking his mini-tape recorder, he raised it to his mouth.

In a quiet even tone he said: 'The window hasn't been tampered with and the front door shows no sign of being forced. The downstairs windows are in good order and the body corporate doesn't lock the entrance at night; I suggest the killer was either invited, or conned his way into the apartment.'

'Yes, it seems the killer was allowed in,' Pete said. McAbbey turned abruptly, the tape recorder in his clenched hand. He stopped the tape.

'If you want to help, move your car and come back with protective gloves.'

McAbbey waited for him to leave the room before continuing to record his first impressions.

—-—

Pete moved his car down the street. As he walked back, an unmarked police car groaned to a halt beside him, the grill twisted and steaming.

Out climbed two men in their mid thirties.

One, Detective Senior Sergeant Jack Turner wore a black suit and stood tall at six–four. With his pallid face and straight black hair, Pete could see how he had earned the nickname of "The Undertaker" in the Squad.

The other, Detective Sergeant Gavin Toohey, was short and wore a tweed sports jacket, the sides of which had no chance of meeting in the middle. Together they looked like a modern day Laurel and Hardy.

'I'm Jack Turner,' said the senior detective. 'We spoke on the phone. But cripes, I didn't expect you to start at an ungodly hour like this—it's barely even Monday!'

'The day starts when we get a call,' Pete shrugged.

Jack pointed over his shoulder. 'Tubby here, is Sergeant Gavin Toohey.'

'Hey!' Gavin snorted. 'That's Sergeant Tubby to you!'

Pete tried not to laugh.

Jack turned to the uniformed cop. 'So where's McAbbey?'

The local cop nodded to the car parked down the street. 'The Inspector's gone in already. I don't think he liked seeing Junior upstairs before him.' He nodded in Pete Vincent's direction.

Jack began walking to the apartment block, placing a lanky arm around the rookie. 'Forget about McAbbey—he'll come around.'

3

Pete followed Jack upstairs, while Gavin headed towards the kitchen.

"I'll just check the pantry for evidence," he said, patting his stomach. The other two grinned and kept climbing.

As he entered the kitchen, Gavin turned solemn. The policewoman was still comforting the weeping mother.

'Judy.' Gavin greeted the young constable, who nodded towards the distressed woman.

Gavin took a seat at a respectable distance from the mother, who was still hunched on the stool with her head in her hands.

'I'm sorry for your loss, Ms Stevenson,' said Gavin, by way of introduction.

She raised her head and studied the pudgy policeman with wet eyes, saying nothing.

'I need you to tell me what happened.'

There was a long moment's silence, and the two officers looked at each other. The policewoman was about to move forward, when, haltingly, Tracey Stevenson began to speak.

'When I came home from work at the Espy I could see her light on,' she whispered.

She wiped her eyes and flicked her hair behind her ears, not noticing that it fell free. 'I called out to her, but she didn't answer. I went upstairs ... and ... saw her on the bed. She was just sitting there. I thought she had fallen asleep with the light on at first ...'

'Was anything out of place when you came home? Was the front door open?'

Tracey shook her head. 'No, the door was locked. I didn't notice anything unusual until I saw … Tania.' Tracey dropped her head in her palms and wept.

Gavin nodded for the policewoman to follow him into the lounge.

'What have you found?' he asked.

'She said that Tania didn't have many friends. I asked if there was anyone who might've had a grudge against them, but she didn't think so.'

'What does Tracey do at the Esplanade Hotel?'

'She tends bar and serves meals. She works casual hours—mostly nights.'

'What about the girl's father?' Gavin asked.

'You'll have to give me more time.' Judy raised a hand. 'She won't talk about it. He's definitely not part of their lives. There's not much family to speak of. The mother's parents are dead and she has no brothers or sisters. Tania was her only child.'

'When did she last see Tania alive?'

'She saw her at eight, but called her from work around eleven.'

Gavin asked a question about the victim's school, then thanked Judy and walked back through the kitchen and upstairs.

McAbbey stared thoughtfully at the deceased. He tried to understand why she would let her killer into the house. The lack of a struggle hinted that she was attacked by someone she knew and trusted. Of course, her family would come under intense scrutiny.

Looking at the girl, he struggled to shake images of his own teenaged daughter. He could see Chelsey's cheeky smile and rebellious attitude in this ghostly-silent young girl. McAbbey's blood boiled with the knowledge that someone had taken advantage of her vulnerability.

'Morning Boss,' Jack said as he walked into the bedroom. Pulling gloves from his suit coat, he approached the deceased. Pete hovered in the doorway.

'Where's your bigger half?' McAbbey asked.

'He's downstairs, talking to Judy and the girl's mother.'

'You didn't happen to see the Chief Inspector's five seconds of fame while you were down there?'

'Ah yeah.' Jack turned around and grinned at Pete. 'He's right here.'

'Swell.' McAbbey turned to face him. 'Come in, kid. What do you think? Does anything strike you as unusual in here—besides the poor girl?'

Pete hesitated. 'The bedroom's clean and there's been no sign of a struggle.'

'Also the bed's been straightened and she's been propped up and tucked in,' Jack added.

McAbbey nodded. 'Sort of thing a parent would do, wouldn't you say?'

They agreed.

McAbbey stood quiet for a long moment, then leant forward and raised the chin of the deceased with a gloved hand, fully revealing the girl's neck.

'She was definitely garrotted.'

A new voice pierced the air. 'I'll make the determination, thank you.' Catherine Smith, the appointed pathologist, stood in the doorway holding a grey medical bag.

Pete looked across to see an attractive woman in her late thirties. She was tall and wore a shock-white gown with her blonde hair tightly pulled into a bun.

Without acknowledging the senior detectives, she went straight to the rookie. 'So you're Pete—I'm Catherine.' She offered a hand.

Catherine was followed in by the police photographer, a cuddly woman in her late forties with short bobbed hair.

Pete moved back against the open door and watched in fascination as Catherine put on protective gloves and worked methodically over the girl. The photographer stood at a distance, taking specific photos of her posture and the mark around her neck. Suddenly he felt weak in the knees realising that he was at his first murder scene—the detectives, pathologists and the shock of the camera flash. Fatalities were common in the Traffic Safety division, but this was murder.

'Jack.' McAbbey knelt in front of the bed and motioned for him to look at the girl's left hand. Jack took hold of her limp arm and inspected the nails.

'Clean,' he said. 'Looks like the killer might have scrubbed her.'

Pete stepped outside the bedroom to make way for Gavin who went over and stood beside McAbbey.

'The girl's name is Tania Stevenson. She's thirteen years old and went to St Anne's College in Brighton,' Gavin said flatly. 'Her mother couldn't give us the names of any close friends. I think we should visit her classmates at school tomorrow.'

'Agreed. I wouldn't mind doing that myself,' McAbbey said, chewing his lip.

Jack glanced at him quizzically and was about to comment when he caught Catherine's eye.

'Why don't you take Pete?' Jack suggested instead, smiling at the rookie.

'He might learn something,' Gavin agreed.

'Yeah—from the kids ...' McAbbey added under his breath.

'What about the father?' Catherine asked.

'Not sure. We know it was just the two of them living here. Judy's finding out.' Gavin said.

'Why is the mother dressed up at this hour?' Pete asked Jack.

'Yeah. Good question, though you'd be surprised how many people are frocked up when we arrive at a crime scene—I've even seen people wash their cars. People react differently to the loss.'

McAbbey rubbed his chin. 'Cath, has the girl been raped or hurt anywhere other than her neck?'

'I'm ready to take a look now.'

Catherine leaned forward and gently pulled back the covers tucked around Tania's waist. Her legs, exposed from the bikini bottom downwards, were a rich colour from blood pooling. There were no bruises or cuts on her lower body.

Catherine examined the rigidity in the girl's neck and then moved the victim's arm forcibly in semi-circles.

'What time was the call made?' she asked no one in particular.

'Just after two-thirty this morning,' Gavin said. 'An ambulance was dispatched but they left here soon after. Her mother said she last spoke to her daughter at eleven last night.'

'Strange,' Catherine said. 'I'd guess she's been dead for six hours, but that can't be right.'

'How do you get that?' Pete asked.

'I'm basing my assumption on the time of rigor mortis. It's not an exact science, but it's a good guide. The girl's still warm, but stiffness has set in. That's generally indicative of about six hours post-mortem for this room temperature. I wouldn't have expected her to be so rigid.'

Catherine took hold of the girl's arm and contracted and expanded the biceps muscle. 'Unless ...'

'What?' McAbbey pressed.

'She has a slight but distinctive body odour, which is suggestive of aerobic activity. She may have been active before she was killed.'

'Why would exercise make her stiffen quicker?' Pete asked.

Catherine raised an eyebrow before answering.

'Rigor mortis is due to a chemical reaction and the time it takes to react is determined both by temperature and initial concentrations of lactic acid in the muscle tissue. High metabolic activity—like playing sport for instance, leads to higher levels of lactic acid and can significantly shorten the length of time rigor mortis takes to develop.'

'Could she have been running from her killer?' McAbbey's eyes narrowed.

There was silence in the room as everyone pondered the question—if she had been running, how did she end up tucked in bed as if nothing had happened?

'Is it inconceivable that she could have died, say about midnight?' McAbbey broke the silence.

'No. She could have—it's just suggestive of outside influence, that's all.'

Catherine opened the girl's mouth and inspected her teeth and tongue. 'She's been drinking Coke.'

'What do you make of her body piercing?' McAbbey asked.

'Interesting—for her age. I count four in each ear and one each through her nose, lip and belly.'

Pete leant closer, surprised to find that he missed the body piercing earlier.

'That's not so unusual these days, boss,' Jack said. 'Don't forget you had to fight to stop Chelsey getting a belly ring for Christmas to go with her hipsters.'

'Yeah, don't remind me. Has anyone found the studs?'

'No,' Jack said as he opened the bedside drawer and shuffled through the contents with a gloved hand. 'Just a few issues of *Dolly* magazine, a couple of multicoloured pens, jewellery and a box of tissues.'

'Maybe the killer took them as a souvenir?' Pete offered.

'I want you to take the room apart,' said McAbbey. 'In the meantime cordon it and make sure the mother knows to stay out.'

McAbbey stepped back so that Catherine could finish her inspection and spoke to the others. 'You'll want to door knock the other apartments now. Don't wait until the morning—the clock's ticking.'

Jack nodded. 'Forensics will be here any minute.'

'Good, I'll be off then.' McAbbey said. 'See you in the office at nine.' He eyed Pete briefly. 'Don't be late for school.'

When McAbbey left, Pete followed Jack and Gavin to the courtyard.

'There are six other units facing the pool,' Jack said. 'Let's take a couple each and meet back here.'

Jack and Gavin headed down opposite sides of the pool to the far end and began door knocking. Pete watched them for a minute and then walked to the next apartment. He rang the bell and cringed as the melodic peal echoed around the courtyard.

After a minute's silence, a light came on and Pete heard shuffling and cursing. The front door opened but Pete could not see through the wire door.

'What the fuck! It's after four in the morning, for chrissakes.'

'Sorry Sir …' Pete paused.

'You'd wanna be.'

'There's been a murder next door. I want to know if you saw or heard anything.' Pete looked at the doormat.

'Why should I tell you, you little twerp?'

'I'm in Homicide,' Pete said, reaching for his ID.

'It's too early for jokes, kid. Fuck off.'

The door slammed shut and Pete held his wallet limply in his hand. He moved towards the buzzer again, but stopped short. He waited a minute, then walked briskly to the next apartment and stood outside.

'Waiting for us?' Gavin chuckled.

Pete stiffened.

'It's OK, Pete.' Jack put a hand on his shoulder. 'I didn't get much either. Sometimes I think they pretend to hear nothing.'

'Let's hope someone here is interested in things that go on in their neighbourhood.' Gavin reached past Pete and pressed the bell hard.

An old lady answered the door and invited them inside. Mrs Tanner was a widow with blue rinse hair, wearing a flannel nightie. She drew a crocheted shawl across her chest, though it was muggy outside. She offered them tea, and after a look at his watch, Jack nodded.

Mrs Tanner put a kettle on the stove and began setting the vinyl top kitchen table.

Jack explained what had happened next door and the lady gasped.

'Terrible business this. I liked that young girl. She often helped me carry my shopping upstairs.'

'Did you hear anything unusual tonight?' Jack asked.

'No, I didn't. Mrs Black from number three called in her cat at eleven, and Mr Thompson in five, came home from his Casino shift at midnight. Tracey came in at half past two.'

Mrs Tanner put out cups and saucers and a biscuit tin of Iced Vovos.

'You said you liked Tania. How'd you get along with Tracey?' Jack asked.

'A hussy, if you ask me. She thinks I'm a busybody—can you imagine? I only expressed my concern for her daughter who spends too much time home alone.'

'Hussy?' Gavin asked, as he took a biscuit.

'I've lost count of the men that come and go. She certainly attracts them.' She poured them tea from a china pot dressed in a pink cosy. 'You don't think it was one of her boyfriends do you?'

Jack put milk and three sugars into his tea and took a sip. 'It's too early to say. Did you know any of her visitors?' Jack asked.

She shook her head. 'She never introduced them to me.'

'Was there anyone who stood out—someone who might've threatened Tania?'

'I'm sorry. I really am. I can only tell you what I see from my window. Sometimes I think they leave from the back door in the laneway.'

'Would you recognise any of her regulars if we put them in a line-up?'

'I think so.' Mrs Tanner walked to the vertical blinds and parted a worn section. 'I've been asking the body corporate to approve better lighting out there. Perhaps now they'll listen to me.'

Jack nodded and waited impatiently for Gavin to finish his third Vovo before leaving.

4

Later that morning, McAbbey picked up Pete from the office and drove in silence to Brighton, a suburb of freshly renovated houses from the Victorian era. He pulled up to the curb under a row of shady elms on Matthew Street, outside St Anne's College.

'Look, you're probably wondering why I was pissed off about where you left your car last night.'

Pete listened.

'Early in my career, I was partnered with a Senior Sergeant who refused to walk. Once he parked in the driveway behind an ambulance. He figured, the man was dead, so why not? He hadn't counted on the deceased's wife, who suffered a heart attack at the scene. They couldn't get her into the ambulance and had to wait for him to move. That poor woman died on the way to hospital, and his car might've made all the difference.'

Pete nodded thoughtfully.

'Let's go in. Just remember—you've got two ears and one mouth. Use them accordingly.'

McAbbey was first out of the car and led the way up a path, which cut its way between box hedges to the main office, a tall brick building built in the 1920s

The principal's personal assistant was an elderly woman who greeted them with a curt nod. She buzzed the principal and announced their arrival.

The principal's door opened and Karen Nicholson gave them a thin smile. Her bottle-blonde hair was teased and she wore ample, yet elegantly applied makeup. McAbbey guessed she was about his age.

She waved them to a seat. Her office was bright and her desk clean. Behind her, a large wooden crucifix was suspended above a neat row of filing cabinets. The view from her window took in the student's quadrangle, primarily a concrete slab with a few token seats and pot plants.

'Thanks for the warning call this morning,' she said. 'As you can appreciate, the girls and teachers are upset.'

'Was Tania a popular student?' McAbbey asked.

Mrs Nicholson eyed McAbbey for a moment. 'Not really. But you know how the death of someone you know can shake you. I think it reminds us of our own mortality.'

'It seems she was popular with administration.' McAbbey glanced at the bulky student file open before her.

'I saw plenty of her here.' She sighed. 'She was quite rebellious and often fought with other students. She had a mouth, and I often had to send her home for wearing body piercing—which is banned.'

'Did you ever feel tempted to expel her?'

'No.' She shrugged. 'Her mother was prompt with the school fees and Tania, for all her shortcomings, was a bright student and passed her grades.'

'But what did you make of her attitude?'

'She craved attention. I don't think she ever knew her father and her mother was too busy to show any interest in her daughter's development. I was the closest she had to a disciplinary figure.'

McAbbey stood. 'If you don't mind, I'd like to see her classmates, then her teachers.'

She led the way to the classroom where Tania had spent most of her time, referring to the student file as she walked.

'Ms Stevenson rarely attended parent-teacher interviews—she blamed it on work commitments.'

McAbbey kept stride alongside her, down a corridor with religious statues and ceramic pot plants jutting from the walls.

'Makes you wonder why she bothered sending her daughter here.'

'I see it all the time. They want a better life for their kids. Sending them to a private school cleanses their soul. They think it's our job to do the rest—including raising their children.'

At the end of the corridor, the principal stopped. 'This is Tania's classroom.'

She introduced them to Mrs Westworth, Tania's form teacher. Mrs Nicholson then excused the teacher from the class and led the detectives to the blackboard at the front.

They turned and faced seven rows of evenly distributed desks. Some of the students had red eyes and held damp tissues.

McAbbey looked at his watch, frowned and turned to the principal. 'I might leave my associate here to talk with the girls. I'm pressed for time.'

Mrs Nicholson nodded approvingly.

'See what you can find out.' McAbbey gave Pete a reassuring nod before following the principal to the staff room.

Pete turned back and faced the class of girls with his hands deep in his pockets.

'Good morning ...' he started, but was unable to finish his sentence with thirty pairs of eyes staring at him.

The staff common room had been maintained in its original state, except for a small modern kitchenette in a renovated alcove. McAbbey noted the absence of radio, television and computers with interest.

The teachers sat on antique couches facing a grand wall-to-wall bookshelf containing student reading material by authors as diverse as Shakespeare and John Marsden. As he expected from a private girl's school, most of the teachers were female.

'Does anyone know who might have had a reason to kill Tania?' McAbbey asked.

There was light chatter and a few troubled looks. McAbbey could not help wonder if they had been briefed.

One teacher looked to the principal before speaking.

'It's a terrible thing, Inspector,' she said. 'Tania was hard work, but she was worth it. She had brains, but spent most of her time using them to frustrate you.'

'She never complied with the school uniform,' her form teacher added. 'One day she'd turn up with fluoro socks, and the next, earrings. One day I caught her wearing a stud through her tongue. I went to get Mrs Nicholson, but by the time I returned, she'd removed it.'

'Please, can you think of anyone who might be involved?'

'I doubt it,' Mrs Nicholson apologised, glancing at her staff.

McAbbey watched his audience for a moment, noting that most of the teachers were sitting forward, but avoiding eye contact.

There was a silence and Mrs Nicholson picked her forefinger with her thumbnail.

She eventually turned to McAbbey.

'Sorry, but my staff have no idea who did this horrible thing.'

He gave a curt nod and followed the principal back to Tania's classroom.

Pete took a few moments when McAbbey left to gather his thoughts.

'I need to ask about Tania,' he said.

After a pause, a tall girl in the back row raised a hand. 'I'm Alicia. I feel terrible this happened, but I didn't like her.'

'Why not?' Pete walked toward the student.

Another answered from the back of the class. 'She thought she was Miss High and Mighty. Like, she fought with everyone.'

'She swore all the time,' a third student volunteered.

'And got away with wearing studs,' said Alicia.

'Was anyone here her friend? Did anyone have lunch, or walk to and from school with her?'

The girls returned vacant looks and Alicia ended the silence. 'She was a loner. She didn't fit into any group.'

Pete scanned the classroom walls, which contained mathematical formulas, bookshelves and panoramic photographs of the Eiffel Tower and the Colosseum.

'What about your teacher, Mrs Westworth? Did she like Tania?'

'Not really, but she's new anyway.'

'New?' Pete asked. 'Is this her first year at this school?'

'No, she was the Year 7 and 8 science teacher. Mr Pearce was our form teacher, but he left last week.'

'Last week? School's been back just a month. Where did he go?'

'They said he went on long service leave ...'

'He was a pervert,' a girl at the front of the class interrupted.

'What?' Pete turned sharply.

'You don't know that!' another girl said.

Pete turned to Alicia for an explanation.

'Most of us reckon he got caught looking up dresses.'

'Did Mr Pearce like Tania?'

'Yeah. Tania was his favourite. She said she'd been to his house.'

A mobile rang and Pete pulled a compact phone from his belt and answered.

'Pete. How's it going out there?' a gruff voice said.

He froze.

'Good,' Pete whispered. He walked to the front of the class and faced a blackboard of scribble.

'It looks like one of the teachers left the school suddenly. He might be connected to the girl's death.'

'Pete. Does anyone else know this?'

'No, Dad. McAbbey's with the teachers.'

'Good. Keep it that way.'

Pete ended the call as McAbbey and the principal walked into the class.

5

'So, how'd you go?' McAbbey grumbled, as he merged back into traffic.

'OK. The girls are upset, but they didn't like her much.'

'I got the same impression, but I reckon they're holding something back. What I can't work out is whether it's just private school antics or something more serious.'

McAbbey's phone rang and he answered on hands-free.

It was Gavin from the apartment.

'How'd it go this morning? Was the principal good to you?' Gavin asked.

'I haven't changed my opinion of teachers, if that's what you mean. You can tell a teacher, but you can't tell 'em much.'

McAbbey cringed as Gavin's belly laugh ended with an unhealthy coughing splutter.

'Remind me not to stir him up will you?' McAbbey muttered to Pete, who grinned.

McAbbey let Pete out of the car before parking underground. At reception, he picked up his messages from his personal assistant, Andrea, and trudged to his all-glass office, nicknamed "the Fishbowl".

A post-it note grabbed his attention—a request to call Harry Vincent. As Inspector, McAbbey reported to Bill Harnden, the Assistant Commissioner of Crimes Division, but Vincent didn't give a shit. As Chief Commissioner, he did as he pleased, answering only to the Police Minister and the government of the day. McAbbey dialled the number, wondering if Vincent wanted a parent-teacher report on his son after his first morning.

'Ryan, good to hear from you so promptly.'

McAbbey looked down at the paper, noting the message was only minutes old. 'Aim to please.'

'Good. A friend of mine from the Carbine Club has a daughter at St Anne's in Brighton. He's also on the School Council.'

McAbbey tightened his thumb grip on the pencil he was holding.

'His daughter went home this morning, upset about a fellow student who was murdered last night—I believe you're investigating that personally.'

McAbbey snapped the pencil in half.

'That little prick,' he muttered under his breath. Only the members in his squad knew he was on the case.

'As a personal favour to my friend, can you wrap up this case as quickly and quietly as possible? It's not just the stigma, but he's concerned that the killer may be stalking students from the school.'

'Sure,' he replied with a snort. 'I might even do it as a favour to the girl.'

Vincent ignored the comment and thanked him in advance for his cooperation. McAbbey slammed the phone down. He grabbed for his coffee cup, but stopped short of taking a swig, noting it was coated with the prior week's dregs. He cursed, reaching into his filing cabinet for a new case folder and headed out of his office.

6

'I think McAbbey's going to be surprised by your preliminary report.' Jack sat on a small edge of Pathologist Catherine Smith's desk. It was otherwise covered with case files, court summonses and legal correspondence. Somewhere behind the skyscrapers of paper was Catherine, who nodded without taking her eyes from a computer screen.

Above a library of case-law, a cluttered photo board caught Jack's eye and he cringed at a snap of an autopsy victim. The photo showed the lower half of a man with his penis hacked off. As the only female pathologist on staff at the Coroner's court, Jack surmised that the photo was a shock statement to reduce her male counterparts to mere mortals.

'That your last boyfriend?' Jack nodded casually, sensing she had noticed his reaction.

'Yup.'

Jack turned from the photo to watch Catherine write her report.

'Did you notice how quiet McAbbey went when he looked at the girl?' Jack asked. 'And what's with him interviewing teachers and students?'

'Yes, I noticed.' Catherine did not look up. 'I've seen it before. A ten-year-old girl was killed in a hit and run about three years ago. He was rather distraught.'

'He didn't look upset as such ...'

'Ryan hides it well, but I know. Why do you think he missed my autopsy and is only coming to hear the preliminary?'

'Because of the school interviews?' Jack cocked an eyebrow. 'OK, but why? He's worked thousands of cases and seen many bodies.'

'True.' Catherine nodded. 'You saw how similar that girl was to Chelsey.'

'She's not that alike.'

'Maybe to us, but there were similarities; the girl was of the same physique and age. He worries about Chelsey a lot.'

Catherine stood. 'McAbbey is meeting me in Theatre One. We'd better get down there.'

They walked downstairs, past the Coroner's courtrooms and into the city morgue, which was attached to the premises.

Jack walked from the theatre door to a lonely stainless steel desk by the far wall. He did not look at the occupied steel trestles, which lay shrouded like stored furniture. He sat on the edge and waited for Catherine to take her seat before continuing the conversation.

'McAbbey once told me they had a lot of trouble having Chelsey and gave up on ever having another,' Jack offered. 'He said the experts were clueless.'

'I was one of those clueless experts,' Catherine glared.

'He asked you for advice on that?' Jack scoffed, waving a hand. 'I reckon you know more about the other end of the deal!'

'Really,' she replied, with pursed lips. 'When he came to me, he was at his wits' end. He'd tried iced water baths, herbal tea, ritual prayer and even a vegan diet.'

'I've heard about the diet. Apparently he complained constantly about the food and was unbearable that week.'

Catherine laughed. 'Exactly. But what's more amusing is that when he came to see me, I'd only been on staff for a few years and had no experience in fertility. He handed me a specimen jar and asked if I would pull a few strings. I was about to tell him where to go, when he mentioned the strain it was having on their relationship and that Lisa wanted him to go to a clinic.'

'Gosh. It took him years before he was comfortable talking about it with us,' Jack said.

'Yeah. He needed someone to share his problem with. I guess he chose me because I'm a doctor.'

'It certainly isn't because of your success rate with patients! Perhaps it was because he saw you as a close friend.' Jack smiled. 'So what broke the camel's back and made him talk to you in the first place?'

'Apparently they had a tiff. Lisa was sick of him delaying a visit to a clinic and demanded he do something. I don't blame her, though apparently she told him he was procrastinating as a way to get more sex than he needed.'

Jack chuckled. 'So why didn't he just go to the damn clinic?'

'He had this thing that "No Porsche-driving knife-wielding doctor was going anywhere near his family jewels".'

'So, what did you do with the sample jar?'

'Fortunately one of the girls in my graduating class worked in a fertility clinic, so I pulled a favour.'

'What was the result?' Jack asked.

'He had an obstruction in the vas deferens, lowering his sperm count. I told him he would probably need a testicular biopsy.'

Jack laughed. 'No wonder you work with dead people, speaking lingo like that.'

Catherine hit him. 'I encouraged him to join the new IVF program at the Melbourne Womens. It took them a year, but they were one of the early couples to succeed in Victoria. There was an article in the local newspaper at the time.'

'After all that effort and Chelsey's the spitting image of her mother anyway.'

'Just as well. Could you imagine her looking anything like him!' Catherine joked.

McAbbey walked into the theatre and greeted them.

'I'd better go,' Jack said. 'I have to get the results from Macleod for this afternoon's meeting.'

Once Jack left, Catherine went to the fridge.

'Guess you want to see ...'

McAbbey did not, but was not quick enough to say so. Opening the unit, she pulled out a gurney. Her autopsy was recent and she didn't need to look at the tag to find the right body.

'Just tell me what you found,' he said.

'Sure.' Catherine shoved the sheet-covered tray back and closed the fridge, clearing the frosty air, which reminded him of chilled rotten fruit.

They returned to the desk, a few steps away from the fridge.

The 'workshop' consisted of two large stainless steel trestles standing metres apart. Beside each table sat a torture tray of scalpels, saws and tongs.

The air-conditioning forced disinfected air onto McAbbey and he sneezed suddenly and rubbed his nose hard.

'Sorry.' Catherine said. 'Is it the new perfume I'm wearing?'

'Very funny. Let's go upstairs.'

McAbbey followed Catherine out of the morgue to her office. He sat in her visitor's chair—a rickety old swivel seat, with a fragile back that encouraged him to lie flat. He waited for her to put on reading glasses and open the file.

'I don't have all the results yet, but I believe the MO was asphyxiation by garrotte. She showed no signs of needle abuse, and I didn't find semen when I ran the ultra-violet over her. The scene and the girl's condition do not point to rape.'

'Any scratch marks—matter under the nails?'

Catherine shook her head. 'I don't think there was a struggle. I'd say it was someone she knew well. There was one thing though ...' Catherine paused and McAbbey motioned for her to continue. 'She was definitely sweating before she died—the presence of oils and salts on the skin are indicative. However, there's a clear spot on her forehead about the width of a thumbprint where there is no sweat. I don't know what to make of it—but I thought you might want to know.'

McAbbey nodded.

'What about the mother? You don't buy that bar worker bit do you?'

McAbbey chuckled. 'You definitely chose the wrong profession, Cath. To answer your question, of course I don't. I'm going to ring the place when I get back to the office. The waitresses I know don't live quite so affluently. See you at our case review this afternoon.'

7

McAbbey was first to return to the office on St Kilda Road and had barely sat in his chair before hitting the intercom.

'Andrea, get me the number for the bar where Tracey Stevenson works.'

McAbbey rang the manager of the Espy Hotel, introducing himself.

'How can I help you?' the manager asked.

'I'd like to know when Tracey Stevenson finished her shift last night.'

'Sure ...' He took a deep breath. 'What's this in relation to? Is she OK?'

'Yes, she's fine. But her daughter died last night.'

'Oh God, how horrible. Let me find last night's time sheets.' The man put the phone down and McAbbey heard paper shuffling.

'She finished at ten-fifty.'

'That's an unusual time ...' McAbbey prompted.

'Tracey's a casual. She works different hours to fit in with her other job.'

'Her other job?'

There was a moment's silence.

'You mean the escort agency?' McAbbey asked casually.

'Oh ... you know? Yeah, her hours here depend on her schedule at the Weekly Stellar.'

'So why does she bother with bar work?'

'No idea. I guess you'll have to ask her that one.' The manager said. 'I can't see how a few extra bucks can make a difference to what she earns.'

McAbbey ended the call. He put his faded briefcase on the desk and rolled the tumblers. He removed his sandwiches and proceeded to munch on Vegemite and cheese as he mused over what he had learned.

In the early afternoon Catherine arrived and acknowledged greetings from the team as she squeezed past Gavin and sat at the conference table for their briefing.

The conference room was a converted office and, as such, the rectangular pine table fitted as snug as an adult in a cubby house. Pinboards were plastered along the inside windows, more for privacy from the remainder of the office than as graphic reminders of the cases they worked. A whiteboard, grey and beyond cleaning, was perched adjacent to the door. Beneath it, at the head of the table, sat McAbbey staring at his case notes.

He spoke without looking up. 'What did you find, Gavin?'

'We searched the place top to bottom. Forensics reckons it's one of the most spotless crime scenes they've seen. They think someone cleaned the room the night of the murder.'

'That might've been the killer making absolutely sure he left no trace,' Jack interrupted.

'That was my first thought, however, Ms Stevenson's a neatness freak. She hires a cleaning lady to come through twice a week and goes through the place with a vac and duster herself on the other days.'

'What about fingerprints?' McAbbey asked.

'There were layers of partially-wiped latent prints all over the room.'

'How many full sets of prints?'

'About a dozen thumb and index finger. If you count partials from individual digits, then plenty, but they'll be impossible to trace. The thumb and index ones are worth checking through the system and we've started that process.'

'So it's possible the killer wiped the crime scene. What other evidence?'

'We collected a few hair follicles from the bedroom, but we think it may have been vacuumed since.'

'Did they empty the vacuum cleaner?' McAbbey asked.

'Yes. They've tried to make the most of a full bag of dust, dirt and hair. Forensics is looking into it—but I'm not expecting anything definitive. There was nothing of note as far as the rest of the apartment goes. No blood, overturned furniture, moved pictures ...'

'What about the mother?'

'We checked her effects,' Gavin said. 'Found nothing—just the usual hygiene products, magazines and trinkets. There's no trace of a man's clothes, photos or toiletries.'

'What about the MO? Did you find any twine or rope which could've been used as the murder weapon?' McAbbey asked.

Gavin shook his head. 'The killer was methodical. I doubt he left the cord lying around after dusting, wiping and vacuuming.'

'Could he have used the power cord from the vacuum cleaner?' Pete asked.

'No.' Gavin dismissed the thought. 'The circumference of the power cord is too large.'

'OK. Let me know the forensic results as they come to hand.' McAbbey made a few additional notes in his file.

'Next—our visit to the school.' McAbbey chewed the end of pen for a moment.

'The teachers were hiding something—I'm sure of it. They looked hesitant to say anything improper about her. They referred to a few minor things and her abuse of school uniform. It was not the sort of response you would expect over a student who was a regular in the principal's office. I think Mrs Nicholson is covering something up.'

'What did the kids say?' Jack asked.

'Not much,' Pete shrugged. 'They didn't like her. She didn't fit in. She fought with the other students and was always breaking the rules.'

'I got the teacher out of the room so you could find out what the hell was going on!' McAbbey glared at Pete. 'Perhaps you can explain to me why your old man called me when I got back this morning, wanting to know what I was doing in Brighton. How'd he know I was out there?'

'He asked me ...' Pete said quietly.

'So what's his interest in this?' McAbbey demanded. 'I don't see how the death of the girl impacts the school unless there's something going on.'

Pete frowned. 'I honestly don't know.'

'Did the kids mention anything untoward about any of the teachers?'

Pete caught McAbbey's stare and took a sharp breath. 'Their class teacher, Mr Pearce, left last week. The teacher they had today is his replacement.'

'The principal mentioned nothing of this. Did the girls say why he left?'

'They were told he went on long service leave, but they think he was sent off. Some of the girls thought he was a pervert.'

'Did you ask if Pearce had a thing for Tania?'

Pete nodded. 'Apparently Tania bragged that she'd been to his house.'

'Right. Jack, get CIU to find this teacher ASAP. I think we should pay him a visit this arvo.'

Jack left to make the call.

'What about the principal?' Gavin asked. 'She's obviously tried to mislead you.'

'I know, but she didn't lie. I guess I didn't ask the right question.' McAbbey frowned. 'I can't see the point in pursuing her just yet. Let's see what comes from Mr Pearce's visit. Catherine, can you update the team on your preliminary autopsy results?'

Catherine stood.

'Her body was in sound condition—no scratches, contusions or bleeding. Nothing was visible which would indicate a struggle or assault. The autopsy confirms no semen or vaginal bruising. The blood pooled in the position we found her. From this, I believe she was propped up in bed soon after being garrotted.'

'What about signs of a struggle—were there any internal injuries?' Jack asked.

'No broken bones, internal bleeding—nothing. No wads of hair removed from her scalp, broken nails ...'

'Are you sure she died from the garrotte wound?' McAbbey asked.

'Though I'm sure, the circumstances which led to it are hard to determine.'

'I think we'll learn more from the mother,' Jack said to McAbbey, who nodded.

'This stinks of an inside job. She's still our number one suspect.'

'Could it be a boyfriend?' Pete asked.

'Possibly, Pete, however stepfathers and boyfriends often sexually assault their victims first. I suppose Tracey could have asked a boyfriend to kill Tania,' Jack said.

'Ms Stevenson's here.' Their receptionist stood at the door.

'Thanks, Helen. Set her up in interview room one.'

Catherine stood. 'I'll get going.'

'Thanks. I owe you again for coming down today,' McAbbey said.

After she left, McAbbey turned to the team. 'What do we know about Tracey Stevenson so far?'

'Very little,' Jack said. 'We have a request in with social security and a credit check is underway. She has no priors, has never held a passport and let her driver's licence lapse a year ago. Tania was an only child and the birth certificate doesn't list the father. Tracey has no brothers or sisters and her parents died in a car crash when she was twenty.'

'Well, let's go see her.'

McAbbey led the way through the main office, which was an ant's nest of activity, with detectives, witnesses and administration staff interacting against a constant ringing of phones in the background. Across from the main foyer was a series of numbered doors. McAbbey chose the first and waved Jack in before him. Gavin opened a second door and he and Pete stepped inside. Jack and McAbbey took plastic chairs and sat before a plain desk. Tracey was standing in front of a large reflective window, which faced the viewing room. Other than the window, the room was a box painted in ceiling white.

Tracey turned. She wore a tailored olive-green dress with matching shoes, handbag and complexion. Her blonde hair was swept into a bun, and covered in a halo of purposefully unrestrained wisps.

8

'Ms Stevenson. Would you like a drink? Tea, coffee …?' McAbbey asked.

'No, thanks.' She smiled thinly and sat before them.

'Thanks for coming this afternoon.' McAbbey nodded to Jack.

'I want to start with Tania,' Jack said.

She nodded, her glum look accentuating the red lines around her moist eyes.

'We've been unable to find any close friends that Tania may have had.'

'She didn't have many. There was a girl who lived down the street in the commission flats—but they moved to Sydney last year.'

'Do you know her name?'

'Caitlin. I'm sorry but I never knew their surname.'

'What about boys?'

'There were a few sniffing around, but I kept a close eye on that. She didn't have a regular boyfriend, if that's what you mean.'

'But you work a lot—and she seemed to miss a lot of school ...' McAbbey prompted.

'You think a teenager did that to my girl?' Tracey said, her left hand finding a hip.

'Not necessarily.' McAbbey lowered raised hands. 'We're required to check all avenues.'

Tracey shook her head.

'At what time did you find Tania?' Jack asked.

'I've already told the policewoman.' Tracey wiped her eyes. 'Please ...'

She sighed. 'I came in after two-thirty. The light was on in her room so I went up to see if she was awake. That's when I discovered her sitting up in bed.'

'And you called the police then?'

She nodded.

'What time did you leave the Espy?' McAbbey asked.

'Minutes before. It's not a long drive.'

McAbbey rubbed his brow. 'Why lie, Ms Stevenson? You must have known we'd check your alibi. You were working at the Weekly Stellar.'

'I guess it doesn't matter any more,' Tracey sighed. 'I work full-time as an escort. I only do about eight hours a week at the Espy.'

'Why bother with eight hour's bar work?'

Tracey dabbed fresh wet eyes with a tissue from under her sleeve. 'I was trying to be a good mother.'

Jack frowned. 'I'm sorry, but I don't understand.'

'What do you think my chances of getting Tania into St Anne's were, with "Escort" written on the parental application? It's not enough that you can afford the term fees—you have to be seen to be the right sort of parent. As it was, it was difficult for me not being happily married to Mr Right.'

McAbbey gave her time for composure before continuing. 'What happened to Tania's father?'

'She never knew him,' Tracey said with a sombre shrug. 'And he doesn't know about her.'

McAbbey nodded. Prostitutes with children were often single.

'Do you have a boyfriend?' Jack asked.

'I've had many. Keeping them is the hard bit.'

'Are you seeing anyone now?' McAbbey asked.

'No.'

'Is there any chance a past boyfriend could've held a grudge? Maybe the attack was not directed at her—but as revenge for something you've done.'

'Look, I don't mix men with my home life—it doesn't work. It's just Tania and me.'

'You called for the police when you saw her?' Jack asked.

She paused before nodding. 'Yes, they were here in minutes. The rest of it's a blur. I don't remember much after that.'

'Did you go to her? Touch anything in the bedroom?' McAbbey asked.

'I was in shock.' Tracey sighed. 'I think I might have walked over to her.'

'Was she a tidy girl? Her room's clean.'

'Yes, but I clean through the house most days and we have a maid. My friends think I'm nuts.' She shrugged.

'Did you and Tania get along well?' Jack asked.

She gave a wistful smile. 'We had the usual mother–daughter fights. I kept trying to get her to do something with her life—you know, school and the like.'

'Do you regularly work Sunday nights?' Jack asked.

She nodded.

'What would be the earliest you'd normally finish?'

'About one—I guess. It's never the same.'

'How do you get home?'

'John Roderick gives me a lift.'

'Is he a friend?'

'Yes—well, no. He drives all the girls home from work.'

'What about Tania—did your driver meet her?'

'They met many times. He adored her—as he adored all of us.' She frowned. 'There's no way John could be involved.'

'One last thing. Was anything stolen—money, valuables?'

'Not that I can think of.' She burst into tears. 'My daughter's gone and you're worried about money? She's the only important thing that's been stolen from me ...'

9

McAbbey stood and Jack ushered the mother out.

Pete turned to Gavin in the observation room. 'Did you think she was a prostitute?'

Gavin nodded. 'She lives too affluently for a bar worker, but her bold classy outfits and confidence were the giveaways for me.'

'What a lonely life,' Pete said.

'Yeah, well that's the sad thing about prostitution. No one to share the money with,' Gavin replied.

McAbbey walked into the observation room.

'Pete, I want you to ring Emergency Services. Get me the tape of her call to the police. Gavin, go to the Weekly Stellar and confirm her alibi for the record. While you're there, speak to Mr Roderick. If he took her home regularly, he'll know if anything was up. Go with him, Pete.'

'Do I need to take anything?' Pete asked Gavin.

'Protection—just in case,' Gavin winked and Pete blushed.

'He means your gun ...' McAbbey glared at Gavin.

When McAbbey returned to his office, he called the Weekly Stellar and spoke with the manager on duty. McAbbey introduced himself and explained the circumstances.

'We were sad to hear about poor Tania.'

'You've heard?' McAbbey asked.

'Sure—we're practically family. Tracey rang this morning to let us know she'd need some time off.'

'What can you tell me about Tracey?'

She thought for a moment before answering. 'Look, I won't talk about my staff over the phone. I believe you are who you say you are, but I'd like to see ID before I talk. You know how nosey the press can be.'

'I understand—I'm sending two detectives out this afternoon,' McAbbey said.

Jack tapped on McAbbey's door and McAbbey thanked the manager and hung up.

'The teacher is Paul Pearce. He's at home, in Balaclava. Do you want to go and see him now?'

McAbbey nodded. 'I want a DNA sample to test against the matter Forensics found.'

'We need to ask his permission,' Jack said.

'I don't want to alarm him. This needs to be an informal chat—he knew the girl, nothing more. Start asking for DNA samples and he might refuse to cooperate.' McAbbey lowered his voice. 'I think a hair might accidentally leave his apartment. We need to know if he's connected ASAP. If we discover anything, then we'll go through the red tape and get a warrant for a legit DNA sample.'

Jack nodded—it had been done before. It would be inadmissible in court, but invaluable for them to determine whether further effort was necessary with the suspect.

'Good. Let's go and see Pearce.'

'We can expect a wait if he wants his lawyer,' Jack warned.

'Bugger his lawyer—we'll get him talking first. Then, if he wishes, he can phone a friend.'

McAbbey drove the short distance south down St Kilda Road to Carlisle St and turned left. He followed a tram at a crawl, past a shopping strip and under a rail bridge then turned right. He pulled up at a terracotta-brick block of flats overgrown with ivy.

Jack led the way up concrete stairs to the second level and pressed the buzzer.

Paul Pearce opened the door and waved them inside.

'Good to meet you.' McAbbey offered a hand and received a clammy grip in return. He introduced himself and Jack and thanked Pearce for making time to see them.

Paul Pearce looked like a middle-aged Charlie Brown, wearing corded pants and a knitted jumper. He was clean-shaven with short brown hair that circled a bald patch at his crown.

He stood and offered them a three-seater leather couch.

'Can I offer you anything to drink?' Pearce asked.

'Yes. Coffee please, white and one.'

'Nothing for me.' Jack gave McAbbey a look of surprise and then smiled.

Once Pearce left the room to get his coffee, McAbbey looked around. It was a single bedroom apartment. His living area was carpeted and opposite the couch was a portable television and video. Above the couch, McAbbey counted twelve sunflowers in a framed Van Gogh reprint. To the side was a computer in a wall cabinet, with books and a stack of compact discs in a shelf above.

Jack stood and wandered across to look at the computer. McAbbey peered under the coffee table in front of him and saw editions of *House and Garden* and *Family Circle's Easy Vegetarian*.

The kettle whistled and Jack returned to the couch. Pearce arrived with McAbbey's coffee.

'So, how can I help you, Inspector?'

McAbbey set his coffee down without tasting it.

'Tania Stevenson was murdered last night. As her former class teacher you're best placed to give us some background on her time at school.'

'What would you like to know? I mean—I was only her teacher for the first month of this year.'

'Was she a smart student?' Jack asked.

'She was gifted—no doubt about that,' Pearce admitted. 'She just had no inclination to study.'

'Can you think of anyone who might have held a grudge against her?'

'No, Inspector. Some of the teachers hated her attitude, but not enough to do that.'

'Perhaps one of the teachers was seeing her?' McAbbey prompted.

Pearce froze.

'Why did you take long service leave?' Jack asked.

'Stress. I needed the break.'

'After only a month back? That's a bad disruption to the kids' learning.'

'I know, but I've been teaching for twenty years without a decent rest. Ask Mrs Nicholson, the principal. She understood that I needed a break.'

McAbbey nodded, having no doubt that the official file in the principal's office would support his claim.

'Where were you last night, Mr Pearce?'

'I was at a church retreat in Wandin, an hour east of Melbourne.'

'Is there someone who can attest to that?'

'Yes, about thirty adults.'

'Was the retreat connected with the school?'

'Um. No ... it's a Christian society, but not affiliated with the school.'

McAbbey stood. 'If you don't mind, I need to use the bathroom before we go.'

He left the room before Pearce could object.

Down the short hall, McAbbey passed the bedroom on the way. He took a look in before opening the bathroom door. There was a large painting of the Virgin Mary on the wall. The bed was made and his dresser was clean, but for a pile of opened mail, newspapers and catalogues, which looked like they had been scooped up from the lounge coffee table in a hurry. McAbbey glanced at the open section of the Saturday *Age* with interest.

In the bathroom he reached into his pocket and pulled out an envelope and tweezers. Kneeling, he selected a few random hairs with follicles attached. Placing the samples in his pocket, he flushed the toilet and washed his hands.

'Thanks for your time, Mr Pearce,' McAbbey said when he returned to the lounge room. 'Please call me if you think of anything which might help us.'

—▲—

'What did you find in the bathroom?' Jack asked when they were back in the car. 'He looked worried.'

'I got a few DNA samples for testing, but it was what I saw in the bedroom that interests me. He had a copy of the employment section of the *Age* and had circled a few gardening jobs.'

'Gardening?'

'I wonder ...' McAbbey looked at Jack. 'If he was ousted for improper behaviour, maybe the school agreed to keep it under wraps if he quit teaching altogether.'

'He seems religious,' Jack said. 'He had a few bibles on his computer shelf and a scroll with Christian quotes on it.'

'Yes, but that's not unusual for a lay teacher at a religious school. Did you get a look at the computer discs?'

'Yes. They were numbered and dated, but there were no descriptions.'

'What do you suppose is on them?'

'Could be anything. He has his own CD writer.'

'Could it be child porn?' McAbbey said.

'Maybe, or it might just be educational software. Do you think he's involved?' Jack asked.

'Yes, but I'm not sure he killed her. You must admit though, he does look like the tidy type who might vacuum a crime scene.'

'Do you want to get a warrant and go through his place?' Jack asked.

'No, let's wait and see what comes of the DNA test. We should keep our eye on Pearce—oh, and confirm his alibi will you?'

10

The sun blazed hot from the west when Pete arrived at the Weekly Stellar Gentlemen's Club. He jumped from his car but before he could close the door, a dapper young man in a tuxedo took his seat.

'Keys, please,' he demanded with authority.

Pete paused, running a hand through his slicked back hair. 'But I'm with Homicide ...'

'No problem, sir. The last guy was a judge.' The valet took the keys and shut the door before Pete could object, and drove off.

From the street the club looked like a private hotel with quiet advertising and glass doors with gold handles. With a furtive glance to the passers-by on the street, he went inside.

Pete was surprised not to find a dingy, dark environment with seventies décor. Instead, he stood in a modern foyer complete with chandelier, comfortable seating and coffee lounge. He glanced repeatedly at his watch until Gavin arrived.

'Sorry I'm late.' Gavin looked at Pete and grinned. 'You're not nervous are you?'

'Of course not!' Pete said, leading the way to the reception desk.

A lady greeted them with a smile. She was dressed in a black business suit, with neatly tied back hair. Standing beside them at the counter, two gentlemen were filling in documents.

'Do you have an appointment?' she asked. The two other men stopped writing and stared at them.

'Yes, I'm here to see the manager. I'm Detective Senior Constable Pete Vincent.' He removed his wallet and flashed his "Freddie". 'We called earlier.'

She looked at his ID and nodded. 'I'm the manager. My name's Barbara Horton. Please come through.'

Barbara ushered them into her office, painted plain white and decorated with six movie posters from old Bogart classics. She proffered them each a black leather study chair.

'What can you tell us about Tracey Stevenson?' Pete asked.

'She's a good worker with a long list of regular clients.'

'How is she with clients—does she make enemies?' Gavin asked.

'She does have a temper, and occasionally fights with them.'

'Do you call in security when that happens?' Gavin leaned forward.

'Oh no. It's up to each girl as to the action we take. Security can be called for, but Tracey generally took care of herself. She even put one in hospital once—he tried forcing her to fellate him without a condom.'

'What did she do?' Gavin pressed.

The manager gave a wry grin. 'Let's just say, like Humpty, they struggled to put him back together again.'

Gavin shifted uncomfortably. 'Could he have a grudge against her?'

'Wouldn't you?' she raised an eyebrow.

'Was she seeing any clients at home?' Pete asked.

'Of course not!' Barbara was horrified. 'It's illegal. Besides this place gives the girls anonymity and security.'

'Is there anyone here, client or employee, who might have a reason to kill Tracey's daughter?'

She shook her head. 'Everyone here loved Tania. She was such a sweet girl—yet so much like her mother.'

'What do you mean?' Pete frowned.

'Her moods, of course.'

'No, I mean did Tania come here?'

'Well, yes. A lot of girls bring their dependants to work. We do have a crèche,' she defended angrily.

Pete apologised.

'Is Tracey's driver, Mr Roderick, here?' Gavin asked.

'Sure.' Barbara disappeared for a minute, returning with a burly man who was shiny bald with a bushy black moustache. He wore a short-sleeved white shirt like a second skin and the tattoos on his forearms had faded green.

'I'm Mr Roderick.' The man squeezed the life from Gavin and Pete.

'You drive Tracey home regularly?' Gavin asked.

'Yes, that's right.'

'Is there anyone who might have had reason to kill her daughter—a client of this club?'

'No one comes to mind. The crèche is always out of sight of the clientele.'

'What about the other security officers?' Pete asked.

'We had a function last night. Every security guard was on duty.'

'Why wasn't Tania at the crèche?' Gavin asked.

'You're kidding, aren't ya? She's thirteen for chrissakes. She hasn't been here since her last birthday.'

'Did Tracey talk about her clients much?'

'She sure did. She bagged 'em all. They either smelt, couldn't get it up, or came too early.'

'What about boyfriends?'

Mr Roderick frowned for a moment. 'You know, in the three years I've been here, I don't think she's ever had a partner.'

'Do you remember dropping her off last night—were there any suspicious cars outside the apartment building?'

'Yeah, but the street's always full of vehicles. There's not much off-street parking. I didn't see anyone hanging around, if that's what you mean.'

Gavin glanced at Pete, confirming they were finished.

'Thanks for your time.' Gavin stood.

11

McAbbey returned to his office in the late afternoon and sent an envelope of hair from Pearce's apartment to Catherine for DNA testing. He took his briefcase and walked out, pausing only to tell Andrea he was going home.

McAbbey drove to Lilydale without turning on the police or commercial radio.

As he reached the outer eastern suburbs of Melbourne, he released the sunroof and soaked in the country air, exorcising the demons of the city. As a seasoned Homicide detective, McAbbey lived and breathed the worst of urban society—his nightly escape from its clutches saved his sanity.

The road gave way to rolling hills, nestled creeks and gum trees of chaotic form, as he turned into the drive of his five-acre homestead. As he pulled up, he noticed his daughter, Chelsey, saddling up her pony for an evening ride. Her hair was plastered to her head by a tightly crammed riding hat. She waved to him as he walked to their double-storey house.

Lisa was by the sink, peeling vegetables. They were the same age, but she looked younger with her trim figure, light freckles and mousy brown hair in a ponytail.

'She done her homework?' he grumbled, as he dumped his briefcase on the kitchen table.

'Chel's finished it already. Remember she gets home at three thirty.'

'Bloody schools—it's bad enough that their holidays are interrupted by semesters.' He sighed, sitting heavily at the kitchen table.

'Why are you home early?'

'I've had enough today.'

Lisa went over and squeezed his shoulders.

'What's on your mind, Ryan? Is it that girl who was found?' Lisa stopped her massage.

'Yeah.' McAbbey reached for the *Herald Sun* and flicked through it aimlessly. 'We have so little to go on. Her mother's a prostitute which means the girl was potentially exposed to her clients. That increases the number of possible suspects.'

'I heard on the news that she was strangled,' Lisa said.

'She's the same age as Chel.' McAbbey continued to turn pages—flicking past the comics and crosswords and into the classifieds.

Lisa nodded. 'I saw the picture.'

McAbbey shook his head. 'She was only a kid, for chrissakes.' His shoulders slumped as he reached the back page. 'Sometimes I just want to go out and belt someone.'

12

First thing the next morning, McAbbey received a phone call from Harry Vincent.

'Ryan, how are things down there?'

'Swell.'

'How's the investigation into that girl from St Anne's going?'

'Not good,' McAbbey grumbled. 'It's been over thirty-six hours. We're finding it hard. There are no witnesses and we've failed to find DNA evidence or a suspect.'

'Shocking. What about family and friends?' Vincent asked.

'She has no friends to speak of and her mother is a prostitute at the Weekly Stellar.'

'Has that got out?'

McAbbey gritted his teeth. 'I seem to be having trouble with the principal from St Anne's. You couldn't speak to your contact there so I can get some answers?'

Vincent let out a forced cough. 'Look, I have to go. I'm meeting the Police Minister in half an hour. Please keep me posted.'

'Arsehole.' McAbbey slammed the phone down.

An hour later, McAbbey went to the conference room for their briefing.

'Morning, everyone,' he said. 'Welcome back from holidays, Ted.'

Ted Dowling was a skinny man in his late thirties with thinning hair and large horn-rimmed glasses. He was a late detective recruit to Homicide and was still a senior constable.

'Hope you had more luck fishing on the Murray than we've had here.' Gavin chuckled.

McAbbey gave him a look as he put a phone on the table and hit a preset number. Catherine answered and McAbbey greeted her tersely,

'Hi, Ryan. There's no doubt she was garrotted with a thin rope or cord and died of asphyxiation. However ...' Catherine paused and they heard rustling of paper over the speakerphone. 'The toxicology results are in and she was drugged.'

'That would explain the lack of a struggle,' Jack said.

'What with?' McAbbey asked.

'An antihistamine. Unfortunately it's a generic, which will be impossible to trace. I checked with Forensics that there were no vials or tablet packets found at the scene. My guess is the killer dispensed it to the victim.'

'Are you sure she wasn't on a prescription?'

'Yes. I confirmed that with Tracey. I didn't uncover any preconditions requiring treatment or medication.'

'I had a call from Forensics about a washed glass we found in the dish rack,' Gavin volunteered. 'It was laced with a fine residue. They were going to run tests on it.'

'Can you be sure she didn't die from the drugging—that it wasn't an overdose?' McAbbey asked.

'Yes, I can. Her stomach had digested the drug. If she'd died before, then her stomach would have ceased to absorb.'

'How was it ingested?'

'From gastric residue, I suggest it was mixed with Coke on an otherwise empty stomach.'

'What effect would this have had on the girl?' Gavin asked.

'It would have made her extremely drowsy, after ten minutes or so.'

'So, the killer spiked her drink, waited and then garrotted her,' Jack said.

'It appears so. The vaginal swab came back clear, earlier this morning,' Catherine said.

'Did you match any DNA on your wiz-bang data box?' McAbbey asked.

'Database ...' Catherine said pointedly.

Jack and Gavin exchanged a wry grin. The national CrimTrac database was one of Catherine's leading projects, which aimed to record all felony offenders for future crime identification.

'Whatever.' McAbbey's ignorance of all things binary made him stand out like a redneck at a Greenies convention.

'So far, no. We've dismissed all matter found as being from either the mother or the daughter.'

'What is the likely success rate if we get you a DNA swab?' McAbbey asked with a frown.

'Not high,' Catherine said. 'Unless the murderer is a formerly convicted offender, the database will be of no use.'

'But haven't you been working to include a wider net of criminals with Forensics at Macleod?' McAbbey pressed.

'The database is new—you know how many obstacles we've had getting convicted criminals and suspects listed.'

'OK, Cath. What about the hair samples I sent you last night from Mr Pearce?'

'If Forensics finds DNA matter matching Pearce in their second sweep of the apartment, I will be able to confirm it for you through a PCR comparison.'

McAbbey thanked her and took the phone off the table when Catherine hung up.

'Jack. What about prints?'

'We put the best partial prints through the computer; however there was no match to any convicted offenders on CrimTrac.'

'What about Pearce?' McAbbey asked.

'I guess he could've left prints. We would need a warrant to take a clean set from him. Do you want to go that far?'

'No. I don't want to alert him just yet. What other evidence were you able to recover from the bedroom?'

'Not a thing.' Jack shook his head.

'Do you think the killer wiped the crime scene?'

'Yes. I don't think Tania would invite a man wearing surgical gloves into her house,' Gavin offered.

'Could the crook have worn a bodysuit?' Ted asked. 'It would explain why the house was free of dermal matter.'

'That's one possibility, but again, it's unlikely Tania would allow him in,' Jack said.

'I want you to check her family and friends again. This stinks of an inside job. How did you go with the neighbours?' McAbbey asked.

'Not great,' Jack said. 'For the most part they keep to themselves. Even if they knew something I don't think they'd tell. We had one decent response from Mrs Tanner, an elderly lady who lives two down. She can see people coming and going to the courtyard apartments through her front window.'

'She said Tracey was a hussy who often had different men visit her,' Pete continued, after a curt nod from Jack.

'Do you think she'd be useful to us if we conducted a line-up?'

'Yes—she took note of what happened around her. Unfortunately the apartments have back doors facing the laneway. I reckon someone visiting Tracey would be more inclined to use a discreet entrance.'

'A regular could get lazy. Jack, I'd like you to have another chat with the people in the apartment block and to those who live down the street.'

McAbbey turned to Pete. 'How did your visit go? Did the brothel manager know of any clients Tracey may have had on the side?'

'No. She said they're not allowed to.'

'That wouldn't stop Tracey doing it without their knowledge.'

'I found out that Tania used to go to work with her mother!'

'They allowed kids in that place?' McAbbey raised his voice.

'They have a crèche. Most of the women who work there are single mothers,' Gavin explained. 'The establishment is a well-run operation.'

'It may be the Hyatt, but it makes it bloody difficult for us to narrow the search if everyone who's ever visited the Weekly Stellar has seen her.'

Gavin agreed.

'It comes back to the mother,' McAbbey said, with a nod in Jack's direction.

'You think she killed her daughter?' Pete looked surprised.

'Not personally, Pete,' Jack said. 'She may have had one of her boyfriends or clients do the job. Parents often lose control—some kick their kids out of home, others bash them senseless and the worst ones turn to murder. Tracey can't even palm her daughter off to the father.'

'You're assuming Tania was an accident,' McAbbey said, picking up the case file. He dismissed them and returned to his office.

13

The following morning McAbbey received a call from Harry Vincent, the Chief Commissioner.

'I'm sorry to say we haven't made much progress,' McAbbey said, ignoring pleasantries.

'That's OK, Ryan.'

He cringed; he was 'McAbbey' on the Force and only Catherine ignored protocol by calling him by his first name. Why was Vincent being polite?

'Where are you at?'

'We have a couple of leads but no witnesses. We need to set up a mobile operation near her house and at the school. I also want to interview the mother for a press statement,' McAbbey said.

'I think you can forget about the mobile.'

'Why?'

'Nothing can come of it. It's best to leave it alone.'

'Leave it alone …?'

'Yes, Ryan. If the mother had taken clients home, just how many men had access to her daughter?'

'Her daughter was murdered. I think by involving the public, someone might come forward.'

'No, McAbbey.' Vincent raised his voice. 'Conduct your investigation through internal means for now. There's no need to involve the public in this.'

'The school won't wear it—is that what you're saying? Does the school really think the parents will take their kids out just because one student is murdered? Or is it because the mother's a pro?'

'You must understand this cannot be good for the local community. It's best forgotten. Her mother invited trouble with her behaviour and put her own daughter at risk. I won't let the school suffer for it.'

'This wouldn't have anything to do with your Carbine Club friend being on the School Council would it?'

'Never mind that—just do your job.'

'What about Paul Pearce—does he have anything to do with this?' McAbbey clenched his teeth at the silence at the other end. Vincent made an excuse about another appointment and hung up.

'PETE! Get the fuck in here!' McAbbey yelled through the glass. Pete came into his office, but stood at a distance from his desk.

'How does your father know that the mother was a prostitute?'

Pete's hands began to shake and he tried to speak, but no words emerged.

'Did you volunteer it?' McAbbey asked.

Pete nodded.

'Don't ever volunteer information on a case again,' McAbbey yelled. 'I don't care if shutting up means you need to stuff a crayfish in your mouth at the dinner table—what happens in our cases stays inside.'

To his satisfaction, Pete's face suddenly resembled a cooked crustacean.

14

After lunch, McAbbey received a reminder from his electronic diary. It was in hardcopy form—printed by Andrea, who entered his messages and reminded him as they fell due.

McAbbey quietly packed his things and walked out to his car. Helen, the receptionist, was chatting with Andrea about nail polish when McAbbey pushed past and told them he could be contacted on his mobile.

He puzzled over the Melways street directory in his car for five minutes and then called his wife.

'You're not thinking of pulling out?' Lisa asked.

McAbbey gripped the steering wheel. 'It sounds so wanky Lise.'

'You told me yourself you need stress relief. Your doctor's concerned that your stomach cramps might be more than just stress—for God's sake put my mind at rest. The Oracle is a great meditation centre. It got me through my pregnancy.'

'I guess any place that calls itself the Oracle of Mental Fulfilment can't be too stressful.'

McAbbey continued south down St Kilda Road to the beachside suburb of Mentone. The home of the Oracle was a late nineteenth century renovated Victorian mansion, painted virgin white with elaborate cornices and religious statues. Most of the internal walls had been removed to form an expansive area with ocean views. There were large photos of sunsets and mountains on the remaining walls and the floor was covered with plush cream carpet and stacks of pillows.

The Oracle resembled an eccentric Tupperware party. The 'tired souls', as one volunteer labelled them, were mostly women with offspring leaving McAbbey to ponder how it was supposed to de-stress the others. Kids ran amok as the mothers sat in little circles on pillows discussing motherhood and stress. McAbbey took a glass of cold water from a passing lady identified by a printed name tag as Sister Sue.

A man wearing an open check shirt walked up to McAbbey and read from his hand written name badge.

'McAbbey … an interesting Christian name.'

'Sorry, everyone knows me by my surname.' McAbbey smiled at the tall athletic man, whose quiet manner belied his Jack Pallance exterior. McAbbey guessed him to be in his fifties, but was surprised by the sparkle of life emanating from his blue eyes.

McAbbey studied the man's badge thoughtfully. It was typed, and thus he was not a visitor. 'How are you, Brother Clive?' McAbbey asked.

'Very well. I'm glad you could join us.' The man moved towards the door to greet latecomers. McAbbey glanced over the new arrivals and paused when he recognised one of them.

'Well, well …' he muttered under his breath.

Paul Pearce walked in, wearing a light brown cardigan with a diamond pattern. Pearce froze when he saw McAbbey staring at him from across the room and spoke briefly to Brother Clive, who gave a cursory glance in McAbbey's direction.

Sipping his water, McAbbey remembered that Pearce's alibi involved a religious sect; did they run this meditation facility as well? McAbbey acknowledged him and Pearce reluctantly walked over.

'Inspector. Here for meditation?'

'I am, actually. Wife's orders.'

Pearce gave a thin smile.

'Hope there's no hard feelings about yesterday,' McAbbey said, noting that Pearce also wore a printed badge.

'None taken. You were just doing your job. Enjoy the relaxation.' Pearce walked away and sat on a pew.

'Please everyone, come together and join us in meditation.' It was Sister Sue. She was a wafer-thin woman in her mid-forties with jagged short hair.

McAbbey begrudgingly made his way to the carpet, chose a pillow and lay down. Sister Sue switched off the lights and a glow-in-the-dark crucifix looked down on them. She stepped aside for an elderly woman, who introduced herself as Sister Mary and spoke with a whisper.

'Many people find solace in prayer. This session is for meditation, however, for those of you who wish for pure cleansing of the soul, please see one of our brothers or sisters after reflection. Our Christian society places strong emphasis on the original teachings of the Bible. We live for tranquillity and purity of the soul. Purity is essential for the journey to heaven. Those without, are doomed to eternal damnation. In this life, we have but one chance to right the wrongs of the past.' The lady closed her eyes and rested her chin on her chest.

'I would like everyone to close their eyes and concentrate on the sound of my voice,' the lady said.

As she droned on in her hushed manner McAbbey found his attention drift and in minutes, he was fast asleep.

An hour later, a man tapped McAbbey on the shoulder and he sat up, embarrassed to see that everyone else was up and talking. They were being encouraged to join the religious movement, of which the meditation was a part.

With the session concluded, McAbbey made a dash to his car without looking back. As he walked out, he couldn't shake the feeling that Pearce was watching him.

15

Two weeks passed and the first chill of autumn was upon them when McAbbey paid a visit to Catherine at the Institute of Forensic Medicine complex at Southbank.

McAbbey often consulted Catherine on his ideas, as her thought processes worked outside the paradigms of a Homicide detective.

'So, you're not convinced that one of the mother's clients was responsible for the murder.' Catherine said.

McAbbey shrugged, 'No, I could believe it if the young girl had been raped. Certainly the mother had nothing to gain from her daughter's death financially. There were no insurance policies etc. Every way you look at it, Tracey and Tania seemed to get on well. The drugging suggests premeditation.'

'A woman or a man of limited strength might have required drugs to subdue her. The fact there was no break-in suggests to me the killer was known to the girl,' Catherine offered. 'I think the killer didn't want to see her suffer pain. It would explain why she was nicely laid in bed. What about the father?' Catherine asked.

'She says he doesn't know Tania existed. I'd say it was a mistake from a client relationship. Jack checked the births record but the father is listed as unknown.'

'Can you force her to reveal his identity?'

McAbbey shrugged. 'I'm beginning to think she may not know which client it was, and that she's trying to protect her own interests. If it gets out, the father may sue her.'

'Perhaps the father is someone famous,' Catherine said.

McAbbey smiled. He loved the way Catherine could prattle on about 'what ifs' and possibilities. Occasionally she rattled his tin with a lead worth pursuing. Other times, like now, she reiterated the thoughts which had been running through his head for weeks.

He dropped his head. 'The mother didn't know her daughter's friends well enough and I doubt one of Tracey's clients will confess. The brothel has refused us permission to photograph their clients for the neighbours to look at. Unfortunately, with so little to go on, I don't think we'll find her killer.'

'What?' Catherine folded her arms. 'You can't tell me that you've given up hope already?'

'No, but look at the lack of evidence, Cath. We've found only fragmented fingerprints, and no DNA. The mother was a prostitute with many clients and she had an alibi for the time of death. To top it off, the Chief Commissioner is thwarting our investigation at every turn and refuses to allow a mobile unit to be set up at the scene ...'

'What?'

'Yes. It's politically motivated of course. I could escalate the case through the press, however it's hard to lead an investigation from the back of the dole queue, which is what would happen if I went around Vincent.'

'The bastard.'

'Yeah. We have no witnesses to any persons entering the premises, yet irate neighbours lost count of the men who came and went.'

'But someone got inside with Tania's blessing and killed her.'

'I know. It's been bugging me but, unless I can get a lead of some sort, I haven't a hope in hell of catching the bastard.'

Catherine shook her head slowly. 'It makes it so much harder when it's all in vain.'

'Well, we're watching Pearce. He's the closest I have to a suspect. I think he's a paedophile, which gives us motive. What I need now is proof that he was at the crime scene. I might bring him in and work him over a bit.'

'If he's a paedophile and she wasn't raped, perhaps he took pictures of her naked.'

McAbbey was angered by the thought.

'Look, I know how you feel, Ryan. I'd be upset too if I had a daughter.' She put a hand on his shoulder. 'I saw the girl and I know how alike she and Chelsey are.'

McAbbey looked away, but did not shrug off her hand.

'The lack of suspects is frustrating. If we rounded up half the suspicious people in St Kilda, we'd need to double the size of the force to process them. I've a horrible feeling we'll never solve this case unless I can link Pearce somehow. I can't shake the feeling he's involved.'

16

Another two weeks later, at night, McAbbey tossed and turned endlessly. His heart raced and the pulse in his temples thudded in tune with his thoughts. He needed to give his job away—but never would. It was on nights like this that he knew he should take the drugs.

McAbbey had strong sleeping pills, but he rarely used them. He did not like the sinking feeling—the chasm through which he fell into the arms of darkness. So potent were the pills that he rarely heard the morning alarm, had no appetite for breakfast and was napping in his office by three in the afternoon.

More importantly, he did not take them because his restless conscience was usually a portent that death was to follow. McAbbey was often wide awake when the call came through to attend a murder scene. Sometimes he had even dressed and shaved before a call.

The investigation into the young girl's death had stalled. McAbbey was constantly plagued by unanswered questions. Was the girl's attacker a client? What was the motive? Was her death related to her mother's prostitution? Was Pearce somehow connected?

They had been unable to find evidence that Pearce was ever at Tracey's house, and though McAbbey's vibes told him Pearce was involved, there was no proof.

McAbbey was puzzled as to why someone was freely allowed in the house, but found it necessary to use drugs. The killer then garrotted Tania and mysteriously tucked her into bed, leaving no fingerprints or distinguishing matter for DNA analysis.

During the investigation, the press had largely ignored the murder. As per Vincent's request, Police Media omitted all reference to her mother's employ and the fact she may have been soliciting prostitution at her private residence. McAbbey withheld information from the press about the murderer's use of drugs and unusual corpse presentation, believing it would serve them better unreported. The lack of evidence found at the scene pointed back to the mother, but they had been there already. She had a rock solid alibi for the two hours before the murder took place.

It had been a month, and lying in bed at four in the morning, McAbbey wondered whether that girl's killer would ever be brought to justice. Somehow he felt he would not sleep well until she was avenged.

McAbbey sat bolt upright; the phone was ringing.

Rubbing his eyes, he reached for it.

'Boss, we have a suspicious death. You might want to come in.'

It was Jack Turner. 'It's in Walnut Drive, Mount Waverley.'

'Be there ASAP.' McAbbey hung up and stretched, his bones protesting. It was six in the morning.

Slipping out of bed quietly, he walked to the ensuite. He glanced back at his wife, Lisa, still lying blissfully unaware of the phone call. He considered himself lucky to live with a heavy sleeper.

McAbbey was not surprised that there had been a murder. Since young Tania, case 15/04, they had investigated only five more. To say they were due was not to say they lived in a violent or dangerous city. But when over three million people resided in an urban sprawl stretching over sixty kilometres east to west, murders were bound to happen.

A shower and shave took McAbbey five minutes. He put on his dark brown suit pants and a tweed sports jacket. He had dispensed with wearing a tie years ago. In his first year with Homicide, McAbbey leant over an autopsy victim and accidentally lowered his tie into the chest cavity of the deceased.

McAbbey surmised that he was a bit like Pete Vincent when he first started. Young, impressionable and gung-ho. Like a new shirt, Pete just needed ironing into shape.

He quickly drank his cup of Earl Grey, though it scalded his tongue. He made his typical Vegemite on toast and rushed for the door with his briefcase.

McAbbey's worn leather briefcase was a source of amusement at work. It was a twenty-first present from his father, who had aspirations of him becoming an accountant. The case had seen many years of action—that was to say, a career of lunches had lived inside it.

On a typical day it contained a Vegemite and cheese sandwich, the latest *Sports Illustrated* and an apple.

Gavin and Jack teased him about the case because he always locked it. They suspected he had something exotic stored inside. One year they actually drew up odds for what McAbbey kept in the briefcase. It appeared that the consensus among his peers was that he was collecting a piece of evidence from each homicide. There was nothing of interest or value in his case but, strangely, it was the reason he secured it. If they were to ever find out the case was nothing more than a glorified lunch box, he would never hear the end of it. He was sure they had rifled through his things looking for the password, but the lock had four tumblers and he kept the code in his head. They would never get it.

A top shelf Commodore came with McAbbey's position, however comfort had its price. The vehicle was used during work hours by the people of the office who refused to clean up their mess. Plastic bottles and brown paper bags littered the passenger and back floors. By the end of the week he usually had to empty all the rubbish out himself.

McAbbey feared the threats to catch the messy crooks fell on amused ears. He felt like the teddy bear of the office—hugged and squeezed occasionally, before being thrown back in the cupboard. He knew he was well liked, but often his easygoing nature left him trodden on.

McAbbey pondered this as he travelled down Burwood Highway with a fleet of cars growing like a river from its source. Peak hour—a misnomer—had started. McAbbey mused that these days the roads were forever busy.

Off Blackburn Road, he found Walnut Drive. The street number was unnecessary. The red and blue light disco at the end of the road was a beacon.

17

McAbbey pulled up outside the house and stepped from his car. A young constable from the local CIU greeted him.

'Sir, we have a young male, aged fifteen.'

'Cause of death?'

'Not sure yet. The ambulance officers were the first to arrive at the scene.'

'Who called it in?'

'The emergency call came from the house—the father I assume.'

'Anyone else here from the Homicide Squad?'

'Yes, sir. Detective Vincent is upstairs.'

It was a double storey home, with a triple garage. It was open and he could see a new Volvo and five-series BMW parked inside.

Greeting another officer inside the door, McAbbey walked through a grand marble entrance into the lounge room.

He introduced himself to the victim's father, Brian Anderson.

'Please explain exactly what happened.' McAbbey was polite and showed respect for their loss, but time was precious.

The father spoke, choking back tears: 'I went to wake Brad at twenty past five. We go running together before he goes to school, but he didn't wake up this morning. I called for an ambulance when I realised he'd stopped breathing.'

'Exactly what time did you call?'

'Five-thirty.' The father was dressed for their run, wearing a trendy Move tracksuit. He maintained his composure, as his wife wept uncontrollably beside him.

'You know,' he said, blinking away tears, 'He was the last of our family's line.'

What could McAbbey say? Chelsey was an only child. He nodded sadly, but insulated his feelings. The Victim's Liaison Officer would arrive shortly to console the parents.

Standing slowly, McAbbey pointed discreetly to the stairs. The constable in the entrance way nodded. Walking up, he forced himself to look at the pictures on the wall. The baby photos commenced at the foot of the stairs. They were followed by pre-school snaps of Brad with a black labrador and then school photos tracing Brad from age five to fifteen. The blank spaces at the top half of the stairs drew bile to McAbbey's throat. There would be no graduation or wedding photos to follow.

Inside the bedroom, he was surprised to find Pete sitting thoughtfully at the kid's desk.

'What's up?'

'There's something about this that doesn't feel right.'

McAbbey frowned. 'Really? What's that?'

Pete never ceased to amaze him. Tania's case was the only cold-blooded murder he had ever seen. Since that case, McAbbey's crew had not been on call to investigate the other murders.

'Brian Anderson called the police saying his son was murdered and an ambulance was dispatched …'

McAbbey listened to Pete, but at the same time studied the scene. The youth looked to be sleeping. He had no marks on his face or visible chest. He was wearing fleecy pyjamas and had a few pillows stuffed under his head. The doona was pulled up comfortably. Pete was whispering as though he did not wish to wake the boy.

'It doesn't look like a suspicious death. He looks to have died of natural causes.' Pete hesitated, reading nothing from McAbbey. 'Why are we here?'

'Patience, Pete. Look around you. This boy was a sporty kid. Every cabinet, bookshelf and available space is taken up with trophies from athletics, footy and swimming. Even if the lad died of a heart attack, we'd still have to follow procedure.' McAbbey paused. 'Why don't you get me a copy of the emergency tape anyway? Let me know what you find.'

Pete nodded. 'Do you think he was murdered?'

'Not yet.' McAbbey had already noted a few anomalies, which would form part of the inquest brief and, though he suspected they were dealing with a homicide, it was up to the Coroner to report the final determination on cause of death.

He pulled out a pair of latex gloves from his coat pocket. Walking to the window, he pushed against it. With a quiet groan, it opened outwards.

'This lock is broken.' The latch was made from a die-cast metal and the wound was shiny new.

A cool breeze and a tall elm, beside the house, greeted him. 'This looks like a convenient entrance and exit for the killer. I want you to go outside and check the tree. Look for footprints, broken branches, clothing fibres, anything.'

'Sure.' Pete turned to go.

'Where's Jack?' McAbbey asked.

'Jack's checking on the neighbours.'

'Good morning, Ryan.' Catherine Smith had arrived.

'Howdy, Professor.' She looked like a nutty scientist, with her magnified glasses, white lab coat and latex gloves. The Coroner's court had a rotating list of on-call pathologists, however McAbbey deemed himself fortunate to have Catherine more often than not.

She moved about silently, firstly inspecting the body, and then the surrounds, using tweezers and clear plastic bags to store potential trace evidence. Maree, the appointed police photographer, followed her, taking pictures with an expensive camera. McAbbey stood with interest, watching Catherine and Maree work.

'What do you think, Cath?'

She wrenched a glove off and rubbed her neck thoughtfully. 'Well, at first glance there appears to be nothing suspicious. It appears likely the kid died of natural causes. But the latch here,' she pointed to the window, 'certainly looks like it was forced.'

'Hey! It's my job to worry about the window. I'm asking if the boy was aided in death.'

'Well, if you're so competent, why is one of your bimbos out there climbing the tree?' Catherine smiled smugly and she and Maree shared a grin.

There was an element of competition between the women and his all-male department. McAbbey stirred Catherine often by stating that his equal opportunity policy was not based on quotas, but on hiring the right 'man' for the job.

Detective Pete Vincent, however, was not one of those. Red with embarrassment, McAbbey opened the window.

'What the hell are you doing climbing the tree!'

'How else would I find evidence up here!' he replied with exasperation.

'Try a ladder.'

Pete disappeared down the tree, McAbbey hoped, to find the Anderson's ladder.

'Anyway, as you were saying?' McAbbey said casually as though nothing had happened.

Catherine grinned. 'At this stage I'd say he died in his sleep. The evidence I've collected and the autopsy may reveal otherwise, but I doubt it was foul play. I'll conduct my preliminary tests to determine whether you need to proceed with a Homicide investigation.'

'Fine. Shall I call on you, say, for lunch tomorrow?'

'After lunch.'

Noting her curt response, he stepped out of the bedroom. The last time he met her during mealtime he made a fuss of her eating habits. Catherine was so engrossed in her work that she returned to the autopsy table at least three times while scoffing down her salad roll. McAbbey did not eat lunch that day.

An hour later McAbbey arrived at the office. Though his crew had been quiet recently, there were always ongoing investigations to deal with. At least eighty cases were open and active, and some fourteen hundred cases remained unsolved.

Throwing his briefcase down beside his desk, McAbbey sat. His first reflex action of the morning was to turn on the computer. He was not sure why, as he rarely used it. McAbbey had computer literate staff to print his reports for him. Picking up his coffee mug, complete with a weekend's fungal sediment, he trudged to the tearoom.

'Morning, boss.' It was DSS Jack Turner. 'Did you hear the news?'

'No, what?' In the periphery of his vision McAbbey could see Andrea, his PA and Helen, the receptionist, watching them.

'The IT department is taking away your computer this afternoon.'

'Mine? I can't believe they'd dare take mine. There are junior officers less deserving, surely?' McAbbey snapped. 'I need it. My office has clear glass panels—the computer screen gives me privacy!'

'But you never use it.'

McAbbey felt the need to turn it on every day. Apart from the habit—it had a screen saver that Gavin had installed for him. It was an Elle McPherson swimsuit edition—his pride and joy.

'I do so use it!' he retorted.

'Did you notice that the mouse was missing?'

'It's there. Unless … you took it,' he accused Jack. He would not put it past him or Gavin to remove it as a practical joke.

'Don't worry sir; we can always print out the pictures of Elle to put on your wall.' Andrea said.

'That has nothing to do with it!'

'Actually, Boss, we took your mouse away last week to see if you were using it,' Jack said. 'I also had the IT department run a system test. It seems you don't even have a valid access code for the database. The system has suspended your login!'

McAbbey turned abruptly and grumbled his way back to his office. He was not reliant on computers anyway. His responsibilities were in the field, not in computer processing.

'Bugger ya. Have the bloody thing!'

He could hear laughter behind him.

18

It amazed McAbbey how quickly the time passed when the day was taken with reading reports and signing off on investigations. He had just spent the last thirty minutes reviewing the Tania Stevenson file.

A recommendation had been made to reduce the priority of the case. A month had passed and they had spent over a hundred man-hours with nothing to show for it. Even the tail on Paul Pearce had gone cold. The Chief Commissioner was trying to reduce spending within the department and a manhunt was expensive to run without a solid lead. As much as McAbbey had driven the investigation, he was also wary of expending energy without results.

Closing Tania's file did not ease the burden he felt. Placing it in the out-tray with five others, he sighed. The paperwork he processed lent an uncannily detached atmosphere to his work. He hated it.

Each shuffle of paper represented some poor dead soul. Generally an inspector was removed from the emotive aspects of a case but, with his added responsibilities as coordinator of a squad crew, McAbbey was signing off on investigations he had witnessed first hand.

⁓

It was a nice afternoon for a walk. Leaving his office, McAbbey strolled casually down St Kilda Road, amid the verdant elms and tolling trams. He stopped briefly for gnocchi bolognaise at the Southbank food court before arriving at Catherine's office.

He could not understand why Catherine ate in so often. She had restaurants, the Melbourne skyline and the Yarra River—all within a stone's throw of her office. Were dead people so intriguing?

The security man at the front desk waved him through. McAbbey had visited the place more often than the bored officer had counted sheep. He went past the lift and walked into the Morgue. Nodding to the receptionist, McAbbey passed through to the left theatre. The smell of enforced hygiene grew as he approached the entrance to Catherine's domain.

He opened the swivel door suddenly and peered inside, expecting to catch Catherine in the middle of some unorthodox procedure. Nothing doing. Catherine was on the far side of the room sitting at a stainless steel desk.

McAbbey could not help but notice a body on one of the sterilised trays. Covered by a stark-white sheet, the features of the human beneath protruded sharply.

'What are you doing here?'

'Our meeting. Remember?' His look of utter exasperation did not soften her resolve.

'I haven't forgotten, Ryan. I said after lunch.'

He sat next to her and watched her open a lunch box containing a smorgasbord of cold meats and salad. He watched in fascination as she cut open a bread roll with a scalpel, then proceeded to place pieces of lettuce, salami and tomato on the roll.

'Why eat it here—why not upstairs in your office?'

'There's less chance of being interrupted down here.'

McAbbey looked around him, hoping she was right. 'Why don't you make the roll at home?'

'I like the roll fresh,' she responded curtly, but sensed his interest was innocent. She glanced at him cheekily, leading him to believe she was about to do something that would incite his indignation.

He was right.

Standing abruptly, Catherine walked to the fridge. She opened the door, revealing a Star Wars-like puff of cold steam and disappeared inside.

Emerging quickly from the mist, Catherine returned to the desk carrying something she had retrieved from inside the air-conditioned tomb.

McAbbey would have to wire his jaw back into place. She sat with a smile, smugly proffering a block of cheese in a wrapper.

Waving a hand feebly, he watched in disgust as she picked up a scalpel and cut slices from the slab. She calmly placed the cheese back in the wrapper, put the scalpel back on an instrument tray and began eating her sandwich.

'Excuse me a minute will you?'

'Sure,' she replied gaily, through a mouthful of food.

McAbbey pushed the exit door wide open and gulped fresh air as he stood in the corridor.

Jack Rawson, the Senior Pathologist, passed McAbbey and grinned. 'Looks like she got you good and proper!'

'Yeah yeah …' McAbbey grumbled. 'It's not the first time.'

Within a few minutes his head cleared. Through the oval window in the door, Cath watched him. With a smile and a wave, she turned and finished her roll.

Shaking his head at her tenacity, he walked back in.

'Ready to see my report yet?' She stood.

'What about dessert?' He motioned to the body on the stainless steel tray, raising his eyebrows with mock expectation.

Catherine laughed. Picking up a file, she led him to the steel table. Removing the sheet, she revealed the body lying underneath.

It was Brad Anderson. The file reported his age at fifteen, though he appeared older, with long straggly blonde hair and facial growth. McAbbey recalled the trophies and pennants in his bedroom. He was not the type to die of a sudden illness.

'So, did he have some special precondition; a weak heart?' he asked.

'No. He was in perfect health. There were excessive mites and cotton fibres in his trachea. The burst blood vessels in the lungs indicate that he was muffled.'

'Suffocated?'

'Yes. With his own pillow. The fibres matched those found in his respiratory system.'

'But wouldn't a person normally breathe in matter from their own pillows anyway?'

'Not to that extreme. I suspect he may have struggled,' she said. 'But he would've been half asleep.'

'So it would've taken a fair amount of force. A man, most likely.'

'Not necessarily. If he were in REM sleep, the killer would have had an element of surprise.'

McAbbey nodded. 'We found no fingerprints, other than a few latents on the window from the boy. What about DNA? Any hair, semen, sweat, bad breath … ?'

'The kid was not violated, if that's what you mean. His parents' hair follicles were retrieved at the scene, but the killer was careful—we found no other traces of DNA in the bedroom.'

'Could it be the mother or father?'

'Maybe,' Catherine admitted. 'Do you think they might be involved?'

McAbbey shrugged. 'It's possible, but unlikely.'

Catherine knew what he meant; they both saw the distraught look on the parents' faces. McAbbey had previous experience with parents murdering children, and more often than not, was able to pick up vibes suggesting their involvement.

'What concerns me is that Mr Anderson called Emergency Services and said the boy had been murdered. Does that sound like the first reaction of a genuinely shocked parent at finding his son not breathing? He had no marks, bruises or wounds. A normal person would not have concluded murder.'

'Good point,' Cath replied.

'Did you find drugs in the boy's system?' He knew that by asking she would suspect he was trying to link this to the Tania Stevenson case.

'No, the toxicology report came up clean ...' Catherine paused.

'What is it, Cath?'

'Well, I agree the kid was about the same age as Tania, and the murderer left the scene as cleanly as her killer, but there's something else disturbing ...'

'What?'

'Did you publicly mention that Tania's killer sat the victim up, closed her eyes and covered her?'

'No.' The girl's melancholy pose had haunted him ever since. 'Your point—do you think the same guy did this?' McAbbey asked.'

'I don't know—that's your job!'

'Well, thank you.' When it suited her, it was his responsibility to fill in the blanks to the 'logic' she fabricated. He believed Cath was the best pathologist he had worked with. She often divulged peripheral information that led to the arrest of a murderer. McAbbey had this thought in his mind, but it was with an unconcerned flick of the wrist that he gestured for her to continue.

'Both victims were redressed post-mortem and both looked at peace. Neither would have looked relaxed if untouched after suffocation or strangulation.'

'Agreed, the change in modus operandi has taken our focus away from the fact the killer's signature is the same in both cases. Tania was strangled, yet Brad was suffocated. The girl was found dead with antihistamines in her system, yet there was no evidence of drugs with Brad Anderson. But in both cases his signature had not changed.'

'Signature?' Catherine frowned.

'Detective-speak. A serial killer learns from his past kills. He discovers what works, and what doesn't. He'll change his MO if it means achieving his ultimate aim more easily. The killer may have found strangulation too noisy, or difficult. The signature, however, is what gives the crook his sense of satisfaction. This is something he will not change, for to change would take away his reasons for committing murder in the first place. In our case here, if we were to draw a long bow and suggest the same killer is at work, his signature might be the posthumous presentation of the deceased.'

'What about the selection process?' Catherine asked.

'It depends on his needs. If he requires the victims to be a certain age or sex, then that would form part of the signature. If he chooses them simply because they're easy to find, I'd label that MO.'

Catherine paused, choosing her next words carefully. 'So when are you going to hand the crew over to Jack?' Catherine asked.

'I'll get around to it.' McAbbey scowled.

'Don't you think Jack's up to it?'

'Of course I do.' McAbbey sighed. 'I just can't bear the thought of being office-bound. I guess it's the reward you get for blood, sweat and years.'

'Want an ice cream?' Catherine broke McAbbey's sombre mood.

'Your shout?' he asked. Lisa would have a fit if she knew he was tempted. He was supposed to be on a diet. Lunchtime gnocchi was also taboo.

Suddenly McAbbey realised where Catherine kept the ice cream.

'Ah, no thanks. I'll be off,' McAbbey said. 'If anything else comes up, let me know.'

'Other than your lunch?' She smiled broadly.

19

McAbbey had a pleasant walk back along the Yarra River and caught a tram up to the office. He felt at peace—his thoughts detached from the outside world, momentarily interlocked with the steady sound of his breathing. How could such a tranquil city be the scene of violence?

McAbbey called it a day after an hour back. His computer was gone, leaving a patch of dust underneath, which gave McAbbey a sneezing fit.

His drive home to Lilydale was better than normal. The roads were not choked with peak hour traffic. In just twenty minutes, he was on the Eastern Freeway heading for the hills.

At home he cleansed work from his mind and thought about what to cook for dinner. Lisa would be at the sandwich shop until four-thirty, so he had time to surprise her and Chelsey with a creative dish.

He boiled hot water for rice and cleared the bench of dishes. He chopped tomatoes, onions and chicken fillets into a frypan. Adding mixed herbs, soy sauce and steamed vegetables, he fried an aroma the chef of Jacques Reymond would be proud of.

McAbbey set the table and found some candles in the cupboard. Lisa and Chelsey were stunned to see him cooking when they came home. They both went upstairs to change.

Rather than discuss his rotten day at the dinner table, he heard all about Lisa's afternoon, taking sandwich orders for the local factories in Bayswater. McAbbey mused how Lisa's stressful moments were almost whimsical—for instance, having to cut fifty sandwiches in just an hour. He would never have shown amusement at the troubles that plagued her for fear of offending, but he sometimes wished for such simple concerns.

Chelsey had played netball for the school junior team that afternoon—her first win as vice-captain. Her studies were progressing well and her particular academic interests were coming to the fore. Rather than follow in her 'daddy's footsteps'—for a long time her preferred path—she had become interested in school teaching.

With dinner finished, Chelsey was up and ready to leave.

'Where are you going?' McAbbey asked, hoping to spend the night with them and perhaps watch a video.

'Out!' she declared.

He could tell that Lisa had already approved.

'Where is she going, Lise?'

'Sorry, Ryan. If I had known you'd be home early tonight …' she sighed. 'Chelsey's going to Matthew's to study.'

'Not wearing that top you're not!' McAbbey snapped.

'Hello! Dad, it's only a belly button.'

'Better to be 'cool' than warm huh?' McAbbey rolled his eyes.

'The kids of today, Ryan.' Lisa shrugged helplessly, reserving a wink for Chelsey.

'Why can't you study here, Chel?' McAbbey asked.

'Because it's a group assignment and we have to team together to complete it. I'm in Year Eight now you know.'

'I could help.'

'Like, yeah. Dad,' Chelsey said. She pecked them both on the cheek and left on the tail of a whirlwind.

'What are we going to do about her?' McAbbey sighed. 'She's growing up way too fast.'

'What do you suggest, darl?'

'How about a tranquilliser?'

Lisa came around the table and sat in his lap. 'Maybe her going out isn't such a bad thing after all. We could retire upstairs.'

'How long do you reckon we have before she'll be back?' he asked with a wink.

'Oh, more than five minutes, dear.'

Slapping her behind playfully, he chased her to the bedroom.

Later, they watched the movie *Kiss the Girls*—a bad idea in hindsight. He had picked a video to satisfy his curiosity with how the Americans investigated their crimes and consequently could not sleep afterwards. He knew Lisa would have preferred a Meg Ryan film.

Matthew's father returned Chelsey at eleven and now that she was home, McAbbey could stop the tossing and turning and get some sleep.

20

'Sir?'

'Yeah?' McAbbey's throat felt choked with cotton wool. The clock starkly declared midnight.

'We have another; I think you'd better come. We're at the corner of Carrick and South Circular Drive, Gladstone Park.'

McAbbey dressed quietly and left a note for Lisa, who had not stirred.

The trip by moonlight from Lilydale to Gladstone Park, near Melbourne Airport, took an hour.

After multiple speed humps and a roundabout, he could see the flashing lights of his co-workers' vehicles. The local sticky beaks were out in force and he had to drive carefully to avoid people standing on the road seeking a better view. With no place to park due to the ambulance and police cars scattered like cyclone carnage, he drove into the middle of the roundabout.

A uniform was directing people around the house and Jack Turner was talking to the first officer to arrive at the scene.

The house was a three-bedroom brick veneer behind a fawn picket fence. McAbbey walked through a slate floor rumpus room and down a hallway to the victim's bedroom. For the second time in twenty-four hours, the deceased was found in bed.

'Her name?' he asked Catherine, who stood beside the bed.

'Sharron Sylvester.'

'Age?'

'Sixteen.'

'Swell. Where are the parents?'

'In the ambulance. The mother's taken ill.'

The girl was a typical sixteen-year-old. Posters of her favourite bands adorned every inch of space on the walls. McAbbey recognised Nirvana, Linkin' Park and The Offspring. He'd heard the noise from Chelsey's room often enough. He wondered if the girl was into the occult as well. The smell of at least twenty candles and incense burners lingered like the aftermath of an acrid bushfire.

Something on the ceiling caught his eye and he turned off the light with a latex-clad hand. Bathed in darkness, the ceiling glowed with the brightness of a clear night sky, thanks to fluorescent stickers cut into stars.

'Cute,' McAbbey said.

'Do you mind? I'm trying to take pictures!' Maree frowned at him for losing a photo to the darkness.

'You have a flash.' McAbbey shrugged. With the light back on, he joined Catherine beside the body.

'There seems to be no correlation with yesterday's murder.' Catherine confirmed his thoughts.

The girl was naked and lying on her other side. She was tall, thin and the crown of her dyed black hair retained its natural blonde. Her hair had matted to the back of her head, congealed with blood from the strike.

McAbbey could not help but think that she'd slumped down onto her side. He moved closer and touched a shiny spot on the bedhead with a gloved hand.

It was blood. McAbbey pulled a tissue from his jacket and wiped his glove clean.

'How was she killed?' he asked.

'She was struck from behind. I'd guess a cricket bat or rolling pin. The autopsy will reveal more.'

McAbbey studied the room. 'Where do you think she was struck from?'

'There is a light spattering of blood on the CD player and wall behind. I think she was sitting opposite the door, facing the player and taken by surprise.'

'So the killer put her in the bed?' McAbbey's pulse quickened.

'He may have, however, she wasn't propped up or tucked in.'

'What about the stain on the bedhead?'

'I wouldn't be surprised if he struggled to get her into the bed and knocked her head against it.'

'It's only a downwards smear. I think the killer sat her up and rested her head—like the others. She must have slumped down on her side after the killer left.'

'It's possible …' Catherine took another look. 'You might be right, you know. I guess there's a first time for everything.'

Nodding curtly, he walked outside to where Jack Turner knelt, marking time in the backyard vegie patch.

'Hi, boss.'

'What did you find?'

'Beans and cauliflower, but I wouldn't recommend the silver beet. It's been eaten alive.' Jack straightened up. 'The killer researched the area well. He came from the street behind and walked through the neighbour's property to this backyard. There are boot prints in the mud here where the killer jumped the fence. The lock on the back door was picked.'

'Could it have been a bungled burglary?'

'Not much chance of that I'm afraid. Muddy boot prints go from the back door directly to the girl's room. The intruder left the same way, taking nothing but the murder weapon.'

'Swell. Another premeditated.'

'Yeah.'

Jack had a son and daughter—fourteen-year-old twins. They were trying at times. He often joked to McAbbey he would probably strangle them before they made twenty one, but he knew how much they meant to Jack.

'I'm going home. Don't forget our meeting at noon today. See if Catherine can have a preliminary finding by then. Have you spoken to the parents?'

'No, they're being counselled at the moment.'

'How about you get Pete involved in interviewing them?'

There was a general resentment of Pete's appointment to the squad. Members of the force frowned upon favouritism by the bureaucracy, and nepotism was its worst form.

'Sure. But if he goes crying to dad again I'll kick his arse!' Jack smiled.

His house was in darkness when McAbbey returned to Lilydale. Melbourne in general was oblivious to the death that had occurred during the night.

It felt a waste of time for him to attend the scene. Jack was an excellent operative and McAbbey knew that one day he'd have to stop procrastinating and promote him to crew leader.

The thought of being desk-bound horrified McAbbey. Attending the murder scene allowed him to see the body 'in situ'. He believed there was a certain detachment to seeing the photos and hearing about a murder scene secondhand. It was like sniffing plastic roses and imagining the real fragrance.

Slipping back into bed quietly at three-thirty, he felt sleep descend like a theatre curtain after an epic.

Today was going to be a long day.

21

Later that morning, McAbbey awoke to open curtains revealing a cloudless sunny day. On his bedside table were the morning paper and a freshly brewed cup of coffee.

'Morning, darl. How do you feel?' Lisa asked.

'OK. What's the time?' he asked.

'Eight-thirty. I let you sleep in. I saw your note.' She frowned. 'I hope there isn't a serial killer on the loose.'

'Is that what they said?' he sat up.

'No. They just reported two murders within twenty-four hours. If anything, I think they shied away from admitting that it was the same killer. When I heard they were both young kids who died at home, I guessed they might be related.'

McAbbey threw back the covers and climbed out of bed. 'I have to get into work. Some of my detectives have been up all night. God knows, even the Commissioner will be after me this morning.'

'Where have you been?' Andrea asked when he walked into his office. 'The Chief Commissioner wanted to see you an hour ago.'

A meeting with the Chief was bad news for McAbbey. Technically he did not report directly to him, but since the appointment of Pete, Harry Vincent was forever calling to discuss his son's progress and meddle in their cases.

He passed Jack and Gavin on the way out and asked how their investigation was going.

'We'll be ready with a profile by lunchtime. Also, Catherine hopes to have a preliminary report by then,' Jack said.

'Good. Ask her if she will join us as soon as she's done. I think the earlier we have this meeting the happier Vincent will be.'

The trip to Police Headquarters took longer than the expected ten minutes. Traffic and tram works slowed the journey up St Kilda Road to Flinders Street in the city.

McAbbey walked to the Chief's outer office; a plush sitting room with thick carpet, wood panelling and Australian landscape paintings.

The Assistant Commissioner, Bill Harnden, greeted him from a leather settee. He was McAbbey's direct supervisor—a short man in his late fifties, who had worked his way up the ranks as a yes man.

'Glad you could join me.' McAbbey said. Bill was hands-off in managing his departments within the Crimes Section, which pleased McAbbey. As head of the Homicide Squad, he rarely spoke to Harnden on day to day issues however; he assumed Bill was invited as his superior in an important matter.

'Been a tough few days, Bill.' McAbbey filled him in on the details of the two recent cases.

'Morning, Bill, Ryan …' Chief Commissioner Harry Vincent pointed them to leather couches.

'I need an update on the two murders.'

'To be honest Harry, it's too early to say,' Bill said, with a look at McAbbey.

'Well, I need answers. I've had a call today from the Police Minister requesting a report by five this arvo. I need to know if there's a link between the two cases.'

'We're making progress,' McAbbey said, to alleviate Harry's impression that they were no closer to the murderer than the next victim. 'I need to sit with the team and formulate a plan of attack, before we hold a press conference.'

'Look, I'll be under a lot of stress if this escalates. All we need is for paranoia to set in.'

McAbbey tensed, but said nothing. He bit his lip for the remainder of the meeting.

——

Back in the office, McAbbey fielded calls from the print, television and radio media. He took a break from the phone and picked up the *Herald Sun*. The cover had "**Murdered!**" splashed across the front. Few details were released, especially about this morning's murder, as the paper was close to going to press at the time.

At eleven, he received a call from Catherine.

'I have some interesting news for you,' she said.

'I need it.'

'Firstly, I will have the results from the tox this afternoon. The food she ate last night was half digested, suggesting she met with foul play around eleven-thirty.'

'Go on,' he pressed.

'She was hit to the back of the head with a cricket bat. There were traces of linseed oil and an indentation caused by the implement. She died instantly from a single strike which caused a massive cerebral haemorrhage. We found foreign hair strands and semen in the bed. I believe the victim had sex before her death.'

'Let's hope it was the killer,' McAbbey said. 'Have the samples gone to McLeod for forensic analysis?'

'Yes, they will be fast tracked.'

Jack tapped on his door.

'Cath, I have to go. Can we ring you this afternoon during our meeting? I'm getting the team together to profile the murderer and compile what we know so far.'

She affirmed.

22

The office of the Homicide Squad was like the ABC on election night. The phones and faxes had not stopped as the press hounded his office and Police Media for exclusives.

McAbbey assembled his crew in their conference room and Andrea, his PA, was present to take notes and pass out documents.

'I'll ring Catherine now.' Gavin brought the phone to the middle of the table.

Catherine answered after one ring.

'Looking lovely today, Cath—as usual.' Gavin winked at Pete.

'Likewise,' was her curt response.

'Right,' McAbbey said tersely. 'We have two cases to deal with here. Brad Anderson on Sunday night and Sharron Sylvester last night. Let's start with Brad Anderson. Jack, give me your opinion.' McAbbey sat forward.

'Brad was the only son of wealthy parents. His father runs a chain of jewellery stores. Brad was athletic and sports-minded. He went to Caulfield Grammar and was in their swimming, basketball and football teams. He did not have a current girlfriend.'

Jack walked to the whiteboard at the end of the room. 'We've reconstructed what happened.' Jack drew a basic diagram of the residence, which included a floor plan, boundary fences and trees.

'The assailant watched the house during the night for the right moment to strike. The killer climbed the tree and entered the room through the window. He picked up a spare pillow and covered the victim's mouth and nose—smothering him. When the boy was dead, he left the same way he came in.'

'Surely the boy struggled?' Pete asked.

'Possibly, but it would've been too late. We can't even assume the assailant was male.' He looked at the phone. 'Is that right, Cath?'

'Yes. The pressure required could've been exerted by either sex.'

Jack continued, 'I visited his father, Brian Anderson, this morning and they had received a call from their son's Internet provider last night, asking if they would like to increase their credit limit. Apparently the boy had been surfing long hours, and until four in the morning on the night of his death. I believe the killer knew he was still awake. When the lights went out in the bedroom, he waited an hour and then broke in.'

'Could our suspect be someone on the Internet?'

'Possibly. Pete's looking into that now. He's asked the Internet provider to supply a full list of sites the boy visited during the past three months. We have a court order and expect to have their database records tomorrow.'

'Cath?'

'Nothing new to report. The victim suffered lung trauma and died of suffocation. We found no traces of DNA in the bedroom, other than from his parents. I asked them about this, as it's unusual for visitors not to drop a hair or shed skin, but apparently the boy had a rumpus room for when his friends came over.'

'So we have nothing to go by. A killer who could be old or young, male or female, murdered a fifteen-year-old and we have zip.' McAbbey groaned.

'I coordinated the neighbourhood meet and greet. No one reported seeing any suspicious cars or people on the night in question,' Gavin said.

'Should we ignore the similarities to Tania Stevenson?' McAbbey asked.

'The Stevenson case?' Gavin said with a frown. 'How's that related?'

'Tania was beautified after being strangled. Her eyes and mouth were closed and she was propped up and tucked in. With Brad, the pillow used to suffocate him was later placed under his head to offer support. His eyes and mouth were closed and the blankets were raised and tucked around his chest. I also believe the Sylvester girl was propped up, before falling on her side, evidenced by the blood on the bedhead.'

Gavin frowned. 'We don't know for sure if she was propped up—but even if she was, I don't think it's enough to tie them together.'

'I've found something,' Pete said quietly.

'Pete, you'll get your chance in a minute.' McAbbey snapped. He was privately annoyed that Gavin disagreed with his assessment. 'Jack, how's the Sylvester investigation proceeding?'

'No witnesses have come forward. The neighbours didn't see any suspicious cars or people around the house. The parents went out to see the latest James Bond film. Upon their return, they discovered her in bed. The father checked her pulse and then called for an ambulance. One neighbour said she heard loud music coming from the house, but saw no one loitering.

We believe the intruder broke in through the laundry door and, because of the music, walked up to her undetected. She was struck from behind with a single blow to the head. The spattering of blood on the CD player confirms this. We think she was then stripped and put in the bed; however, this is out of character with the other murder. It also doesn't explain why there's no blood on the nightie. The only other explanation we can think of is that she was sitting in front of the CD player naked.'

'Cath, did anything come up in the tox?' McAbbey asked.

'Well, it seems our young lady was a bit of a rebel. We found traces of marijuana in her lungs and bloodstream. It appears to have been smoked less than an hour before she died. There were no other substances found.'

'Funny, I didn't smell marijuana in the bedroom,' McAbbey said.

'I think she smoked it outside,' Catherine said. 'The incense burners would have masked the residual smell in her room.'

'Did the parents touch her?'

'Yes, the mother pulled away the doona when she saw blood.'

'We found a set of prints which did not belong to her parents,' Jack added. 'They were all over the stereo, walls, door handles— you name it.'

'This is a change. The killer left no traces in the other cases.' McAbbey then realised Catherine had been interrupted during her report, a sentiment she was reflecting in her stony silence.

'Cath, please continue.'

'Remember that I told you I found semen? Well, it was recent—no older than an hour before she died. A full PCR DNA test is underway.'

'Good work. Anything else?' McAbbey asked.

'Yes, I think so, but I don't know what to make of it. There was a small stain on the pillow which was neither blood nor semen. I gave it to McLeod to look at with the blood and tissue samples. The preliminary report came back this afternoon. It's water.'

McAbbey shrugged. 'So?'

'There were traces of vegetation found in the water.'

'What could it be?'

'It's most likely fragrance. They still have the sample—I was going to ask them to run a DNA test and find out exactly what it's from.'

Jack shook his head. 'We checked her room out. It was full of herbal perfumes and the like. I wouldn't bother.'

'Thanks Catherine, but I think Jack's right.' McAbbey turned to Gavin. 'Do you have any suspects?'

'Actually, yes. Sharron's boyfriend, Justin Tyler, is in the interview room for questioning. We also have Mr and Mrs Sylvester waiting outside the viewing room. They phoned the boyfriend this morning with the news of their daughter's death. He claimed to be at the movies with friends at the time.'

'Good. We need to make sure it wasn't the boyfriend before sending the crew out on a manhunt. Maybe the killer didn't strip her after all.'

'The boyfriend's already cooperated in providing a sample for a blood test. After this meeting Gavin and I are going to interview him and the victim's family. Would you like to attend?' Jack asked.

McAbbey nodded. 'Is either parent under suspicion?'

'Not at this stage. Their alibi checks out.'

'Ted, what about geography?' McAbbey asked.

Ted stood and approached the Melways wall map pinned beside the conference room whiteboard. With a marker, he plotted the three locations. 'No pattern there. Each kill is a fair distance apart. About fifteen kilometres from Mount Waverley to St Kilda, twenty-five from St Kilda to Gladstone Park, and nearly forty from there to Mount Waverley. The kids were all of school age.'

'I think until we have proof tying these murders together, we should keep an open mind,' Gavin said.

McAbbey sighed. 'Maybe I'm trying too hard to link them together. OK. Let's assume we have three separate murders, at least until we have evidence to the contrary.'

'I have evidence to the contrary ...'

23

'What have you got, boy wonder?' McAbbey sat back and chewed the end of his pen.

'I checked the emergency tape, as you asked.' Pete removed a slip of paper from a blank manila folder in front of him.

'Brian Anderson called the police. Here is the tape.' Pete lifted a small tape deck from the floor beside him and hit play.

'You have dialled triple O, Emergency Services. Police, fire or ambulance ... ?'

They heard a man's voice; 'Please come quickly. My boy's dead. The address is 47 Oakridge Street, Mount Waverley. 'Hurry, I think he's been murdered. Thank you.'

There was an audible click, as the caller hung up the phone. The tape continued to roll and they could hear the telephonist.

'Anyone there? Ambulance and squad car out to Mount Waverley to assist ...'

Pete stopped the tape. 'The call was made at five-fifteen.'

'That was not Brian Anderson!' Gavin objected.

McAbbey agreed. 'He sounded like he was ordering a pizza.'

'That was the serial killer. Here is the real Brian Anderson. Consistent with his statement, he called closer to five-thirty. As he said, the alarm woke him at twenty past five—minutes after the first caller.' Pete swapped the tapes.

'Help—please help! We need an ambulance immediately. My son isn't breathing.'

'Your address please?'

Before he could complete his address the lady stopped him. 'Sir, an ambulance and the police have already been dispatched. Please wait.'

Pete stopped the tape.

'The killer called Emergency Services?' McAbbey frowned.

Pete nodded, 'Yes. Brian forgot to tell us that the receptionist said the ambulance had already been dispatched.'

'Anything else?' Pete had more tapes.

'Sharron Sylvester's parents did not call the police. The tape on file actually had a question mark on it.'

'We forgot to check out who made the call.' Gavin shrugged.

'It's OK, Gavin. We weren't expecting this,' McAbbey said.

Pete played the tape.

'Hi, I'd like to report a murder—a young girl.' The man then passed on the details.

'Do you live at this address?' the receptionist asked.

There was an audible click as the man hung up.

After a pensive moment's silence, McAbbey spoke. 'We have our proof that these two murders are related.'

'Three,' Pete said, with a sparkle in his eyes. 'I have the tape from Tania's murder.'

'Don't they wipe them—that was a month ago?' Gavin asked.

'Yeah, except McAbbey asked me to save the tape.'

McAbbey smiled. 'I clean forgot about that.'

'Why did you want it?' Jack asked.

'Just a whim. I couldn't help but think the mother was caught out by the arrival of the police. I later asked the ambulance crew about her reaction and they said she was surprised to see them—not exactly the reaction you would expect after calling for their help.'

'Maybe she was in shock.' Catherine offered.

'That's what the ambulance woman said. She's seen so many varied reactions to their arrival that she doesn't try to read anything into them anymore.'

Pete played the tape after a nod from McAbbey. It was the same man, with a similar curt message.

'You haven't told your father about this?' McAbbey glared.

'No.' Pete's gaze fell, but McAbbey knew it was due to the embarrassment of being asked, not guilt.

'How long have you known this?'

'Just this afternoon,' Pete replied. 'I've been dying to tell you …'

'Good work. I guess we need to rule out the suspects we have. I'm beginning to wonder if it was the boyfriend and not the killer who left seminal fluid on the body of Sharron Sylvester.'

Gavin nodded. 'That makes sense. Unless the killer has found a taste for sex.'

'Possibly, but if our hunch is right and the semen is from her boyfriend, then that would mean …'

' … That our serial killer is not interested in sex.' Jack finished for him.

24

Gavin looked at his watch. I'll go and settle the victim's family in the viewing room. See you down there in five.'

McAbbey nodded. 'So what do you think, Jack? It's unusual for a serial killer to be indiscriminate about the sex of their victims—maybe age is his deciding factor.'

'It's almost like he regrets the killing afterwards and shows remorse.'

'Do you mean the phone call?' McAbbey asked.

'Yeah, and the way he tucks them in. However, he didn't sound apologetic or emotionally attached on the emergency tapes.'

'What he does with the victims may have nothing to do with a guilt trip,' Ted said. 'Some paedophiles like to see them as children, to tuck in at night.'

'Yes, but the last two victims are well into their teens—not really paedophile territory,' McAbbey said.

'He is certainly a difficult killer to profile. I hate to be morbid, but we may need another case to firm his signature—if indeed there is one,' Jack said.

'I have already invited a forensic psychologist to view the files. Dr Chladek,' McAbbey said.

Jack choked. 'You've got to be kidding. That guy makes *The Godfather* look like Sigmund Freud.'

'True Jack, however we need help,' McAbbey said. 'We have no witnesses to any of the crimes and only a suspect for the first murder, who has an alibi and left no trace at the scene.'

McAbbey straightened in his seat and pointed at Ted and Pete. 'I want you two to interview the victims' families and friends again. We might have missed something relevant—especially now that we know all three are related. I also want to know what the victims did in their spare time, what clothes and music they bought—everything. Draw up any similarities between the victims and check them off, one by one.'

'Jack, I want you to profile the murderer. I want to know how they were chosen and why they were murdered. There must be a pattern. He's not working from sexual urges or reckless abandon. Get Gavin to take what we have on Pearce and compare it to evidence found in the other cases.'

As McAbbey walked downstairs to the meeting room, he felt sure the young man was responsible for the semen and subsequent DNA found. The killer was smarter than that.

Gavin stood outside the interview room door and introduced the Sylvesters to McAbbey. He then took them to the separate viewing room.

'His name is Justin Tyler. Catherine will have the blood typing soon. She'll call when it's done,' Gavin said on his return.

McAbbey nodded. 'Let's do it.'

Gavin opened the door and stepped inside, introducing McAbbey. Gavin then explained what they had already discussed.

'Justin was just telling me how he came to cancel his outing to the movies with his friends. He was with Sharron instead. It appears she asked him to come over because her parents had gone out for the night.'

McAbbey gave Tyler a stern look then studied the file. He was eighteen and had recently left school to start a plumbing apprenticeship. He looked like a tradesman, with tanned arms, a number one haircut and a goatee.

What surprised McAbbey most was his self-confidence. Was it just a guise? He would soon find out.

'I hope you realise the severity of this.'

The young man stared back in defiance.

'When did you last see Sharron?'

'I told them already. Last night.'

'What else did you tell them?' McAbbey demanded.

'I went to see her last night. We listened to music and that.'

'What time did you arrive?'

'About nine ...'

'Just after they left for the movies ...' Gavin added.

'What time did you leave?' McAbbey asked.

'About eleven.'

'What did you do in the meantime?'

'We listened to music.' Tyler shifted in his seat.

'When you left, did you notice anyone else around? Were there any cars parked out front? Any suspicious characters walking the footpath?'

Tyler shook his head slowly. McAbbey thought the impact of her death was starting to sink in.

There was a knock and the door opened. Helen poked her head in. 'Cath just called, sir. She said to tell you the test was affirmative.'

'Thanks.' McAbbey stared at the young adult.

'That was the results of testing from the evidence we recovered at the murder scene. You may want to tell us everything that happened after you arrived.'

'We listened to music. We always do.'

'The tests have just confirmed that you were the last person with Sharron before she died. Is there anything else you need to tell us?'

'We smoked some weed,' he mumbled.

'Marijuana?' McAbbey confirmed. This meant that the killer had not used drugs to subdue her.

'Yeah.'

'What else?' McAbbey demanded.

'We had sex.' He looked down at his shoes, refusing to meet the detective's stare. 'She was on the pill—I never forced her.'

'That's not the reason I ask.' McAbbey shook his head and raised his voice. 'You're the prime suspect in her murder. What do you have to say to that?'

Tyler wiped away tears. 'I'm sorry; I really did love her you know ...'

'You can help Mr and Mrs Sylvester by remembering anything which might help. Did you notice anyone outside the house or any suspicious cars? Did she see or talk to anyone strange in the last week?'

Tyler shook his head.

'I want you to call if you think of anything that was out of the ordinary.'

He nodded eagerly.

Gavin led him out and McAbbey went to the adjoining door.

Mr Sylvester came out, holding his trembling wife. 'I could kill that boy, you know.'

'It wasn't him,' McAbbey said softly.

'I know, but my daughter was only sixteen, for God's sake.'

'Were you any different?' Mrs Sylvester murmured softly. 'My parents would've killed you—remember?'

McAbbey gave a sad smile. How often was it the case?

'I know … it's just … different somehow.'

McAbbey allowed them a minute before showing them the door. He promised to be in touch as developments were made.

'Please get the bastard who killed my girl,' Mr Sylvester whispered to McAbbey.

He walked back to his office to find Jack in a guest chair facing his desk.

'Do you have anything yet?' he asked Jack.

'Firstly, I believe the culprit was not expecting us to make a connection between the cases. If he was looking for notoriety, he would have announced himself, rather than calling anonymously. In regard to their appearance, I think it was something he wanted to do, for his or the poor victim's sake—not as a talking point. The changes he makes are minor. It's not as though he paints lipstick or gives them a jagged haircut.'

'Agreed. We have to find the connection. No matter how random these killings seem I think he's highly selective. Could they have done something to upset him in the past? Maybe all three went to the same beach and kicked sand on his towel. Perhaps they made a noise during a movie in his favourite theatre.'

Jack nodded. 'But how are we going to find him?'

'Well, that's why Dr Chladek is coming to see us this afternoon at three.' McAbbey stared at his watch in surprise. It was already three o'clock.

—▪—

Jacques Chladek was a short man in his forties with long black hair, wearing a black Italian suit and shirt. His hands flashed with gold rings, a chunky bracelet and a Rolex.

Chladek walked to the whiteboard.

'I've read your files and seen photos of the victims. I believe your culprit is a man between twenty-five and fifty years of age. He's a professional in a position of trust, possibly a dentist or GP. He's had a tough upbringing and is most likely an only child. I believe he's single and lives in an inner city suburb, like Toorak or Balaclava.'

'What can you tell us in relation to the cases? Is there something we should be looking out for?' McAbbey said.

'Yes.' The doctor frowned at the interruption. 'He's attracted to their youth and zest. I think he feels guilt after he kills the victims—the post-mortem changes are consistent with post traumatic contrition. We may be dealing with a man who believes he has to kill these youths. He may have been betrayed by his peers as a teen.'

'Could the killer be a paedophile?' McAbbey asked, thinking of Pearce.

'He could be,' Chladek replied, hesitantly. McAbbey could tell he had not seriously considered paedophilia. 'But you said there was no physical violation. I think the victims are too old. He's more of a teen killer.'

'Do you think he wants to be caught?' Jack asked.

'Hard to say—the pose he leaves them in and the phone calls tag him, but something makes me think he's on a mission.'

'So you think he'll kill again?' Gavin asked.

'Most definitely—and soon. Only when he perceives his agenda is realised will he stop. If you don't catch him while he's active, he might just disappear back into society.'

McAbbey returned to his office when Chladek left. He had promised the press a statement and the Chief Commissioner wanted a briefing at four.

He pulled a clean piece of paper from the printer, which stood alone since they removed his computer. He had never worked the printer in the conventional sense and was only using it as repository for paper he took to make written notes.

He jotted down a few comments for his press statement, confirming that the two cases were related. He did not make mention of Dr Chladek's profile and omitted reference to the touching up of the bodies. He did write that the killer had called in the two murders, but did not link the Stevenson case to the latter ones. McAbbey hoped to use the press statement to prove that the killer was not seeking notoriety.

Most serial killers liked to play with the law. They often teased and flaunted their "skill" in the face of justice—revelling in the reactions of the public and the press. The offender had received little publicity over Tania Stevenson and had only just been revealed as the killer of the new victims.

McAbbey looked over his completed report wondering if his document might change the killer's approach. What would he do now to find his victims? Would he make a mistake? McAbbey certainly hoped so.

25

McAbbey took out a pre-knotted paisley tie from his side drawer and slipped it over his head, snapping the elastic under his collar. He put on his sports jacket and straightened himself in the mirror briefly before leaving.

At the Chief Commissioner's office in Flinders Street, McAbbey sat in silence, waiting for the Chief and Assistant Commissioner to finish reading his brief.

'So, you believe the same offender killed all three,' Vincent said.

'Yes. Though they were killed differently, the corpse presentation and voice on the Emergency Services tape were the same.'

'But you don't have prints, DNA, eyewitnesses ...'

'Unfortunately not. He's the master of lithe.'

The Commissioner gave him a stern look over his reading glasses. 'What's your next move?'

'We have a detailed investigation plan. I have a hunch he's not interested in fame like most serial killers. His selection process is unknown to us, but we don't believe the victims are random. There's a strong possibility these kids have crossed the killer's path at some point.'

'Do your best to find him before the next murder. The last thing we need's a bloody epidemic.'

McAbbey bit his lip and refrained from mentioning that Harry's veto had impeded their progress in solving Tania Stevenson's death. McAbbey sensed the Chief expected him to have a computer generated image of the killer ready for Crimestoppers and that angered him. Vincent spent his whole career pushing a pencil and had no idea about what a police investigation entailed.

'I'm about to give a statement in the Police Conference Room.'

'I know. I saw the reptiles out there. How much are you going to give them?' he asked, with a frown.

McAbbey handed them a point-form note. 'I'm not going to mention the Stevenson case. I want to keep something up my sleeve. Also, I'm going to suppress the way he presents the victims and tucks them in. What I will reveal, however, is the phone calls made linking the last two victims.'

'Good.'

He wondered whether Vincent thought the outline of his statement was good, or if it was good that he wasn't going to mention the Stevenson case.

'I'm going to set up a taskforce to investigate these murders.' McAbbey said.

'Who's going to run it?' Vincent asked.

'I will.' McAbbey stood, with a look at the time. 'I'm going to second the crew that has worked these cases to the Taskforce.'

McAbbey walked back to the main foyer and across to the Conference Room next to the entrance. He looked at his reflection in a glass display cabinet and straightened his tie. With a deep breath, McAbbey walked to the door. Voices ceased suddenly and the cameras began flashing as he stepped onto the podium.

'I can today confirm that both Brad Anderson and Sharron Sylvester were killed by the same person. A full-time taskforce has been established to investigate these murders. We would be interested in hearing from anyone who noticed anyone suspicious in Walnut Drive, Mount Waverley early Monday morning, or Carrick Drive, Gladstone Park late Monday night. If you have any information, please contact Crimestoppers on our 1300 number.'

McAbbey nodded to the press gallery.

'Yes?'

A man stood. 'Were both victims struck with a weapon?'

'No, Sharron was struck with what we believe to be a cricket bat. Brad Anderson was asphyxiated.'

'Do you mean strangled?'

'No. Technically he was smothered. There's a significant difference.'

'How did you identify that the murders were related?'

'In both cases Emergency Services received a phone call from the offender.'

'Are there any other identifying features?'

'I will not go into that.'

'Were the victims raped or molested?'

'I will not discuss that.'

'Will he kill again?'

'I will not speculate on that.'

McAbbey acknowledged the waning of their interest, though half a dozen hands were waving in the air.

'We would ask that parents take an active interest in the whereabouts of their teenage children at all times. Thanks for your time.'

McAbbey strode to the door before members of the press could block his path.

He returned to his office on St Kilda Road and began preparing rosters and schedules to accommodate a taskforce investigation. At the end of the day, he went home to have dinner with Lisa.

He sat down to enjoy roast beef with hot English mustard and baked pumpkin and peas. Knowing McAbbey would be on the news, she turned on the television. He was not in the mood to see anything about the case but he watched it anyway.

The reporter had little to say. He mentioned that the killer had travelled across Melbourne, from Mount Waverley to Gladstone Park over two nights. They then showed his press statement.

McAbbey was relieved to see that nothing else had leaked, as it so often did. The killer's phone calls were the only identifying attribute revealed and Tania Stevenson was not discussed.

If the killer was after notoriety he would try to identify himself with the Stevenson murder. If not, the courtesy call they received at each scene could be lost to them in subsequent murders.

After dinner, they watched a video and retired to bed.

McAbbey spent the first hour of Wednesday writing reports and re-assigning his crew. He then organised his first Taskforce meeting.

McAbbey cringed at the conference room walls. Every time there was a crisis, the room was pasted with articles, photos and reviews. It was Jack's idea to have them focused on the case at hand.

'This crew is now assigned to investigate the serial murders,' McAbbey said. 'The Taskforce is now your number one priority. A portion of Catherine's time has been allocated to assisting us in the investigation. She will perform all the autopsies and analysis we require.'

'Have you given the Taskforce a name?' Jack asked.

McAbbey paused a moment. 'I was thinking Adonis.'

'Beautiful youth,' Gavin murmured with a nod.

McAbbey asked about the fresh interviews with the victims' families and friends.

'Brad Anderson was a popular fifteen-year-old,' Ted remarked. 'We learned lots about his sporting attributes, scholastic abilities and sense of humour. He had no enemies, but I guess there would've been a lot of jealous school friends.'

'Sharron had lots of school friends as well,' Pete added. 'She played tennis and was clever, though her teachers complained that she only showed a passing interest in school. She went to the craft markets and swam at St Kilda beach every summer, but had never been to Mount Waverley.'

'Trying to link the victims to a common location is going to be difficult,' Ted said. 'Imagine for a minute that the killer is a courier driver. He'd travel from one side of the city to the other in a matter of hours—possibly five times a day.'

'We checked the phone records. The calls were made from the house of each crime and the phones were checked for prints. He definitely wore gloves or covered the receiver,' Jack said.

'If that arse Vincent had let us set up a mobile caravan in St Kilda, then maybe we would've found witnesses who saw the killer leave the house.'

'Maybe you should push him again for a mobile unit at the scene,' Jack suggested.

'Don't worry—I will,' McAbbey growled.

'You could always get Pete to arrange it,' Gavin chuckled briefly until McAbbey glared at him.

'Do you have anything on Tania?'

'No.' Gavin sobered. 'Nothing has changed in the attitude of the locals since the first night we did a walk around. I think some people there have skeletons of their own. It wouldn't surprise me if a few of the locals had spent time in her mother's closet.'

'What about the phone records?' McAbbey asked.

Ted shook his head. 'We're still going through them. Apart from the calls by the families to the police, there's nothing suspicious to report.'

'What about incoming calls?'

'They had calls from family and close friends but nothing from strangers, telethons or surveys.'

'What about Tania? Any calls we can link to clients?'

'There were a few calls to the Espy hotel and the brothel Tracey worked at, but nothing of a personal nature. She must have contacted people on a payphone or by mail.'

'I have widened the search to the Internet as well as both mobile and house phones,' Jack said.

'Good one,' McAbbey said. 'I don't want the trail to go cold on us.'

'What do you think the killer will do, now that the press releases have been made?' Pete asked.

'I don't know.' McAbbey shrugged. 'I just don't know ...'

26

Jack was frustrated by the bane of taskforce investigations— when the leads went cold. Pete was sitting in his office when the phone rang.

'Blake—how's it going?' Jack asked, and then frowned. 'Sorrento? I'll come right away.' He slammed the receiver down and reached for his keys.

'Come for a drive, Pete? It looks like Blake might've found our next victim. Cath's already there.'

On his way past reception, Jack left a note for Gavin, who was out of the office.

'Shouldn't you tell McAbbey?' Pete asked.

'Let's go and see before we involve the boss. It might be a false alarm.'

When Pete and Jack arrived at Sorrento on the Mornington Peninsula, they were greeted by DSS Blake Stone from the investigating Homicide Squad crew.

Stone was much older than McAbbey with thinning grey hair and a ruddy complexion.

'Giving up cases—cripes, what's happened to you, Blake?' Jack slapped the detective on the back.

'Kidding aren't you? It's been a week. You fanatics can have this one.' Blake bit the filter off a Marlboro and drew deeply, blowing rain clouds above him.

'Those coffin nails will kill you, Blake.' Jack shook his head, walking towards the beach house.

'I've seen worse ways to go,' he replied.

Jack cut through knee high grass to the front door, while Pete followed the path past kicked-in rubbish tins.

Pete could see the forensic team, distinguishable in their blue overalls, combing the half-acre yard for evidence. He followed Jack inside to an open living area with patchy carpet, faded orange curtains and mixed furniture. The air was like warm custard and Pete struggled for breath.

He walked to the front window, drew back the curtains and opened it.

Jack was stunned. 'What are you doing?'

Pete paused stiffly. 'The smell—I was just trying to get some air in here.'

'Just as well Forensics has finished, or else it would've been curtains for you.' Pete relaxed when he saw Jack was smiling.

'Come on, let's go see the victim.' Jack led the way down a hall with moth-eaten blankets nailed above open doorways.

'Doesn't look like they ever finished the place,' Pete said.

'You're not wrong.' Jack stopped outside a room. 'Must be this one.' He pulled back the blanket and waved Pete inside.

'See,' Jack said, pointing at Catherine Smith, who was hunched over the deceased. 'I can smell her perfume anywhere.'

Pete laughed and Catherine straightened.

'Come closer, kiddo, you're no use back there.' She smiled thinly.

Pete reluctantly moved forward. The burning in his eyes grew and he could taste bile in his throat.

The girl was sitting upright, with her chin resting on her bare chest and a few pillows for support behind. Pete assumed that Catherine had drawn back the sheets. The girl was chubby around her thighs and hips with cropped brown hair. She was stark naked.

'It's him,' Jack said. 'I'm going to call Gavin and McAbbey.'

'What time is it, Jack?' Catherine asked, deep in thought.

Jack looked at his watch fleetingly and smiled.

'Lunchtime!'

Pete rushed past them and outside.

'Was that called for?' Catherine folded her arms.

'What?' Jack shrugged. He took his mobile out and called Gavin.

When Jack called Gavin, McAbbey was sitting at his desk mulling over their stalled investigation. A week had passed and he wondered if their killer was in hiding.

McAbbey mused that taking calls from the victims' parents was the worst part of his job. The parents grieved, yet found the anger to blast him because the killer was at large.

As a mark of respect, McAbbey allowed the two families to bury the bodies during the week. There was nothing more to learn from them and it allowed the families the first semblance of closure.

'Boss.' McAbbey looked up—his reverie broken. Gavin stood at his office door. He was strangely exhilarated.

'We have another.'

McAbbey looked at his watch. It was one in the afternoon. This was unusual, considering the killer had set a pattern of working at night. McAbbey offered Gavin a lift and they took the coastal scenic route down Nepean Highway to the beachside town of Sorrento.

'Exactly what did they tell you?' McAbbey asked, as they drove.

'We received a call this morning from the local cop shop. They found a body in a holiday house after a tip-off by the family of the deceased. Apparently they hadn't heard from her all week.'

'All week! Has anyone placed the time of death?'

'No. The local GP estimates three days. Catherine's there now.'

'So how did they know it was our killer?'

'The local boys thought it was a regular homicide. Blake's crew took the call and went down. He recognised the way the body was placed and called Jack, suggesting we might want to take a look.'

—-—

The beach house was a typical holiday retreat, with unkempt bushes and long grass. Inside, each piece of lounge furniture was unique and the kitchen had an old wood-fire stove and a Kelvinator disguised with magnets and VB labels.

Determining the method of entry would be difficult, McAbbey thought. Most of the locks on the windows and external doors were already broken and rusted. How long had the body gone undiscovered? McAbbey could not believe the family would let their daughter go away by herself for so long.

They stopped beside Jack outside the end bedroom, which was blocked by a tartan blanket. Jack pulled back the woollen cloth and even McAbbey was taken aback by the smell.

It was a large bedroom. Accompanying the old pine double bed in the middle were two bookcases and a vanity set—from different eras. In the bookcases were volumes of *National Geographic*, dog-eared paperbacks, and old library books—probably purchased from garage sales to fill the case.

A large framed picture of the Sacred Heart hung on the only free wall. It was a Christian painting of Jesus with nailed hands, a forgiving expression and a glowing heart. It was the same picture McAbbey's grandmother had over the bed when he slept there as a child. He spent many sleepless nights staring at it, pondering the consequences of his childhood pranks.

The victim on the bed was partially obscured by Catherine and Maree. They had already moved the body—a sign they had been there a while and had completed their preliminary notes and still photography.

'Do you agree with the local GP about how long she's been dead?' McAbbey asked.

'She's been here from three days to a week,' Catherine said. 'I won't be able to tell exactly because I can't be sure how much the room temperature has fluctuated, but these humid conditions certainly accelerate decomposition.'

'That places her death since the last victim. Where's Pete? I thought he came down with you?' McAbbey asked Jack.

'He's outside fertilising the flowerbeds ...'

McAbbey gave a wry grin—Pete had never seen an enduring corpse. 'What have you got so far, Jack?' McAbbey asked.

'Her name's Joanne MacDonnell. She's a twenty-three-year-old Melbourne Uni student. She was on holidays; apparently returning home to start Uni this week. They have an answering machine here and I checked the messages. There were six. Five from her parents and one was from the University checking on her enrolment. There were no date stamps on the messages, however the phone records show that the first was left on Sunday and the most recent was yesterday.'

'The family asked the local cops to come out and check on her this morning. Apparently she was an independent girl, so the family wasn't too concerned that she hadn't called.'

'How was she found?'

'She was propped up naked in bed, covered to the waist. Her eyes were closed.'

McAbbey studied the narrow leathery-yellow ligature mark around the victim's neck, indicating she'd been garrotted with a thin cord.

'How did he get in?'

'We think he came in through the front door—there was no sign of forced entry. The windows look undisturbed, but the locks are buggered anyway. I guess the parents figured there was little point in security—there's nothing of value here,' Jack said.

Jack left to check the neighbouring properties and McAbbey knelt beside the victim. She was atypical—a large woman with short hair. McAbbey had painted a mental picture of their man as one desiring supple children. All the previous victims were slim, sporty types between the age of thirteen and sixteen. Another quirky aspect of the previous victims, McAbbey had noted, was their long hair. Even Brad Anderson had long locks.

He shared his thoughts with Catherine.

'Yeah, I was thinking his attraction might be their hair length.'

It was typical of Catherine to keep a hunch to herself, but he was often guilty of the same.

'What have you found?' McAbbey asked.

'There's nothing under her nails and she has no bruising on her body,' Catherine said. 'She may have been drugged, though I don't know why. Outside of holidays, I'd say most of these houses are deserted.'

'Ha-hum.' McAbbey cleared his throat, warning her of demarcation.

'Sorry, Ryan. Don't you want to hear my valuable opinion?' She looked up at him as though she had been caught doing something naughty.

'Go on then!' He rolled his eyes, as though he would humour her nonetheless.

'I can't understand why he would have bothered with drugs out here. No one would have heard her struggle ...'

Her voice petered out.

'What?' McAbbey asked vaguely, lost in thought.

'You aren't listening!'

'I am so!' he rejected with exasperation. He heard what she said, but was wondering why the killer had come so far from the city.

'So, what do you think?' she pressed.

'I think you wish you were an investigator, not just a doctor.'

'Really?' She planted her hands on her hips.

Comments like that usually ended in a snide rebuttal, casting aspersions about his growing gut—so it was best he end it there.

'You have a point,' he admitted. 'I don't know whether he's using drugs because he doesn't want confrontation with his victims, or if he's worried that subduing them physically may result in witnesses or his DNA being left behind.'

'What do you make of the fact this girl was found naked?' asked Catherine.

'Sharron was involved in sex just before she was killed. Perhaps Joanne had a male friend as well.'

27

Pete returned from the garden beds as green as pea soup.

'How was the technicolor yawn?' McAbbey asked.

'I didn't think I'd need any Vicks, but boy was I wrong,' Pete said.

Catherine suppressed a smile, but drew satisfaction from Pete's discomfort. Few pathologists wore any form of nasal disinfectant and were repulsed by the idea. It was akin to a ship's captain living on seasickness pills.

Gavin stepped in and pulled the blanket "door" closed, isolating the bedroom. 'The father's here to ID the body.'

'Cath, cover the poor girl. Gavin, get him something for his nose. Jack, where do the parents live?'

'High Street, Malvern. Joanne lived with them.'

Gavin lifted the blanket and the father walked into the room, his eyes sunken and red. He walked over to his daughter and kissed her on the forehead.

'Goodnight, my princess,' he whispered, oblivious to the odour.

McAbbey looked away sharply.

'Excuse me,' Pete asked.

Mr MacDonnell straightened. 'Yes?'

'Did she have a brother or sister?' Pete asked.

'Yes, she has an adopted brother.'

Pete nodded. The man left the room with tears flowing unabashed.

'I'm going. Can we get together at ten tomorrow morning?' McAbbey said, reaching into his pocket for keys.

'Ten should be fine,' Catherine suppressed a yawn, but her eyes watered with the effort. 'I've a lot to do this afternoon. I have the Coroner's reports and your brief to finish.'

'Crack to it then,' Gavin joked. Catherine's look was enough to turn Gavin's grin to a grimace.

—-—

The following morning at ten, they sat at the conference table.

'The killer did not call the police. This is a fair indication that he doesn't want to be identified with the murders,' McAbbey said.

'Yet he still covered up the body and closed her eyes, so he definitely has more than one idiosyncrasy,' Jack added.

'It might be something he's doing subconsciously. He may not be aware he tucks in his victims, or at least thinks we haven't noticed.'

'If this is true, then it's bad news in a way,' Gavin said. 'The crime scenes are going to be difficult to work if we don't find the deceased possibly days or even weeks later.'

McAbbey nodded. The chances of catching an offender diminished with time.

'For all we know, he may have killed again,' Catherine said. 'Joanne died on the weekend; he's had a few days since to stalk his next victim.'

Pete's earlier question nagged at McAbbey. 'Why did you ask if Joanne MacDonnell had a brother or sister?'

'I thought I had something,' he admitted.

'Being?' Gavin pressed, with interest.

'All our victims have been only children—until Joanne. I thought maybe the killer had an attraction to single child families.'

McAbbey nodded. 'Good thinking. Anything on the neighbours?'

Jack shook his head. 'The neighbours from both sides and across the street live in Melbourne. The houses are only occupied during the holiday season. We received permission to check their properties, but found nothing.'

'Cath, what about the autopsy?'

'She was garrotted with a thin cord; it was not recovered. I believe she was drugged first. I found Valium in her system which I think was administered by the killer. She was also under the influence of alcohol at the time she was attacked. I'm assuming the killer spiked her drinks with the drug.'

'We did find a half empty bottle of Jack Daniels and Coke in the fridge,' Jack said.

Helen popped her head in momentarily, motioning to McAbbey.

'What is it?' McAbbey frowned on the interruption.

'Sergeant Davidson from Sorrento just called. They've found another body—a male. This one was washed up under the pier.'

'Thanks, Helen. Call them back and tell them we'll be down there shortly.'

'I have something else …' Catherine continued. McAbbey sensed urgency in her voice and waited for her to continue. 'I found fresh pubic hair follicles from another person in the bedroom, which means she may not have been alone when she was attacked.'

'Semen?'

'No, I ran the ultraviolet. However, I did find traces of a water gel substance, consistent with that employed with a condom.'

'Employed?' Jack questioned, bamboozled by her terminology. 'By any chance do you mean KY jelly?'

Catherine affirmed.

'This latest death may be related. Perhaps the floater is her boyfriend?' McAbbey offered. 'If we deem that the killer is not raping the victims, then it stands to reason another person must have been present.'

Catherine nodded. 'It could well be a boyfriend. Maybe he was also drugged.'

'Jack, take Pete and go back to Sorrento. Find out who the boy is and if there's a connection. Please be discreet, people. We've managed to suppress news of Joanne's death to avoid a panic. We need to be sure our killer murdered this man quickly and find out why. Let's reconvene later.'

McAbbey returned to his office but Andrea poked her head in before he could take his seat.

'Harry Vincent.'

He gave her a look of frustration. 'I'll take it in here.'

'No, he isn't on the phone, he's in reception.'

'What? Shit! Send him in.' He madly cleared his desk of all paperwork, throwing it in a pile on the floor, and furnished the desk with one neat file.

McAbbey greeted the Chief Commissioner with a rare smile.

'How are you progressing?' Vincent asked. 'I'm under a lot of pressure to have this resolved quickly. I understand the Sorrento death hasn't been linked to the others yet. This is good; it'll save panic in the community.'

McAbbey mused at how reporting directly to the Police Minister had made Vincent politically savvy.

'However, once the press do discover this latest death is related, we'll have widespread panic on our hands. Look, I know you're doing the best you can. Pete has nothing but praise for your efforts. Apparently you connected the killings—by the phone calls.'

McAbbey made to interrupt, but Vincent dismissed his attempts immediately. 'No need to be modest with me, Ryan. You're doing a great deal for Pete's development. Anything I can do to help, just buzz.'

With that, Harry Vincent was gone.

'Bloody politician,' McAbbey grumbled to himself, 'Thank God Chelsey's too old for gratuitous kissing.'

He stormed out of his office. 'Andrea, where's Pete? He and I need to have words.'

'Didn't you send him back down to Sorrento?'

'Oh yeah. Bugger it.' McAbbey would tan his hide later.

28

McAbbey spent the afternoon in his office reviewing the cases of the other Homicide Squad crews. The main focus of his position was in managing the entire Homicide Squad, however this had been neglected since McAbbey took direct control of the taskforce.

The day to day running of a homicide investigation was more alluring for McAbbey than paper shuffling; he was fortunate to have competent crew leaders who did not require constant supervision.

Eventually his mind wandered to what Jack and Pete had found at Sorrento. He expected Catherine to free up her schedule to conduct the autopsy as soon as possible.

The phone buzzed. It was Helen. 'It's Cath down at Southbank.'

'Thanks,' he picked up the receiver.

'It was a floater. There wasn't much to learn from where the body was found, so I had it brought straight back here.'

'Done already?' McAbbey glanced at his watch, noting it was three in the afternoon.

'No, I was wondering whether you'd like to come and watch.'

He hated floaters. Those who had been immersed in water after death were not pleasant and McAbbey had no intention of watching Catherine take in afternoon tea while she worked.

'Call me when you're done.' He hung up before she could retort.

His late afternoon walk to Catherine's office took twenty minutes. He liked the exercise, but was even more determined after Chelsey's snide remarks about his growing tummy.

Catherine was finished her autopsy and had returned the gurney to the fridge by the time he arrived.

'What do you know?' he asked Catherine.

'The boy is Andrew Jones. He was a surfer who squatted in the Sorrento area during the off seasons when most people leave their holiday houses vacant. From what his friends said, he was squatting in the MacDonnell's house when Joanne arrived for the week.'

'What does the autopsy reveal?'

'He died of a knife wound to the neck. The killer slit his throat.'

'Can you confirm he was at the MacDonnell's holiday house?'

'Forensics lifted his fingerprints and numerous strands of his hair in the house. The preliminary tox shows he was under the influence of alcohol and a dose of Valium.'

'So you think they both drank from the same source?'

'Yes. I'm guessing the killer stole into the house during the day, spiked their alcohol and waited. I'm assuming they had sex and fell asleep on the bed. The woman was then garrotted in the bedroom and the man was taken to the foreshore where the killer slit his throat and dropped him into the drink. There was no blood in the house whatsoever—I think he was killed at the waters' edge.'

'What about head injuries?'

'None. I guess he didn't need to clobber him as he was already groggy from the mix of drugs and alcohol.'

'Catherine, I don't mind you doing my job but you need to cover all bases.'

'So what have I missed, Sherlock?' She planted a hand on a hip.

'If they were both killed together, why did his body take days to wash up on the foreshore?'

'I've thought about that,' she admitted. 'The body's definitely been in the water for days, possibly a week. I think the body wasn't found earlier because it snagged under the pier with the rubbish that collects there.'

'Do you have photos of the deceased?' It was hard to know the right questions to ask without having seen the body. He flicked through the photos she handed to him and immediately noticed something amiss. The killer had been particular to make death as comfortable as possible for his victims—but this youth was butchered.

'Anything else? Was he violated?'

'Oh yes,' Catherine looked as though she had forgotten one savoury piece of information. 'His penis was severed. We were unable to recover it and I cannot be sure whether it was cut before or after his throat was slit.'

'Shit eh? It's almost like he was protecting the girl in some way.' McAbbey said.

'You mean the killer attacked him because he was sleeping with her?'

'Yeah, maybe they're only his to touch or something. But we have to wonder why this lad was not good enough for our killer ...'

'Well, I've done my bit. That's your job!' Catherine chortled, walking back to the fridge.

29

Jack and Pete had returned to the office by the time McAbbey walked back.

'I've been to see Cath. What did you find out?' McAbbey asked.

'Andrew Jones was found by the owner of the Palms Café while he was out on his morning walk. Jones was buck-naked, face down in the water. However,' Jack looked at Pete, 'our bloodhound here went for a long walk down a short pier and found a backpack stuck to one of the pylons at water level. It had the victim's effects inside. We assume it was dumped at the same time as the body.

'Forensics found fingerprints and hair samples proving that Andrew had been in the house. We spoke to his mates and they said that when Joanne found him there, she let him stay on the proviso he looked after the place. One of his mates said Jones befriended her in no time and they became lovers.'

'I think the death of the surfer is confusing the issue,' McAbbey said. 'I think he was merely in the way of our killer. Joanne was larger and older than the others. Use that difference to find his signature. Get going.'

Within moments, McAbbey was alone again. His crew worked feverishly with the scent of blood, and their killer was leaving plenty behind.

McAbbey shut his files at six. A headache was thudding and he needed a good night's sleep.

At home, he joined Lisa in front of the television. He was interested to see what the press had revealed. He had forgotten to ask Jack whether they had encountered reporters at the beach. Come to think of it, he had forgotten to reprimand Pete for talking to his old man again.

'Earth to Ryan?' Lisa waved a hand in front of him.

'Sorry, darl,' he smiled, placing his arm around her.

The serial offender was the first item on the news:

> The Adonis killer may have claimed his third victim. The body of Joanne MacDonnell was found this morning at Sorrento. Police have declined to comment on the latest discovery, but a statement is expected tomorrow. The twenty-three year old university student was staying at her parents' holiday house for the week.

They showed a picture of Joanne from high school and a location shot from outside the house in Sorrento.

McAbbey was pleased that the local police had contacted them first and not involved the press until his team and the body were long gone:

In another incident at Sorrento today, a body washed up under the pier. Local police have identified the deceased as a twenty-five year old local surfie. He was a squatter who lived in empty holiday houses during the off season. Police have declined to comment, but it's believed the youth was intoxicated at the time of death and may have drowned.

'I thought there were four children killed,' Lisa said.

'Yes, but the media is not yet aware that Tania is one of the serial murders.'

The news then turned to politics.

'Anything else on, Lise?'

She changed the channel before he finished his sentence. They watched a few meaningless American comedies where even facial expressions were an excuse for uproarious canned laughter, then went to bed.

30

At five thirty in the morning, McAbbey was unable to sleep. His headache was gone, but he still tossed and turned.

The phone rang.

'Jack here. We have another victim. We're about to meet at the office and drive out.'

'How old?'

'Seventeen. This one's unusual. He died at boarding school. There were fourteen boys in the dorm and one was singled out. Do you want to come down?'

'Yeah. Where is it?'

'It's out at Sunbury—St Bosco College.'

'I'll be there.'

As he drove into the gates of the college, McAbbey felt a pang of apprehension. His parents had considered sending him to this school, but that was thirty years ago.

McAbbey hated the idea of boarding—the regimen, discipline and lack of privacy. Spending six years of his life with other young men during the hormonal roller coaster ride of youth did not excite him.

He pleaded long and hard with his parents before they decided on St Bernard's College instead, where he was able to catch the bus daily from home and mix with females.

McAbbey followed the signs to the dormitories, making sure he observed the speed limit. He did not wish any trouble with the Christian Brothers.

An elderly brother with a handshake of steel greeted him when he parked outside the entrance.

'Good morning, sir,' McAbbey greeted the man numbly.

The brother smiled at him with a twinkle of amusement. 'Attend a Christian Brothers school, did you? You can call me Brian.'

McAbbey gave a curt laugh.

'This way, boss,' Jack said, appearing from a doorway.

McAbbey followed him down a corridor and into a large room, where beds lined the walls in perfect symmetry. The dormitory was cleared of children and at the far end, Catherine and Maree hovered over a bed.

'The boy is Ben Peterson,' Jack said, as he walked towards them. 'He was in Year Ten. He had a solid academic record and was good at football.'

McAbbey could see the boy was tall, athletic and had exercised regularly. On his bedside table, in what seemed his only personal space, were a best and fairest football trophy and a picture of a girl. The boy was in his pyjamas.

At the other end of the dorm, the headmaster and another brother stood talking quietly with Pete.

'What's he saying to them?' McAbbey asked with a frown.

'Apparently Pete did his schooling here. He knows the headmaster.'

'No wonder the kid takes punishment so well.'

Jack laughed. 'Brother Adams came in to wake them at quarter to five this morning. Every Friday they have an early cross-country run. He left them to dress but when he returned the boys were still asleep. When he roused them a second time, the Peterson boy did not wake and he noticed the mark around his neck.'

'Have you placed the time of death?' McAbbey looked at his watch; it was now ten to seven.

'He's still warm. Cath seems to think he died minutes before Brother Adams woke them,' Jack said.

'Do you think the killer was interrupted by Adams?' McAbbey asked.

'When the brother entered the dorm, he heard a noise and turned on the lights. There was no one there, but the end window was clanging. He closed it and woke the students. As all the boys were present he thought nothing more of it.'

'Maybe someone saw him enter or leave the dorm by the window? Check reception and see who came through—parents, electricians, milk trucks, etc. Someone may have seen a car leave the premises earlier.'

'Already done,' Jack said.

'I wish I knew how the killer researched his information on these kids' whereabouts. He seems to know when to attack.' McAbbey gritted his teeth.

'He was lucky. Just minutes earlier and Brother Adams would've caught him in the act. We almost had a look at the killer.'

'How did he enter the dorm?'

'The same way he left. There was no evidence of tampering with the locks on the door. Apparently the end window had been broken for weeks. His decision to use the window makes sense. Ben Peterson's bed is only two places from it. Somehow I think the school could be sued for not having the lock repaired.'

'Anything else?' McAbbey asked.

Jack looked at Catherine.

'I think the boys were drugged. It would explain why they stayed asleep. We've taken urine samples from three boys to check.'

'Did you personally supervise the sample taking?'

Jack laughed and Catherine went bright red.

'Actually no, I didn't.'

'So you think the killer drugged the boys so he could enter the dorm and kill Ben without interruption?' McAbbey asked.

'Yes. I find it hard to believe someone could get away without being heard otherwise,' Catherine said.

'Jack, can you see what Pete's saying to the principal. I don't need him flapping his gums.'

Jack left them.

'Do you think the killer is wearing a full body suit and gloves to avoid dropping hair and skin?' McAbbey asked Catherine. They had found no trace of the killer at any crime scene so far; only samples from acquaintances and family members of the deceased.

'It's possible,' Catherine admitted. 'I can't think of another explanation for the lack of evidence.'

Her unwavering faith in technology concerned him. Had she missed something in her analysis?

Catherine packed up her kit and stood. 'I'm having the body delivered for the post now. Do you have anything else you'd like me to look at?'

McAbbey shook his head. He walked to where Jack and the principal stood talking in the dormitory doorway. Pete had gone to the loo.

'Boy wonder can come back with me. We have a few things to talk about,' McAbbey said. Jack excused himself and went to supervise the forensics team.

McAbbey stared at his watch, conscious of the brother standing beside him.

'Nice day for it,' he said, ending the stilted silence.

The brother frowned. Fortunately Pete returned and they were away.

'Just what did you tell your old man this time?' McAbbey glared at Pete grimly. 'I thought I told you not to speak to him about internal matters.'

Pete's face glowed like a ripe tomato and he clasped his hands together, white knuckled.

'He asked …'

McAbbey could tell that Pete feared his father more.

For a split second McAbbey wondered whether he should redefine fear, but then realised the pointlessness of being the mirror image of his overbearing father.

'I need you to be part of the team. That means not telling your dad anything that we haven't cleared. A lot of the information is classified and if it were to indiscreetly leak to the press or a friend, it could undermine our position and jeopardise the investigation.'

'I promise not to say anything again,' Pete vowed.

McAbbey was privately concerned that Pete's tone of voice did not suggest complete allegiance but he kept this to himself.

'Good. Fortunately you didn't give away anything important, hence the reason why I'm not too upset.'

McAbbey felt it important to be supportive and so with a smile added, 'And I don't think lying to your father to make me look good is allowed either, OK?'

Pete nodded sheepishly. 'I just wanted to let him know that you were helping me and that your crew have been great to work with. He was a worried as to how you would react to my promotion and thought that you would give me a hard time.'

'You don't think that's the case?' McAbbey raised an eyebrow.

Pete laughed. 'You mean well—even when you're angry. The others say you're bark is worse than your bite.'

McAbbey sported a rare flash of red. Toothless hey, McAbbey mused quietly …

31

In the office, McAbbey hoped to catch up on paperwork in silence, but Pete was still buzzing around.

McAbbey spoke with the rookie detective, who left quickly. McAbbey walked back to his desk with a grin of contentment having seconded Pete to be his official witness at Catherine's autopsy.

'No bite? I think not,' he said to himself. 'Only a heartless person would send him to Doctor Death.'

——

When he returned to his desk, McAbbey was surprised to find a young man with long hair, glasses and a faded Jimmy Barnes t-shirt sitting in his chair.

'Craig Bacon.' The young man stood. 'I'm here to reinstall your computer.'

'What! My computer was confiscated. Some sort of budget cut.'

'Man—they've been having you on. Apparently Jack said there was a problem so I ran diagnostics. It had a faulty motherboard and the mouse was dead. It's all working now.'

'Can you reinstall my Elle poster on the screen?' McAbbey casually asked.

'Cool. You don't mind if I rip it first?' the tech asked.

McAbbey stared at him quizzically. 'You can't, it's on the screen.'

'Oh yeah. Silly me.' The tech grinned. 'Anything else?'

McAbbey had a thought. 'Can you take away Jack Turner's computer?'

'Sure. What's wrong with it?'

'Nothing. You wouldn't have a really old computer to replace it with for a few days, would you? I owe him one.'

'Yeah.' He smiled. 'I've just the computer—an old 386.'

'Great. Can you put it on his desk today?'

'No worries.'

McAbbey had Andrea draft a brief memo detailing cuts in expenditure, which included the downsizing of Jack's computer. McAbbey found it rather ironic, as Jack's replacement looked much bigger than its predecessor. McAbbey returned to his desk, and went through his overstocked in-tray.

At eleven he received a call from Catherine, who had been working on the autopsy and inquest brief for the Coroner. She agreed to a conference call during their Taskforce meeting in the afternoon. McAbbey apologised for sending Pete over. Usually more than one experienced member of the investigating Homicide crew attended the autopsy.

'So how is boy wonder anyway?' he asked.

'Bugger you!' She sighed. 'He's still mopping up the mess he made.'

McAbbey smiled to himself.

McAbbey found the meeting at one o'clock enjoyable. Jack was rambling on about the old computer which had replaced his new one, and Pete was still pasty from his autopsy experience. It was a good start to shaking his soft image.

McAbbey called Catherine on speaker phone and then nodded to Gavin.

'We spoke to the boys in the dorm. Two of them heard noises during the night, but none of the kids actually saw the killer. The boys are feeling lethargic and sickly this morning.'

'There's a good reason for that,' Catherine said. 'They were drugged with a strong dose of Valium. I found traces in the urine samples provided by the other students. I traced the source to the milk they drank with their supper.'

'Cath told us and we checked the milk supply,' Gavin explained. 'Syringe punctures were detected in the tops of all the milk cartons. We brought back the remaining supplies for testing.'

'So, the killer broke into the kitchen and injected the milk without being detected,' McAbbey clarified.

'The kitchen was empty from eight until nine last night. He must have gone through the back door, which is unlocked until security comes past at eleven,' Gavin said.

'What else, Cath?'

'The killer pulled a cord tightly around the victim's neck and throttled him. I think three minutes would have been enough. I doubt the boy struggled or made much noise.'

'Apparently he was a big milk drinker ...' Gavin volunteered.

'Don't tell me the killer knew that too.' McAbbey grimaced. 'Thanks, Cath. Let us know when you have anything new.'

Catherine hung up and McAbbey stood. 'I want each of you to investigate something. I don't care what, but by tomorrow morning I want results. The Commissioner's going to wring my neck if we don't get somewhere soon.'

'Sir, the Commissioner's on the phone.' Helen stood at the door—unwittingly ratifying his statement.

'Thanks.' McAbbey frowned at his team. 'What are you going to do next?'

'I'll go back over the staff and parents who have been at the college in the last week,' Ted volunteered.

'I'll look through those emergency tapes again and see if there's anything else I can tell from his voice and what he said,' added Pete.

'Two good ideas.' McAbbey pointed at Jack. 'I need you and Gavin to continue working on the common denominator—his signature. He's not a random killer. He has a reason and a purpose—but doesn't want anyone to know what it is. Can you also draft up a media statement? There will be no hiding this one from the press. The news has probably already leaked through the bloody parents' network.'

'News reporters had arrived when we left this morning but I declined to comment,' Ted said.

'Good for you, Ted,' McAbbey said pointedly.

As an afterthought Jack handed McAbbey the *Age* and *Herald Sun*. 'I bought these on the way in to work. Seen them yet?'

McAbbey shook his head.

'The *Age* reads: 'The Adonis killer claims number five. Panic to set in'. The *Herald Sun* says: 'Number five. Melbourne's serial killer claims another life—police are baffled.' Jack looked up, noting their reactions.

'Hold on! Five? Are they referring to the surfer?'

Jack scanned the article. 'No. Tania Stevenson. They claim "a source" told them.'

'It's a leak,' McAbbey growled.

'There's nothing you can do about it, Boss,' Gavin said quietly. 'It could have come from anyone inside. I mean there are a lot of people who know the murder is related.'

'Yes, but if I find out it was the Minister ...' A vein in McAbbey's temple bulged.

Helen poked her head in. 'The Chief Commissioner is still on the phone—waiting ...'

'OK.' He turned his attention to the others. 'Get going.'

McAbbey walked back to his office to face the music. As expected, after a few minutes on hold, Harry Vincent wanted blood.

32

That night, McAbbey argued with Chelsey for the umpteenth time.

'Don't you have homework to do, young lady!'

'I've done it already. Mum said I could go out to the movies with Sharee's family.'

'How come you never go to the movies with us? You always go the movies with Sharee.'

''Cos like, they actually go to the movies!' she retorted. 'The last time we went to the movies you took me to *Toy Story*.'

'And it was a great film! You said you enjoyed it.'

'I did! But that was years ago!'

'Oh.' McAbbey made a mental note to take her again. 'Don't be home too late—you have school tomorrow.'

'Der. Tomorrow is Saturday!' He watched her rush out the door and into their car. Sharee's father waved as they drove off.

For the first time in months, McAbbey fired up the spa and he and Lisa had a relaxing night drinking beer and champagne respectively, forgetting the woes of the world.

McAbbey awoke to the sun streaming through the open curtains. Lisa came in with a tray holding bacon and eggs and freshly plunged coffee.

'You're up and about early!' he remarked. 'Most days you make me get my own brekkie.'

'It's one in the afternoon, dear. I thought you might want to do something today.'

'What did you have in mind?' Lisa was positively glowing in the light of the window and McAbbey was more than hungry.

'The lawns for a start. They haven't been mowed in weeks ...'

With an exaggerated groan, he ate his breakfast and flicked through the newspapers.

The Saturday *Age* and *Herald Sun* discussed the Adonis Taskforce extensively and the effect the murders were having on the community. The death at St Bosco College had jolted many schools into placing curfews on their students and increasing security to their premises.

There was no doubt in McAbbey's mind that the killer was close to making his first big mistake. With heightened awareness, people would begin to secure their houses and take notice of stalkers.

McAbbey finished a domestic day of cutting lawns, washing cars and cleaning the house, by having a family dinner at the Taurus Restaurant. McAbbey enjoyed a medium-rare fillet mignon with a dusty cabernet sauvignon from his wine cellar. Before bed, he turned on the answering machine and muted the phone.

On Sunday morning, McAbbey sat on the veranda sipping tea and reading the paper. The sun had settled behind the clouds, lowering the autumn temperature to chilly. He was at peace, the kind of tranquillity he felt when on the verge of solving a perplexing case.

When he went back inside, he checked the phone messages. There were five calls on the machine. The first three were from the night before. All were Chelsey's friends, much to his chagrin; she would give him a serve over that.

The fourth call was from Lisa's friend, reminding them of dinner at their house that night and the fifth was from an excitable Catherine. She had found the link!

Naturally she didn't say anything over the phone, rather suggested that he visit her office as soon as possible. She had left the message at nine that morning—four hours earlier.

'Annette called, Lise. She was reminding us about dinner tonight.'

'You have that look about you. Are you going into the office?' She glared at him.

He nodded sheepishly. 'Catherine says she's found the link between the victims. But I'll be back in time for us to go out for dinner.'

'By five o'clock?' She sighed. 'You do this every time. You know Annette lives in Mentone. It could take us an hour or so to get down to the beach.' She grabbed him by the neck—throttling him lovingly, though sometimes he wondered. 'Just be back by five,' she warned.

33

The traffic at Southbank crawled like ants over a cake. There was a festival on at the Casino and along the banks of the Yarra River.

'Glad to see you could make it.' Catherine laughed at his attire. He had turned up in a pair of jeans and a baggy open necked shirt.

'Just 'cos you live in a white gown. I bet you kiss your boyfriends wearing latex gloves.'

'Very funny. Do you want to hear what I have or not?'

'Sure.'

He sat opposite her desk and she opened a cabinet drawer and removed a folder.

It was the photo file. At every crime scene, the photos taken were stored in a separate case folder. When the same crook was suspected, those folders were combined into a larger file.

She opened the file.

'Look at each victim's photos objectively.'

He took Tania Stevenson's file first.

It hurt McAbbey to look at her again. There were photos of the bedroom and Tania lying in bed. The next shots were taken after Catherine had removed the covers. He studied the close up of her neck bruising and a snap of her bizarrely serene facial expression, which they knew to be posthumous.

The next series of photos were of the second victim, Brad Anderson. Tania's girly room was replaced with Brad's sporting den. His room was littered with clothes, trophies and posters.

McAbbey noted again that the photos failed to show the painful and ugly side of death. He was smothered with his own pillow and, apart from internal haemorrhaging in the lungs, showed no external signs of having died unnaturally. Their killer's efficiency was extremely worrying. If he stopped killing, would they ever catch him? McAbbey doubted it.

The photos of Sharron were the first to reveal blood. She had been struck to the back of the head whilst listening to music. Her room was a myriad of posters, incense, candles and compact discs. The killer had tried to alleviate the ugliness of the strike to the head by propping her up. However this time the victim had slumped down on her side.

The fourth victim was Joanne MacDonnell. There was no sign of a break in, but they knew the killer had drugged her alcoholic drinks. McAbbey believed the young surfer met a brutal end because he was with Joanne when the killer arrived.

McAbbey could see the leathery-yellow ligature mark around Joanne's neck. In the photo she looked calm and peaceful. The actual crime scene had affected his judgement on this. From the photos, it was obvious she had died as painlessly as the others had.

He was wrong in his earlier notion that the killer had a fetish for young, slim youths with long hair. Joanne was a size eighteen with short-cropped hair, yet something linked her to the others, not just the way in which they died, but something else, currently indefinable.

'Review the last two files so I can tell you what I've found,' Catherine urged.

'Why not just tell me now!' he replied curtly.

'I want you to see what I did when I discovered the connection.'

He snatched the Andrew Jones file from her. It was obvious from the photos that this murder did not fit the style of the killer.

'Are you going to suggest he didn't kill Andrew Jones?'

She shook her head. 'I admit the MO is different, but he killed Jones. The killer was ruthless, and I think, waited until the victim was revived before slitting his throat.'

'Agreed, I think he killed him, but not for the same reason as the others.' McAbbey returned to the file.

The final victim was Ben Peterson from St Bosco College. The photos depicted him in the same pose. The garrotte mark on the boy's neck was similar to that of Tania and Joanne. McAbbey initially believed the killer beautified the bodies to give him time to escape, but this was discounted when they realised he called Emergency Services.

Earlier, McAbbey thought the killer was calling after each offence for the thrill of it. However since it was published in the media, the killer had ditched the courtesy. McAbbey now figured his motive for calling was to ensure his victims were cared for quickly and not left to decompose.

Catherine took back the file. 'What's the one thing we cannot discern from all these crime scene photos?'

McAbbey had no idea. 'That Maree's a shocking photographer?'

Catherine was quick to belt him on the arm.

She picked up another file. 'I asked Jack to provide me with a photo of each of the victims. Not a crime photo, but a professional shot, whether it be a school photo or family portrait.'

'There were photos published in the papers—I saw them. So what?'

'These clear copies show us something we've not focused on before; the newspapers print blurred photos, and most of them are in black and white.'

All of a sudden McAbbey felt a chill settle at the nape of his neck; like someone was about to wax the hair from his back.

He took the photos from her and spread them like a poker hand.

The eyes of each victim were an unusually radiant blue.

34

'He hunts down kids with light blue eyes ...' he said quietly.

McAbbey did not see a photo of Andrew Jones. 'Did the surfie have blue eyes?'

'No, green,' Catherine replied.

McAbbey nodded. It proved he was irrelevant and not an intended target.

'Five out of five. The eye colour is identical in every case.'

A ringing phone brought him out of his reverie.

'Well done Cath, I'll call Jack right away. It'd be great if you could join us for our Taskforce briefing tomorrow.'

She nodded. 'I'll be there—and I'll have a think about the connection tonight as well.'

'Tonight?' McAbbey gave her a puzzled look, and then glanced at his watch—in the background the ringing phone was still irritating him.

'Five already damn! I'm supposed to be going out to dinner. Lisa will have my neck.'

He cursed Catherine's work environment, which offered no outside light. 'It could be midnight in here and you wouldn't know!'

She laughed, 'Leave it to me. I have Jack's number. I'll call him. He can call the rest of your crew.' She made some notes on a pad, before inquiring about a time for the following day's meeting.

'Make it nine.' McAbbey frowned, his agitation showing. 'Aren't you going to answer that?'

Catherine picked up the phone.

'Hi, Lisa.' She gave McAbbey a look.

He ran to the door.

'He's already left, Lisa.' Catherine said with a wry smile.

They arrived late for dinner, but Lisa was glad for his breakthrough in the case.

McAbbey sat there biting his lip while Annette's husband, Richard, bragged about his company, which had just gone public on the stock exchange. They had certainly done well for themselves. Their house faced the bay overlooking Beach Road in Mentone. He often wondered what he could have achieved had he not been lured into the Police Force.

When Richard asked what he had been up to, McAbbey started to explain his latest case, but any time he described an event in detail, Lisa kicked him under the table. McAbbey was convinced that with Lisa's censure Richard would think his job was as lame as saving cats from trees.

—

Arriving at work the following morning, McAbbey sensed excitement as he joined his colleagues in the conference room. The portrait photos were already tacked to the whiteboard.

'What have you got?' McAbbey took his seat at the head of the table.

Jack took a marker. 'We've each made our own list of means by which the killer could have found his victims. From Cath we have "Optometrists".'

'Great foresight, Cath,' Gavin said wryly.

Jack wrote the occupation on the whiteboard. Next he wrote "General Practitioner".

'I doubt this will be it. Doctors don't move around that often,' Jack said.

'Maybe the victims travelled to the same crooked doctor?' Catherine defended her suggestion.

'Where would you propose we find a list of crooked doctors?' McAbbey asked, folding his arms.

'How about the Yellow Pages,' Gavin said with a grin.

Catherine sat back in her chair with the poise of a teacher who was unsure whether a fart in her class was funny or offensive.

'I guess it could be a GP,' Jack answered with a conciliatory smile. 'We should check it out anyway—maybe the victims went to the same bulk billing clinic.'

—

By the time they had exhausted everyone's ideas, the board was full. McAbbey stood when Jack finished writing.

'I want you to tackle a couple each. Organize to interview the friends and parents if you have to. Keep thinking of other possible connections as to how they may have met the killer. I'm going to see the Chief to report on our progress.' He dismissed them.

35

McAbbey returned to his desk and made notes on the discovery and the leads they would pursue and faxed it ahead to Vincent.

When he arrived at the Chief Commissioner's office, he joined Vincent and Bill Harnden, McAbbey's immediate boss. They were reading the forwarded copies of McAbbey's report.

'You believe you've found the causal link between the victims.' Vincent eyed McAbbey over his rims. 'Good work. I expect you will find the killer quickly now. I'm under increasing pressure from the Police Minister and the press is circling.'

'This wouldn't be about votes?' McAbbey asked, testily.

Bill shifted in his seat and Vincent glared back. 'It may be, Inspector. But your pay cheque depends on the budget that the Minister attains from the public purse. If the government determines we aren't doing our job, they'll take action. Retrenchments ...' He lingered on his last word as if it were agreeable to him.

'I understand the bureaucracy,' McAbbey snapped. 'But the Taskforce is doing its best.'

Bill interrupted, 'Harry.' He smiled apologetically. 'The work of the Homicide Squad has been the pride of the force. They're a team of truly dedicated workers, often putting in weekends and nights to the cause.'

McAbbey was convinced Bill had chosen the wrong profession.

The Taskforce meeting the following morning began well.

'Jack? How did you go with tracking professions which may have led the killer to his victims?'

'Well, I started with the gardeners, but without success. The Andersons use an elderly handyman—a long time family friend. I rang him, but since his retirement, he only mows a few lawns. The other families maintained their own gardens.'

Jack studied his notes for the next item.

'The victims' medical records were checked re the use of an eye specialist. I had two bites. Sharron Sylvester's father uses contacts and Joanne MacDonnell's brother has glasses.'

McAbbey nodded for him to continue.

'We also cross-checked the GPs visited by the victims. They've never used the same doctor, nor attended the same hospital for an operation. Next was portrait photographers used by the victims' families. There was no connection—nor were they part of a studio chain,' Jack said.

'What about school photographers and chemists that develop film?'

Jack nodded. 'I'll get on to it.'

'Gavin?' McAbbey looked across the table.

'I visited each victim's school and it wasn't easy. Each student had more than a dozen teachers in the past three years. With the way Brad Anderson's private college is structured, he's had thirty-five teachers in the past three years.'

'Heck!' Ted muttered.

'It wasn't so bad. I was able to eliminate the teachers who had stayed put for more than five years. I found one teacher who taught at Caulfield Grammar where Brad went to school, who then moved to St Bosco College. However, he didn't work at any of the other schools, nor was he tutoring.'

'Nonetheless, he's worth a look at,' McAbbey pressed.

'I did. I spoke with him yesterday. Matthew Lescai is a congenial and learned man—and distressed to have known both boys. I had the Crimes Department run checks on him. He's never even had a parking ticket …'

'Some of the worst criminal minds of the last hundred years looked harmless. We should put a tail on him for a few days and see where he takes us.'

Jack nodded, making notes.

'What about Pearce?' McAbbey asked, his eyes narrowing.

'He was at St Anne's for nearly twenty years—ever since he qualified as a teacher.'

McAbbey nodded to Pete.

'I checked the bus lines. No bus drivers swapped to other companies used by the victims during the past seven years.'

Ted's report was brief—only Brad Anderson had a tutor.

McAbbey looked at the list on the whiteboard—it had been completely wiped out.

36

McAbbey wrote a press release that afternoon and sent it to the Chief Commissioner's office for vetting.

He had earlier requested that Vincent suppress the manner in which the killer posthumously positioned the bodies. Now he asked that the victims' light blue eyes be added to the taboo list.

McAbbey received a call from Harry Vincent at the end of the day.

'I've read your brief and press statement, Ryan. I think we have to demonstrate to the public that we're progressing in the investigation. The evidence you've uncovered will be a reflection to the community that you're close to catching the bastard.'

'Harry, when it was headlined that the killer called the police, he stopped calling. Since then we've had a decaying body and cold evidence from the delay in finding the deceased. I believe releasing the other idiosyncratic information will cause him to change tack.'

'You can't be sure of that,' Vincent said. 'You have no evidence that the press statement was the reason he stopped calling Emergency Services.'

He was right. McAbbey sighed. But this was about more than facts.

'I have a strong feeling about this. Serial killers love publicity—the chance to be remembered. This guy wants none of that. He makes no grandiose statements, has not baited police and does not kill in a way that attracts more than the typical hype surrounding multiple killings.'

'What if we release this information and he makes a mistake as a consequence? Is it worth the risk then?'

'We already have six dead. The last thing we need is a serial killer changing his signature. Forgive me if that doesn't appeal.'

'Look, Ryan. The decision isn't mine anyway. I'll give your report to the Police Minister. The right to publish and make a statement is his.'

'Just make sure the vote-grabbing prick gets my message. We'll never catch the bastard if this information gets to him.'

'It's out of your hands now, Ryan. You just worry about doing your job.'

That night after chicken tandoori, McAbbey sat with Lisa in front of the television. He had no interest in the news, but something tugged at his conscience and he changed the channel to the ABC for the seven o'clock update.

McAbbey stiffened as the Police Minister, Gary Moloney, was introduced on the steps of Parliament in Spring Street. Moloney was tall with jet black hair and a nose so keen it could cut butter. He was dressed in an Italian suit with gold cufflinks.

'What's the Minister going to say?' Lisa asked.

'I wish I knew.' McAbbey grabbed the remote and turned up the volume. 'I had no idea the Minister intended to make a public statement tonight. Generally an address from him only comes about when there's something to take credit for, and that worries me. Ministers don't like making statements about failures.'

They listened to the Police Minister's speech:

> As you are aware, a manhunt for the serial killer is underway. The Homicide Squad has made significant progress and I wish to make it known that the killer has a particular interest in young people with light blue eyes.

McAbbey was overcome with nausea.

'I gather this is bad news?' Lisa asked.

'Yeah, not so much that the killer likes blue eyes, just that the Minister is announcing it. We believe our killer has idiosyncrasies he's unaware of. He touches up the bodies to make them look peacefully asleep, rather than leaving them as they died. Though the killer may be aware he's doing this, he thinks we haven't noticed. He was calling the Emergency Hotline until they revealed it.'

'What effect is this announcement going to have? Is the killer going to lie low, or stop killing kids with blue eyes?'

'I don't know. Admittedly, this will prove if his fetish is with blue-eyed kids. I think he'll continue killing because he won't be able to stop what he does. If the eye colour is irrelevant, I think he'll make sure his next victim has different coloured eyes.'

'Maybe he's already finished?' Lisa suggested.

'Personally I doubt it, but I guess it's been a week since the last murder.' McAbbey changed the channel.

McAbbey arrived at work Wednesday after another good night's sleep—a subliminal indicator that the murderer had not killed overnight. He started to wonder—had their killer finished his crusade?

He flicked through the local newspapers for articles about their Minister's disclosure, before opening *The Australian*, which has a refreshing national focus. McAbbey could read about the crime problems of other cities without feeling responsible.

He turned a few pages and eyed an article which curdled his blood. Staring at the page in disbelief, his mind reeled like a weather vane caught in a tornado.

'What the ...'

37

Jack walked past his office and saw the look on his face.

McAbbey showed him the colour picture of a girl and the related article.

The caption underneath read: "Murdered at Home".

Jack stared at the snap. She was a stranger, but her eyes emerged from a school photo in the paper, pleading with them.

McAbbey read the article:

'Twenty-year-old Sue Maryvale was found dead Monday night, brutally murdered. She was in her second year of an arts degree at the University of WA. She was found in her bed.'

Only minor detail followed the opening caption. Something about police working off vague leads—the usual garbage, McAbbey noted.

'Jack, you'd better ring the Western Australian PD and request a copy of all the files pertaining to this investigation.'

Was their killer on the move? McAbbey withdrew from his reverie when Jack returned with a faxed file ten minutes later.

He convened an impromptu Taskforce meeting and made copies of the faxes from WA for them to read. He also passed around the article in *The Australian*.

The table was hushed as they absorbed the details.

'As you can see, this changes everything. It seems our man has been holidaying interstate.'

'Are you sure he killed this girl?' Gavin frowned.

'The MO is different, but we have to rely on his signature—her blue eyes and the posthumous presentation, to link it to the others. I think he has cleverly disguised his efforts to throw us off.'

'It wouldn't be hard to do,' Catherine admitted. 'Each state has its own Homicide Squad and State Coroner. Though I cooperate with the Coroners from other states, I seldom work with them on cases unless they cross jurisdiction. Apart from a monthly report and an annual conference, I have no contact with the other forensic investigations interstate.'

'So you're saying that our killer might be picking victims from around the country?' Gavin asked.

'Possible, but unlikely,' McAbbey said. 'Perhaps she used to live in Victoria. I have Inspector Orford of the WA Homicide Squad checking this out. I must admit I'm excited. This discovery could unveil a previously esoteric link between the cases.'

McAbbey nodded to Jack.

'The young woman shared a flat with three girls. At the time of death, two of the others were home—asleep in their separate rooms. Apparently when the last girl returned after nightclubbing, she noticed the front door open and bloody footprints on the carpet. She followed the trail to the victim's bedroom. The door was ajar, so she turned on the light. From the police report, it sounds like her screams woke not only the other occupants of the house, but the entire neighbourhood.'

'How was she killed?' Catherine asked.

'Her throat was slit from ear to ear. The blood loss was severe and our usually whistle-clean killer trampled blood all over the carpet.'

'How did he get in?' Pete enquired.

'The front door—apparently the last girl in always locked it. He left the same way.'

Gavin grunted. 'Sorry boss, but I can't see how this fits our Taskforce. The killer's never used a knife or butchered an intended victim. There must be thousands of women with blue eyes—why would he bother going as far as Perth?'

McAbbey understood Gavin's objection. Serial killers liked familiar surroundings and rarely moved from their environment. It was the reason why so many mass murderers were given geographical monikers like the Yorkshire Ripper and the Boston Strangler.

McAbbey, however, knew more than his crew, having read the article twice and spoken to the Homicide detectives involved.

'They interviewed the girl who discovered Sue Maryvale. She was upset by how her friend was sitting. I've requested for the original photos to be sent, but they won't arrive until tomorrow.' McAbbey said. 'She was sat up in bed with her head supported by a pillow and an open book placed before her …'

There was silence around the table.

'What about the autopsy and tox findings?' Catherine waded through the notes McAbbey had copied for her, but was lost without her obligatory medical reports.

'I've asked the WA State Coroner to speak with you as soon as the inquest brief is complete and the autopsy reported,' McAbbey said.

Catherine nodded. 'I may be able to assist them in arriving at a finding. I know the Chief Pathologist, Doctor Sarra, well.'

McAbbey smiled, hoping that Catherine would have her own contacts.

'Excellent. We need to know for sure if it's our killer. He hasn't attacked for a while and this may explain why.'

'I wonder if he's come back to Victoria,' Jack said.

'Who knows,' McAbbey said. "How did you go with the photographers?'

'There seems little point now that we know he also kills interstate,' Jack said.

'On the contrary, it's more likely the killer is using a contact at something like a photographer's studio to find his victims. Many studios and chemists have franchises operating in more than one state.'

'So, what did you find, Jack?' Catherine suppressed a smile. Catherine loved it when one of McAbbey's infallible crew members drew a blank.

'Nothing. Not a goddamned thing! I checked the employees of each chemist developer but no staff members moved between them.'

'What about school photos?' McAbbey referred to the photographers hired to do the annual school portraits.

'I checked with each school to find out which studios they had used. Each school had changed photographers more than once in the past five years. We were able to track down each studio and sequester the database information for the schools they worked and the staff used. However, only one staff member had swapped between two of the studios over the period.'

McAbbey stood. 'I want you all to keep an open mind for other ways that the victims may have come into contact with the killer. Make any enquires of the WA police that you deem necessary.'

He turned to Catherine. 'As soon as you have the findings of the autopsy, let me know. I'll have to brief the Chief Commissioner of this before he discovers it from someone else …'

38

Later that afternoon, McAbbey stormed into Harry Vincent's office on Flinders Street. He sat without invitation and Vincent studied him thoughtfully from across the desk.

'To what do I owe this pleasure?' Vincent, for all his bravado, looked uncomfortable. For once, he had not set the agenda.

'I'm here about your hair-brained scheme to reveal our best lead to the press.'

Vincent shook his head, seemingly exonerating himself. 'That was the Minister's decision, not mine.'

'The Minister's a pompous vote seeker. If I'd thought you were going to tell him, I would've kept the lead from you.'

'You would keep information from me?' Vincent was incensed.

'If it meant saving lives, yes.'

Vincent frowned. 'The Minister's a cock. I told him in confidence. I can't help it if his sole concern is his television career. The fact is, he chose to publish the information—not me.'

'Can I have your word that you'll exclude him from any new developments we tell you?'

Vincent gave a nod that McAbbey was loath to trust, but he did.

'The killer's been interstate this week—in Perth. A twenty-year-old woman was murdered last night. We don't have all the details yet, but I believe he did it. She has the same eyes ...'

'Keep me informed.' Vincent dismissed him and returned to his report.

—◦—

On Thursday morning at nine, McAbbey waited impatiently for Catherine to join them. They had received detailed information on the WA case and Catherine had spoken with the pathologist and was privy to the autopsy results.

'What have you got, Cath?' McAbbey asked.

She sat, dropping a stack of folders in front of her with a yawn.

'What's up with you?' McAbbey asked.

'I've been working on the national CrimTrac database. I'm on the committee.'

'What? The DNA link up?' Jack asked.

'Yes. We've always had a fragmented state-based system. The new database references the DNA of all known offenders nationally. The system is already up and running for conventional fingerprinting, but the DNA side's had its teething problems.'

'Does it only cover convicted crims?' McAbbey asked.

'At the moment, yes. The technology's new. In most states, DNA fingerprinting is an optional procedure requiring the approval of the offender or a magistrate. Soon, both suspects in criminal cases and those convicted will be recorded.'

Catherine opened a file and handed out copies of a stapled report. They read the document in silence.

'The killer was professional. The slash severed the spinal cord precisely at the base of the skull. The effect is not dissimilar to death by hanging.' She continued, noting a few blank looks. 'When a person is hanged they generally die, not through a lack of oxygen, but from the whiplash which snaps their spinal cord.'

'So she would have died painlessly.'

'As painless as death gets, I guess,' Catherine said. 'There was no sign of a struggle and the girl was not previously drugged or violated. The killer entered the house, went to her room and slit her throat. He waited for the blood rush to subside and then sat her up in bed with a book.'

'What was the book?' McAbbey asked. The summary made no mention of the title.

'The Bible,' Jack replied.

39

'A religious nut?' McAbbey ended the stunned silence.

'Maybe a priest?' Ted offered. 'That could explain his access to the kids.'

'None of the other murders indicated religious fervour,' Catherine disagreed. 'Could this be a furphy?'

'What if we hadn't noticed a religious element to the other murders?' Jack said.

'Pearce is a religious type.' McAbbey tapped the dull end of a pen on the table.

The Taskforce crew studied the notes before them, in the hope that some quirky detail would reveal itself.

'What evidence was recovered from the victim?' McAbbey asked.

'Very little,' Jack admitted. 'The only DNA and fingerprints found were linked to either her family or friends.'

'The lack of evidence also links this case to our investigation.' McAbbey stood. This assumption had just broadened the Taskforce outside his jurisdiction.

'I want you two to investigate the Bible lead.' McAbbey pointed to Jack and Pete. 'See if there were any religious artefacts moved, spat on, or turned upside down in each of the deaths we've investigated so far. Ted, I want you to check the religion of each family and if they attended the same church. Gavin, find out if Pearce left Victoria in the past week.'

Later that afternoon, Pete waited for Jack in reception. They were to make a routine visit to the Forensic Science Centre at Macleod.

'What's that you're doing?' Pete asked Helen with interest.

She giggled. 'Don't say anything, but I'm doing the Inspector's e-mails.'

'Those are hand written notes.' Pete said with a frown.

'Yep.' Jack had appeared beside him at reception. 'If you must know, Andrea and Helen print and type all his e-mails.'

'You're kidding?' Pete was astounded.

Jack shook his head. 'I encouraged him to go on a typing tutor course, but he kept complaining that his computer played up. I didn't believe him until the day I sat and watched him use the program.'

'Was there something wrong with the software?' Pete asked.

'Of course not!' Jack scoffed. 'The silly bugger was so slow in finding the keys that the power save kept shutting down the computer.'

'Ever since then, we've been typing them for him,' Helen finished, with a wide grin.

After emptying his in-tray of paperwork and expense claims, McAbbey went home and spent the evening helping Chelsey prepare an assignment on the Australian bi-cameral system of Parliament.

Lisa berated him for his snide remarks about politicians in general and Chelsey disagreed with his advice, even though she persisted in asking him for it.

After a night of belittling government officials, especially Gary Moloney, McAbbey retired to bed, wondering what else the Minister could do to damage their investigation.

A ringing phone during the night was totally unexpected. Reaching wildly for the receiver, McAbbey opened his eyes and felt the digital clock burn the time into his eyes. It was midnight. Just two hours had passed since he'd fallen asleep.

'Boss, Jack here. There's been another.'

'Where?' he mumbled.

'Kilborn Court, Mill Park. Are you sure you want to … ?'

'Yeah. I'll be there in an hour.' Reaching for his clothes, McAbbey stumbled into the ensuite. He looked like crap and the worst thing about being called in the middle of the night, was the need to be presentable. He would rather attend a murder scene in rumpled tracksuit, but it would not be considered proper. Gone were the days of the unkempt homicide investigator. McAbbey mused at how he had spent more time recently in ministerial meetings and attending media functions. Even at a murder scene the grieving relatives of the deceased generally sought him out with questions of how and why. The police counsellor always seemed to arrive after he had dealt with the worst of it.

McAbbey parked outside a neighbour's house, twenty metres from the crime scene.

40

A uniformed officer sat with the distraught family in the lounge room. McAbbey passed them, looking for his team.

From the kitchen, a large bay window offered a stunning view of the backyard brightly lit with spot and garden lights. He could see his crew working with a forensic team in the gardens.

As he pulled back the sliding door, McAbbey saw a well-manicured yard with cobblestone paths and neat garden beds filled with plants whose names he could never pronounce. He could not see the side or back fences for creepers and trees. Towards the end of the yard, he noticed Catherine and Maree with the victim.

He walked down the path. Occasional flashes of light from Maree's camera lit up the spa, which, with occasional wisps of rising steam, set a surreal scene. A pot plant held the metal gate open, so the workers could come and go.

Catherine mumbled a greeting when McAbbey stood alongside her.

'Carly Williams. She's fourteen,' she said.

The spa seated six but now held a single occupant.

McAbbey could see that Carly was a pretty girl—even in death. She was sitting propped up in the spa, her hair long enough to drag in the water.

She looked to be sleeping; her chin had fallen to her chest and her arms were lying in her lap under the water. She was wearing a bright yellow one-piece swimsuit.

The scene reignited McAbbey's belief that the killer was interested in her particular age and physical appearance. Most serial killers chose their victims from a narrow cross-section of the community and so Joanne remained an enigma.

He watched Catherine inspect the spa filter, collecting evidence and samples with tweezers and surgical gloves.

'Back to the drawing board.' Catherine walked around the spa from the filter to the body. She raised the victim's head revealing a red-stained bruise from the twine that had contained her final breath. With the other hand, Catherine raised the girl's eyelids.

McAbbey swore quietly. She had brown eyes.

'It's definitely the same killer,' Catherine stated.

'So eyes aren't the deciding factor ...' he muttered. 'Finding his signature is harder than nailing jelly to a wall.'

'Not necessarily.' Catherine sat a supporting hand on his shoulder. 'Perhaps the killer saw the press release on his return from Perth and has changed?'

McAbbey sighed. 'I thought we were closer than this. It's been two months and we still have nothing.'

With a spark of an idea, McAbbey was off down the path. Catherine watched after him with a concerned frown. Inside, he followed the hall lights to the lounge room where Gavin was with the parents.

The mother sobbed lightly and the father sat in a trance. They slowly looked up at McAbbey and he studied their eyes closely.

'I'm sorry for your loss, Mr and Mrs Williams,' McAbbey said. 'My crew will be spending every waking hour to find the answers you need to put this terrible thing to rest.'

McAbbey had approached them with some hope, but he walked away with a gut ache of disappointment; his intuition had failed him. Neither parent had the same shade of light blue eyes.

'What is it?' Catherine had followed McAbbey back inside.

'I had a thought that the killer came into contact with the parents and then chose their child.'

Catherine scratched her hair. 'You mean the parents upset the killer at some point?'

'No. If the killer was attracted to one of the parents because of their light blue eyes, then the child's eyes could be a different colour.'

'Actually, the inheritance of eye colour can go back further than one generation if both parents have recessive genes. Interesting theory, but blue is a recessive gene, so we should have had victims with other eye colours before now.'

'That's something I could live with.'

Catherine watched McAbbey storm to his car.

41

McAbbey joined the Taskforce crew at the conference table later that morning.

'I have to meet with Moloney and Vincent this afternoon and I need more than conjecture. They'd also like to see a summary of the autopsy findings.' He looked at Catherine apologetically.

'I stayed back to finish it.'

'Thanks, Cath.' McAbbey was grateful. It was only ten-thirty.

McAbbey motioned for Pete to start.

'At nine last night, her parents went inside leaving Carly in the spa. She was told to turn it off and be in bed by ten. Alone in the spa, the filter, pump and bubbles would have prevented her from hearing the killer jump the back fence. Jack and I believe he parked a car in the street behind and walked through the neighbour's yard. We spoke with them, but they said it'd be impossible for anyone to get past Rusty and Butch.'

McAbbey raised an eye.

'Doberman pincers. So I asked why the dogs hadn't barked when I rang their doorbell,' Jack said. 'Outside, the dogs were heavily sedated. They had been given a large ham bone by the killer.'

'We searched the yard and discovered footprints in the garden patch, which borders their back fence with the Williams' property,' Pete added.

'Do they match the boot prints found on the floor of the student apartment in WA?' McAbbey asked.

'Err. No.' Pete glanced at Gavin.

Gavin interrupted. 'We received more information from WA. The boot prints don't belong to the killer. I'll get to that later.'

'By scaling the neighbour's fence, the killer was effectively behind the spa. After killing her, he left the same way. His coming and going footprints are in the vegie patch behind the fence. There are heavy depressions from where the killer landed.'

'This tells us the killer is athletic. The indentations have enabled Forensics to make a rough estimate on his possible height and weight,' Gavin added.

'Cath?' McAbbey asked.

'I believe she was killed with the same cord that was used in the other three garrotte murders.'

She opened a file and handed out photos.

'In the cases of Tania Stevenson and Ben Peterson, the cord imprint is clear because the photos were taken soon after death.' Catherine ruffled through her papers and produced another photo. 'However, Joanne was not discovered for days. The pictures reflect this time delay, but you can still see the faded pattern.'

McAbbey took the photo. He could see the mark encircling her throat. It was a touch wider than his watchband and looked like a nasty rope burn.

'Though Carly Williams was soaking in the spa and her skin had waterlogged, I could tell it was the same cord. Unfortunately, this same pattern is used by many manufacturers who make twine and rope for draw curtains, zip cords for lawn mowers and vertical blinds to name a few.'

'I've never heard of a serial killer who was so easy about his method of execution.' Ted frowned. 'Apart from garrotting, he's also bashed, suffocated, and cut victims' throats. He's all over the shop.'

'Only understanding his signature and motive will explain his erratic and secretive nature.' McAbbey motioned for Catherine to continue.

'Though Carly had not ingested drugs, she offered little resistance. Her lungs were full of water, indicating she was submerged. That would have muffled most of her thrashing and screaming. I took hair samples from the water and material from under her fingernails to determine if the killer left any evidence. If she was submerged, his arms might have also been underwater, possibly leaving skin and hair.'

Catherine handed McAbbey the forensic report.

'Unfortunately, a lot of people had been in the spa since its last clean. The filter was awash with hair, dirt, sweat and human faeces.'

'Ugh!' Gavin remarked.

'Yeah,' Catherine confirmed. 'All spas contain trace elements of faeces, just like your bath water does when you soak in it. This can be limited by replacing the water regularly and showering beforehand.'

'I think I might refill that hole I dug for our new spa.' Gavin pulled a face.

'Did you find anything other than Polly Waffles in the spa?' McAbbey asked, with a wink at Gavin.

'The hair and skin samples were from many different people. There was a lot of fat and grease on the surface—from calories burned off by those in the tub.'

'OK. What were you going to tell me about the boot prints found in WA?' McAbbey turned to Gavin.

'The prints were from Sue Maryvale's boyfriend. He cracked during an interview, admitting that he found her but was spooked and ran. Based on his alibi and our information linking the murder here, they have not pursued him. He has no priors and has cooperated thoroughly in their investigation.'

"The killer last night wore Blundstone boots,' Jack said. 'We had the pattern confirmed this morning. Forensics at Macleod has estimated the killer's height and weight at one-eighty-five centimetres and a hundred and five kilos.'

'Has this been released through Police Media? Do patrol cars have it?'

'Yes. The next edition of Crimestoppers will be asking for anyone with information about a suspicious adult fitting the description at any of the murder scenes to come forward.'

'If you'll forgive me Ryan, I'd like to get some shut-eye.' Catherine yawned for effect.

'By all means—this isn't a motel,' McAbbey said.

42

'What did you find out about the families and their religions?' McAbbey asked Ted, when Catherine left.

'Firstly, they were all Christian families,' Ted said. 'But they came from different denominations. Most of the families did not go to church and were non practising. Only Tania's mother and Ben Peterson's parents were the same; they are Catholic.'

McAbbey stood impatiently. 'I guess that's it then.'

'No. We have our report,' Pete said.

'You've got five minutes,' McAbbey glanced at his watch—he had thirty minutes to be at the Police Minister's office.

'We called each family and asked them if anything of religious significance had been taken or moved,' Pete explained.

'Tania's mother could think of nothing,' Jack continued. 'The Andersons had a look and found that a bible given to Brad as a child had been moved to the bookshelf with his most current sports books. Mr Anderson said that those sports books were the only ones Brad ever looked at.'

'Mrs Sylvester couldn't see anything that had been moved,' Pete said. 'But the MacDonnell's went down to their holiday house last weekend for the first time since the tragedy. Mrs McDonnell told me that a religious picture had been moved from the lounge to the bedroom where Joanne died. She assumed Joanne had moved it, though the girl had never been interested in the picture before,' Jack said.

'Did we check it for prints?'

'Yes. All items in the room were dusted for latents. There were none.' Gavin answered.

After a pregnant pause, Jack motioned for Pete to continue.

'I went back to Ben Peterson's boarding school this morning. They reported nothing out of the ordinary, but in the time I was there, I counted fifteen crucifixes, ten religious paintings and many statues. I think if one was missing or moved, no one would notice.'

'What about the statue you told me had been defaced?' Jack asked.

'Well,' Pete shrugged. 'As it turns out, three kids in Year Ten confessed to smashing it.'

'We already know about the bible in the Maryvale case in WA, which leaves Carly Williams,' Jack continued.

'Wait a minute,' McAbbey interrupted, 'Do we know what page the Bible was open at?'

'Yes.' Pete looked up his notes. 'Apparently it was Revelations—the passage about Judgement Day.'

McAbbey made a note on his pad to check up on it.

'This morning I visited Carly Williams' mother, Leanne, but it was difficult. She's still not in a state to talk,' Jack said. He pulled out a photo and passed it around. 'She gave me this today. It's Carly at the beach last year. Leanne told her not to wear her necklace in the water, but she never listened. She said Carly wore it day and night. It was not until I asked about articles of religious significance that she realised ...'

' ... that she was not wearing any jewellery when we discovered her,' McAbbey finished.

'Exactly. I think her mother was too upset to notice that her daughter's necklace was missing.'

'A crucifix ...' McAbbey murmured, staring at the photo of the young girl, so vibrant and full of life.

'He must have removed it after he killed her—maybe as a souvenir?' Pete offered.

'No, not after, before.' McAbbey muttered, still absorbed in the photo.

'That's right,' Jack said. 'The necklace would've affected the ligature mark from the strangling cord.'

'What about Pearce?' McAbbey asked.

'He hasn't been interstate this year. He was at the Christian Society on the night of the murder and I've verified his alibi,' Gavin said.

'I can't help but think Pearce is somehow connected to this.' McAbbey leant forward. 'Jack, call Inspector Creed from Sexual Crimes and get him onto his favourite magistrate. I want a search warrant for Pearce's place. He's the closest we have to a suspect. He knew Tania, and was dismissed under suspicious circumstances. He's also into religion in a big way.'

Jack nodded slowly. 'I think we have to be careful about trying to link Pearce to these quirks. Our victims were not sexually abused.'

'Agreed,' McAbbey said. 'But I want those disks we saw in his apartment. If he's a paedophile, I want him behind bars.'

Jack sighed. 'It's just we've found no trace of the man and he has an alibi for each murder.'

'Yeah. That religious sect—every time.' McAbbey folded his arms.

'I know, but Gavin went through Telstra—he has a mobile. His phone was logged into the network at the times of each murder. He was at the sect—even when the girl was found in Perth.'

'You can tell where a person is from their mobile?' Pete asked in amazement.

Jack winked. 'Better kept as our secret, hey!'

McAbbey frowned. 'What's to stop him dumping his mobile there?'

'Nothing.' Jack gave in. 'I'll call Creed this arvo.'

'I need you all to put your thinking caps on this afternoon and follow any lead you deem necessary. We'll meet first thing tomorrow to discuss your developments. Meanwhile, I have to go and tap-dance for the Minister and Vincent. I'll let you know my score tomorrow.'

With that, McAbbey picked up his files and briefcase and headed out of the office.

43

McAbbey had five minutes to read over his notes, made during the Taskforce meeting. He was not sure exactly what he was going to say, let alone what the Minister wanted.

McAbbey was scribbling on his report when the Chief Commissioner arrived.

'Good afternoon, Ryan. How are Lisa and Chelsey?'

McAbbey raised an eye. 'Well, Harry. Chel is as cheeky as ever.'

'They all end up like that. She's about to start the teenage rollercoaster.'

'You're not wrong,' McAbbey said.

He was uncharacteristically friendly, and McAbbey realised that Vincent was just as apprehensive as he was.

'The Minister's ready for you both.' The receptionist smiled thinly, letting them in.

Gary Moloney stood from behind a spotless oak desk. Probably polished and dusted twice a day, McAbbey thought. McAbbey's adage was that a clean desk was an unused desk. With the mess in his office, he had little choice but to advocate an aphorism like that.

'Minister.' Vincent shook hands.

The Minister then reached for McAbbey's hand. 'Good to see you again, Ryan.'

'Likewise.' McAbbey smiled back.

'Really!' The Minister feigned surprise. 'What was it you said to my wife at the Police Presentation dinner last year?'

Damn! McAbbey was hoping the Minister had forgotten it. The crack he made to the Minister's wife earned him one hell of a reputation. Unfortunately, McAbbey did not know that she was his wife at the time.

'You must tell Harry!' he pressed, astonished by Vincent's utter stupefaction. Even McAbbey was a little surprised that he had not heard about it.

'Gary's wife asked me what I thought of the new Minister.' McAbbey paused hesitantly before continuing, 'I said the Minister was so far up himself, he'd have to swallow to pass wind and if he could have things his way, paper-shuffling pricks would be all that's left of the police force in Melbourne.'

'Mind you, I'm only quoting,' he added haplessly.

Vincent did not know how to react and McAbbey could sense his indecision. If he laughed, would the Minister take it as an affront? At the same time Moloney was chuckling with amusement, probably enjoying their joint discomfort.

McAbbey admitted it was a big mistake that could have cost him his career. Though McAbbey disapproved of the Minister's policies, he respected his straight attitude, which he found rare among politicians.

'Do you have a submission?' The Minister sat.

McAbbey nodded.

'Glenda.' Moloney was on the intercom and his secretary graced them with her presence instantaneously. 'Take two copies of Inspector McAbbey's report please.'

Before he could object, Glenda had efficiently whisked them from the table and disappeared.

'You better have something, Harry. Otherwise we're in deep shit,' Moloney muttered.

Glenda returned his notes and passed out the copies.

'Last night, the killer claimed his eighth victim—Carly Williams. In doing so, he's left the strongest evidence yet. Footprints.'

'Foot ...' Moloney was astonished. 'A snapshot of the killer's boots is hardly going to benefit Crimestoppers.'

'It's not easy. This killer is precise and clean. He appears, kills and then disappears—leaving no trace.'

'Tell us about the footprints, Ryan,' Vincent said.

McAbbey glared at his boss, barely hiding his disdain. Vincent's tone suggested McAbbey had failed them both.

'A forensic expert from Macleod visited the scene and believes he can closely estimate the killer's profile in height and weight.'

'They are confident of accuracy. What about you?'

'I'll answer that when we catch the bastard.'

'If you don't hold the estimate in high esteem, then neither will I,' the Minister concluded.

McAbbey ached inside, just having discounted his only ace.

'I've been fully briefed on your investigation and I know your crew is working hard ...'

Here it comes, McAbbey thought.

' ... but, we need answers and we need them now.'

'We don't have a resolution. If we did, the killer would be behind bars now.'

'Not good enough!' he raised his voice. 'I can appreciate your situation, but you must understand mine. The Premier wants to put the minds of Victorians at rest. We are receiving hundreds of letters each day from concerned parents. We need to show them we're progressing and that the streets will be safe again.'

'How touching,' McAbbey remarked. 'That sounds like real concern, not just a quick fix aimed at freeing the blame from the government for reducing funds to the Homicide Squad.'

'Hang on a minute!' Moloney stood.

'Ryan,' Vincent warned, with his temple throbbing and his face, explosive-red.

'I have an obligation to the people of Victoria to ensure that the Police Force can protect its citizens from serious crime. We're not doing that at the moment and I'm getting a severe rap on the knuckles for it,' the Minister said.

'Severe rap hey? Maybe you should come down to the morgue and take a sweet look at young Carly Williams. Just for a minute stop thinking about your next term.'

'That's enough!' Vincent yelled. 'Another word and you're suspended!'

44

'Cool it, Harry.' Gary Moloney dismissed his outburst and addressed McAbbey sternly: 'I don't mind a bloke who speaks his mind. You of all people should know that by now,' he said.

McAbbey nodded slowly.

'I'll take your advice on board but, at the end of the day, if I don't act on it that's my decision. Disagree with me all you like.'

The Minister turned to McAbbey's notes and frowned. 'Why don't you précis for me?'

'We've investigated a myriad of leads on how the killer makes contact with his victims. Our strongest lead was the fact that they all had the same light blue eyes. That was until someone from your department saw fit to release this. Since then, a girl with brown eyes has died.'

'I was told the information was harmless, but would relieve public pressure ...' Moloney glared at Vincent, clarifying who the adviser was.

'We believe the killer is shirking notoriety and trying to achieve his goal without drawing attention to himself.'

'You've written here that the killer touches up the bodies and makes them appear asleep.'

'Yes, that's how we're able to determine it's the same killer, particularly in the WA case.'

'Do you have a theory about that?'

'No, but I think the killer is fond of his victims—if that's at all possible. In all cases they appeared to die without suffering any pain.'

McAbbey paused to search for the surfer's name in his papers. 'There was one notable exception—Andrew Jones, an unemployed beach-bum who was with Joanne MacDonnell when she was killed. Though her death was painless, the boyfriend was practically tortured. His neck was slit and his body was thrown into the bay.'

'So he's not bound to kill in the same way? You've written here that some were suffocated and others were strangled.'

'His MO has varied, however his intended victims are not violated or tortured in any way.'

'You said that when the eye colour affliction was revealed, he deliberately killed a young girl with brown eyes?'

McAbbey nodded. He wondered where the Minister was leading.

'If that's so, why didn't he kill her in the same manner as the surfer?'

'I've drawn the conclusion that eye pigmentation has nothing to do with his affliction. I think choosing a victim with brown eyes was a deliberate attempt to disassociate himself from the earlier murders.'

'If he wanted to disassociate himself, why didn't he kill her in a completely different way?'

'He's unaware that we know he presents the bodies peacefully. That's how we're still able to identify him as the serial killer.'

Moloney glanced back at the report. 'Why is there a reference to the Bible?'

'It's just a file note. Sue Maryvale from WA was found with a bible in her lap, opened at Revelations.'

'Is that an isolated incident?' Vincent asked.

'Yes,' he lied. No one outside his crew was aware of the religious change in some of the cases.

'Well, you've answered some of my concerns, Ryan. We'll be releasing a press statement this afternoon regarding this latest profile you've submitted, and we'll be revealing the killer's posthumous presentation.'

'What! You wouldn't dare!' McAbbey was aghast. 'If he changes again, we may never find him.'

'On the contrary, if we're to believe your story that he killed a brown-eyed girl because of the press release, then we'd be well-advised to publish this latest trait. He made his first mistake in killing the girl with brown eyes—the footprints. Perhaps by revealing more, he'll make another mistake, possibly a fatal one.'

'Fatal to whom? Him or some poor victim ...'

Vincent glared at him.

'Nonetheless, the decision is mine to make. You've not been able to convince me otherwise, so it'll be announced in the press statement that the killer treats the victims kindly and tucks them into bed.'

'But if he does change, he may decide to punish the victims, torture them and who knows what else. We're able to comfort the parents with the knowledge that their children died peacefully. Please don't take that from us.'

Moloney rubbed a finger on the rim of his nose. 'I'll think about it—but no guarantees. The Premier won't tolerate this dragging on indefinitely.'

Their meeting was over, but McAbbey's humiliation was not.

Outside the Minister's office, Vincent blasted him. 'Another display like that and you won't make your pension!' he yelled, as they stood in the lift together.

Three.

McAbbey faced forward, willing the lift to move faster.

Two.

'You have three days to get some answers, or I'll get someone else to carry on the investigation.'

Ground.

As soon as the lift doors permitted his escape, McAbbey slipped through and out to his car without looking back.

'You're on notice, Inspector,' Vincent yelled after him.

McAbbey drove straight home. His first stop was the fridge and four Crown lagers later, he was able to relax.

That afternoon, Jack pulled up outside Paul Pearce's flat with Gavin and Pete.

Inspector Bernie Creed and a uniform walked across the road to join them. McAbbey's counterpart in the Sexual Crimes Unit was a gaunt man in his fifties with a face like sculptured granite and dark eyes that sparkled.

'Thanks a million, Creed.' Jack shook his hand.

'Not a problem. I owe McAbbey a favour or two. The warrant was straightforward. It's amazing how quickly a magistrate reacts when you wave a heavy submission in front of him. I then sit back with a full glass of water like I'm expecting to take up his afternoon.'

'And Judge Honeychurch bought it?' Jack laughed.

'Of course. I was surprised he didn't notice it was the same dog-eared submission from last summer. So where's the grump anyway?'

'He had a date with the Minister.'

'Figures, I didn't think I was his favourite anymore.'

Creed walked to the apartment building, pulling the warrant from his shirt pocket. He rang the buzzer for Pearce's unit twice with a pause in between.

Pearce answered and reluctantly let them in. As Jack led the way to the unit he instructed the others.

'Pete, I want the disks. There were at least two dozen here last time. Gavin, look in the bedroom—we want any material, mags and photos you can find.'

Pearce was blushed and ruffled when he answered the door, with the chain still attached.

Creed handed him the warrant and began talking. Pearce let them in and they went about their search while Creed explained the intricacies to him. Pearce looked past Creed, his eyes darting from one member to the next.

'I've done nothing wrong!' Pearce protested.

'There's no better way to prove your innocence than by cooperation,' Creed said.

Pete went straight to the computer and rifled through drawers for the disks. He found none.

Jack joined him at the computer. 'The CDs were in a stack last time. He must have hidden them.'

Pete paused a moment, then pulled out the bottom drawer in the desk fully. It fell to the floor with a thud. In the gap behind was the pile of numbered disks.

Jack patted Pete on the back.

Gavin returned from the bedroom with a pile of soft porn magazines. 'Nothing illegal here,' he said with a shrug. 'I have a few of these in my trusty collection.'

Jack gave a wry grin and turned to Pete who had not finished at the computer desk.

'What's wrong, wiz?' Jack asked.

Pete frowned. 'The monitor's hot.' He turned on the PC and waited for it to start up. The 'auto check' started and Pete gave Jack a look.

'What?' Jack asked.

'He must've shut the computer off when we rang the bell.'

Jack nodded. 'This disk scan always comes on when my computer locks up.'

'Or is suddenly turned off without being closed down properly,' Pete said.

The CD player within the computer started up and Pete pressed eject, releasing another CD. The home-made disk had no markings.

Pete collected the disks and the PC tower, and they left.

45

It was Saturday morning and McAbbey was woken by the phone.

He tried to sit up in bed, but his head ached from the previous night's alcohol. He lay back on the pillow and pinned the phone to his ear.

'McAbbey.'

'Aren't you coming to our review meeting this morning?' It was Jack.

McAbbey groaned.

'No matter. I'll chair the meeting,' Jack said.

'Why don't you put me on speaker phone?' McAbbey mumbled.

Jack put the call through to the conference room and McAbbey greeted them gruffly.

'How did your meeting with the Minister go?' Jack asked.

'Shithouse,' McAbbey replied. 'I think Vincent is setting me up for a fall, but don't worry, I'm not about to give in to these pencil pushers.'

'If you're going to hang, you may as well go out swinging!' Gavin chuckled.

'So what did you and the Minister discuss? Not his wife again, I hope?' Jack knew the story and considered it service folklore.

'Very funny.' McAbbey could hear murmuring in the background. 'You can tell them later, Jack. As for the meeting, it went well, until they realised I had nothing concrete to offer. Basically the Minister refuted our argument for keeping the information from the public. He wants to release the killer's signature to flush him out. Moloney said the killer made a mistake last time when he left identifying footprints, and Moloney figures he may make a bigger mistake next time.'

'Stupid idiot. Doesn't he realise the risks involved.'

'Well, unfortunately his argument is sound. I had no comeback.'

'But a kid is going to die.'

'To be brutally honest, the next victim will die regardless.'

'I realise that, but we may not be able to tell which murders the serial killer commits.'

'How many other people under the age of twenty-three have been murdered in the last year? Five? Ten? I think in all honesty, we'll be able to tell.'

Gavin spoke up. 'At least you didn't tell them about the religious inference.'

'How did you know that?'

'It wasn't published. The newspapers this morning have a large spread on the 'Adonis' murders. The Police Minister made announcements to the press. The TV promo suggests it will be the feature story on tonight's news. We assumed the statement was the outcome of your meeting.'

'So he did go ahead with it. I hope he knows what he's doing.'

McAbbey had a sudden thought. 'Pete, if you mention the religious connection to your old man, I swear to God you'll have one fairly soon afterwards.'

'I promise,' Pete said slowly. He was understandably offended, but McAbbey was not in the mood to apologise.

He ended the meeting, wishing them all a relaxing weekend. He suggested they reconvene on Monday at nine to discuss their future.

When the meeting finished, Jack called Pete into his office.

'Did you have a look at the hard disk and those CDs?'

Pete nodded. 'There was nothing on the PC, but the CDs are encrypted with a password. It looks like a complex algorithm. We can't decode it here but I know a guy at Swinburne Uni in Hawthorn. We went to high school together.'

'Ah. The old boy's network!' Jack smiled. 'See if you can visit him Monday morning.'

'He's there waiting for me now.'

'Excellent.'

Pete took Burwood Road to the University and parked in John Street, outside the main building. He took the lift to the seventh floor and the Computer Sciences Department.

An unkempt man in his late twenties with a bushy beard and ponytail greeted Pete in the computer lab.

'Andy.' Pete patted him on the back warmly.

'So, what have you got for me? Porn?' Andy rubbed his hands together.

Pete frowned. 'I don't know, but it's for Homicide. I need you to keep it to yourself.'

'Can do.' Andy walked to a large desk with multiple computers. He took the first disk and put it in the drive.

'This computer has the most grunt.' He looked at the directory structure on the Compact Disk.

'There's only one file. It's a Bell-EnCrypt file.'

'How hard is it to crack?' Pete asked.

'It's one of the best. I'd say he has something to hide.'

'Can you hack it?'

Andy loaded a program. 'This is a cracker that will put every possible password permutation through it, starting with single characters.' He set the program running and sat back with a foot on the desk.

Pete watched the data in a window on the screen as it whizzed through alphabetical and numerical combinations.

'If he's used a long string, it could take days to find the right combination. You may as well go home. I'll let it run over the weekend. Gimme a call Monday and I'll let you know how it's going.'

The first round of the footy season was one of their few rituals remaining as father and daughter, and McAbbey had forgotten. After his briefing he went back to sleep until Chelsey jumped on the bed. Inappropriately donning a footy jumper and scarf for a typically warm time of year, she yelled at him to get up. Turning abruptly, she was gone, the number eighteen on the back of her jumper.

McAbbey enjoyed going to the footy with Chelsey, but hated it when she insisted they sit behind the goals, as he believed the wings were the best place to spectate from. She had become a mad Essendon fan and liked to be up close to Matthew Lloyd during the game. If McAbbey had not put his foot down, she would have insisted they change ends with the players every quarter.

It was a close game, but Essendon prevailed. Chelsey sang the Bombers' anthem on the way home. McAbbey even joined in for a chorus, feeling more relaxed and refreshed than he had been in a long time.

That evening, Lisa suggested he cook a barbecue and they watch a video. He wanted to read over the case files, but gave in easily.

46

For the first time in ages, Lisa elbowed McAbbey to answer the phone.

Reaching to the bedside table, he scooped up the receiver and squinted at the clock. It was Monday morning; five AM.

'It's Jack here, you'd better get up. There's another victim.'

'Is it the same killer?'

'We can't say for sure.'

McAbbey sat up in bed suddenly. The disorientation faded as his mind questioned. How could Jack not be sure?

A cold shower brought McAbbey screaming to his senses—a necessary evil, if he was to drive anywhere.

McAbbey pulled out the Melways and looked up Marshall Street, Ivanhoe before leaving home.

At the scene, a few curious people milled at either side of the driveway, held back by a uniformed officer. The seventies-built double storey flats were the colour of a block of Cadbury's.

Walking up concrete stairs, McAbbey stood on a landing at the front door and swore under his breath. There were bloodstains on the door and front step.

Inside, Gavin nodded to McAbbey briefly. He stood in the kitchen with the mother, who was hunched over in a chair.

Pale sunlight from early dawn penetrated the windows and the only lamp in the room was dimmed.

McAbbey was aghast at the carnage. Rarely did a murder carry through so many rooms. The extended living area was wet with blood spattering—the modular couches, telephone, kitchen vinyl and carpet. His attention focussed on a bloody hand smudge down a wall in the lounge. The smear tapered off near the floor suggesting a harrowing struggle before the victim was dragged away.

Jack joined McAbbey from the passage. He wiped his brow with a forearm. 'Whoever did this is sick and depraved.'

'What do we know so far?'

'Well, the mother came home from Crown Casino about four this morning and was grabbed by who she thought was a burglar.'

'What?' McAbbey said. 'She was grabbed by the killer?'

Jack nodded.

'What was the mother doing out that late?'

'Her name's Karen Johnson. She left here about nine last night, which is apparently her Sunday night tradition.'

'How old is the daughter?' McAbbey asked incredulously. He could never imagine leaving Chelsey home alone all night.

'Melinda is eighteen.'

'Is it our serial killer?'

'Not likely. Nothing matches any previous pattern. Cath also thinks it's unrelated.'

McAbbey was despondent. His mind was heavily focused on the serial killer. It was hard to just start over. They would have to open a new case file and investigate the victim's family and friends, find a motive …

'I'd better take a look. Who's in there?'

'Cath, Maree and Ted."

'Pete?'

'Kermit went home.' Jack gave a wry grin.

McAbbey rolled his eyes. 'Is it as bad as it looks from out here?'

'Worse.'

McAbbey walked down the hallway, stepping gingerly around bloody carpet stains. He passed a combined bathroom and toilet, surprised to find a matted clump of hair on the floor, congealed like last night's spaghetti in pasta sauce.

Following the crimson trail, he passed the mother's room and came to the door at the end of the corridor. Pushing it open, he was dazzled by a bright light, which momentarily blinded him.

'Sorry about that!' Maree laughed, 'I guess now you'll have to be bagged and tagged!'

'Well, I'm innocent ...'

'Don't bet on it.' Catherine looked up. She stood crouched over the bed, tweezers in hand. 'Where I come from, you could be arrested for wearing an outfit like that.'

'Very funny.' Catherine forever made fun of his clothing, but McAbbey realised that today she had a point. He had dressed in the dark and had mismatched a brown corduroy sports jacket with grey-pinstriped suit pants.

With a deep, but silent breath, he studied the room.

Sloppily painted in white, the bed, dresser and bookcase looked to be from the opportunity shop. An old tape recorder with a broken casing and a few neatly stacked dog-eared editions of *Cleo* magazine sat on top of the bookshelf.

A dusty collection of Hardy Boys and Nancy Drew novels filled the bookcase, notably in series order. Her built-in wardrobe was open, so he took a glance inside. All the clothes were hanging in blissful unity. If only Chelsey was this organised, he rued.

47

McAbbey stepped to the window by the far side of the bed. It appeared to be fastened securely but, with the sheer drop outside, a ladder would have been required to reach the second floor anyway. There were no trees or fire exits within reach.

'Have you ascertained the method of entry yet?'

'The killer came and went through the front door. There was no sign of forced entry, but the mother claims the door was locked when she left,' Ted said.

'What about the neighbours directly below and beside? They don't make thick walls in apartment buildings.'

'We're yet to interview the people above, but those next door heard stomping and a brief scream.'

'So they called the police?'

'Actually, no. The mother did, when she came home.'

'What did the neighbours say? Why didn't they call the police? Surely they acted on the noise—the girl must've been hysterical!'

Ted shrugged. 'Jack spoke to them. The neighbours say the mother is divorced and has many male friends. She has a real temper and her arguments generally end in screaming and broken plates. The neighbours were used to tuning out.'

'Great, we get a homicide in a block of flats in a quiet street and we get about as much interest as an Uncanny X-Men concert. Ted, do me a favour. Organise a few extra photos of the girl for me.'

Ted nodded.

'For my friend the Minister ...' McAbbey murmured, as he took his first look at the victim.

She was on her back without a pillow to support her head and her arms and legs were spread haphazardly on the sheets. The doona had been stripped from the bed before she was attacked and was, for the most part, clean. She was naked, but saturated in congealed blood. It was difficult to see the cause of death or main trauma points. She was Caucasian, tall and thin, with brown hair and green eyes.

McAbbey couldn't help but wonder whether the Minister's decision to publish the news of the killer's distinct style had had an effect. Could it be their man?

Though she fitted the profile, he doubted it. Perhaps there was no need to send any photos to the Minister to lay blame on him for the sudden carnage.

Staring into the girl's hapless eyes, he was confused. She cried out to him in same way as the others, yet he could sense this was different. Their serial killer was cold and calculating; fashioning his victims for some reason unknown to them, but he did not brutalise them.

'Cause of death, Cath?' he murmured quietly.

She shrugged, keeping her soiled hands away from her clothes.

'I'm afraid this autopsy won't be completed in a hurry. There are too many trauma points; I can't even begin to suggest what actually killed her. She died about three hours ago—I can assume that much.'

She wrenched her gloves off, sighing with exhaustion. 'There's little more I can achieve here. I'm going to take the body back.'

Gavin poked his head through the door. 'What do you want me to do with Karen Johnson? She's too upset to give us a detailed profile of the assailant.'

'We need her help sooner rather than later; we need that profile.'

'She is staying at her sister's house. I suggest we give her tonight and pick her up tomorrow when she's had a chance to settle. We can interview her in the office and run her impressions through the computer imaging system.'

'Sounds good. Pick a time.' McAbbey turned back to Catherine.

'I'm hoping that the autopsy will prove or disprove whether this is an isolated case.'

He stared at the lifeless body before them. 'What are your impressions based on what you've seen so far?'

She rubbed her tired red eyes thoughtfully. 'I don't think it's the serial killer.' She packed her medic bag as she spoke. 'But we need to wait for the autopsy.'

McAbbey followed Catherine and Maree to the kitchen, leaving behind a ghastly scene that he knew would remain etched on his memory for a long time.

Though he wanted to be out of the flat as soon as possible, he felt the need to stay—at least until the body was removed.

Standing in silence at the kitchen window, McAbbey could feel his anger surging. Gavin had driven the mother to her parents' place where she could grieve with family, leaving the house like a ghost ship. The remaining forensic investigators moved about like lost souls, dampened by the senseless slaughter.

When the morgue's appointed staff finally removed the body, McAbbey followed them out—like a relative, grieving another waste of young life.

As he drove into the city, a stunning day was born. The clouds cleared, providing the sun an open view of the city skyline. This time, however, the vista did not calm him. The panorama was just rose-coloured glass through which McAbbey had to see—somehow—to end the bloodshed.

48

Arriving in the office, McAbbey cursed; he had forgotten to bring his briefcase. Conscious of Catherine's remarks, he left his corduroy jacket on the back of his chair and walked to reception where Helen was sipping tea.

'Helen, do we have the weekend papers?'

She stood briskly. 'I'll check around the office.' Five minutes later, Helen dropped a huge bundle of papers on his desk.

The front page headline of the *Age* read: "Serial Killer's Fetish Revealed."

He took a deep breath before reading on:

> The Police Minister last night revealed that the serial killer stalking our youth has a strangely compassionate side. Mr Moloney is reported as saying that the killer does not cause the victims undue suffering. This unusual show of compassion has the police puzzled. In most cases the murderer has covered the victims' bodies and closed their eyes. One parent, still grieving her child's death, has made mention that she was relieved to know her daughter was not violated or mistreated. She told the *Age* that the police said her daughter had died unknowingly and painlessly. Mr Moloney also hinted that the police were close to an arrest and as we speak an identikit of the assailant is being prepared.

The blurb on the cover led to a more detailed article on page seven.

McAbbey gripped the paper tightly. The revelation that they were close to an arrest was absolute crap.

McAbbey was pissed that the Minister had revealed this information. His comments about the victims not being tortured gave him heartburn. He closed the *Age* and read the article from the *Herald Sun*. Both articles were from the same press release, however, in this paper, there was also an editorial on the manhunt.

McAbbey read angrily from the article written by a journalist named Roger Bateson who questioned the competence of his department.

Pete picked an inopportune time to stand at his door. He sensed McAbbey's volatile mood and was about to go when McAbbey motioned him into the office.

'Here, read this.' McAbbey flicked the paper across to Pete.

'"Nine victims have died yet the police just stand around with their cameras and body bags poised to collect the next victim in the inane hope that one day the killer will make a mistake. After nine murders, there should be ample evidence to convict a saint."' Pete read aloud.

McAbbey slammed a fist on the desk.

'Are you upset that he would tell such lies?' Pete asked quietly.

'No, I'm pissed off that he's probably right,' McAbbey growled, sinking into his chair like an insolent despot.

Pete quietly disappeared.

———

McAbbey waded through paperwork to take his mind off the articles. After an hour, hunger pains drove McAbbey from his chair into the main office looking for food. He approached Jack and Pete in the coffee room.

'Got anything to eat?'

'Why? Did you forget your overgrown lunch box?' Jack asked with a grin.

'It's my briefcase. And it holds more than my lunch, thank you,' McAbbey snapped back.

Jack chuckled. 'Does that mean no to one of these?' He held up a donut. 'I went out to get some for everyone—we haven't had breakfast either.'

'Great, thanks Jack.' McAbbey brightened, taking it. 'Hey, how did you go with the compact disks from Pearce's apartment?'

Jack looked at Pete. 'Well …'

McAbbey stopped chewing. 'You haven't got around to it yet?'

'Yes,' Pete said. 'I took a couple of them to a friend of mine—a computer expert.'

'Really,' McAbbey scoffed. 'And what has your expert discovered?'

'The disks are heavily encrypted. He's running a cracker now.'

'How long has it been?' McAbbey asked.

'Since Saturday.'

'Cripes, kid.' McAbbey sighed, with a look at Jack. 'Never send a boy on a man's job. Get me the rest of the disks now.'

Pete left.

'Do you know someone who can decipher the code?' Jack asked.

'Hell no.' McAbbey smiled. 'I have a colleague in Sexual Crimes who can lean on the software company. Inspector Creed does this shit every other day of the week.'

Jack smiled.

'Get Pete to courier them to him. He'll have them cracked for us in a few hours.'

Jack nodded. 'Pete and I are going to find Melinda Johnson's father now. Gavin has gone back to the victim's house with Ted to check if anything was missing.'

'Good. Let the crew and Cath know that I want to see them at four this afternoon.'

With a coffee strong enough to erode the enamel from his cup, McAbbey returned to his office.

He was reviewing files when Andrea dropped a printed e-mail on his desk. 'This is a confidential memo from Harry Vincent.'

'I wonder what he wants.' McAbbey muttered to himself.

'Vincent wants to see your progress report before a meeting he has scheduled with the Minister tomorrow morning.'

He glanced up sharply. 'Thanks, Andrea!'

McAbbey shook his head in the realisation that someday he would have to learn how to use e-mail. He recalled an incident the previous year when he received an e-mail from his doctor after suffering a bout of diarrhoea. Jack saw the printed message in reception and made sure the entire office knew of his unfortunate situation. McAbbey expressed his anger that it had circulated, but was further ridiculed for suggesting they had a leak in the office.

She left him with a fresh pile of case reports to review.

When he was finished, McAbbey decided to see how Catherine was progressing with the autopsy. He hoped she would have something worth reporting to Vincent.

As he passed Andrea on his way out, she handed him a post-it note.

'Jack called five minutes ago. He's bringing in Ms Johnson at two this afternoon for an interview. She's keen to help us generate an image of the killer.'

McAbbey nodded, thankful for her cooperation in her time of grief.

49

Catherine was hovering over a microscope in the lab when McAbbey walked in.

'What the hell are you doing here?' Catherine glared at him.

'I thought I'd see how things are going.'

'Just fine—until now.'

'You know,' McAbbey said. 'You're attractive when you're angry.'

'More than you would know!' She snapped back, but her manner was almost congenial.

'Your place or mine?'

'Both,' she smiled alluringly, 'You go to yours and I'll go to mine.'

'Gee, thanks,' McAbbey muttered. 'Well if you don't need me, I'll be on my way.'

'Hang on a minute.' She broke into a grin. 'Can you get me the first gurney tray from the cooler.'

McAbbey grimaced, but did as he was asked. He found it difficult to wheel the gurney in a straight line and wondered if the manufacturer had perfected his craft on supermarket trolleys.

She asked him to read out the tag—to be sure he had the right one. Catherine had been burnt before. Once, a body which should have been buried was accidentally cremated.

He held the tag gingerly, trying not to touch the hardened pasty toe of the deceased.

'Who's this?' The reference number was meaningless to him.

'That's Andrew Jones, the surfer. Apparently a few of his friends are going to pay for his cremation and toss his ashes in the sea.'

McAbbey did as she requested and left the shrouded gurney near the lift well for the funeral courier. He returned to her lab bench, where she was studying a sample of something or other.

'Do you have to stand over me like that?' Catherine sighed. 'Why don't you take a look at Melinda Johnson? You know what you're looking at. You may be able to make some preliminary findings.'

'What are you working on now?' he asked intrigued.

'I'm looking at the trace evidence found on the body. The fluid samples have gone to the lab at Macleod for DNA testing.'

'Have you found anything to suggest this is the work of our serial killer?'

She took off her bug-eyed spectacles and chewed on one of the arms thoughtfully. 'I'm almost convinced it's the work of a separate man. Not that I will postulate—as that's your domain.' She smiled briefly. 'But we found what we believe to be seminal fluid deep within her vaginal tract.'

'What! She was raped?'

'As far as we can tell, she had sexual intercourse in the last hour or two of her life.'

'So if it isn't the serial killer, there's a chance we'll have a sample of the offender's DNA?'

'Logic suggests it. The serial killer has not raped a victim before.'

Walking over to the first of two stainless steel beds, he pulled back a damp, soiled white sheet and squinted at the smell.

'Oh. Would you like some of this … ?' Catherine proffered a brand new jar of Vicks.

'Go to hell, Cath!' he said.

Catherine only kept nasal aids for visitors and McAbbey would never become the first to use it.

McAbbey turned back to the body. Catherine had wiped up blood from an area on the victim's arm to access the epidermis; otherwise the body was just as putrescent as when it was first found.

He could not help but wonder; Melinda was of the same build, shape and good looks as the serial victims, but common sense dictated that this was a different case—this killer was a mutilating sadistic rapist.

Perhaps this rapist–killer had tried to copy the serial killer, but was unable to control his sadistic urges.

He found it hard to believe that the serial killer would leave a seminal sample, when to date, he had been so careful.

McAbbey struggled with proper surgical gloves for a few minutes before giving up. At least three fingers from each hand were properly set, but the others were lost somewhere in the glove. He had no idea how Catherine coped with removing them all day.

Inspecting the girl's face first, he could see abrasions on her left cheek and under the chin. Her left ear was caked in dried blood; it was possible her jaw was fractured. She had been hit with a blunt instrument and all over her body were marks of abuse consistent with rape. There were contusions caused by grabbing, around her ribs and breasts and her legs were bruised, suggesting she had struggled.

Sometimes death was a blessed relief from the physical and emotional trauma. Rape victims rarely overcame their fears and were often scarred for life. McAbbey believed that in sentencing, judges failed to understand that the victims lost more than their innocence in the violation.

'Did you notice the girl has many bruise marks but no scratches?'

Catherine looked up from a microscope. 'You're right. There should be light scratches in the surface of the skin, especially in areas where bruising is caused from a hand clench. My guess is he wore gloves. I can tell from the matter under her fingernails that she left him many lasting reminders ...'

'Great,' he muttered. 'Now all we have to do is look for a man with scratches down his back—I guess it eliminates married men.'

McAbbey frowned at something he saw. There was a smudged patch of blood in the middle of her forehead. It looked like someone had tried to wipe the blood clear. McAbbey was about to mention it to Catherine when Louise, her assistant walked in.

'I've got lunch,' Louise said, holding a folder in one hand and a tray of sandwiches in the other.

McAbbey was already feeling queasy and her interruption had not helped.

'Oh.' She was surprised to see McAbbey. 'Sorry. If I'd have known you were coming I would've ordered extra.'

'No thanks, Lou.' He quickly said his goodbyes and walked briskly from the lab.

50

The lunchtime crowd at Southbank was bustling—restaurants and cafes overflowed as white-collar workers commenced their break. McAbbey even stopped to watch some buskers. One played an overturned plastic drum with two tin lids as percussion, while another had converted a wire bed frame and played it like a harp-sized acoustic guitar. Their sombre rendition of 'Knockin' on Heaven's Door' was appropriate, what with McAbbey's superiors looming over him.

With the latest case an isolated incident, his task was now impossibly difficult. He had to choose between handing the latest murder investigation over to another Homicide Squad crew or dividing his Taskforce resources between two distinct homicide investigations. The result being little would be resolved before his meeting with the Minister.

The band had collected their spoils and departed but McAbbey remained there, looking out over the Yarra River, wondering whether the job was worth the stress.

Back in the office, McAbbey saw Karen Johnson sitting at the conference room table. Though he could hear nothing through the glass walls, he could see her tears.

Jack joined him in his office. 'She's not coping too well, so I suggest we talk with her quickly.'

McAbbey agreed.

'I've set up the computer in the conference room. Gavin is proficient with the identikit software package. With Ms Johnson's help we should be able to firm the identity of the killer.'

The file said Karen Johnson was forty, but she looked older. In fairness, the last twenty-four hours had preyed heavily on her appearance. Her dishevelled hair was ash-grey, and her red eyes were almost lost in crow's feet.

McAbbey wondered: where was the father? All he knew was that she had divorced her husband years before.

Jack started the meeting after a brief introduction from McAbbey. 'Karen, please tell us exactly what happened from when you opened the front door.'

'I went to put the key in the lock, but the door was ajar. I called out to Melinda. There was no answer, but I could hear …'

She wiped her moist eyes with a tissue Gavin handed her from the box. He then claimed the used one with cold efficiency.

McAbbey looked past Karen Johnson and waited for her to compose herself.

'I walked into the hall and put down my keys and handbag. That was when I saw a shadow in the passage. He was tall and strong and walked quickly without appearing to. He came straight for me. I tried to scream, but he was quick. He covered my mouth so I couldn't.'

'Was he wearing gloves?"

She nodded, dabbed at her eyes and then excused herself. She walked to the bathroom to powder her nose—or whatever it was that women did in the ladies.

'For Christ's sakes get Helen in here. We need the female touch,' McAbbey muttered.

Gavin leapt to his feet.

Helen was sitting to Karen's left by the time she returned from the ladies.

'He whispered in my ear,' Karen continued with a tissue to her mouth. 'I didn't hurt your daughter. The wretched child is with God. Be thankful.'

She broke into tears again. Helen snatched the tissue box from Gavin and consoled the hapless woman.

Helen held the mother's hand as she continued. 'His voice was calm, yet evil.' She shuddered. 'I honestly thought he was going to break my neck, but he released me and I fell on the floor. He didn't hurt me—and I can't work out why.'

She stared at McAbbey. 'Why my daughter? Did she do something to annoy him? I loved her so much.'

She wept.

Gavin waited until she stopped and then asked her if she could describe the assailant. As she did, he ran the mouse pointer furiously across the computer screen.

'He was tall, with silvery hair. It was difficult to tell its original colour as it was dark. I didn't see much, but I smelt his breath and body odour.'

'What did he smell like?'

'Strong sweat. I don't think he was wearing deodorant.'

'Would you remember the odour if you smelt it again? Jack asked.

'Yes.'

'Did you get a look at his face?' McAbbey asked, leaning forward.

'Sorry, it was too dark.' She shrugged helplessly. 'His face was in the shadows.'

'Did you follow him out? See where he went?' McAbbey asked desperately.

She gave him a horrified look. 'Of course not! I went to find Mel.'

He lowered his gaze. With the benefit of hindsight, it was what McAbbey would have done.

'I have a question,' Pete said, his voice barely more than a whisper.

Jack gave Pete a stern look, but nodded.

'What star sign was she?'

'She was a Leo.'

Pete nodded, thanking her. He made a few notes on a pad, leaving McAbbey and the others intrigued as to the reason for his question.

'Where's your ex-husband?' McAbbey asked, and the poor woman cried again. Jack gave him a look and he dropped it. The interview was over. Karen asked to be excused.

McAbbey returned to his desk and cleared it of cluttered papers, leaving just two files. The first contained a huge wad of documents from the serial killings and the second was a new file for the rape–murder of Melinda Johnson. He began to review the two investigations.

An hour later Jack walked into his office. 'Are you ready for our meeting?'

McAbbey nodded. 'Call Cath and see if she will join us on a conference call.'

Helen knocked on his door and brought in a security sealed internal envelope. 'This was couriered from Inspector Creed.'

McAbbey opened the package and pulled out a stack of compact disks without cases and a note.

'What does Creed say?' Jack asked.

'He's made a copy of all the disks without the password protection. He says they contain medium level porn. Nudity, voyeurism and sexual acts, but no sadistic images or suggestion of paedophilia. Nothing to lock him up over.'

McAbbey put them back in the envelope and handed it to Jack.

'When we finish with Ms Johnson, I'd like you to get the other disks back from Pete and have Creed check them.'

'Will do.' Jack put the envelope under his arm.

51

McAbbey sat at the head of the table and pulled the phone toward him.

'Before I call Cath, let's go around the room.'

'I was able to put together a quick fit of the person wanted for the murder of Melinda Johnson.' Gavin passed around copies.

Apart from narrow eyes and a well-defined chin, McAbbey thought the rest of the face was nondescript. His hair was depicted as grey–blonde. Ms Johnson did not notice his hairstyle, so Gavin assumed a vague part down the left. At the bottom of the picture he had estimated his age as mid-forties and height, at six-one.

It was little to go by, but McAbbey hoped it would suffice in the eyes of the Police Minister.

'Pete. Why did you want to know when she was born?' McAbbey asked.

'For the past few days, I've been studying the lives of our victims, trying to find a connection. I've searched through their personal diaries and talked to their friends but found nothing—that is until I happened to find a horoscope at the MacDonnell's house. Apparently Joanne was interested in astrology and lived by her horoscope.'

'What was her star sign?' McAbbey asked.

'Taurus. She was born on the twenty-seventh of April.'

'Didn't Ms Johnson say Melinda was a Leo?' Gavin asked.

'Yes, I was just wondering. We hadn't conclusively proved whether or not this latest murder was connected.'

'So, the horoscope thing turned out to be a false lead?' McAbbey asked.

'Sort of.' Pete shrugged. 'I had a thought that the killer was attacking youths from a certain star sign and after finding out that Tania, Brad, Sharron and Joanne were all Taureans, I thought I was on to something. However, none of the others were the same.'

'Interesting coincidence, but keep it in the back of your mind,' McAbbey said turning to Jack. 'Have you had any luck with eyewitnesses on the serial killer?'

'No. But the forensic experts have estimated his height and weight based on the imprints left at the scene of Carly Williams' murder.'

'Do you have an approximate age?'

'No. The psychologists are divided on that issue. One believes the assailant to be in his late twenties, while the other two think he's in his forties.' Jack hesitated before continuing. 'They have all ruled out the prospect that the offender is a woman. Unless I see factual evidence to the contrary, I tend to agree.'

'Harry Vincent is on the line for you.' Helen stood at the door. She pointed to the phone on the conference room table.

His crew made to leave, but McAbbey motioned them to sit. He wanted them to hear the political urgency generated by the serial killings.

McAbbey tapped the speaker phone and announced himself.

'By Christ, I hope you've got something for our meeting tomorrow with the Minister,' Vincent began.

'We have a computer generated image of the suspect for last night's murder. The papers will be receiving the portrait for tomorrow's run,' McAbbey replied. 'Doctor Smith is working on the autopsy as we speak and Forensics hopes to have the DNA results on the skin and semen tomorrow.'

'What about the serial killer. Any developments?'

'Not really. We're following a few leads.'

'Like?'

'I've been checking their star signs,' Pete answered and McAbbey glared at him.

'I didn't ask you,' Harry snapped. 'Are you sure last night's murder is not related to the serial killings?'

'They appear unrelated, yes.'

Harry sighed deeply. 'You have a fine way of making friends Ryan.'

McAbbey glanced at the others with a puzzled look.

'The Minister rang me this afternoon about a pack of photos of the latest victim that arrived. He assumed you were blaming him for the change in the killer's approach. If it's not the same offender, you'd better have a good explanation as to why you mailed them.'

He stared at Ted numbly, who was as white as a sheet.

'I thought you wanted me to mail them,' Ted whispered.

McAbbey held his head in his hands. He had only asked Ted to take the photos, not send them ...

52

When Vincent was off the line, McAbbey asked about Ms Johnson's ex-husband.

'Sorry about that,' Jack apologised. 'They went through a nasty split and when we mentioned him, she went hysterical. I was going to warn you.'

'Did he have access to the daughter? He's our most likely suspect.'

'Why would he kill his own daughter?' Pete objected.

'Blood may be thicker than water, Pete, but it sure as hell leaves a bigger mess,' McAbbey said.

'Surely Karen would have recognised her ex-husband?' Pete asked.

'True,' McAbbey admitted. 'But you'd be surprised how many times stressed witnesses don't recognise close family members. Don't forget it was dark and she didn't get a good look at him.'

'It may be possible the killer was hired by the father,' Gavin added. 'Apparently he lives in Sydney. His name is Frank Khan.'

'Get in touch with the police in New South Wales and make arrangements for us to question him.'

Gavin nodded, making notes.

Catherine joined them on a conference call.

'The post is progressing well. I now have the cause of death and the events which led to it,' Catherine said.

'Start from the top,' McAbbey instructed.

'I spent a lot of time with Jack and Gavin trying to recreate the events which lead to her death. We believe the killer broke in and surprised Melinda. She was hit with a cricket bat.'

'Like Sharron Sylvester,' Gavin explained. 'It is probably the same bat—as we found neither murder weapon.'

'Yes. I think he struck her when she came out of the shower,' Catherine said.

'Shower?' McAbbey interrupted, and then remembered the clump of hair on the bathroom floor.

'Yes. She had showered and dressed in her nightie. From the cast off stains, we've determined she was hit three times in the head. There were blood spatters, which indicate she was facing the bathroom mirror. The brain haemorrhaging was severe and it surprises me she was able to resist him, but I believe the killer grabbed her by the hair and then cut her superficially with scissors.'

'Scissors?' McAbbey asked.

'Yes. Her lacerations are consistent with the use of domestic grade scissors.'

'Ms Johnson said there was a pair in the bathroom, but we were unable to find them afterwards,' Gavin added.

'She was then dragged into the passageway, where she struggled free and ran to the lounge. The phone was bloodied and we think she tried to pick it up. There were blood droplets on the couch and from the angle we determined that she was thrown to the floor. It looks like she tried to pull herself up again, using the wall for assistance, presumably while the killer watched. I don't think he was in a hurry to end her misery.'

'What happened next?'

'She was dragged down the passage to her bedroom, where her nightie was torn from her and she was raped. There was skin under her nails, so I'm presuming she was still conscious and resisted his attack.'

'Presuming …' McAbbey cocked his head slightly. 'You don't sound completely convinced.'

Catherine sighed. 'The first strike to her head cracked her skull and the internal bleeding was significant. My instinct tells me she died instantly. Yet,' Catherine chose her next words carefully, 'everything else leads me to believe she survived the attack and fought him off to the end.'

'Meaning?'

'I feel I'm following breadcrumbs. A complicated rape and murder should not be this easy to read.'

'You think it might have been staged? Why?' McAbbey asked.

'Could just be my brain working overtime. It's like the old mind-bender,' Catherine said. 'If there are five birds in a tree and you shoot one, how many remain?'

'Four,' Pete said perfunctorily.

McAbbey's eyes narrowed. 'None.'

'Correct.'

'What's the relevance here?' he asked.

'She was struck three times to the temple. She may not have fallen to the floor from the first strike, but I find it hard to believe she stood there so he could hit her twice more.'

'So you think the second and third strikes were staged?'

'Possibly. But it would mean she was unconscious after the first strike.'

'Which means everything that happened subsequently was faked. Did you find fibres from his clothing?'

'We did. He wore denim jeans and a cotton top—nothing fancy.'

'What about her nightie? I didn't notice it at the scene?'

'It was already tagged and bagged. We found it on the floor in the bedroom.'

'What else have you found? Any word on the toxicology report and DNA?'

'The DNA and some preliminary toxicology results will be available tomorrow. I am using the Taskforce as an excuse to fast track them with Macleod. Gavin has assisted with getting buccal swabs from Melinda's friends and family.'

Catherine paused. 'There's a big chance that the offender's DNA won't be on the CrimTrac database yet, so I'm hoping he will be a friend or relative of our victim.'

Once Catherine was off the line, McAbbey stressed to his crew the importance of following every possible lead in minute detail.

'Do you want me to question Ms Johnson about any change in religious artefacts?' Pete asked.

McAbbey shook his head. 'Not at this stage. I'll take Cath's word that they're unrelated.'

McAbbey caught Ted's eye. 'Next time, at least check with me before sending off case evidence to the Minister! He will have my arse over those photos, especially if he thinks I sent them to make a point that the killer has changed tack.'

'What will you do?' he asked worriedly.

'I'll make him believe I sent them to keep him posted on the latest case. To make it realistic, can you drum together the main points on the Johnson case and fax them to his office?'

He nodded vigorously, to McAbbey's satisfaction.

Helen knocked and entered. 'I have an urgent call for Pete.'

McAbbey gave Pete a narrow stare. 'Patch it through.'

When the phone rang McAbbey hit the speakerphone.

'Inspector McAbbey.'

'Hi, sir. My name's Andy. I was decoding some disks for Pete—to do with the serial killer. I just wanted to say I cracked one.'

'One.' McAbbey raised an eye. Pete had his head down and Jack was grinning broadly.

'Yeah. It took three days. The code was thirty alphanumeric characters long. I can start the second now if you like.'

'No, one's fine. Pete will come and pick them up.'

'Cool—glad I could help.'

McAbbey hung up.

'Gavin, Ted, you're dismissed. He pointed at Jack and Pete. 'Not you two.'

Pete glanced at Jack, who refused to meet his gaze. Jack sat back quietly and waited for what was to come.

'You may have moved up the ranks pretty quick, kiddo,' McAbbey started. 'Regardless, I will not tolerate you speaking to your father on our behalf. I have enough problems without you adding to them.'

'I think his old man will give him enough grief over it,' Jack reminded McAbbey.

'That's Harry's problem. If he trusted me he wouldn't have promoted Pete in the first place.'

'Promoted me?' Pete objected meekly, 'I passed the exams.'

'Really?' McAbbey folded his arms briskly. 'You may have passed the senior constable's exam, but you spent only twelve weeks in the field while you studied at the Detective Training School. Most trainee detectives spend more than a year in a CIU before qualifying for a post in a specialist squad like Homicide.'

'But I passed the exam …' Pete faltered, surprised that McAbbey knew so much about his past.

Jack answered, 'Sorry Pete, you might have excelled in the exams, but you haven't completed the field service required as a detective to earn this post. I also heard on the grapevine that you didn't even have to sit before a district selection panel on your eligibility to become a detective.'

'How do you think that makes an officer like Gavin or Jack feel?' The sting had faded from McAbbey's voice, but nonetheless he felt it was a home truth he was obliged to tell.

'It's not that you haven't had your moments Pete,' Jack said. 'It's just there are many other detectives who have put in the hard yards. Unfortunately for them they don't have connections.'

'Should I resign?' Pete asked, after a stiff silence.

'I don't think that's the answer, Pete,' McAbbey answered. 'It's obvious you were dropped into this. All I ask is that you remind yourself of your situation in future before opening your trap in front of your father, like you did today.'

Pete nodded reverently. 'Why doesn't he like you?'

Jack answered, 'McAbbey dethroned the previous Chief Commissioner. He was taking bribes offered by illegal gambling venues in the city. There was a murder at one of the casinos and the Chief became implicated. After the scandal, McAbbey was promoted to head of the Homicide Squad.'

'I've been the head for ten years now. Your father was appointed as the replacement Chief Commissioner a month after I took up my new post. Harry did not hire me and I think that's partly the reason for his distrust. Sometimes I get the feeling he would have sacked me for making the revelation about his predecessor.'

'So I'm just here to spy on you?' Pete was horrified.

'Now you know why we're touchy when Harry hears things from you,' Jack said.

Pete nodded, eyes downcast. 'I'll keep my family out of it.'

McAbbey gave Jack a look and he nodded, placing a comforting arm on Pete's shoulder. 'Of course you will.'

—

Leaving Pete to mull over his predicament, Jack followed McAbbey to his office where they summarised their information on two sheets, one for the Taskforce and the other for the Johnson murder.

McAbbey faxed a short press statement and the Identikit picture of the new killer through to Harry's office. Once he cleared the statement, it would be released to the press.

When Jack dropped in to say goodnight at six, McAbbey dropped the file he was reading and stood, looking for his briefcase.

'You left it at home remember ...' Jack reminded.

McAbbey smiled. It was past home time, considering he had started the day early, with the worm.

53

McAbbey had a good trip and was home in time for the ABC news.

Lisa was hesitant to turn on the television, but McAbbey wanted to hear the latest update.

The first item was the Johnson murder in Marshall Street. The police cars and ambulances alluded to the sordid events that had taken place therein.

The next shot was a close up of the block of flats taken long after the police had left. The press had no inside photos or video as McAbbey had refused them entry:

Another youth murdered in Melbourne—this time in quiet Ivanhoe. The police are refusing to speculate on whether the Adonis killer is responsible, though it seems unlikely. One neighbour was reported as saying she heard a scream and scuffle at the time the young woman was attacked. The victim's name has not been released, but the Homicide Squad has made a statement and released a likeness of the suspect.

There was a brief pause while the picture was displayed. Even now, McAbbey thought it was horribly vague:

The assailant is described as being in his late forties, weighing ninety-five kilos and a hundred and ninety centimetres tall. If anyone thinks they know this man or have seen a suspicious character in Marshall Street in the past few days, please call Crimestoppers.

'That could be anyone!' Lisa remarked.

'I know. Unfortunately the girl's mother was vague in her description. It was dark when he grabbed her.'

'Was she harmed?'

'No. She was let go. He was only after the girl.'

'Could it be the serial killer?' Lisa asked. 'Surely it's not coincidental that he only wanted the daughter?'

'It might be a copy cat.'

'But what if it's the serial killer? Maybe he's trying to disassociate himself from the other murders.'

'The serial killer doesn't brutalise them.' he said softly, visualising the latest victim.

The news continued with an appended statement to the Johnson case, revealing that little progress had been made in solving the serial killings.

Lisa turned off the television as soon as the story finished.

Actually, there had been no movement on that front since Carly Williams perished, more than a week earlier. McAbbey secretly hoped the serial killer had finished his baneful agenda.

Lisa handed him the paper. 'Read the opinion on page ten. Roger Bateson really has it in for you.'

He reluctantly took the paper. It was a small article, which called for heads to roll over the lack of progress:

> Ten youths have died since February and nothing positive has been done to end the carnage. We must draw the line. Our children are at risk, and now is the time to act. The Police Minister is under increased pressure to sack the senior official in charge of the Homicide Squad, Inspector Ryan McAbbey, over what can only be called a bumbled investigation covered up through rhetoric and inconclusive leads. Protecting the citizens of this city should be McAbbey's priority and it is the job of the Minister, the publicly elected official, to do what is necessary to ensure that this happens.

'Great,' he muttered. 'Did you get the employment lift-out this weekend? I might need it.'

'You can't listen to him!' Lisa was shocked at McAbbey's reaction. 'What does he know about the internal running of a police department?'

'Too much,' McAbbey growled. 'There's a good chance I'll be replaced if I don't make significant progress in this case.'

It was hard for him to convince Lisa that twenty years exemplary service counted for nothing when politics were involved.

'Moloney will have to respond decisively. The usual political gambit of creative inertia won't cut it this time.'

Chelsey returned home from netball, lifting the sombre mood from their evening. They discussed the latest football and netball news and her school friends. Afterwards they put on a movie and settled in for the night. Though McAbbey objected, he suffered through *The Lion King* for the umpteenth time.

Typically, he was the only one awake at the end to see Simba reassert his regal authority. He mused that it was probably why they wanted to watch it over and over—neither of them had ever seen the second half.

As the film rolled through the credits, his mind wandered to the following day's meeting. He hoped the progress they made in the new murder would overshadow their failure in apprehending the serial killer. At worst, he was prepared for the sack.

Maybe he would offer his resignation if he saw it coming.

At eleven, he drove those sombre thoughts from his mind as he carried Chelsey to bed and tucked her in. It wasn't losing his job that caused his chest to ache with every heartbeat—it was the unfinished business which left a serial killer free to murder innocent children. He gave her a peck on her cheek and went to bed.

54

The uninterrupted night's sleep was a godsend. Clean and refreshed, McAbbey was first in the office on Tuesday. His meeting with Harry and the Minister was set for eleven and he was hoping to hear from Catherine first. He called her at eight-thirty.

'Sorry, Ryan. But the complete DNA profile for all the samples we submitted won't be available until lunchtime. I've asked for them to fast track, but it still takes time.'

'How does this process work?'

'The lab here uses the PCR method, which requires tagging only a few regions of DNA to determine a match.'

'So the entire DNA code isn't needed?' he asked, ignorantly.

Catherine was patient. 'The human genome, which makes up our DNA signature, consists of three billion base pairs. A full detailing of a person's DNA would take ages on a supercomputer, yet an accurate match can be made by using a select sample. In the test, variations are tagged and matched with the suspect.'

'OK. Just call me on my mobile as soon as you have the results. Also, can you make time from your CrimTrac commitments to join us this afternoon?'

'What for?'

'I don't know. Whoever's in charge will determine that ...'

For once she was speechless.

McAbbey parked in the old Casino car park and walked to the Chief Commissioner's office. In the waiting room, Bill Harnden, his direct boss, greeted him.

'They roped you into this too hey?' McAbbey asked. He handed Harnden a pack containing their latest information from both cases.

'Harry tells me you're in deep. You have balls sending the Minister a set of original photos from the crime scene.'

'Nuts, more like it—same difference. They're probably going to send me packing.'

'Not if I can help it,' Bill was determined, but McAbbey laughed, knowing him too well. Bill would need his wife's permission first.

At ten past eleven, they were admitted to see the Chief.

The Minister, Gary Moloney, ceased a terse conversation with Harry Vincent when they entered the room. Sitting like two schoolboys, McAbbey and Harnden faced the Chief behind the desk and the Minister to his right.

'Let me have it. The Taskforce first,' the Chief said.

McAbbey handed them his report.

'Talk us through this,' the Chief said, looking over thick reading spectacles.

'The first page shows a profile of the killer. We don't have enough facial or physical features to form a complete image. His height and weight are listed, based on the estimates from Forensic Services at Macleod.'

'How were the dimensions derived?' the Minister asked.

'The killer left prints in a vegetable garden behind the last victim's house. This is an extrapolation from those boot prints.'

'Not exactly concrete evidence, is it?' Vincent looked at him over his glasses, in a pontificating manner. They had already discussed it, but Vincent was obviously happy to dwell on their flimsy evidence.

'No,' McAbbey agreed.

'What else?' the Minister asked.

'We've followed a few false leads. The earlier victims all had light blue eyes and some of the victims shared the same month of birth and star sign, however, these now appear to be coincidental. Our only surety was the way the killer treated his victims posthumously.'

'You mean his lack of malicious intent, or rape?' Moloney questioned.

'Yes, Minister.'

He studied McAbbey with a puzzled look. 'I assumed those photos you sent to me were to prove a point. That the latest murder, the girl ...' he searched the paper for the name.

McAbbey sat in uncomfortable silence.

'Melinda Johnson,' Bill offered.

'Yes. I assumed from the photos, that she was our serial killer's latest victim. Are you saying this is now an unrelated incident?' the Minister asked.

McAbbey nodded slowly. Moloney had received the additional brief from Ted giving the facts of the case, but he had chosen ignorance to make his point.

'So we have two dangerous killers on the loose now? When are you going to catch them?'

McAbbey's tongue escaped the grip of his teeth. 'Hopefully sometime before the next election ...'

Harry dropped his spectacles and Bill almost fainted.

'I beg your pardon!' The Minister yelled. 'You're out of line. To date you've done nothing to instil any confidence in your abilities. We have nine dead youths and a serial killer on the loose—are you not the least bit worried about it?'

'I am.' McAbbey glared back. 'Every sleeping and waking moment I have is spent worrying about it. I eat, sleep and breathe these murderers, trying to find a link, which will bring us closer to catching him. I worry for the public; I worry for my own family. My Taskforce is working long hours under difficult circumstances to try and catch this bastard.'

He could feel emotion taking over and he stopped to compose himself.

The Minister nodded. His outburst was more effective than McAbbey would have liked. He preferred a scalding to sympathy any day.

'What about the other case?' the Minister asked.

'Melinda Johnson was raped and murdered. It appears she was barely conscious at the time of rape though Dr Smith, who conducted the autopsy, believes the girl would have blacked out before the worst of it. For the girl's sake, I hope so.'

The Minister agreed and McAbbey did not need to be reminded that he had seen the photos.

'In this case, the killer left seminal fluid as well as skin tissue under the girl's nails. We have a description and a photofit of the suspect, which was released to Harry's office today.'

'Excellent.' The Minister said. 'We need to catch the prick that did that.'

'We have another matter to discuss.' Harry alluded to the reason why he had been brought in.

'As from today, Bill Harnden will take charge of the Adonis Taskforce.'

McAbbey sat in silence, seething like water on boiling oil.

'From now on, you'll report to Bill. He'll liaise with this office and the Minister on a daily basis.'

McAbbey nodded, realising that in essence little would change. Bill was too reliant on his help to make any waves. In fact, it was a good result, McAbbey thought. An Inspector from another division would have been a greater distraction and hindrance to solving the crimes.

A ringing phone interrupted his thoughts. McAbbey answered his mobile, glad for the interruption.

'Am I bothering you at a bad time?'

It was Catherine.

'Not at all. Please tell me you have something.'

'I've finished the autopsy and have the preliminary tox results.'

'And ...'

'My instincts were correct. The girl died after the first strike. The post trauma was faked.' Catherine took a deep breath. 'This means the girl died suddenly—without pain or knowledge.'

'The serial killer?' McAbbey could see where she was leading, however he knew Catherine wouldn't link the murder solely on that outcome—she had something else.

'Remember the stain I found on Sharron Sylvester's bed that we couldn't explain?'

McAbbey frowned. 'The one you thought was water?'

'Yes. The DNA test came back last week that it was made from rose petals. Rosewater is a commonly used natural fragrance and so we dismissed its importance as the victim's room contained numerous perfumes and aromatherapies.'

'Yes?' McAbbey said tersely; Vincent and the Minister were watching him.

'There was a smudge of liquid on Melinda Johnson's forehead. I had a feeling about it, so I took a swab. It was a match.'

McAbbey's heart rate lifted. He remembered the smudge, before Cath's lunch in the morgue interrupted him. 'Why her forehead?'

'Traditional holy water used to baptise Christians, contains rosewater.'

'Do you think the killer blessed her?'

'Yes, but not just Melinda. I also found a substance on Tania's forehead. I mentioned it to you at the time, but had no answer for it. I think he might have blessed each of the victims.'

'Well done. Anything else?'

'Yes, the rape was faked.'

'Faked?' McAbbey asked.

'Yes. Remember I told you we found seminal fluid deep in her vaginal tract?' McAbbey nodded. 'Well, it was inserted, most likely with a syringe.'

'So the semen may not be from the killer?'

'No, I think it was. The semen was alive at the time of injection. There was no time for him to extract live sperm from someone else.'

'So he wanted us to think she was raped and tortured—no doubt to confuse us,' McAbbey said.

'Yes, I think the holy water blessing is something he feels he owes them.'

McAbbey thanked Catherine and hung up.

'We have proof that the serial killer was responsible for this latest rape and murder,' he announced proudly. 'The killer changed tack to throw us off. Catherine is waiting for the DNA profile from the forensic lab.'

He then explained that the friends and close family of Melinda had given DNA samples, from which they hoped to find the murderer.

The Minister was pleased, but remained puzzled. 'How were you able to determine it was the work of the same man, based on holy water found on her forehead?'

McAbbey was speechless. How could he explain that he had withheld information from them?

'Um. There's this one other matter …'

55

'You look like handmade shit!' Jack said, upon his return.

McAbbey looked as bad as he felt. He motioned the team to the conference room and explained what happened.

' … so I spent half an hour defending our decision to keep the religion lead from them.'

'Surely in hindsight they must've seen the need for it.'

'I think they did, but their egos took a hit. It proved our hypothesis that the killer would change MO to hide his true signature. Anyway, they grilled me, demanding that I agree never to withhold information again.'

'And you gave that assurance!' Gavin was aghast. 'Hell, you've never been able to keep that promise.'

His team agreed with Gavin.

'Of course not!' McAbbey laughed. 'Anyway, they chose to second Bill Harnden as acting head of the Homicide Squad.'

'What does he know about leading a taskforce?' Jack was appalled.

'It's OK. After the meeting, Bill and I had a little chat. He knows his limitations and believes that by quietly accepting their decision, it can be business as usual here.'

'So you'll still be in charge?' Ted asked.

'Yes. But I have to keep the Assistant Commissioner up to date.'

McAbbey changed the subject, ending all discussion on his uncomfortable meeting. 'I want each and every one of you to focus on our last investigation. Double-check everything you reported. There may be something we've missed due to our belief that it was an unrelated crime.'

'Will the Minister tell the media Melinda Johnson is a serial killer victim?'

'He wanted to, but I talked him out of it. Though we'll treat these as separate cases in the eyes of the public, I want you to consolidate your efforts. Make sure you keep this information within the Taskforce.' McAbbey pointed to Jack. 'I want you to set up a mobile police unit in Marshall Street. There may be witnesses willing to come forward if we leave a presence there.'

Jack nodded, leaving the room to make preparations.

'As for the rest of you, get to it. I want statements from the family and friends of Melinda Johnson. We want to know why the killer chose her. Remember to be discreet. As far as the public is concerned, this is just a routine murder investigation and in no way related to the serial killings.'

McAbbey returned to his office to review the serial killer's profile. They had released disparate images of the two killers, which they now suspected to be the same man.

Helen interrupted his reverie. 'The presentation for your twenty years of service has been set for next weekend at the Police Gala Ball.'

'I guess I've ten days to find the killer hey, or else I could be collecting my final cheque as well.'

Helen laughed—too freely for his liking.

'Who will be presenting me with my award?' He imagined Vincent clouting him over the head with the plaque.

'I believe the Premier will be conducting the presentations.'

'Swell.' McAbbey hoped the Premier was looking forward to a finger-breaking handshake.

McAbbey spent the next hour with Pete, reviewing the publicly released profile of the killer. Though the killer's height and weight were incorrect, McAbbey was not going to change it. He did not want the serial killer to know they had made the connection.

'Why do you think he's become so careless?' Pete asked.

McAbbey shrugged. 'It's the one thing baffling the hell out of me. He's left no trace of his presence—until now. But this time, not only does he leave DNA and seminal fluid, he is witnessed.'

'Maybe he wants to be caught?' Pete pondered.

'He could knock on the door of any police station in Victoria and be guaranteed long term accommodation.'

'What do you think?' Pete asked.

'I'd say he was hoping the connection wouldn't be made. Hence, he could continue with his killing, sending us in more than one direction. That being the case, we would have split our resources into multiple manhunts, dividing our efforts for nothing. It almost worked.'

'There's one thing I don't understand,' Pete said. 'He left behind a sample of his semen and blood. He's been manic about covering his tracks; why give us samples to type now?'

'Nothing has been mentioned in the press about DNA and blood types. He might think there's no risk—especially if he's not a felon and he knows we have nothing to compare his DNA to. Having his DNA could still prove useless to us if he's not a known offender or hasn't been added to the CrimTrac database.'

'But ...'

'Even a random set of fingerprints achieve nothing if the killer's not a suspect or on the database.'

'Let's hope he comes up on the DNA database,' Pete said.

'Yes, but what if Cath is wrong and the killer did plant someone else's semen in the girl? What then? We'll be off tracking another bloody herring.'

The phone rang and McAbbey picked it up quickly.

'It's Cath. You'd better come over.'

'Fine. I'm bringing Pete.' She sounded tired, but there was a hint of excitement in her voice. McAbbey prayed she had a DNA match.

56

When they arrived, Catherine stood, collecting a file from one of her many stacks.

'Come with me. We need to see Doctor Walsh, our expert in DNA progeny profiling.'

'Is he a resident expert?' McAbbey asked, wondering if there was enough work in forensics for such a specialised field.

'No. The doctor also works for the Melbourne Womens Hospital. He makes his bread and butter as an andrologist—a specialist in male fertility and paternity testing. He contracts part-time to the Coroner's office.'

'Paternity test ... ?' McAbbey gave her one of his "what the hell are you up to" glances.

They went downstairs and entered a much brighter lab. There were no stainless steel trestles, fridges or body parts in sight. The doctor's desk was bare, except for a shiny new computer.

McAbbey found Doctor Walsh an interesting specimen. Standing only five foot two, his beady green eyes peered through horn-rimmed glasses. The doctor's balding head was hidden by long wisps of hair to the sides, which McAbbey was convinced were cultivated to effect the comb-over.

'Greetings, detective. I've heard all about your work.'

'I'm sorry to hear it.' McAbbey shook his hand, noting his feeble handshake and clammy palms. 'This is my assistant, Pete Vincent.'

Catherine was anxious to get started. 'The doctor has analysed the sample of the suspect and has a profile.' She motioned for the doctor to continue.

'That's correct. I was able to obtain a DNA fingerprint.' He played with the mouse for a moment and a graphical representation appeared on screen.

It reminded McAbbey of a bar graph. There were three bars—each with a different internal pattern that looked like a supermarket scan code.

'These are multilocus DNA fingerprints.' The doctor pointed with a pen. 'As you can see, all three samples are different.'

'Does each bar represent a different person?' Pete asked.

'Yes.'

'They almost look like barcode readings.' McAbbey muttered his earlier convictions, in light of nothing else to say.

'True. The process is like matching barcodes.'

'Which one is the killer?' McAbbey asked.

'Sample one. Sample two is Melinda Johnson's mother and sample three is the girl's best friend. As you can see, they are all different.'

McAbbey nodded. The lines within the vertical barcodes varied in each case.

'So, if you get two samples from the same person, will they look identical on this chart? Even if the samples come, say, one from blood and the other from semen?'

'Yes.'

'Great—so there's no reason why we can't have everyone related to the serial case tested.'

'It's not that easy. There are confidentiality considerations and legislative guidelines to follow.'

McAbbey groaned. It was as though Catherine had bought him an ice cream to watch melt. 'That's all fine and good, but what did you find? Did you call me here just to show me what DNA looks like? Mind you, I am fascinated.'

'I've got bad news and good news,' she replied enigmatically.

'Typical. Let me guess—the good news is that you have the sample.' McAbbey motioned to the graph. 'And the bad news is that our killer isn't a known criminal and there's no one on the database matching his DNA.'

'OK then. I've got two pieces of good news.' Catherine nodded to the doctor.

'I put up a sample of the victim's DNA and, at the same time, placed the sample from her mother, best friend and the killer on the same screen.'

Working furiously, Doctor Walsh recreated the display.

The graph flickered momentarily and four bars emerged. McAbbey and Pete studied them. They were all different.

'So what?' McAbbey asked.

'Exactly! This proves nothing,' he said. 'Some of the bars match between samples, but there's no obvious link.'

McAbbey gave Catherine a look that said: Is this guy for real?

'We usually stick with PCR, which involves a visual inspection of the strands. I showed you, because this means of testing can be limited when it comes to visual inspection. As you see, this shows no correlation between the samples. But another method, which uses Polymorphic Single Locus Genes such as VNTR genes, does prove a link ...'

'Show him what you found using the other method,' Catherine prompted, seeing McAbbey's impatience.

'The DNA is extracted from the specimens and cut into fragments. Within those fragments, the highly variable regions are tagged. The collective tags produce the DNA identity profile. The computer then compares the profile with the database samples for matches. We use this in paternity testing.'

Doctor Walsh cleared the image and a different chart appeared—one that showed multiple lines across the screen, like a heart rate monitor.

'This is an easy to follow graphical representation of the data. The top sample is taken from the victim, the second—her friend. As you can see there's no direct correlation between the peaks and troughs. He clicked the mouse and the lower heart-line disappeared and was replaced with another. The change was visible—the new line had different peaks and troughs.

'As you can see again. There's no connection between them.'

McAbbey was tiring of the detail, but Catherine was convinced of its importance.

'Now, the next. See anything unusual?'

McAbbey strained to see.

'Some peaks and troughs are identical,' Pete answered, with a wide-eyed stare like a virgin on the brink of discovery.

'Exactly.' The doctor clicked his mouse again and he copied all the like peaks and troughs to form a new, albeit uncompleted line below. 'These are matches,' the doctor explained.

'The killer?' McAbbey asked eagerly.

'The top sample is from the victim and the second sample is from her mother.' The doctor rubbed his hands together before adding another line to the graph. 'This new line represents the killer. See here—it also matches the girl in places.'

He clicked the mouse to highlight them. Like adding the final pieces of a jigsaw to complete a puzzle, he copied the congruent sections from the killer's line to the partially formed match between mother and daughter. A replica line to that of the girl's DNA was created from the selected fragments.

'But what does it mean?' McAbbey asked.

Pete answered, 'It means that the killer must be her father …'

57

'Are you sure?' He couldn't believe it. They had cracked the case at last?

Catherine nodded.

'How sure?' McAbbey asked, suspicious of the technology.

The doctor answered. 'People will typically have two different sized fragments of DNA at each chromosomal location, one sized fragment from their mother and the other from their father. It's a foolproof test and forms the basis of the paternity testing I perform.'

'How foolproof?' he pressed. He preferred a clean set of fingerprints any day.

'Ninety-nine percent. We analysed four chromosomal regions, which is more than enough to ensure beyond a doubt that the girl's father raped and murdered her.'

McAbbey picked up the phone on the desk and called the office. They had to move fast.

'Jack, have you found Frank Khan, Melinda's father?'

'I've located him, but he hasn't been contacted. I doubt if he even knows his daughter's dead.'

'Good. I want you to get in touch with Inspector Oliver of the Homicide Squad in Sydney. Have him go and pick up Mr Khan.'

'That's not necessary. He's living in Parramatta and can drive into town.'

'No Jack. He's it—the serial killer,' McAbbey said.

'Our serial killer ...' Jack was dumbfounded. 'How'd you find that out?'

'Just a little old fashioned detective work,' McAbbey said, then met Catherine's look. 'I need you to commence extradition proceedings immediately. So make sure they read the manual and arrest him properly.' Murder trials had been lost on technicalities because officers had neglected procedure.

McAbbey walked with Catherine back to her lab, while Pete stayed with the doctor to document the findings.

'This DNA technology is fantastic.' McAbbey remarked.

'See, computers aren't all about doom and gloom.' Catherine smiled.

'Yeah. Feel like a beer?'

'Sure.'

It was a muggy walk to Southbank and his shirt clung to his back like a wetsuit.

'So how's your love life going?' McAbbey asked Catherine with a grin.

'Terrible.' She laughed. 'I took a guy that I met at an engagement party into work the other day. He said he was fascinated with what I did and wanted to see it first hand.'

'You're kidding!' McAbbey laughed. 'I gather you showed him the worst of it and grossed him out.'

'Sure did,' she boasted. 'I had a few cases to review.'

He shook his head in disbelief. 'You just don't want them around, do you?' he remarked. No other person in their right mind would consider such a bizarre courting ritual.

'I just wanted to see whether he was full of as much bravado as he had displayed.'

'What—and if he passed the test, you would be in the mood for anything?' McAbbey was bewildered. 'At least your patients don't complain about lying on cold steel trestles.'

PJ O'Brien's Irish Pub was coolly air-conditioned, relieving them of the sultry evening. With a lager for Catherine and a pint of Guinness for himself, they sat by the bar in momentary silence.

'Penny for your thoughts,' Catherine asked.

McAbbey smiled. 'Sorry. I was wondering how Khan managed to make contact with all those girls.'

'I know. It seems unlikely.'

He glared at her. 'What do you mean?' McAbbey was worried that Catherine had changed her mind about Khan being the killer.

Catherine paused to sip from her lager.

'He must have spent a lot of time stalking the streets and houses of his victims. Are you suggesting Khan caught a plane down for a few days, stalked and murdered a victim and then returned home to Sydney?'

'Maybe he takes short plane hops back and forth. His job may require him to travel.'

'But why would he bother going so far to find his victims?'

'I agree that it doesn't make sense.' McAbbey continued, 'Maybe he thinks he can get away with it by going interstate?'

'You may not find any evidence he travelled to Melbourne—especially if he used an alias.'

'I know all that.' McAbbey finished his pint and decided against another as paperwork awaited him back at the office.

'Thanks for the drink, Cath. I must get back.'

'When are you expecting Khan to be here for interviews?'

'Tomorrow. It will be conducted at the city watch-house. You're welcome to attend if you like.'

With a light buzz in the head from a pint of black soup, he strolled back to the office.

58

As McAbbey walked back into the building, he noticed a car parked out the front in a police reserved zone. There was a press pass displayed in the window and he gritted his teeth. Inside, McAbbey walked past the waiting room and saw a man writing something into a leather notebook.

It angered McAbbey that the reporter had parked there, even with his pass. It was for police emergencies.

'Who's that?' McAbbey asked Andrea at the front desk.

'That's Roger Bateson to see you—from the *Herald Sun*.'

'Swell. What does the bastard want?'

She was taken aback.

'Sorry, Andrea. Did you read the article he wrote about our department?'

'No need to apologise, sir. I most certainly did.'

'Good. Call the council and get a Grey Ghost down here to book him.'

'Certainly,' she said with a smile. 'Shall I keep 'the bastard' waiting a little longer?'

'You'll go a long way, Andrea,' McAbbey replied.

McAbbey called Bill Harnden first, to update the Minister and Chief Commissioner about the new developments.

'What do you have?' Bill asked, after McAbbey introduced himself.

'We have a match for the skin and seminal fluid samples taken from Melinda Johnson. The killer is her father.'

He explained in simple terms how the DNA results were derived and that it was damning evidence.

'Great,' Bill said. 'I'll let Harry know.'

'I think you'd better make it ASAP. I don't want the press to find out we have a suspect before the Minister does.'

'Will do. Are you sure he's the serial killer? You say he was the last victim's father?'

'We hope to prove that tomorrow. At this stage, all we have is a solid suspect in the rape and murder of Melinda Johnson. We're bringing him down to Melbourne for questioning.'

'I'll inform the Chief straight away,' Bill promised.

'By the way. I have Roger Bateson here from the *Herald Sun*. Should I send him away, or offer him the news that we have taken a suspect into custody for the rape and murder case?'

'They may already know of Frank Khan's extradition from New South Wales. Maybe it's best to inform him.'

'Good. Remember, they aren't aware of the connection between the latest victim and the others.'

When McAbbey ended the call, he cleared his desk and placed all pertinent files behind him before asking Andrea to show in Mr Bateson.

McAbbey did not bother to stand and greet him.

Bateson was of average height, wearing a neatly pressed navy suit with a mustard shirt and bright blue necktie. He sported a manicured five-day growth and his hair was pulled back in a pony tail.

'What can I do for you?'

He smiled, revealing nicotine-stained teeth.

'I would like a statement. I've heard rumours that a man's on a flight from Sydney tonight, possibly to answer charges relating to the Johnson murder?'

McAbbey tried to sound disappointed. 'I was hoping you wanted to hear my side of that bullshit article you published recently.'

Bateson's smile disappeared. 'I can only report current affairs as I see them. You must admit, your Taskforce has got nowhere in the last couple of months.'

'Sit and I'll give you a statement,' McAbbey said.

Bateson sat poised on the edge of his chair with a pen ready.

'We've called in the father of Melinda Johnson for questioning. He is a suspect, but charges won't be pressed until he's been interviewed, at which time more information will be released.'

'Do you believe he raped and killed his own daughter?'

McAbbey shook his head vigorously. 'We cannot make those sorts of assumptions until we've spoken with him.'

'But you must have some damning evidence to warrant his return to Melbourne?'

'Yes, but nonetheless, he's merely a suspect at this stage.'

'I would say if you're extraditing him, his DNA was found at the scene.'

'You're extrapolating—cut out the conjecture,' McAbbey snapped.

'Don't worry, Inspector, I'll stick to the facts. Besides, conjecture is your forte.'

McAbbey felt a tingling warmth in his cheeks. Moments like this reminded him of his love–hate relationship with the press. He had to admit, the majority of journalists were helpful and he was able to rely on their accurate reporting of events. The media was a vital tool in the arrest and capture of offenders.

On the other hand, there were a few journalists, like Bateson, who were careless and sensationalist in their reporting. Even when spoon-fed the facts of a case, they managed to turn a suspect man into a woman, and a red sedan into a blue wagon. McAbbey could recall three such incidents where Bateson's attitude had inadvertently freed crooks and undermined investigations.

After the interview, McAbbey walked him to reception and turned abruptly, without a farewell. When he sat back at his desk the phone rang.

'Hi, just me.' Andrea chuckled. 'The parking officer got him.'

'Consider yourself promoted Andrea.'

59

McAbbey arrived home a little after seven. All he wanted to do was sit in front of the TV with the air-conditioner breathing on him, however Chelsey was studying in the lounge so he was barred.

He joined Lisa in the kitchen.

'How was your day, love?' he asked, pecking her on the cheek.

'Horrible. I had too many abusive customers today. Can you believe that people would buy a sandwich with onion and later complain that it ruined their breath?'

'No, I can't.' He was honest. With the problems he had in the world, who cared about a little bad breath?

'Sorry, Ryan.' She smiled. 'How did your meeting with the Minister go?'

'I still have my job, I guess. I have to report to Bill Harnden now.'

'Haven't you always reported to Bill?' She asked, puzzled.

'Yes, I have. I suppose they've just rearranged the deck chairs.'

'Isn't that good news? Won't it insulate you from the Minister and the Chief Commissioner if Bill has to report to them directly?'

'Yes, it's a godsend really. No wonder Bill didn't look happy.'

McAbbey drifted to sleep peacefully that night; the ceiling fan silently blew a tardy summer breeze from above.

—

'Khan was brought to the watch-house at eight this morning,' Jack said, the next morning. 'I've been on the phone all night, making preparations for our interrogation.'

'Well done,' McAbbey patted him on the back.

'Shall we make a move?' Jack asked, glancing at his watch.

McAbbey nodded. 'What about the others? I invited Cath too.'

'So I heard. She rang first thing this morning.'

First thing? He imagined what that meant. It was only nine o'clock.

'Gavin, Ted and Pete will meet us there. Cath's going to make her own way over.'

'I guess that leaves just the two of us.' McAbbey grabbed his files and closed his office door behind him.

In the foyer of the watch-house they were greeted by the sergeant in charge of the facility.

'Take a seat, Boss. I'll go and prepare the suspect.' Jack followed the resident sergeant.

The smell in the centre was offensive—a constant battle raged between disinfectant and body odour. A watch-house was a horrible place to stay and, though he had not had the privilege, McAbbey had spent the early years of his career checking in drunken and drugged people picked up from the streets. Some of the holding cells smelt worse than the toilets at the footy.

McAbbey began to shift uncomfortably—the plastic chair was built for a hunchback midget. Where were the others?

The lobby was quiet. The receptionist and guard ignored him, keeping busy with nothing to do. It was an art form in the public service that McAbbey affectionately referred to as creative inertia.

Suddenly the external doors slammed open and three policemen came in, manhandling a swearing youth.

He caught McAbbey's eye. 'Listen, man—set me free. I'll make it worth ya while.'

McAbbey's old suit gave him the appearance of a defendant. The lapels were shabby and the inside pocket had split, and as a result, McAbbey had stopped carrying his gun. He hated wearing a holster and didn't really need the weapon anyway. His gun had been locked in the bottom drawer at the office ever since Lisa spat it after finding it in a sock drawer at home. Even without ammunition and the catch on, she refused to have it in the house.

A few minutes passed before Jack appeared.

'About bloody time. What's taken so long ...'

Jack frowned. 'You'd better come through.'

'Did everything go to plan? Do you have him?'

'Yes.' Jack covered a yawn. 'The others are in the observation room.'

They walked through swivel doors into a dingy corridor. McAbbey peered into the open doorways as they passed. Most were change-down rooms for those being remanded overnight. At the end of the corridor, a guard opened a barred gate and they were inside.

'The first door on the left is the observation room. The second has the witness.' Jack paused outside the former. 'Do you want to conduct this interview?' he asked.

'I'd be more than glad to.'

'Good.' Jack looked relieved. 'Do you want to check in with the others first?'

McAbbey nodded and they entered the observation room. A technician stood near the door, working a complicated system of video and amplification equipment. Catherine and his team members sat in elevated chairs. McAbbey waved to them curtly before stepping out.

He motioned for Jack to open the second door. 'Let's get this over with.'

Jack waved McAbbey through first. As he had done many times before, McAbbey casually took his seat in front of the captive without looking at him. Generally, a perfunctory approach disconcerted the suspect.

He looked up and stared into Frank Khan's eyes with all intention of burying the sucker.

He could hear the ticking of the clock.

It was pounding.

Frank Khan stared at the Inspector quizzically, waiting for him to speak.

McAbbey's head sank and he held it in his hands.

Mr Khan was black.

60

'Are you Frank Khan?' McAbbey wondered if his voice was loud enough for him to hear.

'Yes, I am.'

McAbbey wanted to walk out. Melinda Johnson was Caucasian. He turned to the two-way glass looking for Catherine—her foolproof tests were a crock.

'I'd like you to meet my assistant, Senior Sergeant Jack Turner,' McAbbey said. 'He will explain why you're here.'

Khan nodded graciously; probably pleased to finally find out why he was arrested and transported down amid intense security and scrutiny.

Jack coughed, 'Well, you see …'

McAbbey cut him off. Karen Johnson had refused to talk about her previous husband—maybe he knew something they didn't or perhaps she had had more than one husband.

'I have bad news,' he said.

Khan swallowed heavily, realising the next statement would explain the reason for his detainment.

'Your daughter, Melinda, is dead.'

Khan stared vacantly past him.

McAbbey leaned closer, giving him a few moments to absorb it. 'Do you have anything to say?'

He shrugged sadly, but was calm. 'That's a tragedy. She was a lovely girl.'

'You knew?' McAbbey asked. Most offenders feigned grief.

'I suspected as much.' Khan nodded. 'I still read the *Herald Sun*. I lived in Melbourne for years, you know.'

McAbbey casually agreed. The truth was, his arrest had happened too quickly for them to uncover his past.

'When I saw the pictures and realised it was Marshall Street, I knew there was a possibility it was Mel.'

'But you didn't call to find out?'

'No. Karen …' He paused a moment and a tear welled in his eye. 'She won't talk to me. Nor would she let me talk with Melinda.'

'But you're her father. Surely you had the right to talk to Melinda if you wanted to?'

'No, and that's what sucks about the Family Court system! I could have saved her—had I been there.' He held his face in his hands.

McAbbey glanced uncomfortably into the two-way mirror.

'Maybe you should tell me what happened between you two?' McAbbey asked.

Khan looked up. 'We were happily married for ten years. Then she started the gambling. She used to love a weekend up on the Murray at the pokies, but when the machines were introduced here, she went berserk.'

'How'd you discover she had the problem?' Jack asked.

'Well, occasionally I'd call her from work, but she'd be out. Later she'd say she was shopping or in the garden, but I knew it was a lie. I called her many times during the day and she was never there.'

'How were you sure she wasn't in the garden?' McAbbey pressed.

He laughed briefly. 'The backyard looked like a wildlife park you drive through with your windows up. She hated gardening and that's why she now lives in the flat. Not only that, the cupboards were bare though she claimed she went shopping twice a week.'

'What did you say to her?' Jack asked.

'Well, I was giving her money for food and clothing and every week she would ask for more. One day before I left for work, I happened to notice Melinda's tattered school uniform. I asked Mel why she wasn't wearing the new dress we'd promised and she said that I couldn't afford it.' He glanced at McAbbey, with exasperation. 'Can you believe that? I worked fifty hours a week in a factory to keep her daughter and Karen was using me as the excuse for why we had no money.' Khan stood angrily.

'You said her daughter …' McAbbey paused. 'Why?'

It was bloody obvious, McAbbey thought. Melinda was as much related to this man as Skippy was to Lassie.

'Karen desperately wanted a child. I did too, but I was willing to wait—she was not.' Khan sat heavily.

'She went to the Reproductive Biology Unit at the Melbourne Womens Hospital and filed for donor sperm. She was pregnant before I could do anything about it. There were papers, which I unwittingly signed. She told me they were for a fertilisation program. Eventually she told me what she'd done. I guess she knew that once the baby was born, I'd be able to tell.' Khan sighed. 'I was devastated. I loved Mel—I still do, but she was not mine and I had no recourse after the proceedings.'

'What do you mean?' McAbbey asked.

'When I was sure Karen had a gambling problem, I sought help. She refused to participate in rehabilitation and was extremely bitter at me for suggesting it. I was working during the day and could not restrain her from spending everything we had. When Mel's education and clothing began to suffer, I took action. I rang Social Services and asked them to investigate.'

'What did they report?'

'They saw Karen at home, cooking tea and ironing. She must have seen the letter advising they were coming to inspect the house. They came and left, calling it a waste of their time and I was told not to ring them again.'

Khan pounded the table with a clenched fist. 'The system can be so cruel.'

'When did your marriage end?'

'Soon after my failed attempt to have her rehabilitated, she filed for divorce in the Family Court. She beat herself senseless one day before going to see a counsellor. The next day an injunction was slapped on me. I was barred from my own house, my kid …'

He cleared his throat before continuing. 'I didn't stand a chance in the Family Court. It made a mockery of justice. She declared I was a habitual woman basher and a risk to Mel. I was given no rights to see my daughter—the girl I'd raised as my own with loving care.'

He looked McAbbey in the eye. 'If only you knew what it feels like to love one that's not your own. Believe me; the connection is stronger than an umbilical cord.'

McAbbey nodded slowly—his composure weakening. 'I know what you're going through, believe me,' he said quietly. It was victims like Khan and his daughter that kept McAbbey fighting for justice.

'I paid half my wages to keep them both. My only satisfaction out of this will be severing the funds for her gambling obsession.'

'Why did you go north?'

'I wanted to get away. I couldn't bear living in the next suburb. I had a mental breakdown and my psychiatrist decided the best thing for me to do was leave. I hoped that when Mel grew up, she would seek me out.' He looked at McAbbey with a wistful smile. 'We used to have a lot of fun together.'

'Will you submit to a DNA test?' McAbbey asked. At least then Khan could get back to the life he had started over.

He looked up at McAbbey with surprise. 'Why?'

McAbbey took a breath. He did not want to burden him with the full atrocities. 'We found DNA at the scene. It was from Melinda's biological father.'

'So, that's why you had me arrested,' he said. 'I'll submit to the test, officer, but on the condition you won't sleep until you catch the bastard who hurt ... my daughter.'

'Why didn't Karen tell you that I wasn't her real father?'

'Maybe she thought you did it,' Jack offered.

'Not even Karen—as heartless as she is—could accuse me of this.'

The interview was over.

61

'Well, wasn't that just fantastic?' McAbbey was fuming. They returned to their offices after the interview and met in the conference room.

'At least that explains why Ms Johnson didn't recognise the killer,' Pete offered inanely.

McAbbey glared at him with the countenance of a father who had solved the riddle of his missing condoms by discovering his daughter was sexually active.

'Why the hell didn't you tell me?' McAbbey banged the table with a file. 'Not only did you put me through hell, but that poor innocent man as well.'

'There wasn't enough time,' Jack apologised. 'We didn't see him until the interview.'

'What? Neither you nor Gavin had bothered to check him out first?'

'No.' Jack shrugged. 'He was the Frank Khan that Karen Johnson was formerly married to. Even the New South Wales police thought they had the right man.'

'Except for one thing—they didn't.'

'They couldn't have expected this, Ryan,' Catherine said.

McAbbey knew it was his frustration speaking. 'What help do you need to sequester the name of the donor from the hospital?'

'It'll probably have to come from a magistrate,' Jack said. 'Maybe two days.'

'What if it's an emergency?' McAbbey asked.

'Three days.' Jack shrugged.

'Bullshit! It will happen tonight, even if I have to call Judge Judy myself,' McAbbey snapped.

'I'll get on to it,' Jack offered.

McAbbey nodded. 'Use the Chief Commissioner's name if you have to.'

'I have two samples to process now,' Catherine offered. 'If I'm to confirm that Khan's not the biological father, I need time with Doctor Walsh.'

'Take all the time you need with the nutty professor; just get me the results as soon as possible. The Minister knows we have a suspect. I want to be able to say more than we got it wrong.'

'As for the rest of you …' He was suddenly annoyed at the sight of them sitting idly. 'Go and do something.'

McAbbey spent the afternoon working through the other crews' homicides. He kept an eye on the clock, but neither Catherine nor Jack called with an update.

He rang Bill Harnden late in the afternoon.

'The biological father is the true suspect. The man we had arrested was the child's stepfather,' McAbbey explained.

'So you're back to square one?'

McAbbey could tell by the tone in his voice that Bill was reluctant to call Vincent with bad news.

'No. We still have the DNA sample. We'll be able to sequester the documentation which will identify the sperm donor.'

'How far away are you from a name?'

'As soon as the judge approves, we'll have a suspect and make an arrest.'

'If you have any problems with the warrant, call me.'

McAbbey hung up, pleased that Bill was a supportive buffer between them and the egos at the top.

Picking up the *Herald Sun*, he found an article on page three:

> Suspect arrested in latest rape/murder case. Detectives hopeful.
> However, no progress has been made in the serial killings dogging Melbourne's reputation as the world's most liveable city. Even with calls for his resignation, Inspector McAbbey remains none the wiser.

'Bloody lovely,' he muttered as Gavin knocked on his door. 'Found anything?' McAbbey asked.

'Yes and no. Remember what Pete asked Joanne's parents?'

'Yeah—if she had any brothers or sisters. Why?'

Gavin sat. 'He asked because the other victims were only children. I just wondered whether they were only children because the parents had trouble conceiving and they used donor sperm.'

'Are you saying that someone with access to records may be killing these children?' McAbbey asked.

'I was thinking that, however, I rang Mr Williams—Carly's father. He said Carly was their biological daughter. However, I did learn something; Carly's mother died when she was three and Mr Williams married again—Leanne, his wife, is Carly's stepmother.'

'I think it's worth checking the others.'

Gavin nodded.

Wednesday passed quickly into Thursday. McAbbey sat at his desk first thing and was immediately given good news.

'The donor's name is André Barrett.' Jack handed him the report.

'Did you have any trouble?'

'At first I did. The doctor at the hospital swore over his dead body that the records would not leave his office.'

'Shall I inform Cath she has another autopsy to perform?' McAbbey winked.

'No.' Jack smiled. 'I had our Minister's office call the Health Minister. Barrett's address is in Buckley Street, West Essendon. Gavin and Ted have already left. They're working with the local police. Apparently the area has been secured.'

'Good. Do we have a picture of him?'

'Unfortunately, no. They don't allow pictures as the customers aren't permitted to identify the donors. They merely read a detailed description.'

'Does the profile match?'

'Yes, it seems to agree to Ms Johnson's recollection.'

'What else does the Barrett file say?'

'Not much. It has the official documents on his medical history and the results of a physical examination. The hospital provides a sheet with the donor's details for prospective clients, discussing their general appearance, hobbies, occupation and the like. This is still useful to us, as it gives us a dossier on Barrett,' Jack said. 'There's one more thing. They found a frozen sperm sample from Barrett in the hospital archives. Years ago they kept random donor samples for genetic research. We're fortunate for this anomaly, as most sperm donations are destroyed after ten years in Victoria. This means we can run a DNA test to confirm our conviction.'

'Finally some luck. Have Cath report the findings as soon as possible. Has she checked Khan's sample yet?'

'I believe she's with Doctor Walsh now. Also I have word from Sydney. There's no surprise, but Khan's alibis for the nights of each murder check out.'

McAbbey nodded. 'Get Cath to call me when she has something.'

An hour later, McAbbey received a call from Gavin and Ted.

'We're at the address. There has never been a house here. We're on Buckley Street, but in a dell where Steele Creek runs through to the Maribyrnong. The local council has confirmed it is scrubland.'

'Understood. I want you to go to the state records. Find Barrett in the births and work your way from there. Get all the help you need.'

McAbbey ended the call and picked up his briefcase. With a quick glance around, he entered his code and watched the tumblers click free. Inside was his lunch.

Soon after he finished his sandwich, Catherine called.

'You'd better come over,' she advised.

McAbbey passed Andrea at reception on his way out.

'Get Pete for me. Tell him to be at Dr Walsh's lab as soon as he can.'

62

When McAbbey walked into the lab, Pete was already sitting beside Catherine, watching Dr Walsh on the computer.

'What have you got?' McAbbey asked.

'The results of the DNA sample from André Barrett's file confirm he is Melinda Johnson's biological father.'

'Finally something concrete.' McAbbey took a chair and sat with them.

'There's more. While we were waiting for the results, we conducted a few other tests. In the Tania Stevenson case we found no DNA evidence of the killer, yet we found hair follicles from her mother. We thought nothing of it at the time.'

'Hold on! How did you know the hair was from Tania's mother?'

Catherine smiled. 'Very good, Ryan. At the time, the follicles were compared with Tania's DNA to eliminate extraneous evidence. When Dr Walsh realised they were from a parent, they were dismissed.'

'But how could you determine it was the mother, and not her father?'

'We didn't. It was assumed to be from Tracey because there was no father in the picture.'

Doctor Walsh continued. 'We can determine parentage with assured accuracy, however to know if you're testing for the mother or father, you need more information. In the paternity tests I conduct, we have the sample of the child and the mother. The child will have two different sized fragments of DNA at each chromosomal location; one sized fragment will be from their mother, the other from their father. In other words, the father's DNA completes the puzzle.'

'But what happens if you don't have the other parent's DNA?'

'We can still determine parentage. It's just that usually we know whether we're taking the sample from the mother or father. However in this murder investigation, we guessed incorrectly. The sample matched as a parent of Tania—we just logically assumed it was from the mother.'

'So, what have you found?' McAbbey asked.

'Tracey provided a DNA sample early into our investigation, which we never used. We ran it through the DNA compiler, proving it's different from the sample we thought was hers from the bedroom. We used the program to compare Tracey's filed DNA and the sample from the bedroom with Tania's profile.'

'This was the result.'

The doctor opened the program and three heart lines appeared on the monitor. The doctor clicked furiously with the mouse, then sat back to admire his handiwork.

McAbbey watched in fascination as the program selected segments from each of the top two samples and placed them below the third heart line to form a fourth. The third was labelled Tania Stevenson. When the program finished, the fourth line was identical to the third.

'So you see,' Catherine remarked. 'Tania's father was there.'

'Are you saying that Tania's father killed her?'

'No. From this we can't be sure. But we do know that Tania's father was in her room recently, even though Tracey believes he has no knowledge of his daughter.'

'So, if he didn't kill her, he may have witnessed her death,' McAbbey said.

'Oh. He killed her, but finding the sample alone is not proof that he was her murderer,' Catherine replied.

Doctor Walsh cleared the screen, leaving only the father's strain. He inserted another profile, which the computer overlaid exactly. 'This is …'

'Let me guess,' McAbbey interrupted. 'The serial killer?'

Catherine nodded, 'From the semen and skin samples found at the scene of Melinda Johnson's murder.'

McAbbey stared trance-like at the word Match, which flashed bright red across the screen.

'We have our link!' Pete was ecstatic.

'Maybe Barrett is one of Tracey's old boyfriends?' McAbbey pondered aloud.

'Or customers,' Catherine added.

63

As McAbbey walked back into his office, Helen handed him two post-it notes and a printed e-mail. He sat at his desk and read the messages.

The first note was from Gavin, asking him to call urgently. The second was from Roger Bateson who wanted another interview. The e-mail was from Bill Harnden, requesting his attendance at the Premier's office in Treasury Place that evening.

Just the thought of such a meeting had him in a cold sweat. He was not one for social graces or tact. He was sure to unwittingly upset the Premier. His reputation was deplorable to say the least.

Maybe their idea was to encourage him to slip up so he could be disgraced and dismissed?

McAbbey put the e-mail down, refusing to speculate further on such nonsense. At least he would go to the meeting with a name. All going well, they would soon have him in custody.

Jack came into his office and McAbbey asked him to ring Tracey Stevenson to organise a visit. When Jack left, McAbbey rang Gavin's mobile.

'Where are you?' McAbbey asked. The phone signal was weak and Gavin's words were disjointed.

'At Fawkner Cemetery.'

'What's wrong?'

'We checked with state records and we found André Barrett's birth certificate. He was born in 1955,' Gavin paused. 'And died in 1957. We're at Fawkner to check the death record and his gravestone. He was buried here. Do you want us to exhume the body to be sure?'

'Forget it. Come back to the office as soon as you can—I need a written report of your findings. Take a photograph of the tombstone as well as all documentation regarding the birth and death of the real Barrett,' McAbbey answered. 'Gavin, I really need that report by five. I have to see the Premier this evening.'

McAbbey hung up and began collating their results. He did not trust himself to explain the science and theory of the DNA findings adequately, so he called Catherine and asked for her to summarise it on his behalf. When she was finished, Catherine would e-mail the file directly to Helen, to combine it with his document.

Jack walked into McAbbey's office.

'Tracey Stevenson's home now, if you like.'

McAbbey stood and collected his jacket.

When they arrived at the apartment block in St Kida, the security door was open and Tracey was sitting by the pool with a glass of chilled white wine.

'What can I do for you?' She smiled wanly. Tracey was stunning in a verdant bathing suit with her hair spilling freely over her tanned shoulders.

'We need to ask about Tania's father,' McAbbey said.

'Are you suggesting he had something to do with it?' She turned from McAbbey to Jack and studied their reaction.

'We were wondering—was Tania planned or did she happen by accident?' Jack asked.

'Are you asking if Tania was the outcome of sex with one of my clients?' Tracey raised her voice.

'No,' McAbbey said calmly. 'Jack was merely wondering whether you were still in touch with the father.'

'Don't patronise me, I know what he was getting at!' She stood. 'Do you think I'm stupid? We take precautions to avoid complications and diseases.'

'Tracey. We need to know who he is.'

'I told you already, there is no father.'

'Listen, I've read about the birds and the bees ...' McAbbey folded his arms and waited. Tracey looked to be thinking it over.

'Alright.' Tracey sighed heavily. 'If you must know, I used donor sperm.'

They were quiet for a long time—the implication burdensome. Though this cemented their belief that the serial killer was Tania's father, it allayed their hopes that she might have known him. They needed to know who had donated the sperm using Barrett as an alias.

'It's not easy to find a good man in my profession—a father for my child.' Tracey wiped her eyes.

McAbbey nodded sympathetically.

'I wanted a baby—and I wasn't going to use a client. I did it the proper way.'

'Which hospital did you go to for artificial insemination?'

'The Melbourne Womens.'

'How did you get through the protocols?' McAbbey's eyes narrowed. Until recently, single women were not allowed to receive donated sperm.

'I had a male friend who claimed to be my de facto.'

'Thanks.' McAbbey nodded to Jack and they left Tracey sipping her wine to replenish the tears their visit had drawn.

64

McAbbey threw his crumpled jacket onto a chair in the conference room and sat.

'What have you got? I'd dearly like to go into the Premier's office with more than just twenty years of meritorious service.'

McAbbey handed out a copy of the typed three-page summary he had prepared.

'You think the killer murdered the other children?' Jack asked.

'Well, he's murdered two of his own biological children. If the others were also the products of his donation, then we have our link,' McAbbey said.

'Don't forget that Mr Williams said Carly was his daughter,' Gavin reminded them.

'Perhaps she's an exception?' Catherine shrugged.

Gavin frowned. 'Do you think he intended to track down his offspring and kill them later?'

'Premeditation? No, I don't think so,' McAbbey replied. 'It's hard to imagine.'

'How else can we explain the fact that he lied on his donation form?' Gavin asked.

'Gavin, the registrar at the hospital said falsifying details was common back then,' Catherine explained. 'Firstly, they lie for anonymity and secondly, to enable them to donate more often. There's a ceiling on how many times one can donate and, as each trip earns them money, it stands to reason they can make more if they forge their applications.'

'Not a bad way to make a quid,' McAbbey admitted.

'Cash in hand!' Gavin added wryly.

'Guys!' Catherine admonished. 'I checked with the registrar and though she said people try to forge their forms, few succeed. They now cross-check all records with government databases. But back then, they didn't have those checks.'

'What's your next step?' McAbbey asked Catherine.

'Well, Doctor Walsh is cross checking the DNA found at the other murder scenes for matches. Rather than being incredibly adept at leaving no trace, I believe the serial killer did leave evidence, which has been misconstrued as belonging to the parents of the deceased children. As neither parent has been suspected at any point in time, we've never bothered to follow up on these samples.'

'Excellent. Jack? Gavin?'

'I've already contacted the hospital and requested the records on each application for Barrett's sperm. His file was referenced eight times. Of those, we know two, Melinda Johnson and Tania Stevenson.'

'How long before we can get the records?'

'Maybe Tuesday week,' Gavin estimated.

'What!' McAbbey was incensed. 'I'll explain that to the Premier this afternoon and see if we can hurry them up.'

'It isn't as easy as that. Each client is listed on Barrett's file as a reference code. It's a matter of someone going through archive boxes to find the client record that matches the code referenced on the donor file.'

'You found Melinda's easily,' he reminded him.

'We were lucky. We couldn't find Tania's file. There are hundreds of archive boxes with thousands of records. Some files have been water damaged, others eaten through by silverfish ...' Gavin shrugged helplessly. 'Whoever was in charge of the records going back more than ten years obviously knew he wouldn't be around later to search through them.'

'By Monday our DNA testing should confirm whether all the victims are related—before the manual file search is completed,' Catherine said.

'There's more at stake here, Cath. I'm more concerned with finding Barrett's client list to determine who else might have received donations.'

'Right. We can find his next victim before he does,' Jack agreed.

'It'd be good to save a life for once,' Gavin added.

'If we knew his next move, we might be able to lay a trap. To be honest, this may be our only chance to nail him.'

'Why do you think he's trying to kill his children?' Pete grappled with the sadistic concept.

'Maybe he found God?' Jack shrugged.

Gavin laughed. 'An interesting way to repent for your sins.'

'No, Jack has a point. In some cases we've found evidence of religious tampering,' McAbbey reminded them.

He stood, collating his notes and summary. 'Thanks for your input into this document. I want you to find those records—number one priority. I'll speak to the Minister about resources, but you might have to get down and dirty on this.'

'I guess if you're about to get on your knees, we can too!' Jack replied with a wry smile.

McAbbey packed his briefcase and adjusted his shirt and tie in the washroom. By the time he walked out to the car park, his car was the last one left.

65

'Welcome.' An immaculately presented woman in her mid-forties greeted McAbbey at the door. 'I'm the Premier's personal assistant. Follow me.'

It was five to six and for once McAbbey was early—but not early enough.

Opening a grand oak door, she announced his presence to those in attendance and he was scrutinised.

'Welcome, Inspector.' Moloney, the Police Minister, stood and beckoned him to a leather couch in front of a grand oak table that made his look like a dirty park bench.

Present were Bill Harnden, Harry Vincent, the Police Minister and the Premier. It seemed the meeting had commenced without him.

'I'd like to introduce you to the Premier, Fred Allen.'

'Nice to meet you, Mr Allen.' McAbbey reached over with a firm handshake.

'Call me Fred.' He smiled. 'Can I call you McAbbey?'

'Sure.' McAbbey suppressed his perfunctory response that 'only my friends call me McAbbey.'

'We've never actually met, but I've admired your work over the years.'

McAbbey was surprised. He had never expected his career to be of interest to a politician.

'I've heard you shoot straight,' the Premier said. 'So give me a frank update of your progress.'

McAbbey handed out copies of his summary and spent the next ten minutes running through the major points of their investigation to date.

The Premier ran his hands through his thinning hair thoughtfully. 'Do you think finding these records are our best chance of catching him?'

'Definitely.'

'What about Crimestoppers? Any calls of value?'

'Not really. One of my operatives liaises with Crimestoppers daily. If we had a more accurate likeness of the killer we would receive a stronger public response.'

'When will you have the records?'

'I'm working on that, however, if we could have the clout of your office behind us, we may be able to wade through the administrative bullshit a bit quicker.'

'You have barriers to the information?' The Premier asked.

'Yes. The data is highly confidential.'

'Leave that to me. I'll make sure it's available tomorrow morning.'

'Thanks.' McAbbey added, 'The records may find other children sired by his donations. This is our best chance to save lives or catch him in the act.'

'What about the holy water blessings? Any significance there—or is the killer just looking to be different?'

'The killer blesses them because he wants to; however, he doesn't want us to know he's killed others. Thus, every time we reveal something distinctive about the manner in which he kills, he changes his approach. Likewise with the holy water blessing; he will stop if he discovers we're using it to link him to the crimes.'

'If I get you the data, I want him caught before the weekend is out,' the Premier said.

McAbbey nodded.

'Good. On a lighter note, I am looking forward to presenting your twenty years certificate next Friday night at the Police Ball.'

'Does that mean I'll still have a job?' McAbbey joked, relaxing a little.

'Well,' the Premier gave a wry smile. 'The ball is still a week away ...'

66

McAbbey threw his jacket and tie on the bed, much to Lisa's annoyance.

'How'd your meeting go?' she asked.

'It seems I've got a job for another week,' he said. He felt like an employee who demanded a raise, but somehow accepted a pay cut.

'That bad?'

'Yeah. The Premier's going to present me with my twenty year certificate next Friday night at the ball.'

'Next Friday night ...'

'Don't tell me you've forgotten? You're invited too.'

'No. Well, yes I remembered, but Chelsey thinks you're taking her to the footy. Essendon are playing Hawthorn at the MCG. You promised her the other day.'

'Yeah well, I probably wasn't listening.'

'Really!' Lisa feigned surprise.

'Well, I need a good night's sleep,' McAbbey said, yawning uncontrollably. 'I have another big day tomorrow.'

Lisa looked like she was about to object, but thought better of it. 'Will we see you this weekend perhaps?'

'Maybe. Are you missing me?'

'No, but the lawns are.'

Arriving at the office the following day, McAbbey was handed two e-mails and three post-it messages. One was from Lisa, to remind him of dinner with the Uptons in St Kilda that night. The second and third messages were from the media, requesting interviews. McAbbey asked Helen to call them and decline their request, but suggested they call the Police Minister's office.

Both e-mails were from Roger Bateson, requesting information. He threatened to publish a scathing attack on their failures, unless they gave him an exclusive. Let him do his best, McAbbey thought.

Once he had settled at his desk he called Andrea.

'Where is everyone?'

'They're down at the hospital. Apparently the approval to inspect all the records came through first thing this morning.'

The Premier worked fast. Now it was their turn. There was little else he could for the Adonis Taskforce, so he spent the morning signing paperwork and meeting with his other crew leaders. The Homicide Squad had another ten cases open, from suspected suicides to a spate of hit and run incidents; there was always something for him to review.

After lunch Jack called.

'We're knee deep in dust down here,' he said.

'Good to hear. Have you had any assistance?'

'Yes. We have five administrative staff down here with us. They're keen to help us now.'

'I think the Premier may have had something to do with that!' McAbbey smiled. 'Let me know as soon as you find his file.'

Jack hung up and the phone rang again.

It was Catherine. She requested he join them at Dr Walsh's lab ASAP.

'We already have some results,' Catherine admitted proudly when McAbbey arrived.

'You and Doctor Walsh are working pretty close—is there a possibility of a little romance?' he asked with a wink.

'Not likely!' she snapped back, 'But he's a better chance than you!'

The doctor returned from the men's room oblivious to the goings-on.

He had adjusted his comb-over while in the bathroom and his hair was freshly wet. He sat down at the computer and McAbbey distracted Catherine by staring at his head. She belted him quietly while the doctor unwittingly typed.

'We tested four samples of DNA which were originally thought to belong to the parents of the victims,' Catherine reported. 'We started with the DNA samples from Brad Anderson's bedroom and discovered that the killer was definitely there.'

'Hence, Brian Anderson is not Brad's father,' Dr Walsh continued.

McAbbey drew a deep breath. 'My God. I'm willing to bet that Barrett has light blue-coloured eyes.' All of a sudden, something that previously had not fitted the mould did. McAbbey felt it was the logical explanation for why only some victims had blue eyes. The mother's genes had influenced Carly's and Melinda's brown eyes.

Catherine agreed, continuing with her report.

'We then compared hair follicles that we thought belonged to the fathers of Sharron Sylvester and Carly Williams, but they again matched Barrett. That makes five positives.'

'What about the others?'

'We didn't find any DNA trace evidence at the scene of Ben Peterson's or Joanne MacDonnell's murders. As for Sue Maryvale who was murdered in WA, I have a trace sample being processed by the WA Forensic Science laboratory. We should have the results any day now. That leaves Andrew Jones, the surfer. He is not related to the killer.'

'Joanne MacDonnell is a mystery. Her father was upset when we asked if he was the biological parent—he believes he is,' Pete said.

'Can't you just check her DNA to see if it matches the killer's?' McAbbey asked.

'We will.' Catherine lowered her voice. 'It's just that we misplaced her DNA profile and have to perform the test again. Doctor Walsh has offered to do that tomorrow on his day off.'

'Thanks for that,' McAbbey said. 'Did you find the missing sample?'

'Err no. I have pulled a favour and recovered her heel prick test from birth. That blood sample will be sufficient for a DNA test.'

'Why do you think he's doing this?' Catherine asked. 'Is there a name for killing your own kids?'

'Progenocide?' McAbbey guessed. 'As for the reason—I think it would take another nut bag to understand it.'

'Well ... that is why I asked you,' she retorted.

—◦—

Back in the office, McAbbey penned two quick letters; the first was addressed to Gary Moloney, with copies to Harry Vincent and Bill Harnden:

> We are waiting on the results of DNA tests, which we believe will confirm that the serial killer is the biological father of the victims. We have access to the client–donor records, thanks to the Premier's speedy intervention and hope to have Barrett's files in-house by close of business Friday. If you require any further information, please do not hesitate to call me.
> Kind Regards, Inspector Ryan McAbbey.

The second letter, He addressed to Roger Bateson:

> I apologise for not responding sooner, however I have had more serious issues to attend to. Wasting my time with briefings does not help my department come closer to a resolution in this case. Feel free to make idle threats, but be warned, I have chewed up tougher men than you. In future, I suggest you wait until the press statements like everyone else.
> Signed
> Inspector R. McAbbey

He hurriedly handed both letters to Andrea for typing and sending to the respective recipients.

Sitting back in his office chair, he heaved a sigh of relief. His chores for the week were complete and for the remainder of the day he would tidy the paperwork on his desk in peace.

67

At ten to five a call came through from Gavin.

'We've been unable to locate any more client files.'

'What's the problem with finding them?' he asked.

'The Barrett file referenced a code each time the semen was used. We have to find the client reports that have the corresponding codes on them, but the files are in disarray. It should be just a matter of finding the right archive box for the relevant year, but ...'

'Sounds like fun.'

'Very funny. Jack, Pete and I are leaving now. We're taking turns in managing shifts. Ted will stay to oversee the file search this evening.'

'Good. Let me know as soon as you find anything important.' McAbbey hung up and Andrea stood at his door.

'I have Roger Bateson on the line. He wants to speak to you immediately.'

'Really!' McAbbey was taken aback. 'Tell him I'm busy.'

'I have Harry Vincent on the line too.' Andrea was suddenly pale. 'You'd better take that call.'

'What is it?'

She backed out of his office without a response.

'Got your update,' Vincent replied curtly when McAbbey introduced himself. 'So did the Minister and he's mightily pissed.'

'We're doing the best we can, Harry. I promised resolution by Monday.'

'You won't have a job by then!' he yelled down the line. 'What do you think you're trying to pull? The Minister's ready to kick you out of the force.'

'What are you on about?' McAbbey asked, totally mystified.

'Fancy telling the Minister you've chewed up tougher men than he! Are you bonkers?'

The penny dropped and, with it, McAbbey's jaw.

Andrea knew why Vincent wanted a word with him. She must have sent the wrong letter to Roger Bateson ...

McAbbey apologised and explained the gaffe, somehow managing to convince Harry it was a mistake.

'ANDREA!' he yelled when he hung up from Vincent.

She appeared quietly at his door.

'Did you send the wrong letter?' his voice boomed.

She began to sob lightly. 'Sorry sir. I put the wrong name on the envelope ...'

It was policy to make a duplicate of every document for the file. McAbbey inspected the copy of the letter that had inadvertently gone to the journalist.

'Get Roger Bateson on the line for me.'

McAbbey spent an hour righting the mistake. He had to plead with Roger not to print the document, by firstly threatening to give the other newspapers a first look at any new developments, and secondly, by explaining that the police would hold him personally responsible for any murder as a consequence.

The harder task was to convince the Minister, Gary Moloney, that it was a genuine mistake. McAbbey faxed him a copy of the intended letter and apologised. It did not help his cause that the correct letter had anticipated Barrett's files by late that afternoon.

Andrea was shaken by it, so McAbbey sent her home. He had already forgiven the mistake, having made a few clangers himself over the years.

Looking at the clock, he grabbed the mobile and his briefcase and rushed out the door. He would be late again for dinner.

Rod and Corina Upton were Lisa's toffy friends. A triple storey house and two German cars alluded to their life of pomp and caviar. Rod owned a printing business and since making his first million, talked of nothing but the high life. They generally bored McAbbey to drink.

'Well, next March, we're off to the Caribbean for three weeks—can you believe it?'

'Yeah,' McAbbey muttered, munching on brushcetta as he read the restaurant menu.

She explained their itinerary and McAbbey found himself listening. Perhaps it would be fun to visit ruins and walk in sand as soft as talc on bright blue beaches.

'Maybe we should take a trip, honey.' Lisa took hold of his arm.

It had been three years since their last holiday and he needed a break. He agreed, and they chatted with the Uptons on the hows and whys.

By the time mains were served, the discussion had returned to their family business and McAbbey was quick to switch off.

His thoughts began to drift back to work and he wondered how Gavin and Ted were progressing. He thought of grabbing the mobile and excusing himself to make a call. The notion ceased when he reached down for the phone by Lisa's handbag and her foot planted itself firmly on his thieving fingers.

Corina had taken to complaining about her new BMW, which apparently was not as good as the Mercedes she used to have. McAbbey was relieved when the mobile's shrill ring interrupted.

'Excuse me a minute—this might be the Premier.'

Lisa shot eye daggers at him as he walked out to the rest room.

68

'Gavin here. We're missing only one document. We found the records for Tania, Brad, Sharron, Ben, Carly and Melinda. Plus we also found the application for the Maryvales from Perth. The donor record shows that her parents used to live in Melbourne.'

That was seven, McAbbey mused. 'What about Joanne MacDonnell?'

'We're still looking for that file. Did Catherine find out if Barrett was Joanne's biological father?'

'Not yet. She had to re-acquire a sample to test and probably won't have an answer until Monday.'

'Could this mean that the killer is finished?' Gavin asked.

'If Joanne is the last, then I guess we can assume so. It makes sense; Melinda died last Sunday. Time will tell. Call me when you can confirm the eighth name.'

McAbbey returned to his seat and refilled his glass with another Morgan's Yarra Valley Cabernet.

Once the bottle was empty, Lisa handed him a large glass of water and he took the hint.

When the phone rang an hour later, McAbbey was eager to escape their discussion on the merits of private health insurance.

He quickly excused himself.

'We have the name of the last couple,' Gavin said. 'They are James and Melissa McKenzie.'

'Not the MacDonnells?' McAbbey was shocked. 'Either the killer has made a mistake, or he's not just killing his offspring.'

'We've confirmed where the McKenzies are currently renting.'

'Have you contacted them yet?' McAbbey felt a sense of urgency.

'No. Ted has tried twice, but the phone rings out.'

'Where do they live—have you sent a squad car out?'

'We've just dispatched one. They live in St Kilda.'

'Whereabouts? I'm in St Kilda.'

'They live on Park Street—the Albert Park side of Fitzroy Street.'

He memorised the details. 'I'm on my way.' Hanging up, he walked briskly back to the table. 'I have to go—it's an emergency.'

'How will I get home?' Lisa demanded.

'I'll be back in an hour. Here, keep the phone and I'll call you soon. So nice having dinner with you,' he apologised to the Uptons with a wan smile, as though leaving was the last thing he wanted to do. He could sense however that Lisa was not impressed and not entirely convinced there was an emergency.

In the street, McAbbey paused seeking his bearings. He was not so much lost, as overwhelmed by the crowds of people in the street.

There was music and a wave of people wandering aimlessly— couples, groups and singles. There was an amazing array of clothing and affectations; people with rings through anything that could be pierced; others with torn clothes and unusual hairdos.

Turning right from Acland Street into Fitzroy Street, he pushed his way through the crowd, ruing the festival which hindered his progress. It was a balmy evening in the mid-twenties and most of the youths were dressed for the beach.

Green trams crawled like tortoises, bleating continuously amid the people who had congregated in the middle of the road. Buskers used inane objects to make music as the crowd bustled around them jiving to the beat.

Turning left into Park Street, McAbbey broke into a light jog. He watched for the house numbers. Fifty metres from the festivities, he found it.

Looking around for suspicious cars was a waste of time. The street was awash with vehicles from the festival. People were parked in no standing zones and covering driveways.

McAbbey paused downstairs, wondering whether or not to buzz the apartment—but Ted had already tried calling.

The outer door was ajar—the lever broken from years of use. McAbbey stepped inside. The foyer carpet was worn, exposing the concrete underneath, and a plastic plant to the side had long since died.

Flat four was upstairs. He climbed up as quietly as the creaky stairs would allow and listened for activity—but could hear nothing.

McAbbey knocked on the door and waited for a response. When no one answered, he tried the knob. It was securely fastened.

McAbbey heard voices downstairs and walked to the landing to catch a glimpse.

A young couple started walking up the stairs, barely able to hold each other up. They were singing and carrying on. She was a slender beauty with long brown hair, wearing a bathing suit and sarong and he was tall and muscular, wearing cut jeans and a singlet.

Not wishing to draw attention to himself, he walked to the end of the landing so he could watch them from a distance.

Giggling and flirting with the young man, the girl drew keys from a bag and opened the door to flat number four.

She was the McKenzie's daughter.

McAbbey was in two minds about approaching. It would be hard to explain the current predicament when she was drunk, so he decided to stand guard. She would be safe until the squad car arrived.

When the youths went inside, McAbbey walked to the door and tested the handle. They had left it open.

McAbbey glanced quickly at his watch. It was only minutes since he had spoken to Gavin and he assumed the local cops would arrive soon. Another five minutes passed and then suddenly the door opened.

McAbbey lunged to the left of the doorway, but not quickly enough.

'Can I help you?' she asked gaily, her clothes barely returned to their rightful place.

'No, just waiting for someone.'

She plodded downstairs, holding the rail for much needed support. This left him in a quandary.

'Should I stay or should I go?' he muttered hesitantly.

Eventually he decided the latter. Following her downstairs, he was relieved when a squad car pulled up. She walked towards the festival, blissfully unaware that her life was in danger, as McAbbey approached the cop car.

'Howdy, Macca!'

It was Mick Payne, the Senior Constable from St Kilda CIU who was at the scene of Tania's murder. For once in his life he was not eating, but the remnants of sugar and sauce on his face and clothes were proof of him having eaten jam donuts earlier in the evening.

So conditioned was Mick to this lifestyle that McAbbey was convinced his wife served him his dinner in the car with a plastic knife and fork, and coffee from a polystyrene cup.

'Mick, we need to follow that girl—but I'm afraid, with the festival, it'll have to be on foot.'

'Sure.' He double-parked the car and Mick and his young partner walked with McAbbey.

'Found that serial killer yet?' Mick asked.

'No, but we have reason to believe she's his next victim.'

'No shit?' With the Senior Constable's daily diet, it was impossible for McAbbey not to take him literally.

They reached the intersection with Fitzroy Street, when McAbbey was struck with a sinking realization.

'I have to go back. Mick, stay close—don't let her out of your sight.'

McAbbey ran back to the block of flats. He had assumed the offspring was female, but what if she was just a girlfriend and he was their son?

69

Hearing a splintering of wood followed by a scuffle inside, McAbbey twisted the doorknob. It was now locked.

He wavered with indecision. Should he break in? Had the youth only fallen over drunk?

The department was as strict as ever on breaking and entering without a warrant. When McAbbey heard a muffled cry for help he stepped back into the corridor and ran at the door with all his weight. With a crash and great deal of pain he bounced off the door, which had barely budged. Rubbing his shoulder harshly, he went back for another go. He cursed not having his gun to shoot through the lock. Taking a quick breath and tensing his muscles, McAbbey ran at the door again.

Before he could halt his approach, the door opened and he went lunging into the darkness beyond. Struggling for balance, he tripped over something resembling a coffee table and fell headlong across a couch.

The flat was bathed in darkness and though his bones ached like mad, he was OK. He strained to hear, but the silence was deafening, like the ringing in the ears that remained long after a rock concert.

He could sense a presence. He resisted the temptation to move, as the lights were out, but then he reminded himself that whoever had opened the door was already used to the darkness. McAbbey was camouflaged like a guerrilla in a clown suit.

Turning suddenly, McAbbey saw the silhouette of his assailant with something raised above his head. McAbbey froze in shock as his eyesight adjusted.

It was him. The weapon the killer held glinted in the light of a passing car below and reflected on the killer's sharp, determined features. He held a large syringe with a three inch needle!

The killer swung the hypodermic maniacally and he managed to duck. Suddenly in defending a possible victim, he was himself, under threat. McAbbey backed away.

The man lunged again at him. With no time to think, he was fortunate his instincts were decisive. He grabbed a seat cushion and raised it in defence.

McAbbey felt the syringe pierce the fabric of the cushion and was momentarily mesmerised by the shiny needle-point which pushed through the cushion, just inches from his eyes. The killer retracted the needle and McAbbey dropped the cushion and darted into the kitchen. His assailant strode after him.

The killer was taller than McAbbey and he could see substantial grey in his otherwise fair hair. As McAbbey suspected, he had sapphire-blue eyes. Occasional glimpses of his physique were possible with passing cars throwing light into the room. His features were parched and his muscles tensed giving him the appearance of a mad soldier. He was more powerful than his guise with maniacal intent fuelling his rage, like cask wine to a domestic dispute.

Opening drawers and searching the bench tops, McAbbey grabbed wildly for anything that could be used as a weapon. A clamour ensued from the glasses and plates he accidentally swept onto floor.

His fingers grappled with a heavy wooden article on the bench top. A rolling pin! McAbbey brandished the weapon and suddenly the killer tossed the syringe and lunged, reaching out with talon-like hands. McAbbey fell backwards, hitting his head on a cupboard. The rolling pin clattered to the floor and he felt the killer's fingers constricting his throat. McAbbey was weak from the fall and felt helpless to relieve the grip. Dizziness quickly took hold.

McAbbey felt so sleepy. 'Backup is on its way …' he mustered the energy to whisper.

A siren screamed and the killer let go.

'Get off my back, McAbbey—or I'll come after you,' he said. As quickly and quietly as he had moved about the house, his assailant was gone.

Holding his chaffed throat tenderly, McAbbey stumbled after him. When he stood out in the street he realised that there was no police assistance. What he had heard was an ambulance, probably out to rescue some fallen reveller from the street festival. Little did they know they had already saved a life.

McAbbey searched the crowd and spotted the killer walking calmly towards the festivities. McAbbey broke into a run, determined not to let him out of sight. He did not have time to make a call at a phone booth.

As he rejoined Fitzroy Street, McAbbey jostled and bumped his way, following a tall silvery head, as it bobbed its way through the crowd. Though he did not seem to be in a hurry, McAbbey struggled to keep up with him.

'Hey! Watch where you're going old man!' Angry revellers shoved the detective back and forth as he pushed his way through them.

This was one of the few times he wished he wore a uniform.

His assailant moved at a brisk pace and McAbbey's throbbing throat was not helping his shortness of breath.

As they reached the Esplanade, McAbbey's breathing became more and more sporadic but he trudged on, determined to keep him in sight.

McAbbey lost him in a crowd huddled around a busking band. They were pounding a beat his heart struggled to keep time with. Amid the jiving and cuddling of near naked youths, McAbbey searched hopelessly for his tall target. He was about to give up when outside the Espy Hotel, he caught a glimpse of the killer's head.

Misjudging a wild dancer's next step, McAbbey tumbled and fell among the revellers. By the time he disentangled himself and stood again, the killer was gone.

70

McAbbey loped purposefully through the stalls, people, rubbish and music. The killer could have stepped into any number of restaurants, bars or alleyways.

McAbbey stood still for a few minutes, hopelessly convinced he would reappear. He eventually walked back down the Esplanade and through a side lane to Acland Street.

Resting on a brightly-tiled public stool he closed his eyes. The throbbing in his throat was intensifying and he was light-headed from the chase.

'Where the hell have you been?' Lisa stood in the restaurant doorway. 'Did you leave just to come out for some fresh air?'

McAbbey was surprised to find he was back where he started. Lisa gasped in shock at his appearance. 'Ryan! What happened?'

'I had a run in with the killer,' he muttered. 'At least this time we'll have an excellent likeness for Crimestoppers.'

'Stop thinking about work for a minute.' She frowned, walking to him. 'You're injured.'

Ignoring her pleas, he confiscated his mobile from her, which began to ring as he opened it.

'You there, boss? Christ! I was worried sick,' Gavin said.

'I'm OK. I just chased the bastard halfway across St Kilda.'

'Did you catch him?'

'Hell no. But I had a good enough look. Tomorrow Crimestoppers will turn him into a frigging celebrity.'

'Are you OK?' Gavin asked.

'Yeah, but I'm a little buggered. He had the strength of ten men.' He then realised why Gavin was concerned for his wellbeing.

'How is the kid? Did I get there before the killer had time to …?'

'Sorry, boss,' he answered slowly. 'I'm at the flat now and Jack and Pete have just arrived. Are you coming back?'

'Yeah.' He glanced at Lisa. 'I'll be there as soon as I can.'

'Be where?' She stood with her hands on her hips. 'You need medical attention.'

'Look, I have to go back. We have another victim. There'll be an ambulance there to check me over.'

'OK.' Lisa's look was one of sympathy and resignation.

By the time he arrived back at the flats, the area was alive with police.

'We've got every possible resource combing the St Kilda area for a man fitting his description,' Jack explained.

Gavin joined them. 'The victim's in the bedroom. You were right, Boss. When I asked if I could speak to you, they told me you'd returned to the flat. I guessed why, so I told them to make contact with the girl and find out for sure if she was the daughter. They had followed her to the beach before they asked. She was his girlfriend and had her own keys.'

'What's the victim's name?' McAbbey asked.

'Matt McKenzie. We've been able to contact his parents; they both live and work in Geelong. They kept the flat for their son while he was studying at Melbourne Uni.'

'How old was he?'

'Twenty.'

McAbbey followed Jack and Gavin into the bedroom.

Matt had struggled valiantly. His stereo had fallen from the cabinet, littering CDs all over the floor and his bookcase had been overturned spilling books everywhere.

'What happened when you came in?' Jack asked.

'He lunged at me with a hypodermic.'

'We saw the cushion.'

'Yeah, I ended up in the kitchen and he started throttling me. I told him reinforcements were on the way—and fortunately for me, an ambulance went past. He panicked and I chased him.'

Pausing for a moment, he glanced at the body. He was lying on the bed face down. McAbbey wondered if the killer had intended to bless the victim.

'What was in the hypodermic?' McAbbey asked.

'From the physical reaction and smell of it, I'd say heroin. His idea was to leave the victim with a self-inflicted drug overdose. The boy was held down and injected in the arm. He was convulsing when we arrived but the ambulance crew couldn't revive him.'

Catherine stepped in quietly behind him. 'What do we have?'

'Twenty-year-old male. Possible heroin overdose.' Jack said.

She donned gloves and checked the body briefly.

Catherine turned her attention to McAbbey. 'Give me a look at you.' She prodded the bruising on his neck and wiped blood from the back of his head.

'Not so hard!' McAbbey grumbled. 'Go away. I'm not dead yet!'

'There's an ambulance out the front. Have them check you over.' Catherine gave Jack a wink. 'And next time, don't block with your head.'

McAbbey rolled his eyes. 'The ambulance is for the victim, not me.'

Catherine sighed. 'You need a medic to bathe the wound. Go!'

With one last look around, McAbbey left.

He was quickly given the all clear and a couple of aspirin for his throbbing head. Pete was standing beside the ambulance when he came out.

'We heard what happened. Are you OK?'

'Fine, thanks.' McAbbey smiled briefly. 'Have them call me on my mobile if they need anything. I'll go down to Southbank first thing tomorrow morning to file a computer image of the suspect for Crimestoppers and mobile police units. Get Jack to call Bill Harnden and report what happened here tonight.'

He stumbled back to the restaurant and collapsed at the table beside Lisa.

'I need a stiff drink.'

71

Saturday was thankfully quiet for McAbbey.

After breakfast, Lisa drove him back into town so he could sit with a computer technician, who was also a forensic psychologist.

They used the database compositor to draw a likeness and the results were startling. From his piercing gaze to his hardened parchment-like face, McAbbey could actually sense an evil purpose emanating from within the computer generated image.

An hour later, McAbbey was back in the sunshine. He walked up to Melbourne Central where Lisa was buying herself new clothes—much to his chagrin.

Apart from a phone report from Gavin and Catherine, he had no other contact with work that day. The rest of the weekend was spent working around the house. McAbbey mowed lawns, laid more garden beds and cleaned out the shed.

Who needed a holiday when he lived at 'Camp Commandant'?

McAbbey was first in the office on Monday and was overwhelmed by the memos and notes from each member of the Taskforce. Preferring a face to face to reading reports, he organised to see them at ten.

Opening his bottom drawer, McAbbey removed his Glock 22. Also in the drawer was a brand new holster. He was taking no more chances. The killer had threatened him personally. Next time he would be prepared. He holstered the weapon. From now on it would be his friend, day and night—until the bastard was caught.

Just before their impromptu meeting, McAbbey received a phone call from the Chief Commissioner, Harry Vincent.

'Apparently Senior Sergeant Jack Turner called Bill Harnden Friday night. I'd like to congratulate you on your efforts. How are you feeling?' He sounded suspiciously congenial.

'Not too bad. I have a sore head—he gave me a belting.'

'All the more reason to catch him, hey!' he laughed. Typical Harry; never give a sucker an even break.

'I've told the Police Minister of your valiant efforts and he's most pleased. Apparently he intends to make a statement tonight on the news regarding the closeness of the Squad to a resolution.'

'Wait a sec,' he interrupted. 'We haven't caught him yet. An accurate photofit doesn't mean an arrest is guaranteed.'

'But Turner said your taskforce has determined that the killer is the biological father of those kids. Surely now, with this information, his arrest is imminent. Five minutes earlier and you might have caught him and prevented a death.'

'Yes, that was Matt McKenzie. But he was the last of the children found to be sired by Barrett's donation—or whatever his name is. This may be the end of his vendetta.' McAbbey added, 'If he has a good disguise, or heads interstate, we may never find him.'

'Do you believe that?' the Chief pressed. 'Didn't he say something about coming after you?'

'Yes, but it was an idle threat. He has no desire to kill me—unless I get in his way again.' He patted his gun for reassurance. McAbbey had a gut feeling, but was not willing to chance his luck a second time.

'My point exactly. Why would he need to threaten you if his vendetta was finished? There could be more to come.' The Chief was sounding irritable again. 'Well, Ryan, I was hoping for optimism, but you're not delivering.'

'Optimism is a handcuffed criminal in the dock,' McAbbey muttered angrily. 'I'll let you know if anything comes to hand.'

The silence at the other end, followed by a click, was proof enough that his boss was unhappy.

'Let me have it.' McAbbey muttered, not looking up from his notes.

An unfamiliar face to their taskforce meetings sat at the opposite end of the table.

'I'd like to introduce Doctor Walsh, for those of you who have not had the pleasure,' Catherine said.

The doctor nodded graciously. He was excited at the prospect of participating in a Homicide investigation.

'Ian MacDonnell denied that his daughter was the result of donated sperm, but nonetheless it's true,' Catherine stated. 'We found Joanne's DNA sample and it was a progeny match.'

'Damn,' McAbbey said.

'Why does it matter if she's another of his?' Pete asked.

'Only eight samples were donated under the name Barrett. As we already know, Barrett was the pseudonym the killer chose—but what if the killer has another alias?'

'How far have you got with finding the name of Joanne's donor?' McAbbey asked.

'We've checked through all records from the Reproductive Biology Unit at the Melbourne Womens. We referenced by name and year, but drew a blank in both instances. There is no MacDonnell record,' Jack said.

'Yet the killer sired the girl?'

Catherine nodded.

'And Ian MacDonnell is convinced she is his daughter?'

Again Catherine nodded.

McAbbey rubbed his bruised head thoughtfully. 'Then we cannot exclude the possibility that the killer donated sperm to other hospitals,' he replied, feeling his stomach tighten. 'This isn't over yet.'

72

A dark cloud descended over the meeting and their good spirits were dampened. One positive was his near miss with the killer, resulting in a computer generated image.

'We'll start a check of every hospital that has a donor program,' Jack said, making a note.

'If you think you have a job ahead, don't forget I will have to inform the parents that the biological father killed their child,' McAbbey said.

'What are you going to do with the MacDonnells?' Ted asked.

'I'll wait for Doctor Walsh's official report before speaking with Mr MacDonnell. If he doubts us, a DNA paternity test will prove it to him.'

'What does that mean? Did his wife lie?' Pete asked with a frown.

'He spoke little of his first wife; she died during Joanne's birth.' Jack answered. 'She may have applied for donor sperm without his knowledge or consent.'

'But why go to those extremes?' Ted asked.

'Apparently they tried for years to have a child and then she suddenly fell pregnant,' Jack said.

McAbbey could not help thinking, albeit with twenty-twenty hindsight, that it sounded suspicious.

'It's quite common,' Doctor Walsh told them. 'Almost thirty percent of children do not belong to their alleged fathers— whether it's due to an affair, adoption, or the use of a donor. I know a surgeon who does transplants and he claims it's like confession. Husbands are willing to donate organs and marrow to kids that are not related. Some mothers beg him not to tell their partners the truth.'

'If it were me, I'd find the 'milkman' who was responsible and make sure he donated something,' Gavin replied wryly.

'I want you blokes to find out where the killer donated the sperm used for Joanne. This is your number one priority.'

McAbbey had a sudden thought: 'Did anyone see the Crimestoppers ad?'

Jack nodded. 'It was clear and concise. If I saw the bastard in the street, I'd recognise him.'

'Good. Considering we know the killer's been to WA, can you make sure the ad is run interstate?'

Jack nodded.

Helen poked her head into their meeting. 'Sir, have you read today's paper?'

'No.'

'Anyone?' She asked with a frown.

No one had.

'What does it say?' McAbbey asked.

Without a word, she placed the *Herald Sun* on the table. The heading, "Serial Killer—the Biological Father", was blazoned across the front cover. McAbbey cursed aloud and banged a fist on the table.

'Mr MacDonnell called five minutes ago.'

'I hope he hasn't seen this ...' Catherine muttered.

'That's what he wanted to talk about.' Helen added, 'He's devastated.'

'How'd they find out?' Catherine asked. 'Did the Chief leak it?'

'No. Roger Bateson's behind this.'

Pete took the paper and read aloud:

> The Homicide Squad is waiting on the results of DNA tests which look like confirming that the serial killer is the biological father of the victims. There is some doubt whether all the victims are related, however forensic experts are close to confirming this. It is understood that Premier Fred Allen has fast tracked access to the necessary records.

'Whoever leaked this should be strung up!' Catherine declared.

'It was us, Cath.' McAbbey's reply was barely audible. He had forgotten to tell her about the memo debacle.

'You're kidding!' She said, reacting like a teacher whose star pupil had been caught cheating.

He explained the gaffe, without mentioning the culprit within the office, but he did mention the deal he made with Bateson.

'You had an agreement that he wouldn't publish this. For the sake of the victims and the lives of those unwittingly implicated ...'

If looks could kill, McAbbey thought, Bateson was doomed to a cold slab with Catherine poised with scalpel in hand.

'So what are you going to do?' Catherine asked—as though McAbbey could just knock on his front door and punch him in the nose.

'Damage control.' He shrugged. 'I have the upset parents of nine victims to speak to. They'll want to know why they weren't told beforehand. Plus,' he added, 'I'm sure to receive a phone call from the Minister.'

'What can I do?' Catherine asked angrily.

'I need you to prove to Ian MacDonnell that he's not the biological father. Jack, get him to go through their papers again. I'm hoping there is a record of the sperm donation hidden away in his deceased wife's papers.'

Once they left, he returned to his office with nine phone numbers. He would even have to find the family of the surfer, Andrew Jones.

Stopping briefly for lunch, he resumed calling the parents, dealing with their anger, grief and hostility for not having been told earlier. By four o'clock, he was a husk with nothing left to offer.

Andrea insisted that he go home and McAbbey quietly packed his things and left.

At home, he threw his briefcase on the coffee table and lay on the couch. A headache was pounding his erratic heartbeat through the confines of his head, his bones ached and his emotional resolve was wire-thin. Both physically and mentally, he felt ready for a wooden box.

When Lisa came home, she took one look at him and picked up the phone.

'Phoebe's on her way,' she said after a terse phone call. Phoebe was Lisa's high school friend who was into natural therapy.

Lisa made him a warm Milo and put out chocolate cake. Her philosophy was that stressed in reverse spelt desserts.

'I saw the paper today; have you told the parents?' He nodded and Lisa sighed. 'Surely they have a counsellor to deal with it?'

'They do,' he said. 'But I feel personally responsible for the information reaching the press. I owe it to them.'

'You owe something to your health. You're not a trained counsellor,' she admonished, albeit sympathetically.

For the first time, he looked forward to seeing Lisa's friend Phoebe. She was one of those arty women who read tarot cards and listened to the stars.

She was not coming to read cards today, though. She was a brilliant masseuse, whose music and fragrant aromas seemed to somehow relax him.

When Phoebe arrived, she set up her portable table and started a music tape of chirping birds. McAbbey dutifully stripped to his boxers and lay on the table.

'You really are tense.' Phoebe remarked quietly as she pressed her fingers deeply into his back. 'Have you thought of trying Tai Chi?' She asked.

'No thanks, I'll stick with Twinings.'

Lisa glanced wryly at Phoebe.

McAbbey exhaled deeply, feeling his tension sink through the floor, laying his stress to waste.

73

The following afternoon McAbbey joined Gavin, who had returned from digging through hospital records. The office was otherwise deserted; the office girls were on a flexi-break and the Taskforce detectives were out coordinating the search through various hospitals.

'I'm sick and tired of archive rooms. The sooner these files are copied onto a computer the better. Few records dating back ten years or more have been transferred. I guess the hospitals had better things to spend their time and money on.'

'Any luck though?' McAbbey pressed.

'Not yet. We've been through the records of three Melbourne hospitals for the names MacDonnell and Barrett, but so far nothing.'

'Have you spoken with interstate sperm banks?' he asked.

'Yes. But they're not as helpful when we're a thousand kilometres away. They don't have the resources or time to go digging in their basement. We are working our way through the hospitals in Sydney and Brisbane at the moment. Though they say they will look I'm inclined to believe that they won't want to help.'

'Why not?'

'It has something to do with the revelation that the killer was a sperm donor. I think they're fearful of bad publicity.'

'Let's wait and see if Mr MacDonnell can find something in his deceased wife's effects.'

At that moment, McAbbey had a sudden premonition—the implications of which he could not yet fully grasp. He was contemplating the difficulties of Gavin's search through the files, when it suddenly dawned on him. If they found it so hard to find those records, how the hell did Barrett?

'Don't they keep donor records confidential?' he asked Gavin, who yawned loudly beside him.

'Yes, in those days the parents using the sperm were given no access to the biological father—and in some cases the donors were completely anonymous anyway.'

'Yes, but what about in reverse? Did Barrett as a donor, have access to the parents who used his donation?'

'No way.' Gavin followed his reply with another yawn.

'Then how does Barrett know who his offspring are, let alone where to find them—years later?'

Gavin shrugged.

'Perhaps Barrett had an insider working at the hospital,' McAbbey said.

'Someone who has access to the records,' Gavin mused. 'That would explain why we've found it so hard to find them. An insider could have tampered with the files. It could be a cleaner or security officer.'

'Get onto it straight away. I want dossiers on all staff working at the Melbourne Womens.'

Gavin nodded. 'Have you rung Cath yet?' he asked.

'No. Why?'

'She left an urgent message for you to call earlier. I assumed someone would have told you.' Gavin added, with a hint of exasperation, 'I mean, I asked her what she had found, but she wouldn't tell me.'

'Figures.' McAbbey smiled.

'Give her an inch and right away she thinks she's a ruler.' Gavin shook his head.

'Go home, will you?' McAbbey excused Gavin, who had resorted to pinching himself to stay awake.

McAbbey picked up the phone and dialled Catherine's number at the office but it was her assistant, Louise, who answered.

'Where are you?' she asked briskly.

'I haven't been well. I only just got the message.'

'Cath told your office it was urgent. She's on her way to the airport. You're supposed to be going to Sydney with her.'

'What?'

'They found the MacDonnell's adoption card in the mother's effects—the hospital is in Sydney.'

McAbbey glanced at the clock. He had just over an hour to be on the plane and would be lucky to make the airport in time. So much for stress release, he thought.

Jumping in the car with his briefcase and a newspaper, he gave his wife a quick call and explained why he was heading interstate. As he joined the Tullamarine Freeway, he received an incoming mobile call.

'Where the hell are you?' It was Catherine.

'On my way—I only just found out from Gavin.'

'You've got half an hour. I suggest you leave your car on the departures deck and ask for one of the others to pick it up later.'

'Gavin told me Jack found Joanne's records,' he hinted.

'Yes. Her deceased mother, Emma MacDonnell, went to Sydney to be inseminated. I'll tell you more—if you make it.'

Who's investigation was this? McAbbey was starting to think that Gavin was right about her.

—⁀—

McAbbey flashed a badge to security when he arrived at the airport and left his car in the standing zone.

He ran directly to the terminal, hearing the last call for QF438 to Sydney. Collecting his ticket from the counter, he pushed past the hostesses and ran his own boarding pass through the computer. He grabbed a headset and walked down the ramp to the Boeing.

'Glad you decided to come.' Catherine sat with her arms crossed.

He ignored her, sitting heavily. 'What did you find?' he asked, once he was settled with a Foster's.

'Ian MacDonnell agreed to a paternity test. I also asked him if we could run a sperm count. Testing his count is a quicker way to determine if he can father children. At first he was hesitant, but then I think he wanted to know for sure.'

'When was this?'

'Yesterday afternoon. I sent the samples straight to Doctor Walsh. I asked him to fast track our request—which he did.'

'Told you he likes you,' he replied, and she went red.

She whipped a piece of paper from the file on her lap and handed it to him.

He glanced over the finding. 'He's infertile?'

'Yes,' She said, taking it back. 'I rang Mr MacDonnell and broke the news to him. Naturally he was devastated.'

'How come he hadn't suspected it before?'

'I guess he thought they were lucky. His second wife, Mary, was unable to have children anyway so they adopted Joanne's brother, Kane.'

'After Joanne, he must have assumed he was firing on all cylinders.'

Catherine raised an eye. 'Something like that. Anyway, he invited me over this morning, saying he had found Joanne's birth papers.'

Catherine reached inside the file, retrieving crumpled documents. 'He said these papers were filed with the letters Mrs MacDonnell's mother had regularly sent from Sydney. He found it sadly amusing, because she knew he'd never bother going through his mother-in-law's letters.'

She handed him the documents from the fertility clinic first. As a nervous flier, McAbbey split his time between glancing at the pre-flight safety demonstration and the papers Catherine provided.

'What do you think our killer was doing in Sydney?' McAbbey asked.

'Your guess is as good as mine.'

'Maybe there was some limit to how often he was allowed to donate in Melbourne?'

'OK,' Catherine sported a wry smile. 'My guess is better than yours. I think he moved house from Sydney to Melbourne.'

'This would explain why Joanne is the oldest victim.' he muttered, through gritted teeth as the plane began its acceleration.

'Yes. The other victims range from age thirteen to twenty. Joanne was twenty-three. So it seems the killer moved from Sydney sometime between twenty and twenty-three years ago.'

The plane lurched forward and McAbbey sat back, momentarily riding the acceleration rush. He hated the take-off but Catherine seemed unaware of his discomfort.

'How often do you think these planes crash?' he asked, with his white knuckles gripping the arm rest.

'Just the once.' Catherine smiled.

Changing the subject quickly, he told her of his deduction regarding Barrett.

'Interesting.' She nodded thoughtfully. 'I think you've hit on something there. He would have to know more than an ordinary donor does to be able to find these kids. Is one of your crew going to check out the hospital staff?'

McAbbey nodded.

'Good. 'Cos I don't have the time.'

He glanced at her with amusement.

74

The flight was blissfully uneventful. They landed in Sydney an hour and ten after departure and, with only hand luggage to speak of, were into a taxi in minutes.

McAbbey stared out the window, trying to gain his bearings. He hadn't been to Sydney in ten years, but little had changed other than busier roads.

They passed by Circular Quay and a brief view of the harbour, then turned down a side road to the hospital. McAbbey let Catherine pay the cab driver—he hated filling out expense claims.

Catherine took the lead, introducing herself at reception. Within minutes, Doctor Baurim joined them. He looked like Lurch from the Addams' Family with cardboard-stiff brown hair. McAbbey had seen better rugs in a dog kennel and healthier human specimens on Cath's steel trays.

She got wind of his thoughts, elbowing him when McAbbey shook the doctor's hand and referred to him as Doctor Barium.

The doctor ushered them into his office and quickly closed the door behind them.

'I understand the confidentiality aspect of this,' he said with a German accent. 'I just hope you do too. We don't need bad publicity.'

'I understand,' Catherine replied warmly. 'It's just that we might save lives.'

'We have many checks in place these days to ensure that nothing can go wrong, that no one can be incorrectly inseminated.'

'We believe you, Doctor.' McAbbey said. 'We just have a few questions regarding one of your patients.'

'I've already briefed the doctor,' Catherine explained.

Doctor Baurim picked out a file and handed it to Catherine. 'Here. The donor's name is Ken Marrott.'

Catherine and McAbbey studied the papers intently. Marrott was twenty-nine years of age at the time of donation—which made him fifty-two now.

'If he started donating here, it's more likely this is his real name. It's less likely he would fake his details the first time,' McAbbey said.

'Do you have any available resources?' Catherine asked the doctor. 'We need access to your administration records.'

'Not really,' he shrugged, 'We have four accounts clerks and a receptionist. Our medical staff have no time to dig in archives.'

McAbbey grabbed his phone. 'We need backup, I'll call Jack. It's best that they get a forensic team up here as soon as possible.'

McAbbey had a small contingency budget for just such an occasion. Sending the whole crew north would probably blow that budget, but then he figured what else was it there for? It was rare for them to make interstate trips, as their jurisdiction was only for Victoria. Occasionally he was required interstate on multi-jurisdictional cases, but rarely spent the allocated budget each year.

'How soon can you be here?' McAbbey asked Jack, after explaining the reason for the call.

'I'll tell the Taskforce to meet at the airport,' Jack replied. 'How long are we going for?'

'I can't say for sure, but pack an overnight bag.'

McAbbey gave him the address for the hospital.

'It sounds similar to his alias, doesn't it? Barrett ... Marrott ...' Jack said.

'It does—maybe he was unimaginative and chose an alias similar to his real name.'

'Ted can check out the name—he'll be staying in Melbourne,' Jack said.

'Good. He can be our liaison with the aristocracy. Did you get anywhere with the staff at the Melbourne Womens?' McAbbey asked.

'No,' Jack replied. 'Not yet.'

'Have Ted follow that up too,' McAbbey said, hanging up.

McAbbey watched Catherine study the Marrott donor details for an anomaly. The file also contained an information page—used by the hospital as a marketing sheet for the prospective recipients to determine whether or not the donor was of suitable stock.

It was from this sheet that Catherine read aloud:

'" ... Born of tall and healthy English parents, the donor is a strong and fit twenty-nine-year-old male ..."'

'No shit! Not many women donate,' McAbbey remarked.

The doctor laughed, but Catherine frowned before continuing with the blurb:

'"He's an active sports person—basketball, football and cricket. He is one hundred and ninety centimetres tall with light blue eyes, blonde hair and weighs eighty-five kilos." Makes you wonder why he would need to donate ...' Catherine pondered.

'Marrott's description ties in with the man who attacked me.' McAbbey said.

That evening, they received a call from Senior Sergeant Exton of the New South Wales Homicide Squad. McAbbey took the call. Thanking the man after a brief conversation, he informed Catherine of the news.

'He says they checked the state records for a Ken Marrott of the approximate age and nothing.'

'So it's another alias?'

'I don't know. Surely he would have needed ID to donate.'

'The laws were less strict in New South Wales. Even now, there's still no legislative requirement to dispose of the sperm after a set period. We should check all states.'

'Agreed. We can assume he lived in Melbourne for the last twenty years. The local victims range from thirteen to twenty.'

'Could he have been raised in a third state before moving to Sydney and then Melbourne?' Catherine offered.

'Possibly. I'll get Ted to coordinate a search of the birth and social security records of Ken Marrott's throughout Australia.'

As they were about to retire for the evening, Jack, Gavin and Pete arrived with overnight bags. To their amusement, McAbbey introduced them to Doctor 'Barium' and they briefly discussed what they had discovered. McAbbey then suggested they find a hotel for the night.

75

The team began the following morning before dawn with a cooked breakfast of Eggs Benedict, strawberry crepes and fresh coffee.

Upon arrival at the Sydney Womens Hospital, Jack and his team seconded the office clerks and went to the archive room.

'All we have to go by is the code on Marrott's file, which will appear at the top of each client file—for example the MacDonnell's,' Catherine explained.

'You mean we have to search though the files manually?' Gavin groaned, having already coordinated the search for the Barrett files. 'At least last time we had the names of victims,' he added.

'Yes. Unfortunately, we don't know how many times the donor sperm samples were used, as the Marrott file doesn't show each donation. On Barrett's file, each of the eight donations was represented by the corresponding client code.'

'Can we get some hired help?' Jack frowned. 'This could take ages ...'

'The doctor has assurances that we'll be discreet, which means only police representatives will be allowed inside the archives. We have to accept this, as we are out of our jurisdiction and don't have official sanction to be here.'

'Well, we'd better get started then,' Gavin replied grimly.

Meanwhile McAbbey and Catherine reviewed the management documents dating back to the era of the MacDonnell donor application. Doctor Baurim joined them in his conference room, carrying three folders of memos and notes.

'These documents relate to the sperm bank donation policies of the time. As you can tell, a lot has changed. Our current operations not only keep a DNA reference for each donor, but also ensure that they have proven their identity. This is still kept a secret from the recipient couples during the selection process.' He left them with the files to attend a meeting.

They spent most of Wednesday perusing the documents. McAbbey handed anything of interest to Catherine to determine its value. He was unfamiliar with many of the medical terms, but was learning quickly.

Halfway through a policy and procedures manual from 1978, McAbbey slammed it on the table. 'We'll never find anything but silverfish this way.'

'We have to keep trying,' Catherine urged.

McAbbey was frustrated at the archaic record keeping. He conceded, however, that it was impossible for the hospital to have anticipated that semen could one day provide a DNA fingerprint.

'This is interesting.' Catherine underlined a paragraph in a document.

She read aloud: '"In all cases of donation, the recipient's code is to be referenced back to the donor's file—so that in case of serious illness, required assistance from the biological father can be attained. It is a state offence for this information to be divulged to a member of the public, the recipient or donor without prior consent of a Magistrate."'

McAbbey waited for Catherine to place value on the clause.

'Marrott's file was not cross-referenced with the codes of each donor.'

'But the MacDonnell's record named Marrott as the donor,' he objected.

'So why wasn't it cross-referenced?' Catherine asked.

'If the impregnator had an insider working here, they could have forged documentation and attained the names of the victims. Maybe they erased all reference to Marrott from the forms.'

'The impregnator?' She frowned momentarily. 'I'm not convinced. Does the killer have a network of insiders? We're talking about two hospitals in two different cities. I find it hard to believe that the killer was privy to staff in both ...'

'Unless ...' McAbbey eyed her with conviction. 'The killer worked here as well.'

She nodded thoughtfully.

The extension at the doctor's desk rang and Catherine picked it up tentatively. With Doctor Baurim out of the office, Catherine was reluctant to answer his phone.

'Catherine Smith—Doctor Barium's office.'

She glared at McAbbey for her slip up. She listened a moment, then covered the mouthpiece.

'It's Bill Harnden.'

McAbbey gripped the receiver like an asp. 'Ryan here.'

'Ryan.' the Assistant Commissioner of Crimes sighed. 'How soon can you get back here?'

—-—

Sitting at the back of the plane on his return to Melbourne, the drone of the engines echoed his sombre mood. His phone conversation with Bill was terse. McAbbey was required back in Melbourne for an update meeting the following morning with the Premier and Police Minister. The Chief Commissioner was also upset that his Taskforce was in Sydney without his prior approval. McAbbey explained that he hoped to secure the help of the New South Wales Homicide Squad by proving a link between their Taskforce and an unsolved homicide in Sydney. McAbbey believed their search of the files would do just that.

76

When McAbbey arrived at home he rang Catherine and Jack on a conference call to check their progress.

'Sorry, Ryan,' Catherine apologised. 'But we have little to show for the day's work.'

'We're halfway through the records, but are yet to find any relevant donor recipients,' Jack added.

'I have to see the Premier again in the morning. I was hoping to have more than that.' There was no sting in his voice, just wearied frustration.

Before bed, McAbbey turned on the late news and a Crimestoppers ad came on during a break. McAbbey had not seen an update since he provided the identikit a few days earlier.

The image of the serial killer appeared exactly as he remembered it from the computer. With piercing blue eyes, he was a tall, athletic Caucasian in his early fifties.

The Crimestoppers bulletin remained their best chance of stopping him. He was becoming increasingly doubtful that anything in the files would lead to a real name or address.

McAbbey arrived at the office early Thursday morning, leaving him an hour to prepare for the meeting. As he left for the Premier's office, Ted arrived at work.

'I have some bad news,' he offered with a grimace. 'Marrott doesn't exist in any state.'

'You found no one called Marrott?' McAbbey asked incredulously.

'There are sixty, but none with a Christian name of Ken. We ran backgrounds on all the others and they check out—none match the killer's profile.'

'Have all states been running the Crimestoppers ad?' he asked.

'Yes. It's been aired throughout the country since Monday. I'm seriously considering the reward for myself,' he joked.

McAbbey's look wiped the grin from Ted's face.

'Mr McAbbey.' The Premier shook his hand warmly. Beguiling charm was the mark of a good politician, and it worried McAbbey. He was expecting to be relieved of command as he was unable to learn the identity of the killer or secure an arrest by the Monday morning deadline.

'We've been apprised of your situation,' the Premier began.

'What developments have you made since yesterday's report?' Harry inquired.

McAbbey took a deep breath. 'We've determined through a state by state search, that Marrott is just another alias. I have three members of my Taskforce and Doctor Smith at the Sydney Womens Hospital coordinating the search for other donor recipients. This is our best chance of catching the killer.'

'Why has the search taken so long?' The Premier asked.

'The donor recipients are not referenced on Marrott's file. We literally have to search the client database for files which list Marrott as the donor.'

'Are you hoping to find other potential victims?' The Police Minister asked.

'Yes. Our best chance to save lives is to find his potential victims before he does.'

'But surely that's a matter for the New South Wales police?' Harry countered.

It sickened McAbbey to think Vincent was willing to handball the investigation on the grounds that the death of an innocent victim was another state's problem. They had a chance to stop it. Fortunately he was prepared for this argument.

'True, however, what if Joanne was not the only recipient who migrated south to Victoria? What if there are more deaths to come? Imagine the hysteria and publicity that would create.'

The Premier cringed.

'Can we take that chance?' McAbbey glanced around the room. 'If we find potential victims, it'll guarantee the cooperation of the New South Wales Police Department. At the moment, they don't want to know about it, purely because of demarcation—the deaths happened in Victoria. If I'm right, we could be credited for saving lives. How many—I don't know.'

The Premier nodded thoughtfully.

'I'll ring the Premier of New South Wales personally. I'm sure he'll provide support if it can be shown that he ... I mean the people, stand to benefit from it.' His cheeks reddened and McAbbey imagined the same logic also worked for him.

'You have until Monday, Ryan,' Harry warned. 'We're running out of time to resolve this. If you can't find him by then, I'll ask you to step aside.'

McAbbey walked out with Bill Harnden, who was deeply apologetic. 'I know what you're going through Ryan, believe me, but Harry has overruled me on this. I'm sorry.'

'That's fine.' McAbbey even managed a wan smile. 'I'm surprised they even gave me until Monday ...'

Bill frowned. 'I think that had something to do with the Premier presenting your award at the dinner tomorrow night.'

'Bonza,' McAbbey muttered under his breath.

McAbbey returned to his office and began opening the mail. He had a pile of fresh letters and documents requiring his signature. Alongside that, were a series of court summonses and requests from the press.

They would have to wait.

He waded through his documents looking for anything of relevance to the Adonis Taskforce, but nothing beckoned. In his phone messages he was surprised to find one from Tracey Stevenson. The post-it note gave a number. What did she want?

Holding the note aside for a moment, he called Catherine, who had also left a message.

'We've found one! Just an hour ago, Jack brought in a file with Marrott's code. The family name is Neuharth. He called the local police to track them down as quickly as possible. The child would be about twenty-two years old now.'

'Thank God,' McAbbey muttered. 'Let me know when you have him or her safely under surveillance—keep up the good work.'

His first responsibility was to Bill Harnden. He called him post-haste, to report their first piece of good news in days. Bill promised to pass it on.

When McAbbey finally cleared his desk, one message remained.

Tracey Stevenson. There was no indication of the urgency or subject matter, but he called her anyway.

'What can I do for you?' McAbbey asked.

Tracey's voice was broken and she sniffed lightly.

'I saw the killer on Crimestoppers last night.'

'I'm sorry, Ms Stevenson.' McAbbey knew it must have been difficult.

She broke into tears and McAbbey held the cradle under his chin momentarily.

'I know it's hard, but we need the public's help to identify him.'

She sobbed lightly. 'I know who he is …'

77

He was momentarily taken aback.

'You know him?'

'Yes. He was the hospital administrator.'

McAbbey was stunned—unable to respond.

'He's older than I remember, but those eyes. As soon as I saw his picture I realised what happened.'

McAbbey bit his lip and waited for Tracey to continue.

'When I went for my final visit before insemination, I was told I had to meet the administrator—a Doctor Halliday ...'

At last, McAbbey thought, the name they'd been seeking for three months.

'I had no idea why he wanted to see me. We talked for about ten minutes and he asked me all sorts of questions about my health, family history and well-being.'

'Is that unusual?' McAbbey was puzzled. Surely it was their job to question the health and safety of the donor applicant.

'I'd already been for my check-up and counselling. He seemed to know nothing of that, but was obsessed with my past. It was all rather strange. He never wrote anything down, though he had files opened in front of him.'

McAbbey thanked Tracey and promised to organise a counsellor to visit her.

When she hung up, he planted his finger on the receiver and released again without putting down the phone. His mind was racing faster than his heart.

Did Tracey realise that the administrator had used his sperm instead of her intended donor? She must, considering the biological father was revealed as the serial killer.

He rang Catherine first. 'We already thought the killer might have been an insider. As administrator, he would have access to every record—no questions asked,' McAbbey said, after explaining his discovery.

'My first plan of attack should be to call the two hospitals,' Catherine said.

'Please. Ted was casing the staff, but I was hoping you might speak to the administrators. Also—can you find out what the AMA has on him,' he said. 'Your medical credentials will be useful.'

'Fine. Jack wants to speak with you. We have some news too.' She did not sound happy.

Catherine handed over the phone and McAbbey updated Jack.

'We need to find Halliday right away,' McAbbey said. 'I'll get another homicide crew onto that. We need the manpower today.'

Jack agreed.

'What did you find?' McAbbey asked.

'Another three recipients of Marrott's donor sperm,' Jack said. 'I'm having them checked out now.'

'What about the donation you discovered earlier? Neuharth?'

'We checked it out. The Neuharths live in Penrith.'

'Do you have the child under surveillance?'

'Err, no. It was a boy.'

'What do mean was?'

'He died in an accident two years ago—riding his bike on a main highway. A hit and run.'

'Oh. Well, keep looking then.' McAbbey hung up and rang DSS Blake Stone, one of his crew leaders. McAbbey explained what they had found and asked him to assist in finding Halliday. McAbbey then called Bill Harnden.

Bill was relieved to hear that they had made a breakthrough. McAbbey pleaded for him to play down their discovery for the time being.

McAbbey waited ten minutes and rang Catherine.

'Have you spoken to Barium yet?' he asked.

'Gimme a break!' she laughed. 'I was going to call him next. I've already spoken to Doctor Walsh.'

'And?'

'He didn't know a Doctor Halliday.'

'Oh.' McAbbey frowned.

'But he went through the records and discovered that a Doctor Halliday was Chief Administrator of the Reproductive Biology department from 1982 until 1992.'

'Why did he leave?' he asked. The timing was right! Tania was thirteen, born in 1991 and Sue Maryvale was twenty—born in 1984.

'He was sacked—for alleged improper use of client sperm.'

'What?' McAbbey asked.

'That's right. He was dismissed, but the charges were never proven. It was all hearsay but, apparently, he was witnessed taking donor vials.'

Catherine had a call waiting and was gone for a moment.

'I have Doctor Walsh on the other line,' she said. 'Wait a sec and I'll see if I can get this onto a conference call.' She was more efficient with technology than McAbbey and had the connection in moments.

'Nice to hear from you, Doc.' McAbbey said.

'Boy, do I have some news for you. Our friend Clive Halliday was actually found by a resident nurse swapping sperm.'

'Why was it alleged? How could they not prove it was him?' he asked incredulously.

'They didn't have DNA testing back then,' Catherine said.

'It was the nurse's word against his,' Doctor Walsh added, 'Apparently a few other staff members at the hospital had reported incidents to the board, so he was sacked.'

'You'd better call Doctor Barium as soon as possible,' McAbbey said to Catherine.

'What an unfortunate name!' Doctor Walsh laughed.

'I'll call him now, but you'll want to speak with Jack again,' Catherine explained, once Doctor Walsh had gone.

'Good news?' he asked.

'No, extremely disturbing news.'

McAbbey figured that coming from Cath "you chill 'em and I'll drill 'em" Smith, he'd better brace himself ...

78

'We've found another three,' Jack confirmed.

'That makes seven, if you include Joanne,' McAbbey confirmed.

'Yeah.' Jack then updated him on the search for Halliday.

'Have you got in touch with any of the parents yet?'

'We've contacted the first three.'

'And?'

'The first boy died eighteen months ago—car crash. His stepfather also died in the accident. The car suffered brake failure. Both the second and third children were killed in different hit and run accidents a year ago.'

'Were they were all deemed unrelated at the time?' McAbbey asked.

'Yes. Wouldn't you? They had no reason to link the cases.'

McAbbey sat with the phone frozen in his hands for a long time after Jack had hung up.

Halliday had been killing for much longer than three months. He shook his head in wonder—how many kids had lost their lives through accidents?

Late in the afternoon, Catherine called.

'I've spoken in depth with Doctor Baurim. He's been most helpful,' she defended.

'What did he say?' he asked suspiciously. Doctors tended to stick together, and if Baurim had withheld something from them, McAbbey vowed he would burn for it.

'Doctor Halliday worked here from 1976 until 1982. He became Administrator in 1978.'

'Did Barium suspect Halliday might have been involved?'

'No, but ...'

'Either he did, or he didn't, Cath,' McAbbey pressed.

'He wondered if Halliday was behind it, yes. When Ted asked him about staff members who might've helped the killer, he became concerned. When we confirmed the birth dates of the Sydney victims were between the years of '78 to '82, he told me. He was not willing to go out on a whim without being sure.'

'You mean a limb—maybe he was fearful of the repercussions the hospital would face if it was revealed that their administration was involved in such a breach,' McAbbey said. 'When did Barium start there?'

'He was a junior doctor who started in 1983, after Halliday was dismissed. Apparently Halliday was caught inseminating recipients with his own sperm.'

'And he was not disbarred!' McAbbey was outraged. 'How the hell was he allowed to continue this immoral bastardry in Melbourne?'

'The board decided to cover up what had happened—for fear of losing their licence, funding and sponsorship. Halliday was even given a reference.'

'Fuck …' McAbbey was dumbfounded. 'Someone has to pay for this disgusting lack of work ethic. What are Jack and the others up to now?' he asked.

'They're on a plane back to Melbourne—I'll be flying out tonight.'

'Home? Are they sure they've found all the recipients Halliday impregnated?'

'No, but since the discovery of the 'accidental' deaths, the local Homicide Squad has opened an investigation. They're combing the records now.'

'About time,' he muttered.

'Any word on where Halliday might be now?' Catherine asked.

'Jack's been coordinating the manhunt. His last known address was Templestowe, but the place was sold two years ago. We've no idea where he is at the moment, however Jack is searching for his name through credit card transactions, registrations, bills—you name it. They'll find him.'

'He's distinctive. Someone will recognise him soon,' she agreed.

'I hate to say it Cath, but he may have been disguised when I saw him.'

'I hope not,' Catherine replied with a groan.

'I know you'll be tired tomorrow, but could you join us at ten?'

'Sure.'

'Thanks, Cath. I owe you again.'

'Just add it to the list.' She sighed.

———

Both his heart rate and brain activity raced to extremes during the night. McAbbey stared at the ceiling for long periods, thinking about the case—wondering if he would get a call. He even dreamed about the Premier making lewd comments at his expense during the award ceremony. Fortunately Lisa was able to sleep alongside him and was not distracted by his constant tossing and turning.

———

That night after the trip back from Sydney, Pete could not sleep either. It was after midnight when he stabbed his computer with a finger and waited for it to power up. Lights shone from everywhere as Pete settled into his leather chair and pulled a series of disks from his work satchel. They were the decoded versions of the numbered disks from Pearce's apartment. He felt guilty checking them out of inventory, because of their sensitive nature. Forensics had been through them and found nothing to indicate paedophilia. Pete still shared McAbbey's belief that Pearce was somehow involved in Tania's death. Perhaps that meant Pearce was linked to the other deaths? Another look through the pictures might reveal some connection previously missed.

He put in the first disk and opened a viewer. He was presented with a plethora of images, most of youthful women under thirty. They wore less than Eve on her first day and smiled seductively at him.

He clicked through the images in rapid succession, storing each only for a brief moment. Blonde, brunette, redhead, twins, implements ...

The first disk became predictable after a dozen photos, but nonetheless he ploughed through more than a thousand images. When he finished, he took it from the drive and read the sticker attached, which indicated the date it had been cracked.

He sighed and placed the next disk in the drive.

It took him two hours to reach the end of the pile. He was tired and his eyes ached.

The last disk was old and scratched. The sticker indicated that it too had been viewed. Pete was about to throw it on the used stack of disks when he frowned and raised it up to the light.

'Funny. This is one of the originals,' Pete murmured. It was the unmarked CD that was in the computer drive when they confiscated the collection. Why wasn't this one copied and cracked like the others?

He inserted the disk and realised why. There was no encryption.

The CD was broken up into meticulously labelled directories. He read from the list and one caught his eye. He clicked on the directory and opened the first file.

It was a young child in a tiny concrete backyard. There were dolls in a pram behind.

The next few photos were taken on the same day. After those images, time jumped a few years to show the girl wearing a school uniform. All the images so far were scanned from original photos.

Suddenly Pete caught his breath.

This disk had nothing to do with paedophilia and he knew why Forensics had found nothing. The images looked like innocent family snaps, whereas Forensics was looking for illegal porn. The disk was not encrypted and Pete wondered if they had figured it was harmless as a result.

He scrolled again through a few more images, feeling a wave of excitement and the sweat built up in his mouse-hand, making it difficult to keep control.

He could sense something. The pictures, though catalogued and in date order, were amateurish in nature. The children were distant and preoccupied—unaware the pictures were being taken.

He scrolled to the next image and froze. It was recent. A girl was sunbaking by a pool. Pete recognised the pool and the girl. She was Tania Stevenson.

Pete was fixated by her image. Her exposed skin was tanned, which contrasted the coldness Pete saw in her death. He thought Pearce was game taking such a close-up. He shut his eyes briefly and closed the directory. He chose another and began perusing. He looked through three directories, each of a different child, before he was stopped by something else he recognised.

A young lad was being presented with a trophy at an athletics meet, but this photographer was lousy at capturing the moment. The photo was taken from behind a crowd of people and Pete could only see the handle of the cup. The image was squarely focussed on the boy—their second victim, Brad Anderson.

The photos were not sexually driven and Pete wondered if Pearce was wrongly labelled a paedophile. One thing was certain though; he was connected to the serial murders.

Ted was first to sit with McAbbey in the conference room the following morning.

'My wife, Sue, has spoken to Lisa. They're going to drive into the city together tonight. She said you'd be going to your presentation straight from work.'

'I am going home to change.' McAbbey laughed at Ted's questioning glance at his attire. 'Do you think I'd wear work clothes to a presentation?'

'Yes,' Ted smiled. 'Anyway, I think the women have an ulterior motive—shopping. They're leaving about five.'

'Typical.' Sue and Lisa often did things together when they worked back late.

The rest of the Taskforce crew and Catherine joined them in the conference room. Jack and Gavin were yawning and Pete rubbed his red eyes.

'I hope you're all coming to the Police Ball tonight?' McAbbey was concerned by their crumpled appearance.

'Yeah,' Jack grumbled.

'What do you have?' McAbbey said, with pen and paper in hand. He was hoping to visit Harry and impress him with some serious progress.

'All together, we've found six aliases,' Jack started.

McAbbey sucked wind. 'That many?'

Jack nodded.

'Most of them were properly cross-referenced with the recipients, so we were able to quickly access the files. Twenty-three children ...'

'Are you sure?' McAbbey asked.

'The New South Wales Homicide Squad has begun exhuming bodies and re-opening investigations.'

'Exhuming.' The implication was clear, but McAbbey refused to believe it.

79

'You can't mean they're all ... dead?' Catherine asked, taking the words out of his mouth.

'No,' Jack replied. 'Two are still alive and are currently under police protection.'

'Two!' McAbbey was aghast. 'What happened to the other twenty-odd?'

'Various means of extermination.' Jack said. 'There were seven cases of road accidents. He must've followed them, until he had a chance to run them over. Witnesses to one accident said the killer attended to the victim before driving off. We think he blessed the child.'

Jack handed him the file, which collated the names and details of each victim.

As McAbbey held each piece of paper in turn, he could not help but feel the despair at knowing every single one represented a child ...

'There were five suicides, four suspected robberies that ended in murder, three drug overdoses and two deaths of a similar method to what we've seen in Victoria. He's disguised each crime to avoid being detected as a serial offender. Secrecy is definitely his game.'

'Was,' McAbbey said. 'We have him by the balls now. He can't kill again without us knowing he committed the crime. Everyone in this country will be looking out for him.'

Jack continued his report. 'The Squad is still checking through the records, trying to find other possible forgeries.'

'How'd you know which donors were the aliases?' McAbbey wondered.

'Easy.' Jack gave a wry smile. 'His ego. Obviously he wanted his offerings to sound overly masculine and desirable to anyone looking for a donor of solid stock. We analysed every file that referred to the donor as being tall, athletic, blue eyes, etc. They were like Man-Power advertisements, all worded the same.'

'So you've checked with the recipient families?'

'Correct,' Jack replied. 'We think the first victim died in 2000. He's been killing them ever since—for more than three years now.'

'Why has he killed so many in the past three months?' McAbbey asked, puzzled.

'Maybe he has a timetable?' Gavin offered.

'What else have you found out about Halliday?'

He had addressed the question at Jack, but it was Gavin who answered.

'I've been working with DSS Stone. Halliday was born in Thornbury, went to Parade College and studied medicine at Melbourne University. At the age of twenty-three, he worked many positions as a locum—his longest stint was at Melbourne's Epworth Hospital. There he showed a great interest in their reproductive unit and worked extensively in the area of infertility. After two years, he transferred to Sydney in 1976. By 1978, he was Administrator of the newly-founded donor department. He was reported as being highly ambitious, yet he seemed keen on administering an infertility clinic—apparently it's not considered the Mercedes Benz of doctoring.'

'His intentions in andrology are now rather clear,' Catherine said.

'When he was quietly removed in '82, he used the reference to take over as administrator of the Womens Hospital in Melbourne. In '92, he was sacked for tampering with samples and has never been heard of again in official circles. His license to practice medicine was revoked and he was struck off the register.'

'What about personal life, friends, family, etc?' McAbbey asked. 'We have to explore every avenue as soon as possible.'

'DSS Stone is on to it.' Jack shrugged. 'Unfortunately, he doesn't seem to have any family or friends. According to the doctors who have worked with him most recently, his mother was admitted to a nursing home in the mid-nineties. We're trying to find her now. She may know where he is, but our best hope is that someone's memory will be jogged by the details of his name and appearance on television last night and in today's papers.'

'So you believe he may be living under an alias now?'

Jack nodded. 'The last time he used a credit card or registered a car under the name Halliday was in 2002. We're starting our search from his last known transactions.'

'Damn this bastard. He's like a chameleon. What about the records at the Melbourne Womens Hospital?' McAbbey asked. 'Were any more aliases found? The killer had five aliases at the Sydney hospital, what's to stop him doing the same here?'

'I have to admit, our focus has been on Sydney,' Jack replied. 'However yesterday, we took charge of a dozen Forensic officers in Melbourne.'

'Good. Find anything yet?'

Jack shook his head. 'Unfortunately not. They're working around the clock in shifts searching the records for similar characters.'

'Do we need more resources?'

'No,' Jack replied. 'Your mate the Minister made a few calls and called up half the police force. We have officers manning Mobile Units at each Victorian crime scene as well. Cath is working on the AMA and medical profession to see if any doctors kept in touch with him. We are concerned that he may still be practicing medicine. Ted is coordinating our efforts with the other states on this.'

'What about you, Pete?' McAbbey asked.

'I'm going through everything we know about Halliday, trying to find commonality. Maybe he visits a regular bar or drives a certain car? At the scenes of some crimes, we've received descriptions of vehicles found in the vicinity. One of those may match a car from a hit and run in New South Wales,' Pete explained.

'Excellent. It appears my presentation may go smoothly after all.'

There were a few wan smiles from around the table as they packed up.

McAbbey stood to leave, but Jack and Pete were standing there. Pete produced an evidence bag and they sat again.

'I have something,' he said to McAbbey.

McAbbey motioned to Jack who shut the door. He nodded and Pete took a seat. He explained his discovery and McAbbey held the aforementioned disk and studied his reflection in the scratched surface.

'I was able to work out who the youths were from looking at the files. Some were from Sydney, but they have all since died,' Pete said.

'Why didn't you ring me as soon as you found this?' he asked.

Pete shrugged. 'They were already dead, and it wasn't something I was asked to look at. Plus we also know Pearce is innocent.'

'Innocent?'

'His DNA hasn't been found at any scene and he has an alibi for each murder.'

'What? That bloody sect?' McAbbey said.

'Get Pearce on the horn. I want to ask him about this one.' McAbbey turned to Jack. 'Find out exactly where this Armageddon sect is.'

As McAbbey wandered back to his office, Gavin followed him and sat opposite while McAbbey picked up his briefcase.

'Do you mind?'

'Not at all …' Gavin smiled. It was obvious that he wanted to see what McAbbey had in his briefcase. He kept the contents a secret because they would pick on him for what he carried in it.

McAbbey held the tumblers close to his chest. 'Only I know the combination.'

'Why lock it?' Gavin scoffed, 'It only holds your lunch!' He was talking loudly and people in the office were milling outside.

McAbbey had the feeling he was being framed somehow. This usually happened around his birthday, but obviously his anniversary presentation was a worthy opportunity to mock him.

'You seem to be having trouble with the lock, Boss. Want me to open it?' Gavin offered.

'A hundred bucks says I can do it,' Jack said, standing in the doorway.

'Done.' McAbbey handed the briefcase over and Jack fumbled with the tumblers for a minute, with a puzzled expression.

'Guess you're right …' he said with a frown.

The others seemed to lose interest and they disappeared.

McAbbey grabbed the briefcase smugly and rolled the tumblers. Releasing the clasps, he drew back the lid.

To his horror, a superfluous supply of confetti spilled onto his lap, the desk and floor, leaving debris everywhere. Diving his hands into the myriad of coloured paper, he was upset to find his lunch missing.

'My briefcase's been tampered with!' he exclaimed angrily.

Flustered, he looked up to find everyone laughing in the corridor.

Jack returned triumphantly, holding his lunch box.

'Guess that's a hundred you owe me.'

McAbbey glared at the crowd and they dispersed quickly, leaving Jack.

'What do you want?' McAbbey folded his arms.

'The Armageddon sect has three hundred acres off the Warburton Highway in Wandin.'

'Excellent. Let me ring Pearce first.'

McAbbey put the phone on hands-free, rang Pearce and explained the reason for his call.

'I already told you about the disks. They're harmless. You can get them through any Internet subscription.'

Pearce was relaxed and that irked McAbbey. It was time to shake things up a little.

'What about the writeable disk without markings—the one with the pictures of Tania Stevenson and the other youths?'

'I don't know what you're talking about. There were a lot of disks. I never got around to them all. Perhaps I missed that one.'

McAbbey caught Pete's meaningful glance.

'It was the one taken from your computer—which you shut off just before we arrived with the warrant.'

There was a brief silence.

'What of it?'

'What of it!' McAbbey raised his voice. 'This CD implicates you in her murder. On that disk are ten directories of different youths including Tania. They have all since been killed. At the moment you're an accessory to murder—that's a guaranteed life in striped pyjamas.'

'But I had nothing to do with that.'

Finally McAbbey had shaken him.

'I'll ask you one last time. Where did you get the disk?'

'I found it. The other disks came from a mail order house.'

'Found it? Where?' McAbbey asked.

'The Society. Computers and technology are banned, but I found the CD behind a bed in one of the guest rooms.'

'Whose was it?'

'Disciples of the Society stay from time to time to claim absolution and see the pontiff for enlightenment. It could've been anyone.'

'Do you know a Clive Halliday?'

Pearce took a breath. 'Yes, he's a disciple.'

Jack and McAbbey shared a look.

'Do you think the disk could be his?' Pearce asked.

'It might be.' McAbbey was giving nothing away, but he pictured Halliday keeping records of his intended victims. He wondered if Halliday knew the disk was missing.

'We're heading out to the Society now. Is there anything else we should know?'

'Please don't tell them I had the disk. They'll punish me.'

'What? Fifty lashes?'

There was a pause at the other end.

'They may expel me.'

'Sounds like a good thing,' McAbbey replied. 'Going by Halliday's predicament I'd say their price of membership is a little steep.'

McAbbey ended the call. Jack left his office as Andrea buzzed on the intercom.

'You have two visitors,' she called over the intercom.

'Who?' he snapped, with a look at his watch.

'It's your boss and his boss.' Andrea whispered into the phone, as though sharing a schoolgirl's secret.

Sitting in the plastic foyer chairs were Harry Vincent and Gary Moloney!

McAbbey smiled graciously at his guests. It was unusual to host a visit from the Minister. He showed them to his office, cringing at the mess before them. The floor was lined with files, folders and thanks to the others, confetti. McAbbey brushed down his visitor's chairs and offered them a seat.

'No thanks,' Moloney looked around them and frowned. 'What's going on here?'

'The guys just played a trick on me. Being my twentieth anniversary and all,' he shrugged with embarrassment.

'Not yet ...' Moloney replied with a hint of amusement.

Changing the subject quickly, McAbbey brought them up to date on the latest developments.

'So what do we do now?' Vincent asked. 'You seem to have him cornered.'

'True, however we're trying to locate Halliday's family. We believe his mother was admitted to a nursing home in 1995. She may know his whereabouts. Also, I am heading out now to a Sect in the country of which Halliday is a member. My crew is working with the police in the other states and at the hospitals Halliday worked at to find other aliases that he may have had. Doctor Catherine Smith is giving professional input to this search. So far, we have two potential victims in protective custody. There may be more children we can save.'

'Cripes ... How many kids have you found so far?'

'Nine from Victoria—though one of those died in Perth. So far we've lost twenty in Sydney.'

'You mean thirty in all?' Vincent was aghast.

'Not all from Victoria ...' Moloney added, inanely.

McAbbey glared at him.

'Is the media aware of the extent of the murders?' Vincent asked.

'Not yet. However the Sydney Homicide Squad has re-opened unsolved cases and opened files on deaths initially thought to be accidents. The press is sure to find out sooner or later. It may be time to make a statement.'

'Agreed. Well done, Ryan. See you tonight at the presentation.'

McAbbey showed them out quickly.

80

McAbbey picked up his keys and grabbed Jack. As they passed reception, he asked Andrea to call Gavin at the hospital and have him meet them at the Society.

'So how did you break into my briefcase?' McAbbey asked as he pulled out into traffic on St Kilda Road.

'I didn't break into it!' Jack laughed. 'I merely opened it.'

'So you spied on me!' McAbbey replied indignantly.

'No. I guessed your code, that's all,' Jack replied.

'I don't believe that with all the possible combinations you just happened to guess the right one.'

'No, you're right.'

McAbbey felt triumphant. If Jack had used devious means to obtain the combination, he could rescind the bet.

'I know you too well, Boss. Besides, do you think you're the first to use your year of birth as a combination?'

McAbbey drove in dumbfounded silence, determined to change it as soon as possible.

They stopped briefly for take-away at McDonald's on Maroondah Highway in Lilydale. McAbbey scoffed his burger before they reached Warburton Highway, where the city's outskirts gave way to strawberries, vines and fresh air.

They drove past the gates of the sect twice before spotting it; such was the anonymity of the place.

A small rusted tin plate nailed to the gate read: "Christian Armageddon Society." McAbbey opened the rusted gates and they drove in, ignoring the faded motif, "Trespassers will be shot."

The Society was a long way from the road. High fences and old gnarled gums followed the track closely on each side. They travelled at least a kilometre before the side boundaries disappeared and they arrived.

In the valley below they could see established buildings. A church, barns and small bungalows littered the landscape. They passed a glistening dam, infested with reeds. Families of ducks swam in single file and sheep grazed beside it.

'Peaceful,' Jack remarked, mirroring McAbbey's sentiments.

They parked behind Gavin, a short walk from the settlement. Gavin got out of his car and joined them. A few people from the Society congregated, staring at them with open hostility.

It was then that McAbbey noticed that their cars were the only ones in sight.

'I wonder if they still use a horse and cart?' he murmured, reminded of the Amish community from the film, *Witness*.

McAbbey felt buck-naked, though he was clothed and carrying a gun—such was the magnetism of their unnerving stares. He approached a man in his sixties, who appeared to be the most senior. He was a farmer, wearing old denim jeans, a flannel check shirt and a straw hat.

'I'm Inspector Ryan McAbbey,' he paused, 'I need to speak to whoever is in charge here.'

'God is in charge,' the man answered mysteriously.

McAbbey remembered what Pearce had earlier said.

'Is the Pontiff here?'

'I'll go and see.' He turned abruptly and walked off down the hill, disappearing behind a series of bluestone buildings.

They waited a long time for the man to return, under the watchful stare of a half a dozen faithful.

'Nice day,' McAbbey said to an old woman who ignored him. Her skin was like baked leather and her tightly-pulled grey hair and threadbare clothing suggested she had worked the land all her life.

The man return from the settlement. 'Come with me. The Pontiff will see you in his office,' he said.

McAbbey raised an eyebrow. 'An office. Well ain't that sweet.'

The man walked at an even pace, as if their deliverance to the Pontiff was part of some ceremonial procession. McAbbey frowned at Gavin, who annoyingly copied the man's exaggerated walk.

They passed a chapel and hay shed before stopping at a high-ceiling villa. It had full windows which faced the other side of the valley.

They were led down a hallway dotted with sculptures of religious significance into a magnificent room filled with large wall paintings on one side, and an extraordinary view over a small stream and green fields opposite.

'Please have a seat. His Excellency will be with you shortly.'

Jack and Gavin admired the view while McAbbey studied the paintings closely. There was a smaller version of Michelangelo's 'The Last Supper', and oil paintings based on segments of the Sistine Chapel ceiling. At one end of the room was a large mahogany desk in front of a fireplace surrounded by oak panelling.

'Not bad. God must pay well,' Gavin remarked.

'Indeed he does, gentlemen. But only on Judgement Day do we truly cash in.'

The Pontiff had a booming voice—an evangelistic talent, McAbbey thought. The man had entered the room through a hidden doorway in the panelling behind the desk. He sat, beckoning them before him. Jack and Gavin sat, and McAbbey stood behind them.

'What can I do for you?' The Pontiff asked regally. Though his form was disguised by pastel robes, McAbbey could see that he was over six feet tall, thin and wiry with receding dark hair which had greyed around the ears. McAbbey pegged his age at fifty.

'I'm Inspector Ryan McAbbey.' He introduced his associates. 'We're from the Homicide Squad.'

The leader was taken aback. 'And what would the Homicide Squad need of me and my little community?'

'We're investigating one of your followers with respect to some recent murders.'

'Who?' The Pontiff folded his arms.

'Paul Pearce,' McAbbey said, wanting to work his way up to Halliday. 'He was found with a series of CDs, one of which contained images of children who have since been murdered.'

'Brother Paul would not have possession of such an item. It is forbidden.' The man shook his head resolutely.

A brief smile passed McAbbey's lips as he handed a document to the Pontiff. 'This is the police record of the inventory collected from his flat. Pearce has since agreed it was in his possession, though he claims not to know who it came from.'

'You realise this accusation has grave implications for Brother Pearce?' The man frowned at McAbbey.

'Absolutely,' He maintained eye contact with the religious leader. 'While you go about re-lecturing him on the evils of technology, perhaps you might include his fascination with pornography and young teens.'

'You mock me, Inspector. This isn't a country club. God is not something we take lightly. Our sect is built on age-old traditions, before there were such things as planes, computers and cars. It is a sin to infect your lives with technology. It makes you physically frail and spiritually weak. Just look at the major religions today—at the beck and call of every slight change in questionable morality. Women priests, lay preachers, divorce, married ministers, contraception, sex before union, abortion, euthanasia ... Nothing is sacred anymore. Religion these days has the convenience of fast food with a side of fries. And when their popularity falls, what do they do?'

McAbbey waved for him to continue.

'They lower the standard ... move the goal posts back. It's much easier than attacking the evils of this world.'

'Do you believe in forgiveness?' McAbbey asked.

'Of course—as does God. We take in every lost soul who comes to us. But here, forgiveness is not just bestowed like a driver's licence. We expect our disciples to reform. You only get one shot at repenting. You cannot sin over again.'

McAbbey actually liked the Pontiff's mantra. Too many criminals became born-again Christians just to improve their chances with a parole board.

'It seems forgiveness is not that forgiving,' McAbbey said, thinking of Pearce, who was now up the creek, paddle-free.

'Inspector, would you release a murderer on a second and final chance?'

'I wouldn't let them out at all.'

'See, so we are more forgiving than you.'

'Did Pearce come to you for guidance after he was dismissed from the school?' Jack asked.

'No. I suggested Brother Pearce leave the school. He has a sickness. His physical being was unhealthily attracted to youths.'

'You mean paedophilia?' McAbbey growled.

'Call it what you want.' The Pontiff's gaze narrowed. 'The man was ill. He wanted help. Can you label someone guilty for feelings he has, yet neither wants nor likes? I merely suggested he remove himself from the temptation.'

'Did he admit to any offences?' McAbbey asked, leaning forward.

'I refuse to discuss it. His place in our sect and path to God are internal matters.'

'It's a police matter actually,' McAbbey said.

'Then I leave it in your capable hands.'

A twitch in McAbbey's upper lip might have been construed as a smile, but under his cool exterior, Jack knew how angry he was.

'Perhaps you could fill us in on one of your other inmates,' McAbbey said. 'Clive Halliday.'

'What of Brother Halliday?' There was no change in the Pontiff's stony stare.

'We believe the compact disk Pearce had in his possession belonged to Halliday.'

'For what purpose would Brother Halliday have a disk of youths?'

McAbbey took a deep breath. He was concerned about forewarning Halliday, but he felt it necessary to pressure the sect for information.

'It is a catalogue—he was keeping tabs on the youths since their birth.'

'Why?'

Gavin glanced at McAbbey who answered. 'He is the illegitimate father of more than thirty children. We don't know whether it started as fatherly concern or an obsession, but one thing's certain, in the last few years he's been killing them.'

'Thirty? Are they all bastard children?' the Pontiff asked. He was looking pale and McAbbey was beginning to think he had no idea Halliday had committed mass murder.

'Bast …' McAbbey gritted his teeth, wondering if he was trying to lighten the burden of his advice. 'They are children; end of story.'

McAbbey paced behind Gavin and Jack. 'Are you telling me you knew he was doing this?'

'I'm not saying anything.'

'But you have already. They're bastard children to you—formed from an unholy alliance. You've given Halliday his chance to redeem himself haven't you? I think he lied and told you there were only a couple of illegitimately sired bastards—not a huge sacrifice to free the conscience of one of your coffer-paying subjects. That explains why he was changing his MO. He needed the murders to appear like accidents or unrelated deaths. If you'd discovered his lies and the number of children he was talking about, you might've rejected his claim for redemption.'

'I had no choice. His right to redemption is assured. Whether he has deceived God with his actions is not for me to judge.'

'How long ago did he approach you with his problem?' McAbbey asked.

'He came into our family five years ago, but it took him a year to admit his sin and plead for forgiveness.'

'You mean kill innocent children?' Jack snapped.

'Our teachings suggest you must put right your wrongs, but I most certainly did not advise him to murder anyone. Alas, when you said he had killed youths I realised he might have misinterpreted the word.'

'So, if righting wrongs did not mean killing, what did it mean?' McAbbey frowned, wondering how hard it would be to pin the Pontiff as an accomplice to murder.

'He has a duty as a brother, to ensure the children were not damned to purgatory.'

'Surely you don't believe that. Purgatory's a place created to scaremonger people into becoming Christian.'

'Absolutely I believe,' The Pontiff said. 'Baptism is the first step to bringing those wretched souls closer to God. It gives them a chance to be accepted into the Kingdom of Heaven.'

'Hence the rosewater,' McAbbey said to Jack and Gavin. 'If blessing the children brought them salvation—why did he kill them?' he asked the Pontiff.

'His own path is much more difficult. He's forever damned if those bastard children live.' The Pontiff sighed.

'So, he's a selfish son of a bitch. He's increased the killings in the past six months; does Halliday have a deadline in which to redeem himself?'

'I can only think of Armageddon.'

'Armageddon?' McAbbey asked.

'Yes, the end of the world is imminent. We have five months until Judgement Day.'

81

'So what does your Armageddon mean?' McAbbey asked.

'The beginning of the end is written in Revelations. All scores are tallied and those who have lived within the guidelines of the Lord will rejoice in heaven. Have you done enough to pass through the gates?'

McAbbey was taken aback. 'Well, no, but I'd be pretty lonely up there.'

Jack and Gavin exchanged a grin.

'Where's Halliday now?' McAbbey asked.

'I don't know. He dropped in a week ago, but spends little time here now. He occasionally helps out at our meditation centre.'

It came back to McAbbey. It was the same centre that Lisa had suggested to him. He did not recall seeing the Pontiff, but he remembered Brother Clive, the man who talked to Pearce.

'Tell me, how does the talk of Armageddon assist relaxation?'

The man smiled sadly. 'Panic is not the mood we try to nurture. We give our disciples a reasoned approach to the afterlife. It is just a new beginning after all.'

McAbbey nodded to Jack and Gavin. He handed the leader a business card.

'Call me immediately if Halliday comes back.'

'Call you on what?'

McAbbey looked at the vacant desk.

'Send a horse and cart if you have to.'

The Pontiff nodded indifferently and McAbbey glared back.

'Just remember he's murdered many young children. Do what your God would expect of you.'

With that, McAbbey turned and left. The Pontiff stared at the space McAbbey occupied, long after they left.

—∼—

They walked back to their cars under the watchful eye of a few followers who stood by their vegie patch with hoes and rakes.

'Could he really be protecting Halliday?' Jack was aghast.

'Perhaps, but I don't think he realised the extent of what Brother Halliday has done,' McAbbey said. 'He looked shaken by it all.'

'What now?' Jack asked.

'Let's check in with the office.' McAbbey plugged his mobile into the car and called Ted.

'We found her. Mrs Halliday is at the Ringwood Nursing home. An officer from Ringwood CIU is with her at the moment. She's coherent.'

'Excellent.' McAbbey took down the address details.

'You two can go back to the office. I can handle the nursing home.' McAbbey looked down at the settlement. 'On your way, have the local police place surveillance on this funny farm. Anyone who comes and goes gets a tail. See if their neighbours would be willing to let us use their land to observe the Sect. If Halliday comes here I want to know straight away. Then call Bill Harnden and explain our situation and see what pressure he can place on God's right hand down there.'

When Jack and Gavin left, McAbbey asked Ted how the search was going.

'We've found three more recipients, all from the second alias at the Melbourne Womens Hospital. We hope to find every last recipient by tonight,' Ted reported.

'What about those you've found so far?' McAbbey asked, hopeful.

'Sorry, Boss. Would you believe four hit and runs and two drug ODs. Cath studied the pathologists' findings of the overdoses. Apparently both victims had never tried heroin before, yet mysteriously overdosed with large hits. There were questions over the findings but the Coroner eventually ruled the deaths as accidental.'

'OK. Call me if you find anything else. I'm off to the nursing home.'

'Don't forget to write!' Ted laughed, hanging up.

McAbbey frowned at the phone.

82

The smell of death lingered in nursing homes. They reminded McAbbey of his grandmother, who was admitted to a home when he was a child. The repugnant odour flooding his senses resurfaced the clinical and unfriendly memories of a confused ten-year-old child.

Passing a sitting room, he could not help but feel reprehensible about looking in on the occupants. Each resident sat focused squarely on the television, with warm brightly-knitted blankets covering their knees. The room was cold and he wondered why they did not turn up the heating.

McAbbey followed a nurse down a corridor, painted brightly like a kindergarten, to another sitting room with a garden view. A uniformed officer guarding the door greeted McAbbey.

'This is Monica Halliday,' the nurse said, leaving him with her.

The elderly lady exuded a scent of eucalyptus and mothballs. She raised her eyes to meet his gaze and smiled weakly.

'So you're in charge, Inspector.' She seemed satisfied with his presence. 'Why are you wearing a gun—do you fear me?' she asked McAbbey. He was surprised she noticed the lump under his blazer. He had forgotten about his Glock, having already become accustomed to wearing it again.

'I'm a policeman, Mrs Halliday,' he exaggerated. He did not have the heart to explain to her that he was wearing it because her son had scared the crap out of him.

'I want to ask you about your son, Clive.' he said comfortingly.

'Is he OK?' she asked McAbbey.

'Yes. But we need to speak to him urgently.'

'I'm sorry sir, but I don't know where he is. He doesn't visit me anymore.'

'What can you tell me about your son? What was he like as a child?'

'Clive is a loner.' She smiled wanly. 'Even as a boy he preferred to play alone, rather than mix with other children. At school, he excelled at sports and his studies, but was quiet. If other kids teased him he would go into a rage. He has a bad temper and was expelled many times for hitting other students. He was a good fighter.'

'Why'd he become a doctor?' McAbbey asked.

'Because doctors make good money and he wanted to be rich,' she explained. 'He loved the trust and power that a doctor holds over his patients. People trusted him with their lives.'

'What happened to his father?'

'He died in a car accident—drunk as usual. He used to beat me and Clive. Harold was cruel at times but it was the alcohol that made him so abusive.'

'When was the last time you saw Clive?' McAbbey asked. He did not want their conversation to drift. They could discuss the reasons for his psychosis later, but now he needed something that would bring him in.

'About four years ago. He came to tell me that he could mend his ways in the eyes of God. He had joined the Christian Armageddon Society.'

'What did he say about them?'

'He said they follow a strict interpretation of the Bible. Clive said he needed to cleanse his soul before God came to pass judgement. Any transgressions had to be righted.'

'Do you believe Clive was acting on the advice of the society?' McAbbey asked.

'Clive wanted to belong. He wouldn't tell me the sin he'd committed, but he said the Pontiff had the solution to his problem and he was going to follow it to the letter. I'm sure it has something to do with the fact he never married. It was not as though girls didn't ring for him—I was forever taking messages. I think relationships scared him, which is sad, as he saw children as an important part of his life.'

'That would explain the lack of depravation in the killings.' McAbbey said to himself.

McAbbey said goodbye to Monica Halliday, who was sad to see him leave and begged for him to call again. He felt sorry that her loneliness would soon grow when they caught her son.

83

McAbbey went home to change for the Police Ball that night and Chelsey greeted him at the door. Lisa had already left to go shopping with Ted's wife before the Ball.

'How was your day?' McAbbey asked, wrenching the tie from his neck, totally exhausted. He threw his briefcase full of confetti, his jacket and his mobile phone on the couch.

'Horrible. God, I'm so stressed. No one ever told me being a teenager was going to be so hard!'

He chuckled to himself.

'What's so funny, Dad?'

'You've got problems! I've been flat knacker all week chasing a mass murderer and I've come close to being fired a dozen times.'

'Yeah. But you're an adult. That's not my fault,' Chelsey replied. 'By the way, Mum said to let you know the school gardener is coming this afternoon to trim the hedges and mow the lawns for us.'

He followed Chelsey to her bedroom.

'What did you say?' McAbbey asked. 'I mowed and worked in the garden last weekend.' He rubbed his brow in frustration. 'Don't tell me she knew about this last week.'

'OK. I won't.' Chelsey replied cheekily. 'Mum didn't want them to come and find our place a mess.'

'So I did the hard work for him,' he muttered. 'How much do I owe him for nothing, or has Mother-dear paid already?'

'They charge fifty dollars—it goes towards the school's provident fund,' she defended.

'Heck—as if the school fees I pay aren't enough. When's Sharee's mum picking you up?'

She gave a loud sigh. 'Later, Dad—don't stress. I'm staying with them tonight.'

'Good.' McAbbey had argued many times with Lisa about Chelsey staying home by herself at thirteen.

McAbbey went upstairs and pulled out his good suit from the back of the cupboard and stripped out of his work clothes.

After a shower and shave, he felt much better. The pressures of the day were cleansed from his mind and he was able to look forward to dinner with his team and a few cold beers.

Once dressed, McAbbey went back downstairs to say goodbye to Chelsey. She was sitting at the kitchen table doing her homework—probably for show. He dodged Chelsey's protests and defences and pecked her on the cheek.

The phone rang and Chelsey squirmed past him to pick it up first.

'For you, Dad.' She sounded typically disappointed.

It was Catherine. 'We found another recipient in Victoria and she's still alive. Jack has sent two squad cars over to protect her.'

'Excellent. Are you coming to the dinner tonight?'

McAbbey knew she would rather eat a kidney pie during an autopsy than attend an official presentation dinner.

'I'll be there,' she promised.

As McAbbey walked to his car, an old Valiant ute pulled up. Attached to the back was a trailer full of dirty hedge clippers, lawn mowers and other assorted objects.

'Afternoon, sir,' the old man politely said. 'Everyone calls me McVeigh.' He put out his hand and McAbbey shook it firmly.

He wore a sloppy, once white hat, which covered a number one haircut. McAbbey could not help but think he had seen the man before, yet couldn't place from where. Though the man looked tired, his dark brown eyes sparkled with life. McAbbey admired the fact he took time out to help the school with fundraising.

'My daughter is inside and she has the money for when you're finished.' McAbbey began to walk to his car when he had a thought.

'Listen,' McAbbey proffered a ten-dollar note. 'For a little extra, would you consider cutting the lawns real low ... ?'

'Why sure,' he laughed. 'In other words, short enough so they don't need to be done for weeks.'

'You're the man!' McAbbey grinned.

'Funny,' the gardener studied their lawn. 'It looks like it was mowed recently.'

'Yeah. Don't ask,' McAbbey said. 'Could you also cut the hedges right back?'

The gardener pulled out a pad and removed a pen from behind his ear. 'I had better write all this down. The school will kill me if I get it wrong again.' He shrugged and gave a wry grin.

McAbbey laughed. The man wore a faded wedding band and obviously knew what it was like to be told off.

'So, mow the lawns low, prune back the hedges and Chelsey has the money inside when I'm finished,' he muttered to himself as he made the notes.

Satisfied, McAbbey hopped into Lisa's car and took off. On weekends, he rarely drove his work car. It was like a taxi driver using his cab on a day off. It spoiled the fun. McAbbey would listen to the police channel and, if there was an emergency, head off to a crime scene that his presence was not required at. Not tonight.

He drove down Maroondah Highway and onto Springvale Road. Taking a hard left, he was on the freeway.

It was just before six. With some luck, he would be at the Crown Palladium in thirty minutes. Lisa's little Excel buzzed down the freeway. He turned on the radio which interrupted the regular program for a news update on the Adonis Taskforce:

> Detectives believe they are close to finding the mass murderer allegedly responsible for thirty youths aged between thirteen and twenty-three. Detective Senior Sergeant Jack Turner from the Homicide Squad said:
> 'Please be on the lookout for a man in his mid fifties—tall, greying-blonde hair and sapphire-blue eyes. Be aware that he may be disguising these features. Anyone who has seen this man should contact Crimestoppers or their local police. Do not try to approach the killer yourself in any way. He is extremely dangerous.'

It sounded silly, McAbbey mused, but it was surprising how many idiots tried to tackle a murderer. He remembered one fool who tackled and beat a robber senseless, only to find out later the man was innocent.

His mind kept wandering back to the gardener and his dirty lawn mower sitting in the trailer. Was there something unusual about it?

He laughed at himself—thinking shop again. He tried singing along with AC/DC, but his thoughts wandered back.

He was constantly looking for flaws in everything he saw—it was the detective in his nature coming to the fore. During work hours it did him credit, but when his mind did not switch off afterwards, it became a millstone.

He succumbed momentarily to the conviction of his imagination.

All of a sudden he was hit with a series of revelations which froze him in a trance. His eyes glazed over and, as hard as he looked, he saw nothing.

'Oh God ...' he mouthed, but no sound passed his lips.

84

Fragments of his subconscious tugged at his grey matter and the implications were heart-rending.

'Be aware that he may be disguising these features ...' Jack's warning came back to haunt him.

But McVeigh had no hair. Perhaps he shaved it recently?

He was the same height as Halliday.

But his eyes?

A strong brown—almost vivid.

Yet he had seen that before. Once, Chelsey came home from school with bright green eyes. He went off his rocker about kids and drugs until she showed him her coloured contacts.

The lawn mower in the trailer was missing its zip cord. The source of the cord used to strangle the victims had concerned him for weeks—yet now, when it was too late, he knew the answer.

McAbbey recalled his forgettable trip to the Oracle for relaxation therapy where "Brother Clive" addressed him. He was tall and wiry, like McVeigh, but did not have the short haircut. Take away the haircut and contacts ...

McAbbey felt paralysed by snake venom and now the serpent of truth was constricting the life from him.

Just after the Bulleen Road overpass, he regained control of his actions. Swapping lanes without indicating, he crossed over four lanes to the median strip.

Seeing an emergency vehicle crossover ahead, he slammed on the brakes and wrenched the wheel hard to the right. McAbbey left the bitumen and skidded beautifully across the grass in between the traffic.

Just as he was about to slide into the oncoming cars, he hit the bitumen crossover. The tyres screeched angrily as traction took hold. McAbbey was now facing home though still moving sideways.

He slammed back into second and kicked the accelerator. The little Excel screamed, but found footing in the tar.

Glancing casually at the outbound traffic, he merged, leaving behind an impressive half donut and a scattering of dust and debris.

It was almost six-fifteen. Time was against him. Tears flowed unabashedly, as he hit one-forty.

One-fifty.

One-sixty.

The little Excel was screaming for mercy.

So was he.

McAbbey lost interest in his own safety—almost daring himself to go that step further. He had nothing to lose.

He remembered Halliday's threat. McAbbey assumed it would be a personal attack, not one on his family. He bashed the steering wheel, ignoring the constant tooting and obscenities thrown at him. McAbbey weaved in and out of the freeway traffic, blaring the horn at anyone sitting in the right lane doing less than one-thirty.

He again looked at his watch—six-twenty.

At the end of the freeway, he careened into the emergency lane and skipped though the traffic lights and onto Springvale Road. Narrowly missing a passing truck, McAbbey waved back, as though the driver's one finger salute was welcome.

He contemplated pulling over and calling one of the team on a pay phone, but he would lose valuable minutes—time which could mean the difference between life and death for Chelsey.

McAbbey cursed himself for leaving the mobile phone at home with his ...

Gun.

Oh shit.

Turning onto Maroondah Highway, McAbbey glanced briefly at his watch. Ten minutes away. Hitting one-forty through Ringwood, he was dismayed to find that not one policeman had taken notice.

How typical.

He passed through Croydon, trying to ignore the voices in his head. Images of Tania flashed into his mind like a photo album and he squeezed tears from his welling eyes.

McAbbey left the highway at Lilydale and sped up his street, hitting one hundred before the first bend. Slamming on the brakes, he stopped outside his neighbour's front yard, twenty metres down the road.

Jumping out of the car, he ran quietly to the house, using the trees lining the front paddock for cover. Halliday's Valiant was still parked out the front. A mower and hedge clippers lay prostrate on the half-cut lawn.

McAbbey strained his eyes in the last light of dusk, but Halliday was nowhere to be seen.

Hunched over like a bag lady, McAbbey sprinted to the front door. He could hear nothing, but from an upstairs window he could see a dull flickering light.

He took a deep breath and wrenched the door open.

McAbbey headed for the couch, where his gun was secured inside his jacket.

A shadow jumped out, lunging at him.

With a start, McAbbey braced for impact.

85

'Dad?'

It was Chelsey.

She was fine ...

'Since when was I so scary?'

His lungs sucked like a black hole. Was he having a heart attack? Had his imagination completely taken over?

'What the hell are you doing with the lights off?' McAbbey found the energy to shout.

'I was watching TV. It's only just gone dark. Are you OK, Dad?' She looked at him with a frown. 'Aren't you supposed to be at your presentation?'

He managed a weak smile to allay her concerns over his startled appearance.

'Yeah ...' McAbbey could not think of anything to say. He did not want to alarm her. His premonition was wrong.

The phone rang and he jumped. McAbbey answered it with a degree of trepidation.

'McAbbey.'

'Hi, it's Cath. Thank God I finally caught you. Don't you have your mobile on?'

'I do now,' McAbbey said. He reached for his mobile phone in his pocket and turned it on. 'What's wrong?'

'We've found an IVF record that you need to know about.'

'IVF?' He was puzzled. 'I thought we were only interested in donated sperm cases?'

'Yes, but some IVF files were mixed up with the donor submissions and I happened to recognise the recipient of one of the applications.'

'Whose was it?' he asked, her damp enthusiasm barely maintaining his interest.

'Yours.'

'That has no bearing on the case,' McAbbey snapped, with the conviction of a cardboard cut out.

There was silence at the other end.

'They must've filed it in the wrong place,' McAbbey said, unnerved by Cath's silence. The breach would certainly form part of an official review of the hospital's procedures in record keeping ... unless?

'It was signed by Clive Halliday,' Catherine confirmed grimly.

McAbbey gagged, unable to arrest the surge of bile in his stomach.

'Are you nervous about getting an award from the Premier?' Chelsey asked, poking fun at him as she so often did.

He couldn't speak, nor could he cry out. Catherine's voice was reduced to a frantic jumble of words, which ceased suddenly.

McAbbey watched as the cordless phone fell from his hands in slow motion and landed softly on the carpet. He was numb—disbelieving.

When he finally met Chelsey's eyes, her composure had changed—she was staring at him in open-mouthed horror. She raised a hand and let off a startled scream.

McAbbey turned too late, and a dizzying kaleidoscope of purples and reds grew before his eyes. It was not a matter of Halliday avenging his investigation any longer.

He was after McAbbey's daughter, Chelsey.

Halliday's daughter ...

He now understood why Tania and the other victims reminded him so much of Chelsey. They were related.

Halliday swapped the sperm.

McAbbey cursed his procrastination all those years ago, as if it would have made a difference. If he had visited the clinic earlier, would it have guaranteed a different outcome? He doubted it. But who else could he blame?

Haemorrhaging tears clouded his thoughts and vision, sinking him further and further to blackness.

With every fibre of his being he tried to retain his tenuous grip on reality, but it was in vain. Night fell swiftly.

The last thing he heard was his mobile phone ringing.

86

McAbbey had no concept of time since the assault.

His eyes opened, registering immense pain when he tried to shift his weight. He forced himself to move but his grip on consciousness slipped again.

⌁

'Where's Jack?' McAbbey asked Catherine. 'He was supposed to be here hours ago.' It annoyed him that Jack would miss his presentation.

'He said he'd be here,' Catherine shrugged.

'Another drink?' She held a flagon of red in her hand. Taking McAbbey's empty glass, she refilled it.

'No, thanks,' he rubbed his forehead, cursing. 'I've got one hell of a headache.'

Jack arrived, placing McAbbey's briefcase on the table.

'Look what I found,' he joked. 'Let's see what we have today!'

'Let me have that!' McAbbey angrily grabbed the case from him. Turning the tumblers close to his chest, he rolled the numbers until they revealed his password.

'Damn—wasn't I going to change that?'

Opening it, McAbbey expected to find more confetti, but he jumped back in revulsion.

Inside the case were bloodied locks of hair—Chelsey's hair.

——

With a sudden gasp, he woke again.

It was now dark, but McAbbey could not guess how much time had passed. Lying on his side with his cheek pressed to the floor, he could see a soft light upstairs.

'Chelsey?' he groaned.

He shuffled gingerly along the floor to the couch. McAbbey tried to raise himself to sit, but the throbbing pain numbed his efforts.

He had no time to contemplate his actions, and instead relied on instinct and police force acumen, built up over years of service.

'Finish me, before I call the office,' he yelled out, teetering on the brink of unconsciousness. He hoped that Halliday heard him. He did not have the energy to yell again, let alone find the phone.

'You should've listened to me.' Halliday suddenly appeared at the top of the stairs. He had removed the gardening guise worn earlier. The affable grin and hat were gone, revealing a shaved head and a scowl—and thankfully, no blood.

'Why are you here? I never wanted this to get personal,' Halliday said, starting down the stairs.

McAbbey blinked to clear his fuzzy vision.

'We know all about you. We've spoken to your mum and the Society. You can't get to heaven by killing these kids. Leave her be. Please.' McAbbey pleaded again, 'Please ...'

'You found my mum?' Halliday stopped suddenly. 'What have you done to her?'

'Nothing and you have a chance to do the same. Let Chelsey go.'

Halliday walked slowly towards him. McAbbey closed his eyes momentarily, finding inner strength. He opened them again and turned to the couch. He gritted his teeth at the back spasms resulting from the abrupt action. McAbbey's fingers stretched for the coat pocket, where his gun was.

'Looking for this?' Halliday asked.

McAbbey turned back and slumped heavily against the couch.

Halliday flashed his police-issue Glock pistol.

'Shoot me.' McAbbey groaned in pain. He hoped the neighbours would hear the shot. He expected that Catherine would have called the police. It was a matter of delaying him until help arrived.

'I never wanted to kill you.' Halliday said. 'I'm sorry it had to end this way, McAbbey.'

Halliday raised the gun slowly.

McAbbey closed his eyes, resigned to fate.

A gun went off and McAbbey felt consciousness slip and his pain ease.

Floating ...

Was he dreaming?

When he could open his eyes, McAbbey was stunned to find Halliday lying beside him, breathing erratically. It took a few moments for him to realise what had happened.

Ted Dowling had arrived and shot Halliday.

It was then that McAbbey spied his gun just out of grasp. Using all his energy he leant forward and picked it up.

Losing his balance and short of a hand to counter, McAbbey was forced to use the gun to hold himself up.

With the barrel pressed heavily into the carpet, burdened by his weight, McAbbey precariously maintained his poise. He was able to rest back, supported by the couch. McAbbey raised his wavering arm and aimed the gun at the monster lying before him.

'Why ... ?' McAbbey asked.

Halliday opened his eyes, delirious, but nonetheless aware. His breathing sprayed blood through clenched teeth, like a sated vampire.

'You think I'm a monster ...'

'Why did you kill them?' McAbbey pressed.

'The Pontiff told me that the blessing freed them from the curse.'

McAbbey's nerves pumped bolts of pain through his outstretched arm and the gun weighed like an anvil. He had to shoot now.

'I made a mistake years ago,' Halliday spluttered. 'Those poor souls need to be saved. Can't you see that?' he pleaded. 'There are more. Please, you must let me finish. I must redeem myself in the eyes of God.'

'Did you ever take a look at the young kids you were eradicating?'

Halliday did not answer.

'I think you did. That's why you tortured Joanne MacDonnell's boyfriend.'

'He was violating her. It's a cardinal sin. A holy union comes only with marriage. They are forever cursed—abhorrent in the eyes of God.' His softened demeanour faded.

'You did all this to save your own yellow skin,' McAbbey spat. 'Even the Pontiff thinks you're cursed for what you've done. You'll rot in hell.'

'Well, if Armageddon is what you want, then why wait for Judgement Day?' McAbbey felt the pressure of the trigger as his finger squeezed, his face impassioned.

'No, McAbbey!' Ted shouted. 'He must stand trial for his crimes.'

McAbbey's gaze did not waver, nor did his trigger finger. He had seen the justice of the courts. This man would never get the chance to finish his vendetta.

'Murder's not the answer.' Ted's warning was as background as elevator music.

Halliday gripped his chest in sudden pain. His breathing was shallow and his eyes were without focus. McAbbey watched as the earlier gunshot wound took its toll on the serial killer. A final exhale expunged the lustre from his eyes and Halliday was still.

McAbbey slumped against the couch and released the gun. The nausea and throbbing returned and he passed out.

87

McAbbey awoke to the sound of policemen chatting. He had been moved to the couch and could see the CIU branch officers checking Halliday's body.

McAbbey sat up slowly, looking around. Ted was gone. Using the couch for support, he stood, wavering a moment before taking a step towards the stairs.

He could hear voices upstairs and one of them sounded like Chelsey!

He hobbled upstairs, using the side rails for support. Behind him the police were engrossed in a sombre conversation and did not hear him pass.

McAbbey reached the top of the stairs and Ted stood in his path. 'How did you get up here?' Ted asked. McAbbey pushed him aside and Ted watched him hobble to Chelsey's bedroom.

In the doorway, he could see Catherine and Jack sitting on the bed, talking to Chelsey.

Jack turned and saw McAbbey. He whispered something to Catherine and stood back.

'Thank Christ Ted got here when he did.' McAbbey was surprised at how raspy his voice sounded. He looked down at his hands and wiped them on his clothes before sitting beside Chelsey on the bed.

She was propped up with a pillow, her hair spilled freely, obscuring her face. Catherine stopped running the back of her hand through her hair and gave him space.

'I got him, love. Everything's OK now.' McAbbey whispered, parting the hair from Chelsey's eyes. She was fast asleep and McAbbey dared not wake her after such an ordeal.

As he flicked her hair, he wiped the sweat gently from her forehead.

McAbbey looked at the moisture on the back of his hand and frowned.

It was cold … rosewater …

McAbbey went faint. He turned to Catherine, but she looked away. Tears fell from her cheeks in rapid succession.

Cath never cried.

'But I heard you …' McAbbey moaned softly, holding Chelsey in his arms. He placed a hand on her face, trying desperately to warm her.

Her cheeks were cool, her lips pale.

McAbbey rubbed her hair despondently remembering her first smile, her first steps, and how cute she looked in his footy beanie.

Uncertainty was a rolling fog clouding his future. He could no longer look forward to her graduation, the walk down the aisle at her wedding, or grandchildren.

McAbbey had no more wings to pull. He hugged her lifeless body and cried.

Lisa would be home soon. He wanted to believe they would sit with Chelsey that night and watch *The Lion King* for the umpteenth time. As usual, Chelsey would fall asleep halfway through and he would carry her to bed.

In the morning, everything would be alright … it always was.